FATHOM

Mikel Parry

Mikel Parry Publishing, Salt Lake City, UT

Copyright © 2015 by Mikel Parry

ISBN 978-0-9976383-1-8

Cover Design: Lindsey Parry

Editor: Jo Spring

Copy Proofing and Interior Formatting: Brooke Lee

FATHOM

Mikel Parry

Contents

CHAPTER 1	CUERPO MORTO	1
CHAPTER 2	DEAD CANARY	19
CHAPTER 3	FREEZING HOT	35
CHAPTER 4	UNFINISHED BUSINESS	51
CHAPTER 5	DOWN THE RABBIT HOLE	67
CHAPTER 6	WANDERING DUCK	85
CHAPTER 7	REAL IMAGINATION	99
CHAPTER 8	BOOGIE NIGHTS	111
CHAPTER 9	TORA TORA	125
CHAPTER 10	BUSH ZOMBIE	141
CHAPTER 11	FLAMING FELINE	161
CHAPTER 12	PRANK CALL	193
CHAPTER 13	DUNGEONS AND DRAGONS	201
CHAPTER 14	ICE TOMB	217
CHAPTER 15	GHOSTNAPPED	229
CHAPTER 16	DARK HORSE	247
CHAPTER 17	LAMB TO THE SLAUGHTER	259
CHAPTER 18	CHECKMATE SUICIDE	273
CHAPTER 19	KILLING GOD	281
CHAPTER 20	FREAK FAMILY	291
ABOUT THE AUTHOR		297

CHAPTER ONE

Cuerpo Morto

"Blood, blood spatters, and more blood. It's always got to be blood."

The empty streets of a barely held together neighborhood encapsulated the harrowing words describing a scene that was still unfolding.

"I never understand why you act so surprised. It's just another Monday."

Two men, standing in the center of a small street that was now clearly a festering ghetto, were having a conversation. One of the men fidgeted nervously, scratching his arm and slowly scanning the streets. He was slightly taller than most men and had a wiry frame that belied his meager muscle mass. Jet black hair sat atop his head like a messy plop of spaghetti. His eyes were a light hazel color and seemed to adapt to his emotions the same way a chameleon's skin changes according to its environment. His mixed ethnicity made him look both plain and exotic at the same time. He dressed in an old, fuzzy suit that had long since needed to be retired. Along the ground dragged his worn, scuffed dress shoes, his failed attempt at professionalism made obvious. The man's name was Demotrius Ward, or as his friends, family, and most of the human population knew him, Demo Ward. Apart from the name, he appeared as nothing more than another face, passed then forgotten on the street.

"Is that what you're imagining, or is that what you've been told?" asked Demo, staring at the other man walking by his side.

The other was a scrappy looking Irish man who looked like he had dragged himself out of bed moments before. His eyes had red runways, which etched their way through his sockets, revealing great signs of sleep deprivation and stress. He smelled like a familiar brand of soap; Irish Spring, ironically. His face was a shabby mess. Atop his head, dirty blonde hair gave way to a pale complexion. Bob Cathy Briar was his name, emphasized by the very un–masculine chime of his middle name. He preferred to be called Bob Briar. Ironically, everyone had dropped the Briar resulting in his being called Bob Cat; a name that always struck a nerve with him. His body was covered in the tattoos of a violent past. These scars proved that Bob Cathy Brier had graduated from the school of hard knocks.

"I'm imagining. But to be honest, it's always the same thing. I can smell the crap from a mile away. And it's a big pile of steaming crap," said Bob Cat, glaring at some teenagers who were jumping over battered fences.

"Look at these hooligans, running amuck without any parental supervision. It's no wonder we keep coming back to places like this."

Demo shook his head, allowing only a sliver of his eye to catch Bob Cat's.

"They aren't all that bad. Or have you forgotten where we come from?"

Bob Cat snorted at his response, his nostrils flaring a bit.

"Yeah, that's why I'm worried about 'em."

Demo pushed himself a few steps in front of Bob Cat, who was obviously caught up in a memory. He began assessing the situation, putting all objects of interest front and center, leaving the rest muted for the time being.

The area was obviously poor. Years of ghetto rehab and rehabilitation had stuck the proverbial needle in and out of the downtrodden society so many times, that all that could be seen now were the track marks. Run down homes, broken–down cars, trashy yards, and flocks of feral, street children were at every corner. The only items of distinction were the occasional ghetto–rich cars, surprisingly clean and well kept. Demo closed his eyes and let his mind take it all in. He needed to adopt this place, understand it, feel it, become it.

"Look! Another one of those little pricks just eyed our car! I'm going to pull out my gun to show him I'm serious. Punks like that need to learn a lesson. I never understand why we have to park a mile away from the scene and walk. It's a waste of valuable resources."

Demo now looked straight at Bob Cat, showing him how agitated he had become by having his focus broken with such mindless banter.

"Look Bobby, you know why. I've explained it to you a thousand times. I've got to understand the area and its people to get the gears moving. I can't just show up to a crime scene and know what to do."

Bob Cat shook his head, looking up at the clouds.

"Talk about your dog and pony show. Well, if you think I'm bad, wait till we get up to the blues. I can't wait to see what you're gonna say then."

Bob Cat ripped a piece of gum from his pocket and stuffed it in his mouth, chewing it viciously.

"Still trying to quit?"

"I quit—just chewing the gum now," he snapped back.

"I think the point of quitting is that you stop chewing the gum. You've just switched addictions."

Demo paused, making sure he had been heard.

"Still not sleeping? Still fighting?" Demo pressed further.

Bob Cat snarled, reminding Demo of his place. He went back to assessing the area.

Worn tires on many cars hadn't been replaced, which indicated commuters with low income jobs. Cigarette butts were as common as sand on the beach. The occasional smutty magazine had made its way into the gutter. Vice, vice, and more vice—the one thing that flourished in places like these. The only obvious fauna was the violent dogs that would occasionally lash out at them as they passed. The teenagers hopping the fences were more than likely members of a gang. Undoubtedly, they were up to no good, but not enough that he cared to pursue them, especially with a murder investigation underway.

I wonder what this place used to look like in its day? It's good to be home.

"Oh, thank anything holy we're almost there. I can see the blues parading around still striping up the place."

Bob Cat's words snapped Demo back into reality. It was then that he finally saw the house of interest.

The house wasn't much different than the rest—broken, busted, trashy—similar to the home he'd lived in all those years ago. This meant there were plenty of holes in its foundation that extended far beyond the tangible. Weeds overran the yard, with the occasional beer can mixed into the fray. Outside sat a truck with a faded construction company logo plastered to its side. Demo sped up to the truck, leaving a bewildered Bob Cat behind.

"I hate it when you do that!" yelled Bob Cat, still gnawing on his nicotine rich glob.

Demo was on his way to the car when he was abruptly stopped, breaking his focus yet again.

"Sorry, sir, this area is off limits. This is an official crime scene."

Demo looked at the finger that led to the hand that connected to the police officer. He was having a hard time returning to normal behavior. Instead, he stood there blinking blankly.

"Is there something wrong, sir?"

"He's fine," said Bob Cat, catching up as he heaved and panted.

"He's with me, and I'm…*we're* part of the detective team."

The police officer looked utterly confused. He peered at Demo who was still staring blankly back at him.

"You walk here?" asked the police officer.

"I told you that was stupid," Bob Cat mumbled to Demo underneath his breath.

"What was that, sir?" continued the officer.

"Nothing…just hashing things out with my partner. I'm Bob Cathy Briar, and this is my partner Demotrius Ward. We're the consultant detectives."

The officer raised one eyebrow to an almost cartoonish height.

"Consultant detectives, Demotrius?" the officer questioned.

It was then that Demo decided to chime in.

"Yes, Demo for short. Don't ask. And we've got a lot of work to do here, so if you don't mind."

The officer hesitated while he tried to gather his thoughts. The prospect of gaining his permission looked rather dim.

"Demo, Bob Cat, we're all inside. Come on in. Don't mind him, he's the new guy."

The voice came from a slender, professional looking woman. She had beautiful tanned skin that gleamed in the afternoon sun, and she was carefully adorned in pricy clothes that fit her body perfectly. Her teeth were almost blindingly white, and her eyes a piercing green that could only be trumped by her wild, streaky hair. Various shades of blonde and brunette covered her head, all purposefully placed with immaculate detail. By the way she carried herself, she clearly felt in charge. Her name was Jacky Stockholm.

The officer glanced at Jacky before nodding his head reluctantly, still caught up in the awkward situation.

"About time I saw a familiar face around here," said Bob Cat, blowing past the officer on his way towards Jacky.

Demo followed, giving a small nod to the dumbfounded officer before peeking inside the car; beer cans, piles of crumpled fast food wrappers, and a paper bag filled with protein shakes, bags of almonds, jerky, and a stick of lip gloss in a weird shade of burgundy.

"I know it's a strange name. I'll explain it to you later," Demo said to the officer over his shoulder as he went.

Jacky gave off an intoxicating scent that had been liberally dosed all over her body. Both Demo and Bob Cat shook their heads upon arriving within its alluring radius of effect. But Jacky was all business, dismissing the formalities quickly.

"And where in this ghetto have you two been? I put the call in over an hour ago."

Bob Cat stepped behind Demo, shaking his head.

"Out for a nice stroll through the park, as usual," he mumbled from his hiding place.

Jacky looked at Demo for a moment before coming to an inward conclusion.

"Still haven't quit, have you?"

Bob Cat's face grimaced in annoyance.

"I've quit. I'm just chewing the gum," he said loudly, catching the attention of a couple of police officers standing close by.

Jacky grinned, waving her hand, beckoning them to follow. She cleared a path with her mere presence. Any pathetic creature caught in it would glance up, realize its error, and flee for its life. Her heels clicked and clacked as she walked on the patchy cement walkway that led to the house. Demo glanced over to catch Bob Cat staring at her swaying hips.

"You really shouldn't look, you know. It'll just make things worse," Demo said, trying to catch Bob Cat's attention.

Bob Cat grunted in response but ignored Demo's suggestion, his eyes following Jacky's every step.

Within moments, they had arrived at the front door. Inside was a beehive of commotion. Men and women darted back and forth, putting up lines of tape while pointing out potential evidence on the floor. The room was as worn as the outside of the house. The carpet was an off color brown that had perhaps been a livelier, lighter color at some point. The walls were covered by one mystery stain after another. Towards the far wall was a couch, whose back was riddled with holes, burns, and even more stains. On it sat a man with his head buried in his hands, sobbing. On the unkempt walls surrounding him was the occasional photo. The smell of mildew and unwashed clothes permeated the air, drowning out everything else—including Jacky's scent, unfortunately. On the floor was a wide arrangement of clutter, just a few cat litter boxes short of a hoarder's paradise. The objects ranged from clothing, shoes, leftover pizza boxes, to unwashed dishes and the occasional empty carton of ice cream. Demo looked up at the photos on the wall and paused for a moment. Many appeared to contain multiple slots, much like any family would have. He tried to imagine what it would feel like to come from such a nurturing garden of emphatic love—he couldn't.

The room led to a filthy kitchen, where stacks of dishes and pots seemed to work their way upward like proud achievements to human apathy. At the kitchen's entrance was a bag filled with construction tools of every kind. It was surprisingly well organized, and the tools inside gleamed, indicating the care they had received. Demo continued analyzing the room while he walked towards the train wreck of a man on the couch.

"Ok everybody, I need you to clear out for a minute," Jacky said, letting her voice be heard.

Demo and Bob Cat looked on as the stammering commotion came to an abrupt stop and began to move outside.

"I like it when she takes control," said Bob Cat.

As the people passed the trio heading outside, Demo felt their stares burning right through him. He knew what he was weird. Taking them away from doing their jobs while he did his was an ongoing battle he had to wage, case by case.

"Not you," said Demo, seemingly out of nowhere, pointing at the man reluctantly getting up off the couch.

Jacky pursed her lips in preparation to clamor away at Demo's remark.

"It's fine, sweet cheeks, he's obviously got him flagged," said Bob Cat, smiling.

Jacky spun around to meet Bob Cat directly.

"I'd watch your loose talking mouth. If you were on the force I'd have you canned in a week."

Bob Cat rolled his eyes, waving both his hands in the air.

"Oh no, please don't."

Demo stepped forward, leaving the two bickering back and forth. He had locked onto his target and was moving in quickly. Just like a torpedo heading to sink a ship, he took the most direct path, stepping over piles of junk, clutter, and the occasional piece of furniture. His lanky legs moved with a ballerina–like precision and purpose, his eyes now in an unbroken stare with the sad looking man on the couch. He arrived just in time to see the man fall into another spout of digression. Tears streaked down his face leaving a salty residue behind. But he was interrupted by a rather odd question.

"Paper or plastic?"

The man stopped sobbing and raised his head, showing his confusion.

"I'm sorry?" he said, now looking at Demo who seemed delighted with his response.

"Paper or plastic—when you go shopping, which do you use?"

This befuddled the man further, who gave a timid response.

"Whatever you get, I guess…never really thought about it."

"Well, that answers that," Demo said proudly.

The man looked towards the quarreling duo at the door as if pleading for help. But Demo pressed on.

"Build the house yourself?"

The man shook his head no while remaining completely confounded.

"How long have you lived here, would you say?"

The man looked further taken aback, but realized there was no escape.

"I don't know…five, maybe six years. It's been a while, I guess."

"Kids, no kids?" Demo probed further.

"No kids. We haven't had much luck that way—Tracy had a hard time with it—and now she's gone!"

At the mention of his wife's name, he sobbed uncontrollably into his hands.

It was then that Demo looked at the couch more carefully. The man sat in a time-shaped indentation that conformed almost perfectly to his shape. To his left was a much smaller indentation that must have belonged to his wife. A few yards away from the couch was the centerpiece of the room; the television. Demo focused on the TV for a moment. In an instant, he sat down to the right of the man on the couch.

"She sat here?" Demo questioned, looking at the man sternly.

"No, Tracy used to sit…"

"I know; I just had to hear it. I need you to look this way," Demo said, nodding his head slightly towards his shoulder.

"Say *my wife* instead of *Tracy*. Say it to me direct and nothing else."

The man's face was now completely plastered with confusion. Again he glanced at the door to see that the once quarreling duo now stood within ear's distance, silently listening. Bob Cat met the man's gaze and gave a stoic nod. Hesitantly, he turned to Demo and did as he was asked.

"My wife used to sit here."

"Again, please," said Demo, looking straight into the man's eyes.

"I don't see the point. Could you please tell me why we're doing this?"

"Again, please," demanded Demo, now with a harsher tone to his voice.

The man took a deep breath, trying to control his emotion before responding.

"My wife, Tracy, used to sit here."

Demo now took a deep breath as if annoyed by the response.

"I said to only say *my wife*. You added *Tracy*."

The man looked agitated with Demo's presence.

"That's because Tracy is her name."

"*Was* her name," corrected Demo, interrupting him belligerently.

The man stood up. He was much taller than Demo had realized. He loomed over him like a shadow cast from a mountain.

"You've got a lot of nerve, amigo. I don't think I'll be talking to you anymore."

Demo ignored him completely and kept looking at the two

impressions in the couch.

"What do you do for work?"

The man stepped away from the couch.

"What does it matter?"

Demo broke his gaze from the couch and put it upon the man under question. He waited silently.

"I work in construction. Like almost everyone in this garbage hole. So what? You could ask anyone around here what they do but it don't mean nothin'."

"Double negative, amigo," said Demo. "Did you want to be a construction worker when you were young?"

The man shook his head.

"No, I wanted to be a basketball player."

"That's why you came?" said Demo pointing at the floor. "That's why you came to the US?"

The man nodded his head grudgingly.

"They said this was the land of opportunity. All I see is a bunch of fat pigs and wasted time."

The man's transition was remarkable. Bob Cat went to say something, but was shushed forcibly by Jacky's finger over his mouth.

"You met your wife here?"

"Yes, we met in college. I was an exchange student."

"Lots of overtime in construction, isn't there? Did your wife work?"

The man looked down at the floor for a second, hiding his face.

"No, no, Tracy doesn't, *didn't*, work."

Demo looked at the man one last time before staring at the TV.

"They sure don't make those like they used to. A literal tank of entertainment, solid couple inches of glass going back to a cathode tube or whatever they call it. Those things are almost unbreakable, keeping everything inside."

The man shrugged not knowing what to say, when out of nowhere Demo sprang up and extended his hand toward him.

"Thank you for your time, Mr.—?"

The man's hostile stance relaxed slightly.

"Paul. Paul Ortega."

Demo paused as if he had just seen something, then continued.

"Well, thank you Paul. We'll figure out whoever killed Tracy and bring them to justice."

The man nodded before sitting back down on the couch. His sobbing came shortly after.

Demo paced over to the team, looking like he had just seen a ghost.

"The body, where did you find the body?" probed Demo.

Jacky pointed to behind the couch. She went to say something when Bob Cat nudged her in the side.

"Thank you," said Demo, retracing his steps carefully until he arrived behind the rugged piece of furniture.

From there his eyes grew wide. Scanning the floor he saw remnants of the vicious, bloody attack in the form of small droplets of blood dotting the walls and carpet in a malicious pattern.

"You found Tracy here?" Demo yelled without looking at Paul.

"Yes, she was dead by the time I got here. Who would do this to her?" he responded, tears streaming down his face.

"*Who* isn't what I'm looking at right now."

Demo went back to the front door, shoving his way between Jacky and

Bob Cat, splitting them in two. Once at the front door, he took a deep breath and closed his eyes. Underneath his breath a million words flew out of his mouth, as if he were rehearsing them from memory, until a moment of clarity arrived. Turning toward Bob Cat he whispered something. Bob Cat nodded his head immediately.

"I'm Paul Ortega, overworked construction worker from who–knows–what Spanish speaking country. My dreams of becoming a word class athlete fail and I end up here, just another run of the mill house in the ghetto, as far away from the limelight and prestige as possible. I'm married to Tracy who I met in college before embarking on what had to have been a wonderful idyllic set–up of the American dream. Only the dream never came true. It died off and disappeared, faded by time. Until one day I come home from a hard day's work to find my wife dead on the floor, brutally attacked by some undeniable presence that then left the scene. Sounds like the classic smash n' grab leaving me, Paul Ortega, the woeful widower."

Demo paced towards the couch where Paul was sitting.

"We spend most of our time here looking out of the digital window at the world that passed us by. Who knows what rants this television has had to put up with? But wait; there are always children."

Demo glanced at Paul who was now intently focused on his seemingly directionless train of thought.

"Children can make anyone feel accomplished. Pull you out of your self–pity that can seem so suffocating. Repair those burned bridges. But I, Paul Ortega, don't have any kids. But why?"

This struck a nerve in Paul and he stood up.

"Just what the hell are you talking about? You're some sick freak, you know that? You've got some real nerve talking like that! You don't know nothing about me!"

Demo vaguely smiled as if Paul's response had come right on cue.

"Because we, the happy couple, can't have kids—or worse—we tried and failed. Miscarriages can scar someone for life. This always comes as the most unpleasant surprise and can really put a hook in things."

The man arose and approached Demo aggressively. But Bob Cat

stepped in between, blocking his path.

"Suddenly there's no light at the end of the tunnel. Happy couple isn't so happy anymore. Time starts to drive a wedge in their relationship, and before you know it, you're roommates. The thing about roommates is that they have an uncanny ability to nitpick you down to every detail. They take for granted what they see every day."

Demo looked at Paul who was weighing the consequences of attacking him outright. Bob Cat kept a ready hand on his sidearm sensing Paul's growing hostility.

"She was overweight, jobless, depressed, and without child; probably because of a direct relationship between those items, in no particular order. You start to blame your emptiness on her as if she were holding you back. Things would have been *so* different in your skewed reality, if only she hadn't been your wife. Your temper did the rest. All it took was the right recipe."

"Say one more word and I'll put my fist through your head! Don't you dare talk about Tracy like that!" Paul screamed, now pushing forward only to be met by Bob Cat's outreached arm.

"I wouldn't," Bob Cat said, making sure the man could see his hand at the ready on his sidearm.

"I live here. Every day I see this mess. Every day I see what was supposed to be a fairy tale falling further and further into this. My once radiant wife is now a blistering eye sore reminding me of my failures as a man and as a husband. But there's one thing I pride myself on in a hate–love relationship; my work. The only damned thing that makes me a man now is my work. A low paying, stressful job that I'd have never dreamed of taking all those years back. And, of course, I have my tools. Each one carefully accounted for like the children I never had. Like a compartment of emotion where I could proudly look at them and say, at *least* I have that. But then comes the day when the boss lets me go. Me, the man, the provider. What am I now? I'm a broken man, I'm nothing. I come home and take it all out on the only target I can blame that's left—the only logical scapegoat—my wife."

Demo now took a more emotional tone as if the character he had assumed was weighing him down.

"We sit at our usual spots before getting into another argument. I tell her the news and it appears this may be the last straw. She threatens to leave; lets loose her bottled up emotions about my infertility, my lack of so many things; she can't live like this anymore. I lost control."

Demo walked over to the tools sitting inside the large bag, heading into the kitchen, his eyes now watering greatly with conviction.

"I'm Paul Ortega—a victim of circumstance, a resentful husband, an unemployed construction worker without his hammer."

Paul's stance suddenly shifted. His sobbing burst wide open, even greater than before. He collapsed to the ground beating his fists against the aged carpet.

Demo approached him cautiously, to the shock of Bob Cat and Jacky. Standing within arm's reach he continued.

"I'm Paul Ortega, and after killing my wife in a passionate rage, I've just realized how much she actually meant to me."

With Demo's final words Paul's emotions erupted free like a volcano that was long overdue.

"I didn't mean for any of this. I didn't want us to live like this. We were supposed to have the baby; the baby would have brought us back together. I want to change this; I want to bring her back," wailed Paul.

Demo's eyes continued to water. It appeared as if he was on the verge of crying himself.

"But the baby never came, Paul. The baby's gone, just like Tracy."

Paul's sadness was almost palpable when to the utter shock of everyone present he let loose his guilt.

"It happened so fast. I was so angry. We were yelling so loud."

Demo nodded at Jacky who ushered in a pair of cops who handcuffed Paul swiftly.

"I didn't mean to—"

Demo nodded his head, staring at Paul directly.

"I know Paul, but you did."

Jacky and Bob Cat let out an extended gasp for air. They had been unknowingly holding their breath in anticipation. Jacky shook her head in disbelief while Paul was escorted out of the house, sobbing uncontrollably.

"I don't know how you do that. All I know is it saves us tons of money on legal fees. Only problem is, we have a verbal confession but no murder weapon."

Demo wiped his eyes before responding.

"It was his hammer. In a burst of violent rage it was the first thing that came to his mind. It won't be far from here. He didn't plan this."

Jacky rolled her eyes.

"Well, there goes the premeditation. Mars is going to try and take us around the block on this one if he gets it, that slippery snake. It would have been easier to have Bob Cat shoot him in self–defense."

Jacky turned and waved her hands, ushering the waiting crowd from outside back into motion.

"Look for a hammer. It can't be far. Don't wipe the prints or I swear on my life I'll wipe you from existence!"

Demo frowned. He had just solved a case in a matter of minutes, getting a confession on the spot, but somehow he still felt the void that Paul had left behind.

He just wanted to live his dream. He just wanted to be the man he thought he was. Why can't murder be more black and white?

"Seriously though, your little parlor tricks work for the blues as long as you get a confession or hard evidence, but I need some answers to how you did that," Bob Cat urged, standing close to Demo's side.

Demo paused as if rewinding the tape within his head. He began where it started.

"First was the area. Low income, ghetto, and jot full of broken dreams. But that's not what was special. First there was the yard, a literal forest of weeds. They didn't care what anyone thought at this point. Then came the car…"

"The construction car?" asked Bob Cat, as if his small piece of detail could help.

"Yes, that car. Inside were wrappers of what had to have been years of fast food binging. This could mean many things, but to me it meant he didn't give a damn, and neither did she at this point. But then there was the paper bag filled with protein shakes, almonds, and an off shaded lipstick. Could the husband have run to get some groceries? Was he just helping out? That's when my question gave the answer to; paper or plastic? He didn't have a clue. Not too surprising as to who might remember that? Except it was paper. You usually have to choose paper if given the option, or ask for it yourself. This required thought. The fact that he had no recollection meant he hadn't been the last person to drive the car. But what would drive someone who never leaves the house to get in the car in the first place? Ironically enough, weight. Inside it was blatantly apparent that nobody was even slightly concerned with the garbage kingdom in which they lived; pure and utter laziness. This led to the obvious conclusion that they, like most people in this situation, spent most of their time in front of the mind tube. Upon inspecting the couch, I discovered the indentations that had been made over their apathetic timeline. Paul's was obviously the larger, being a big guy, but next to it I noticed that her indentation wasn't a far cry from his. I'm not a physics guy but to me that says overweight, and significantly so. No doubt this had been part of the heated conversation that threw Tracy out to the car for a thoughtful drive. She bought what seemed to be health supplements out of naïve desperation before buying something that at one point made her feel beautiful. An off shade of burgundy that's no longer in style, she was trying to go back in time to find herself again. The fight probably restarted at the car when she returned, thus the abandoned paper bag of goodies. I pressed Paul for his history and status quo to feel what could drive him and his wife over the edge. That's when it hit me; *kids*. Along their wall were dated frames that had enough slots for a family to fill—a family they didn't have—but *almost* did. This was a big risk to pursue, but the fact that some of the aged frames had actual pictures in them and others did not, gave me reason to believe they'd been expecting. When I brought this up it enticed an almost violent response, and *BINGO!* Now to find the murder weapon … I hadn't seen her body, so this was going to take some creative slander. But it was Paul's last shred of pride that doomed him; his *tools*. They were the only thing he cared about anymore, his last shred of manhood. Each meticulously organized within his emotional safe house that came burning down by being let go. But the most important detail was the missing hardware; his hammer. What kind of construction worker losses or misplaces his hammer? Well many do, I'm sure, but not when it's your last piece of twisted humanity. It made sense that he would use that. It's almost poetic really; rage, passion, regret, and years of a smoldering volcano erupting within moments. Paul did love her. His emotion was genuine. But it was his pride that damned him in the end."

Bob Cat blinked then blinked again before shoving a fresh piece of gum into his mouth. His gnawing ensued.

"You're a freak. You know that, don't you? But whatever you gotta do to pay the bills," said Bob Cat, grinning.

Demo smiled faintly, quickly fading back into his somber state of emotion.

"He spoke Spanish. I wish I could have seen the dead body. Not like I wanted to, but they can tell so much. Cuerpo morto," said Demo, pondering everything that had transpired.

"Cuerpo *what?* I'm not following you," responded Bob Cat.

"Cuerpo morto. Isn't that how you say *dead body* in Spanish? I took Spanish in college back in the day," said Demo again.

Bob Cat shook his head and put his arm around Demo, escorting him past all the obviously agitated eyes of the crime scene team.

"It's cuerpo *muerto*, Demo. You think you'd get that one down working so many scenes with so many ethnic backgrounds," said Bob Cat.

"Are you sure? I could swear it's cuerpo *morto.*"

"Stick to what you're good at, buddy—pissing the right people off, and putting on a wonderful magic show—I'll be the one who talks and walks," smirked Bob Cat.

"Talks, walks, and practically swallows his nicotine, all at the same time. Someone who can multitask."

Bob Cat rolled his eyes and stared down the street towards the car they had arrived in over a mile away. A group of teenagers scattered upon seeing the car's owner, now carefully watching.

"These kids, I swear, they have no respect. I'd take a belt to each and every one of them," mumbled Bob Cat.

"Patience Bobby, you never know; maybe someday they'll be the ones fixing this place up," responded Demo.

Bob Cat let out a gargled chuckle beneath the amassing pools of nicotine–rich saliva inside his mouth.

"Fat chance, buddy. I was right about the blood, wasn't I? Always with the blood."

Demo gazed down at their beat up ride, still sensing nostalgia in the air.

"You were right. There's always more blood."

CHAPTER TWO

Dead Canary

A white bustling edifice built with the sole purpose of bringing justice to the people. But on this day it looked more like a paparazzi gauntlet of probing cameras, officious questioning, and calumny wordplay. The press were out like buzzards picking up any scraps they could, no matter how rotten. Alongside them came the timely protests of the community, each holding a makeshift pole of scrabbled emotion, all bearing their weight in words shouted loudly at anyone that looked of interest. For cars trying to get through, it was a maze of human emotion.

Demo and Bob Cat had solved the *Cuerpo Morto* case days earlier. Despite Bob Cat's correct assertion that the words were being entirely mispronounced, Demo would always remember it that way. It would be cataloged along with the others, for better or worse, in a library of morbidity. The duo was out looking for one of their less insidious desires. They were hungry and heading over to their favorite Italian sandwich place. It was just a hopscotch game away from the courthouse and had some of the best spicy beef subs in town. What had started as a logistical convenience was now a thing of habit. Their many visits to the courthouse had unknowingly led them into a predictive schedule of Italian bovine. The pair sat silently in their car until the commotion came into plain view.

"Now what are these idiots doing?" said Bob Cat.

Demo looked at the crowds outside of the courthouse, imagining them as little children screaming at the adults to make it all better.

"Looks serious," Demo said back.

Bob Cat took the speed of the car down a notch. The crowds appeared now like impervious walls of upset flesh.

"This is going to take forever. Is that Jacky?" mumbled Bob Cat, feeling his growing hunger pains getting the better of him.

Demo glanced over just in time to see Jacky standing outside the doors to the courthouse wrangling with the belligerent reporters, like a lion protecting its kill from the hyenas. She was obviously flustered and angry. But Jacky had a way of looking good no matter what the situation. Her teeth, like white headlights, flashed on and off as she spoke.

"She looks worked up. This must be serious. It's not like the courthouse to get such celebrity treatment."

Bob Cat moaned. He knew Demo's curiosity would overtake the need to feed. He wanted to get it over with.

"Fine, I'll park the car. But we aren't walking a mile this time. Even I can feel this one out," said Bob Cat, upset.

Demo nodded his head while his scan continued. People of various backgrounds were there. Some looked poor, while others, the cream of the avarice crop.

"What a cluster. You think people could at least park in some reasonable fashion," said Bob Cat, reaching into his pocket to look for one of his chewy, addiction sticks.

"Forget it. Just leave it in space. We'll deal with it later," said Demo, signaling towards the back of an old Volvo.

Bob Cat screeched the car to a stop inches from hitting its back. He was still fishing in his pockets for some nicotine relief.

"Damn it, I must have left the pack in my other pants," he mumbled aloud.

Demo shook his head as he scratched a dry patch of skin on his wrist before creaking the car door open. For Demo, getting in and out of their company car was an evident reminder of how slow the consultant detective business could be.

"You have other pants?" asked Demo, stepping out of the car.

Bob Cat gave him the appropriate answer through use of his clever hand configuration. Demo smiled before breathing in some of the cool air.

Is it autumn? I can't even remember what month it is.

Bob Cat joined him outside the car with a nicotine fit fueled slam of the door. A dictionary of curse words followed that could have made even the most seasoned sailor tear up.

"Bobby, you've just gotta go cold turkey. Those things are affecting your brain."

Bob Cat put up a fake smile that obscured his true feelings.

"I don't know what you're talking about? I'm hungry, depraved, and stuck outside the last place I wanna be. How could this day get any better?"

"Wish you hadn't said that," said Demo, seeing an all–too familiar set of white, pearly pebbles heading his way.

"There you two are. I was wondering when the garbage guys would show."

"How does she do that?" mumbled Bob Cat. "Woman's got a freaking radar dish on her head or something."

Demo smiled politely at Jacky who, as usual, was dressed to kill. Behind her followed a group of ravenous, media driven scavengers, all waiting for her to slip. Jacky seemed oblivious to their presence. She strode like a woman with purpose. It was this that frightened Demo the most. A woman like Jacky never sent birthday cards, and as sure as her pants were always one size too tight, was never that excited to see them.

"Jacky, it's been ages," said Bob Cat, throwing his arms in the air as if enticing Jacky to enter into his previous embrace.

"Oh, no, no, never. I appreciate the gesture though," said Jacky arrogantly.

"Apparently not long enough," Demo whispered into Bob Cat's ear.

Bob cat snorted, and then instinctively shoved one of his hands into his pockets, still looking for his lost golden sticks of relief.

"I swear they were here? Maybe that old hag took them, just trying to make my day worse."

Demo grabbed Bob Cat by the shoulders.

"You really shouldn't talk about your wife like that, Bobby. You've got to start fixing things, not make them worse," said Demo, a decibel too loud.

Jacky snorted holding back an inappropriate laugh.

"I thought she was your parole officer. Shows what I know," she said, still doing her best to keep it professional.

The trio sat tightly packed as they spoke, but the relentless probing of the media was starting to break their professional defenses down.

"Let's get out of this crap storm. I need to talk to you guys inside."

Bob Cat mumbled another verse of profanities underneath his breath, his stomach grumbling loudly. Demo nodded without speaking. He hated being in the spotlight, especially with the mangy vultures of the media. He'd had one too many run–ins with them, and what came out of his mouth never seemed to read the same way in the papers. Off the trio went, carving a path through the media with Jacky in the lead. She sliced through the crowd like the butcher she was. No one dared stand for too long in fear of facing her infamous wrath.

It took them a few minutes to reach the front of the courthouse. The cool feeling from moments before was replaced by the sweltering heat of the amassed crowd. Demo found it hard to breathe. He couldn't remember the last time he had been near such a large group of people. It was an ongoing paradox that never quite fit together; a man who hates crowds and works in a big city. No wonder he was so miserable all the time.

"Clear out of the way!" Jacky screamed.

The buzz was unreal. People picked at Bob Cat and Demo like they were the ones being ushered in for atrocities they'd committed. Death threats and obscenities made a thick, deafening wall of noise.

"Why are they so angry?" asked Demo, doing his best to scream over the crowd.

"Just get inside and we'll talk."

Once the trio burst inside the courthouse doors a wall of blue uniforms united to push the mob back. Demo gasped for air. He wasn't sure what phobia he had, but it had something to do with what had just happened.

"Stinking vultures, they'll do anything for a story," said Bob Cat, directing the conversation at Jacky.

"Well they've got good reason to be. We're bringing in a big perp from witness protection today. A perp who they believe has been involved in decades of murder and says he knows about some long gone thug who helped orchestrate them. Probably just another schmuck who snorted his last line."

Demo's eyes widened. He glanced back and forth between Jacky and Bob Cat.

"Does this have to do with the blood legacy murders?" Demo probed.

Jacky rolled her eyes giving a look of solicitation at Bob Cat to say something. Bob Cat laughed and then pointed at Demo.

"What, you think he wouldn't figure that out? He's a straight up nerd on this stuff."

Demo's eyes glistened with curiosity.

"It is, isn't it?" Demo continued, ignoring Bob Cat's remarks.

Jacky looked around the courthouse as if searching for anyone who might be eaves dropping on their conversation.

"Look, I'm not going to say that it is or it isn't. But what we've got going on here is way above even my pay grade," Jacky said, looking nervous.

"But those murders have been going on for decades. Why the sudden interest here today? Haven't they stopped?" Demo asked.

Jacky now looked as jittery as ever. It was apparent that the subject was really pricking at her nerves.

"Look, let's just say this recent murder was a person of interest, someone that caught the butt end of some bad PR."

Bob Cat let out a growl of anger.

"Someone of *interest?* Wow, you put that sentence together well, sugar. So whose rich kid was it? Some millionaire, politician, or celebrity?"

Jacky shifted on her heels and let out a high pitched squeak on the freshly waxed floors.

"It was the Governor's son. But don't you two idiots leak a peep of that. If you do, I'll trace it back to you both and roast you on the hot seat, got it?"

Demo's smile faded. He looked at Bob Cat, who also didn't seem to like what he just heard. Jacky went to say something else, but stopped when she saw a flashy suit she knew all too well.

"That rat fink decided to finally show up," Jacky said, forgetting to hush her voice.

Demo and Bob Cat turned just in time to see the living offspring of hubris and ego. The man's cat–like eyes had already found them, and he was coming at them fast.

Bob Cat looked at Demo, giving the go ahead to run. But Demo knew there was no escaping at this point. They'd have to endure what was known as the Mars effect.

"Mars Baloducci," mumbled Jacky.

Mars Baloducci was his name; yet another peculiar signature amongst the ethnic, churning sea that was the city. He was an average sized man who made up for it tenfold with an obvious ego. He had a comprehensive ensemble of clothing that was exhaustively placed, layer upon layer, displaying the greedy exuberance he so loved. He had a perfect touch of grey amidst thick straws of pampered, auburn hair. Each hair was meticulously placed. His eyes were an off shade of blue that starkly contrasted against his artificially baked skin. His name reflected his attitude of being as close to deity as earthly possible; a god walking amongst mere men. An engrossing, masculine aroma permeated the air, waging an unseen war against the luscious feminine scent of Jacky's perfume. The two mixed together like oil and water. The outcome of their combined smell was one of pure nausea.

"I'm walking down the hall and see my favorite trio. Sulking like always, probably dodging the public eye? And I'm thinking, why would Miss Stockholm bring in the two amateur magicians? Is there a circus in town? Well, what exactly *are* you doing here?"

Bob Cat furled his lips in preparation for a verbal onslaught. Jacky interjected just in time to stop the chaos before it started.

"We're just discussing a past case that we solved—nothing more, nothing less—and it sure isn't any of your business, Mars."

Mars haughtily laughed, taking an expensive looking phone from his pocket. His retort came just as quickly.

"Oh, yes, Mr. Ortega. He's my four o'clock tomorrow. I'd love to read you the number of broken injunctions I pulled from the interview alone, but it'd probably slip right through those waxy ears. And have they found that magically disappearing hammer yet? I'll spare you the details, but I'd bet your entire year's salary that he walks."

Jacky practically hissed beneath her breath at Mars's arrogant remarks.

"We'll see about that. That's why it's a courtroom and not a Turkish bath. I wouldn't expect you to understand that, seeing as you spend so much time in one, and so little in the other," retorted Jacky, pursing her lips to try to control her emotions.

Mars grinned from ear to ear with an almost seditious glint of pleasure.

"Oh, how I love to see you, Jacky, even with your two incompetent sidekicks keeping you company."

Bob Cat snapped forward.

"You watch it, Mars. I'm not beyond wiping that smug, pampered face all over the floor."

Demo put an arm on Bob Cat assuring that the situation wouldn't escalate any further.

"Let it be. This guy is a waste of time," Demo whispered to him.

Mars, now content with ruining the attitude of everyone, plunged his overpriced phone back into its silk lined pocked.

"I'd love to confer with you all some more about the intricacies of courtroom etiquette, but I have a case to win that's going to launch me even further up those pearly steps," said Mars, pointing at the granite stairs leading to the belly of the courthouse.

Jacky shook her head.

"You'd do anything for the right price wouldn't you, Mars? A regular old gold digging sham. You took the case, didn't you? You're the one who struck the bargain? Do you know how many people have died leading up to this? Have you not seen outside? This place is on the verge of crumbling down."

Mars put one of his manicured hands out in front of him. He examined it carefully as he spoke, ignoring the machine gun blast of questions.

"*Alleged* murders, of which my client may have nothing to do with. I'd watch your accusations if I were you. Your little flea circus might work on the outside, but believe me when I say I'm the king of the courtroom. And If I feel even a prick of a hair on the back of my neck that you three are somehow mishandling my client's information, I'll file enough injunctions on you to fill a library."

Mars felt his pocket buzz. Without a second thought he snatched his opulent phone out of his pocket and placed it to his ear.

"It's probably nobody important. You know how these things go."

Upon answering the call, his face went from smug to horrified.

"He's gone? What do you mean, he's *gone*? I had him on queue for today! What do you mean his car's gone?"

The group listened as Mars's voice began to shake. It was obvious that something had gone terribly astray. At that very moment, an ensemble of terrified screams came from outside the courthouse doors. Without thinking, Demo swung the doors open, barely missing a reporter's face before he saw what had started the commotion.

It took a moment for it all to sink in. But how could it? None of it seemed real to the slightest degree. However, there it was; the tangible embodiment of the crowd's horror. On the very street that Demo had just been on was an old Cadillac, off–white, almost yellow in color. But what was on the inside is what shook his soul. In the driver's seat was a man covered in blood, struggling to keep his foot on the pedal. His eyes looked faded, almost empty. He was completely naked apart from a worn pair of underwear. The car parted the crowds and stopped suddenly at the front of the courthouse stairs. Everyone watched in horror as the man exited the car. He was barely able to navigate his way around the car to the stairs below were Demo stood. Blood trickled down his exposed body leaving a grisly trail of horror behind him. No one dared to approach him. Reaching the bottom of the stairs, the man collapsed to his knees and brought what appeared to be a blindfold into plain sight. The man rattled away, fighting off the obvious signs of an impending death. With one last burst of energy he secured the blindfold around his head and put both arms up in the air. Within seconds, he collapsed, leaving a body and a pool of blood behind. The once bustling crowd transformed into a sea of petrified statues. No one knew what to do.

It had all happened so fast that even Demo found himself still trying to catch up. His mind didn't work like what most people might call normal. His past had molded him into some sort of sentient being that had a remarkable skill for assimilating a victim's or criminal's mindset. He had honed it through the years to a fine witchcraft. It was almost unbelievable to most people that someone could solve cases by ignoring hard evidence, details, and even motives, relying only on pure intuition. But it worked. However, whatever skill set he possessed was sitting quiet and numb in a stupor of lost thought and feeling. He had to know more. Leaving the group and forgetting any protocol, he approached the collapsed man.

"Who are you?" Demo asked with a shaky voice upon seeing the barely moving chest of the man.

The man turned his head ever so slightly before responding. His eyes now looked grey and cloudy, and his life essence was quickly evaporating into the air.

"He told me he'd kill them if I didn't believe. Now I believe," whispered the man, letting out one final gasp for air before falling to his concrete resting place.

Demo's head began to spin. He felt faint and sick to his stomach. But his mind was still acquiring the details. No visible wound, yet what looked to be gallons of blood. And the car. He hadn't been paying attention to the car.

"Demo, step back!" screamed Jacky, now fully functional again.

"Everyone clear out of here now! This is officially a scene of interest!"

The silence erupted into panicked screams of fright. Tears streamed down the faces of many of the onlookers in the crowd. The disgusting apprehension was all too real. Cameras fired away like artillery shells exploding in the sky. Demo watched the photographers trying to get the best disturbing picture of the dead man, to accommodate the front page news that would engulf the media in the weeks to come; the iconic symbol of the courthouse being torn down by an enigmatic symbol of death. Demo needed space and he needed it now. Without warning he began sprinting through the crowd, desperately trying to get back to his parked car. His mind had taken in so much; perhaps too much. He couldn't handle it anymore.

"Demo, what are you doing? Wait for me, would ya?" hollered Bob Cat, following behind.

Demo heard Bob Cat and glanced behind to see the chaos still unraveling. Jacky was now caught in the midst of waves of criticism raining in from all sides, and drowning out even her undeniable presence. Mars soon joined her outside, more than willing to placate the media with empty promises of justice for a price. All the while the image of the blindfolded man covered in blood flashed before him, igniting his dendrites like brush fire. But even he could find no point of clarity, no beginning to the maze. Whoever had done this had planned every detail.

Demo opened the door then slammed it behind him. He still felt ill from the spinning photomontage in his head.

Why would anyone do this? Why would they do it in broad daylight in front of everyone?

"Demo, I said *wait*! I'm getting tired of trailing you all the time. Jacky's got the whole precinct out tracing this!" Bob Cat paused to see a small slip of paper stuck in the windshield wiper. He seized it, glanced at it, then threw it into the parking lot.

"Well at least it looks like officer do–goody still had time to write parking tickets. This whole system is corrupt!"

Demo closed his eyes, doing his best to bring himself back from the pandemonium. Calmly he began to speak.

"Justice is blind," he said, eyes still closed. "The man blindfolded himself."

Bob Cat paused to reflect on the sudden change of direction. His eyes vibrated back and forth from the stress of it all, consummating in the moment.

"Demo, it doesn't matter if the guy's dead, and Jacky's saying the perp is missing as well."

Demo looked at his hands as he listened to Bob Cat's rambling.

"Why did he put his hands up in the air? Was it symbolic or out of a last moment of desperation? None of this makes any sense, none of it." Demo whimpered, feeling helpless.

"It's just another mob job. It has to be. Stuff like this happens, Demo. We've got to pull this together and see what we can get out of it."

Demo closed his eyes again and rested his face into his palms.

"We need to figure out the car."

Bob Cat shook his head.

"We've got a dead guy and half the precinct scattered about, and you're worried about that guy's car?"

Demo was about to say something when his window began to shake under some furious pounding. He rolled the window down to take a better look. It was Jacky. She looked like her once tenacious self had been torn into a thousand pieces. Her eyes had a wild look to them, of both confusion and rage.

"You two come with me. I don't give a damn what you've got going on, this is more important!"

Bob Cat spat out his window in disgust, still hankering for his missing gum.

"We don't do ride–alongs. I'm not getting mixed into this right now. You can thank your boys for being Johnny on the spot with their parking tickets, though."

Jacky smacked the car in frustration. Her normally poised demeanor was wearing away, exposing her more human side. She started to yell but was blocked by Demo's sudden inquiry.

"Where's the ticket?"

Bob Cat winced as if expecting pain upon hearing Demo's comment.

But he knew all too well that there would be no stopping him now. Warily, he opened his door and tracked down the miniscule piece of legality. Without thinking, he tossed it into the car directly at Demo's lap.

"It's just a ticket, Demo. Some jack wagon trying to hit quota for the day, poaching at the courthouse."

Demo opened the ticket quickly and scanned every detail. All seemed in order. It was all filled in correctly except for the date. Demo never could keep track of the days, but it was the year that bothered him. Squinting his eyes, he read it aloud.

"April 10th, 1975."

Jacky hung her head in close to take a look for herself.

"What's that supposed to mean? That's decades ago."

Demo shook his head in confusion.

"I don't know. Why would someone leave it on our car? We've had nothing to do with this case."

Bob Cat grabbed the piece of paper from Demo's hands. He, too, looked over the paper scrupulously. He let out a boisterous grunt of anger.

"It's gotta be a warning. Dirty bastards want us off their tail. Maybe we stepped too close. What with all the cases we've helped on, I wouldn't be surprised. Mob practically runs this town. It's a dead canary."

Jacky stomped her foot, smacking her heels like clogs against the pavement.

"A dead canary? Do you ever *listen* to what you're saying? You sound like an idiot."

Bob Cat's eyes narrowed, obviously upset at the blatant disrespect he thought he was enduring.

"Says one who has never lived a less than privileged life—I'll explain it to you, honey—a canary is put in a cage to warn somebody if the going's good or not. Good canary, good time. Bad canary, well just look at our little friend over there. Mob probably put the guy up to it then offed him as a warning to stay out of their business. I'd suggest we listen. There's no need to get involved in that."

Jacky ran her slender fingers through her hair, wafting it out of her eyes.

"Do you honestly believe the mob, if there even is one, would even notice you two lowlifes playing detective? That's insane! Demo, are you hearing this?"

Demo went to nod but was yanked back into a thought he couldn't shake. The thought kept lingering like bitter smoke swirling about his mind. *The car.* The car was out of place. It was ancient. You just don't see that type of car rolling down the street anymore.

"The car," Demo mumbled.

"The *what*?" asked Jacky and Bob Cat, almost in unison.

"The car doesn't fit. Why go through all the trouble?"

Jacky and Bob Cat's shoulders slumped. He had lost them completely.

Demo pondered the significance of the car but kept hitting one mental roadblock after another, until it dawned on him.

"Bob Cat, give me that ticket again."

Bob Cat did as he was told, like an unwilling child giving up his toy. But once Demo had the paper he locked on decisively.

"What's the license plate number on the car?" Demo asked, looking straight at Jacky.

Jacky appeared slightly caught off-guard by the question.

"Why does that matter?"

"Just do it, please," said Demo, grinding his teeth.

"Whatever," Jacky snapped back, whipping out her mobile phone as she stepped away from the car.

Bob Cat drew close to Demo to try and see what he hadn't been able to see before. The smell of an old time musk filled Demo's nostrils with his proximity.

"You taking her out tonight?" Demo questioned, startling Bob Cat on the spot.

"She says she likes the scent, reminds her of better times. Figure we'd give it another try."

Demo nodded, still analyzing every detail. Jacky returned, waving her phone like a victory flag.

"Alright weirdo, you ready?"

Demo said nothing. He sat motionless, staring only at the scribbled–in marks placed in the license plate number slot on the ticket. As Jacky spouted out the last digits of the plate, suddenly the dizzying world of details came to a screeching halt. Folding the paper carefully he placed it into his pants pocket. Bob Cat looked bewildered and decided to speak up.

"Don't give me this *guess what I'm thinking* crap. Tell me, what did you find?"

Demo ignored Bob Cat and instead leaned towards Jacky.

"Check the plates against the list of stolen cars in the area. If I'm right, we may have a lead."

Bob Cat raised his voice, still prying for information from Demo's mind vault.

"Not one second more of this, unless you *spill* it!"

Demo looked at Bob Cat with sincere worry etched across his face.

"The plate number on the dead man's car is the same plate number on our ticket. Someone knew we were coming, knew our car, saw us leave, and placed it; someone who obviously wants us out of the picture. Dead canary."

Bob Cat cringed.

"We ain't getting out of this one alive," he said, holding his chest and simulating a heart attack.

"No, I think we're all in more danger than we realize. We all might die."

CHAPTER THREE

Freezing Hot

Demo tossed and turned all night, watching the horrific scene at the courthouse play over and over like a video stuck in loop. This, mixed with his own prolific demons that plagued his mind like a cancer, made it a truly unbearable night. So many questions had arisen in so little time. It wasn't like him to be involved in something seemingly so big. He was just a little fish, now being swallowed by the whales. He needed to get outside. He needed some air.

Stepping out onto the street from his apartment complex, he couldn't help but notice the quiet calm before the storm that was the early morning. The magical hour when most people were fighting the urge to sleep in and let go. In mere minutes they would awake and drag themselves back into the grinding stone of life. But in this brief moment, the streets had lowered their voices to a whisper. The peace was dispersed in a heartbeat with the clamorous ringing of the cellphone vibrating in his pocket. Demo cringed realizing that a call this early could only mean bad news. He didn't want to, but he did it anyway and answered the phone.

"Demo, it's Jacky. I need you to come down. No time for chit chat. I've sent Martinez to pick you up."

Demo began to say something but only received the monotone cat purr from the phone in response. He perused over the past details of recent events catalogued away in his mind. So many pieces seemed to be a significant part of a much bigger puzzle. But ironically, several pieces also seemed to fit into a mob style warning. *Tread lightly detective*, Demo thought. Suddenly the quiet was ruptured by the wail of a siren. Demo didn't need to see it to know it was coming for him. The streets had a way of echoing the sound that seemed to pinpoint his location like a bat swooping in for a moth. He stared at the ground and sincerely hoped none of his neighbors were watching. That would be the last thing he needed in his otherwise innocuous existence. Tires screeched to a stop, expending a rich, burnt, rubbery smell that stung his nostrils.

"Hop in. Jacky wants you to come with me. Got to get you to the docks, as of *yesterday*."

Demo peered inside the car to see two young eyes staring back at him.

They were an almost rustic brown that had a relaxing aura. The man's complexion was clean shaven and professional. He had dark brown hair, and an athletic build. He appeared dependable and trustworthy, a real unshakeable personality. It was no wonder that Jacky relied on him as her errand boy. His complexion told the rest of the story; serious and with purpose. His name was Richard Martinez.

Demo paused, feeling a tennis ball sized lump grow in his throat. If Jacky had sent Martinez, something had just hit the fan. Demo knew that if he got into the car, he'd pick up the nightmare right where he'd left off. What troubled him the most, was the puppet master of this nightmare, pulling on his strings like a helpless marionette. Reluctantly, he got in the car. Immediately he was greeted with the traditional city cop smell of old spice and mouthwash, the two essentials you need when being rushed out the door. The car squealed away with the lights blaring.

"We're officially knee deep in this, Demo. Whatever is going on has got Jacky straight wheeling. It's not like that girl to get so shaken up. She didn't even tell me what's going on. Word is they're bringing in some of the big boys."

Demo couldn't help but notice the influxes at certain points in the sentence, divulging the seriousness of the matter. As the buildings whizzed by, Demo's mind wandered. He wanted more details about anything they had found. For once his intuition was getting him nowhere. Evil always had a method, no matter how chaotic. The mind of even the most seditious killers still had similarities with the drug enticed, violent morons. He just had to find that common point, assume that mindset, and follow the path. After all, he himself was a murderer—at least in his mind. Demo leaned back against the battle–worn seat of the police car and took a deep breath, staring out of the window at the meshed collage of images passing by. He hoped he had what it took to solve this case and cut the puppet master's strings.

"We're almost there. When I pull up, stick with me and I'll walk you in. This place is absolutely bumping so leave all the talking to me."

Demo shook his head, coming back out of his daydream.

"Where's Bobby? Did Jacky call him, too?"

Martinez shook his head.

"Don't know. All I know is this one hits close to home with Jacky."

The car pulled up outside a large warehouse, which sat among rows and rows of other warehouses that all looked practically identical. Towering roofs sat overhead, worn from the elements. The warehouse of interest was a buzzing beehive of activity. Men and women darted in and out of the rusty doors, clamoring as they went. Demo noticed the distressed look on some of their faces; this wasn't just a random murder.

"Follow me, she's inside," said Martinez, signaling for Demo to follow.

Demo stepped out of the car into a surprisingly brisk atmosphere. The air seemed full of tiny floating icicles. He hadn't dressed for the occasion. The cold was only amplified by the bleak outlook of the crime scene. He had seen this before. People had different ways of dealing with an unwanted reality, and looking occupied was one of them. A few footsteps towards the warehouse he reached a conclusion, which solidified the further he went forward.

Martinez reached back and grabbed Demo's wrist thrusting it to his side. His sudden burst of strength was incredible. Demo flailed forward like a ragdoll.

"He's with me. We're looking for Jacky. Is she inside?"

The policeman looked at Demo once before responding.

"She's there, but I wouldn't go near that woman right now. This one's got her rattled."

Martinez nodded. It appeared he, too, was reaching some conclusions of his own.

Demo shook his hand free from Martinez's vice–like grip on his wrist. He didn't like the feeling of being dragged around like a schoolboy. He carefully inspected the details of the warehouse from the outside in as they entered. Metal siding and an old vintage sign filled with holes being the only discernible marker between this warehouse and the herd of others. Upon entering, a round of chills attacked his vulnerable exposed skin and made him physically shiver. The inside was even colder than the outside.

"What is this place?" questioned, Demo looking around.

Martinez shook his head while scanning the room.

"Don't have a clue. Just looks like some old, abandoned warehouse to me."

But to Demo it was teeming with questions. The inside was some sort of chemical factory. Old conveyer belts retired from their once vivacious, laboring life stood in rows. Widgets of every kind painted the walls, exhibiting the wonderful innovation that must have birthed the warehouse in its day. Demo looked down at the floor. His aging dress shoes stared back at him reminding him of how down and out he really was. Solving cases seemed so much more glorious in the movies, and came with more money. Looking at the rusted, deteriorated floor below his feet, he smiled. This place and he shared a lot in common; a tangled dichotomy of glory to rags. Demo reflected briefly on his own glory days. The mornings when he loved waking up seemed so distant now. His nerves of steel were finely polished by his days at the academy. And then there was his partner, Mike, who he couldn't think about anymore. The clouds were forming in his head already. Dark clouds filled with remorse and anger. He had to control them or suffer their thunderous rage.

"There—Jacky's there" hollered Martinez, who was by now a surprising distance ahead of Demo.

Demo followed Martinez's finger, doing his best to break free from his torturous trance. With a subtle nod of the head, he set his course. On his way things started to get interesting, almost as if the people around him had disappeared. In his mind they were muted. The only points of interest were those now talking to him as he went. Sets of tools, bags filled with clutter, empty canisters, and a trail of cords all lead to two massive, metallic doors. Demo imagined himself as the killer, glancing behind his back as if being watched. Had he dragged the body here from somewhere else? Or had he done it all in–house? Both seemed viable, but ultimately there could only be one answer. A sober feeling of doubt swept over him. If this was the same killer—the killer who had set the car scene up to ensure it would never be forgotten—his work would be truly cut out for him. But then again, maybe the killer had been in the car that day… Just then, looking like the grim reaper himself, Jacky burst through the doors. At her side was Bob Cat, whose eyes looked blank and empty. Jacky, however, was a fiery maelstrom.

"Demo, get over here!"

He did as he was told and approached the coiled up Jacky cautiously.

"Tell Martinez to drive faster next time. I needed you here earlier."

Demo shrugged his shoulders. He looked into Jacky's eyes to see blood filled subway tunnels rushing in and out of her cornea. Her hair was in a ponytail, which was never the case. Her makeup looked rushed, and it was clear she hadn't been sleeping. Demo glanced at Bob Cat who responded with a vague headshake. Demo couldn't handle the suspense anymore. Bravely he stepped forward trying to get inside the two thick steel doors. Jacky's hand jutted out, smacking dead center into his chest.

"You're not going to like what you see. I want to find this bastard and stick a needle up his arm. Don't fail me on this one, Demo."

Demo listened to Jacky's words as they passed like echoes through a massive cave. The level of stress in the room was beyond manageable. Each person was sitting on the edge of letting go.

"It's the witness, isn't it? The witness and…"

Demo's words stifled Jacky who put an arm over her face, holding back tears. It was then that Bob Cat filled the holes in the only way he knew how.

"They're blues, Demo. Someone is gutting us from the inside out," Bob Cat said somberly.

The news wasn't news at all to Demo. He had come to this conclusion already. In his head a loud snap erupted as two pieces of the puzzle seemed to fit together. The overall emotion of the scene showed the true signs of what ordinary people feared most. That those set apart to protect them were now as vulnerable as they were. Dead cops were always the last thing anyone wanted, especially Jacky. Jacky was charged with caring for them, at least in her mind. Losing a cop under her watch was no less than losing a child for her. This must be devastating.

"I'll need to be alone," said Demo, looking at Jacky.

Jacky looked away for a moment, trying desperately to control her emotions.

"It's already done. Be quick, as the feds will be here soon."

Demo didn't hesitate any longer. He stepped from the splotchy light of the warehouse into the double doors of the murder scene. It took a great deal of effort to push them open, but as soon as he did it was obvious why. The air shot past Demo with a blustery whoosh, bringing with it bitter cold. He was walking into a massive freezer. If he had been ill equipped before, he was reeling in regret now. The freezer's air bit at him like a rabid, ice–toothed dog. He immediately felt his body shiver. He had to keep moving and fast.

He focused on one corner of the room and began scanning while forcing a murderous mindset on himself. He needed to not only formulate the questions, but also come up with the answers. He did this until something made him pause. His stomach churned like an acidic sea in a storm. He dry heaved, letting the sick emotion out in a physical manifestation. He hadn't been ready for this.

In the middle of the room was the source of his sickening emotion; the scene's details now etching into his mind like a chisel into stone. Two men sat in prayer–like positions, each frozen solid and obviously dead. Their adoration was directed at yet another man, whose figure was also that of a venerating man, but unlike the others, his hands sat high up in the air. He was frozen stiff, much like the others, except his eyes were missing. More accurately described, they were gouged out, leaving two gaping holes where his visual connection to the world had been removed. But the heinous artistry continued towards his back. Meticulously designed in every wicked detail were angel's wings, carved from ice with expert–like precision. Demo fought the urge to puke, caught up in its beautiful evil. *How could anyone be such a monster?* Turning away to pull himself together, he was met by yet another appalling sight. Above the freezer doors were the words,

EYES OF BEAUTY

They were etched into the steel walls of the freezer in detailed strokes. Whoever this was had taken great pride in their work. It sickened him to the core to think of all the time spent in this room with the corpses; a truly desensitized predator playing humanity for sport.

You sick freak.

But it was the freak he needed to understand. Jacky was depending on him to pull something out of the room that no one else could. He needed to pull out the emotion, the purpose—and the killer's motive. These things went past mere evidence alone. Even though it racked his resolve greatly to do so, the dog and pony show must go on.

He closed his eyes. He had to be quick as at any moment a higher authority equipped with badges would kindly escort him out. He retraced his steps back to the door. He had to find a connection between the two murders. One seemingly chaotic string tied together with the other. But what strings *were* there? The location was ambiguous to any style of murder. Warehouses were notorious for being excellent stages to play out savage exerts of human cruelty. That's not what made this unique. It was the *style* of the murders. There was an obvious connection between the blindfold, the gouged out eyes, and the posture of the victims. What didn't make sense was *why*? The first victim was still being identified, but he had willingly driven himself to the heart of the city's justice system. Or maybe in the victim's mind the complete opposite of that rang true. Maybe it was the centerpiece for corruption. Maybe to the victim, the whole *system* was corrupt, and this was his way of telling the world he'd had enough.

A suicide...? Perhaps vindication came through a self–fulfilling prophecy invented in the man's deranged head. If he was going to kill himself, then making every detail of the event perfect would be all–consuming and all he could think about. *But then why these men? What was so special about these particular men?* Demo shivered from both the cold and the sudden shock that hit him. He took a long, drawn–out breath. He needed to take a closer look. Approaching the frozen, angelic–styled corpse, he looked over every detail of its design. This would have taken hours. The emotional attachment to this man must have been significant. Or was it what the man represented? Demo kneeled next to the man, mimicking his posture. He imagined the killer removing his eyes before finishing the job, imagined him pacing around his soon–to–be notorious work, practically glowing with satisfaction. Demo followed the eye line being produced by the dead man. The killer had wanted him to see those words, even in his death. This was becoming far deeper than anything Demo had ever experienced. He needed more information and space. Taking one last close look at the gaping holes left for eyes, he realized that the body appeared to be completely exsanguinated; he made a mental note. He turned to leave, barely able to feel his arms, when the two doors burst open. Instantly, he found his face plastered against the ice cold floor. His lungs collapsed under a weight pinning him down as he desperately tried to catch his breath.

"I can't breathe!" Demo screamed what ultimately came out as a whimper.

The small of his back screamed in pain. The force bearing down on it was agonizing.

"Hold still and shut up!" growled a mysterious man's voice.

Demo felt the cold creeping into his bones. He needed to get out *now*. Just as he was deciding that maybe he should just give up hope and become another frozen corpse, he heard Jacky's feisty voice. He had never been so happy to hear her.

"I said he's with me! You guys can't come in on my crime scene and start pushing your weight around! There's a damned protocol for this!" Jacky screamed, shoving her finger into the chest of a black suited man.

The man stood firm. He stared at Jacky without breaking eye contact despite her aggressive nature. He was an older man with a thick head of grey hair neatly combed to one side. His face was a chiseled block of manly features containing deep green eyes that never seemed to blink. It was obvious, without the overtures of badge flashing, that he was now in charge. The Feds had arrived.

"You brought a civilian in on this, Jacky? What on earth were you thinking? What happened to keeping this case professional?"

Jacky paced back and forth before slapping the head of the man who was holding Demo down.

"Get off of him, you idiot! And I was done with our professional facade the second two of my cops went missing and were found dead! No one has come *close* to catching this guy, and desperate times call for desperate measures! You *know* I'm not just going to walk on this one, Roslin!"

Roslin stepped back. His eyes scanned Demo on the ground, taking in everything they could.

"Stand down and let the man go. But if I ever see him sniffing around again, I'll take you down with him, Jacky! This has officially escalated beyond your pay grade."

Jacky let out a belligerent snort. She wasn't used to being put on a leash. She'd been the one yanking for so long she'd all but forgotten the feeling. Although Jacky and Roslin's conversation was vicious, there was a familiar undertone to it that intrigued Demo greatly. They had a history.

"I can't believe how you people work. You show up after the dust settles and take all the credit. What a pile of political BS."

Roslin ignored her, rolling smoothly off and away towards Demo who was struggling to get up. He watched without helping as Demo finally got back to his feet, shaking wildly from the cold and all that had transpired. He looked like he had just fallen down a flight of stairs. Roslin's interrogation iron, however, was red hot and ready to press.

"Demotreus Ward, isn't it? I've heard about you. I'm Agent Tanner, Agent Roslin Tanner. I heard you put on quite the show at crime scenes. You like to mix things up."

Demo locked eyes with him for the blink of an eye. What his radar received was a man who would do whatever it took to win, no matter the cost. Letting his eyes drift, he also noticed a peculiar pendant attached to Roslin's shirt just inside his suit. Three triangles locked together, some sort of symbol? Upon seeing Demo's probing eyes, Roslin quickly covered it up. It would be best to stay out of his way.

"Can we step outside? I think I have hypothermia." chattered Demo, starting to look ill.

Roslin motioned for his men to clear a path. Demo spotted the man whom had thrust his knee deep into his back. He did his best to look mean, but looked far more pathetic than he had realized. Once outside, the authority war was in full swing. Agents recanted credentials like actors rehearsing lines, each busting at the seams with suppressed anger for the sudden power grab. Demo could understand their sentiment. He even felt cheated by the abrupt nature of it all, and he no longer carried any credentials apart from some crumpled up dollar bills and a driver's license. Standing alone, he knew he had been flagged, marked a crime scene pariah who could never return. This thought agitated him greatly. Murder wasn't just a protocol, a cut and paste effort; each case was as different as the individuals involved. Demo had to reinvent himself with every detail. But this case was paramount. It had drawn him like a moth to a flame. He couldn't help but obsess. Roslin's authority wouldn't keep him from turning over the stones they certainly would miss.

"Demo, we're over here!" shouted Jacky, standing with her arms crossed at the entrance of the warehouse.

Demo paced through the warehouse quickly, leaving a dumbfounded Roslin behind. He didn't need to take his time now. His dry sponge was oozing with all that he had taken in; a million pieces of the puzzle that he needed to start putting together. Demo approached Bob Cat who still looked sick to his stomach.

"That's one sick freak, Demo. I think we're way out of our league on this one," Bob Cat said, staring over Demo's shoulder at the commotion.

Demo looked at Bob Cat while he spoke.

"Who was the judge going to be?"

Bob Cat looked on, realizing all too well that the question had not been thrown his way. Jacky's clacking heels froze in place.

"Demo, you better be going somewhere with this. I put my badge on the line every time we play these games."

Demo turned his head slowly and gave Jacky an empathetic look. He knew what she did for them measured far beyond that of mere status alone. She was part of their twisted family. Demo, Bob Cat, and Jacky had spent years together in less than desirable situations. Their family unit could be described as that of a juicy, rotten peach core. Sweet, aged, and disgusting all at the same time, but a core nonetheless.

"Jacky, do you have a name on this?" probed Demo further.

Jacky spun around, looking away from the vivid crime scene. Her cogs were turning as rapidly as ever. Her alluring perfume passed through the doorway just as another breeze wisped by. The scent somehow seemed to warm the air as it went. Or maybe it was the sinuous flow of body heat that Jacky was emitting, caught up on a roller-coaster ride of emotion.

"Lyle, Lyle Ridding. That's the judge who was going to take the case. But he's done hundreds of these so I don't see why he'd be so special or of interest."

Demo shook his head.

"There are a lot of things right now that don't make sense. But I need to check every angle. And if I'm going to track this guy down, I've got to start thinking like him. No matter how sick the process is."

Jacky stood still for just a moment. She looked upon Demo with an almost sisterly endearment for a spark of time. But her stone–faced, killer self soon returned, assuring that Jacky Stockholm still had control over herself.

"Fine—do whatever you gotta do—doesn't really matter to me anymore anyways. Roslin's taken all my thunder and kept me at arm's length from any details. I don't know why I'm acting surprised. It's just the same song played to a different tune. He hasn't changed at all. Just promise me you can keep it low key. If Roslin finds out he'll start throwing the book at anyone who steps inside his coveted investigation."

Bob Cat smiled. Jacky was bringing him back from the nightmare.

"Demo, you did it again. Even over the head of the blues and Jacky. You were right about this being the blood legacy murders."

Jacky produced a storm cloud of anger that looked poised to strike Bob Cat down. But Demo saved him by trying to lighten the mood.

"I might have been. The connection hasn't been made in my mind yet. Until then, I've only got what's in front of me."

The comment made Bob Cat shake his head in disagreement. He began to say something but then paused, taking from his pocket a stick of his favorite vice. Bob Cat was practically drooling by the time he formulated a response.

"Demo, I love you and all but sometimes you're a blooming geebag. If the Feds are here then the connection has been made. We're now a part of a mess that goes back decades," Bob Cat said as he stuffed yet another stick of gum into his soggy bite.

Demo nodded as if agreeing, but in truth was just trying to placate his distasteful partner.

"Bobby, please ditch the Irish tough guy act. It's nauseating," Jacky said, rolling her eyes.

Bob Cat looked at Jacky with a flash of surprise before his all too familiar deviant smile crept across his face.

"You just called me *Bobby*. I knew you cared a *little*, but I had no idea."

Jacky immediately regretted her choice of words, so dispatched Bob Cat from her mind with a few flutters of her eyelashes. She was now fixated on Demo.

"Demo, why do you suddenly care so much about the judge? He's probably at home simmering in a hot tub with a glass of wine from some country I can't pronounce. He's had no part in this."

Demo scratched his wrist nervously at the prospective conclusion he was about to release. He hoped he wasn't right in his assessment, but if he was they needed to know.

"It isn't who he is; it's what he stands for. He was the one who was going to take on the case. The murderer or murderers could still be out there. In their minds he'd be the logical next choice. What's more poetic than cutting the head off the justice system you've learned to hate? I think we need to find him now. If I'm right, he may already be in danger."

Bob Cat and Jacky looked at each other, confused.

"Do whatever you want. But remember what I said. I'm going to be rather indisposed until Roslin gets his ego filled, so don't count on me for anything," Jacky blurted loudly.

"Well, I was hoping you could give me a little nudge while you still can," suggested Demo timidly.

Jacky could see it coming from a mile away. She responded with clear and succinct sentences.

"Victim had been absent from work for a couple weeks; divorced; and minus some traffic tickets, clean. Oh, and that car you had us call in that was supposedly stolen? It wasn't. It was his car. He bought it at an auction months ago. And I know I shouldn't, but it'll be out soon anyways; his name is Kevin Randall. Oh—and please do keep in mind that this could all be a murder suicide," Jacky said proudly.

"Year and model?" Demo continued without missing a beat.

Jacky's once confident face melted back into confusion.

"I don't know—I'd have to look it up—but that seems like a complete waste of time. You saw the car, just like I did. Wasn't that enough? And what is it with you and these pointless details?"

Demo closed his eyes, trying to remember the car more vividly. He opened them slowly as if in a trance.

"The pointless details are what drive this mad man. The deeper I'm getting into this, the more it feels natural to look at something so stupidly obvious that everyone might miss it. These aren't just murders. These are milestones on our killer's quest."

"A quest for what?" asked Bob Cat.

"I don't know. But there's a connection here that I'm not seeing; a connection that goes back to decades of bloodshed. I just don't know what it is."

Bob Cat looked apt to heave his guts out at the response. There was no mistaking his objection to the matter.

"Demo, we don't want to be in this. This is too thick—too thick even for *you*," Bob Cat, said with concern.

Demo placed a shaky hand on his shoulder.

"It's too late. In the killer's mind, we're already part of this."

Bob Cat spun away, letting out a grunt and moan of regret. Jacky surprisingly also tried to grab his shoulder but missed, grasping thin air. This gesture surprised Demo. Even Jacky was showing signs of kinship with their family unit. Demo's face then turned a hundred shades of green. If he could see Jacky as a connection then so could the killer. Even she wasn't safe anymore.

"Take care of yourselves, alright? I'm going to head out, but you know where to find me for emergencies," said Jacky, distancing herself.

Demo was stumbling for the right words to say when they just tumbled out.

"Jacky, you're in danger too. If the killer could find us so easily he has probably already found you too."

She continued walking without stopping. With her right hand she patted her side affectionately.

"Then let him try. I'll blow his face off. Besides you two goons I don't really trust anybody, and you're still a stretch."

Bob Cat mumbled out his appreciation of Jacky's less feminine qualities. Demo was not amused. The killer had taken down two cops, a witness, and a mystery man named Kevin Randall. This wasn't something he found comical in the slightest. There was no telling who would be targeted next. This case was spiraling out of control. Demo could feel Bob Cat's emotions beginning to stick in his gears and grind him to a stop. There was something wrong with Bob Cat.

"Demo, I need a couple days away from this. It's putting a wedge in my life that I just don't need right now. You understand what I'm trying to say?"

Demo did, but then again, he didn't. Bob Cat's timing couldn't have been worse. And without Bob Cat to muscle and voice his way through obstacles, Demo would be on his own. He wasn't afraid of the idea of being alone on an investigation; more the idea of failing. It would all be on him. Demo nodded and Bob Cat walked away. Maybe it would be a good time to take a drive and forget things for a while. He wasn't getting paid to go the extra mile. In fact, he was barely getting paid at all. Why did he keep pushing himself into such small boxes in life? Forgetting it all, letting it go, he turned away from his mind boggling fixation and attempted to be normal.

He hailed a taxi after walking a few blocks alone. He'd more than likely caught a cold already, and could feel his nose leaking like an untightened water hose. But his mind overcame his physical self. As the taxi driver drove up he looked out to see the water on the bay. It was cold and silent; winter must be coming. Looking inside the cab, the taxi driver asked the expected, reaching an arm out as if already requesting payment. Then it hit him; there was a giant piece of evidence missing. As the taxi driver belched out commands at Demo to hurry up and get in, Demo resumed walking. His eyes now truly opened, his mind was ready. Walking down the warehouse row, he arrived to the exact destination he had spotted—a dock—completely underwhelming in every detail. Nothing stood out, no hidden clues, just a plain, old dock like any other. But in Demo's mind he wasn't at this dock, per se; he was gallivanting around the city looking for where the killer would have done it. Where had the disappearing act taken place?

Looking up and down the water's edge, he studied it, looking for just the right spot. It had to be in a place with low visibility. It needed to be a quiet street. The splash needed to be muffled. But it needed to be within walking distance. The warehouse had given out more detail than he had expected. The crime scene had undoubtedly been found by happenstance by a very rare visitor. That would give the killer time; time to do things right, not expecting anyone to find anything. But the witness had been missing for days, not weeks or months. Maybe, just maybe, this one object was a loose end.

Demo turned and ran alongside the river's edge. The frosty, humid air filled his lungs as he went. The picture seemed clear; he just needed the right evidence to validate it. His pace quickened. The sun was peeking over the horizon when Demo came to an abrupt stop, welcoming its warming rays with a smile. Maybe things were beginning to brighten up after all. Smiling, he put his hand down on the ground. The rugged leftovers of a car's velocity met his touch on the pavement, telling the missing part of his story; tire tracks leading to the dock's edge. The tracks felt freezing cold to his fingers, but in his mind they were blazing hot; hot with the activity of details, motives, and gaps being filled. *The freezing, hot trail of the killer*, thought Demo, smiling even more. Seditious planning, artistic murdering, and a royal screw up. He closed his eyes. It made sense to him now. The killer was so proud of his accomplishments he had put them front and center to be sure they were seen; so proud that one object had slipped his mind. The killer, like everyone, needed transportation, and this area was perfect for coming and going. But cars had a nasty way of picking things up—damning things that could put someone behind bars for a lifetime—or worse. The killer had been so occupied with his artistry, his perfection, that the *mode* of transportation had slipped his mind. Demo picked up his phone and dialed the only number that made sense at the time. It rang just once before being answered.

"This is Mars Baloducci. How may I help you?"

CHAPTER FOUR

Unfinished Business

Demo had been waiting for hours. He hated that he was sitting in the last place he wanted to be on a day like today. But necessity had a way of forcing you into this kind of thing. He glanced at his phone assuring himself that he was in the right place. To his dismay, he was. The thought crossed his mind that perhaps adding another cold body to the tally wasn't such a bad thing. After all, many would probably applaud him in his endeavor; he wasn't the first to want this man dead. But the idea of murder brought an onslaught of harrowing guilt—the guilt he perceived from his own past—a past where his failure had led to murder. He still had this lingering guilt that had attached itself to his heart forever. He carried demons that could either drive him, or destroy him, depending on how it all played out.

He looked back at his phone. Jacky had called a few times. She had probably left essay long messages, with most of the details buried in visceral vulgarities. He didn't have time for her to distract him. He was onto something and needed to chase it before it was too late. The only itching matter that just wouldn't go away was Bobby. Why hadn't he called? Just as Demo's will to wait was about to break, the polished glisten and gloss of an expensive sports car caught him just inside his blind spot. He let out a long sigh of relief, mingled with frustration. This man was completely unbearable. Off went the motor that purred like a tiger and out came Mars with a slam of the door.

"You'd better not be lying about this," Mars said as he approached, forgetting any cordial greetings. "I just don't do favors."

Demo nodded. He needed to make sure this would work. He knew that Mars would take the bait. Without saying anything, Demo looked up at the large golden gate he was standing by. It was beautifully detailed with angels and clouds riding up to a starry heaven. Opulence, grandeur, and enough pretentious decoration to make his head spin; this was an area as foreign to him as a good night's sleep. Although just the other side of the city, it looked as if he'd need a passport to get through this. Mars, however, was right at home, dressed to impress as always. It didn't matter what the occasion, he was a prince in his own mind.

"I've never really been this way before," said Demo suddenly.

"Not surprising," Mars replied casually as he stopped next to Demo.

"They actually kill the roaches out here instead of letting them breed."

Demo's body instinctively tightened, but quickly relaxed again—he had expected this—he'd just have to endure the Mars effect.

"I hate to repeat myself but my doubts in this are high. You honestly have something solid that's telling you that my life is in danger? I mean, you've got me spooked, I'll admit, but you better have something to back it up."

Demo snapped back at him surprisingly fast.

"Look, this hasn't exactly been a joy ride, okay? I've seen a lot of things I wish I never had. But in my head it's adding up. And believe me; if I didn't think it was real enough, I wouldn't have called you. You need to know what I've got."

Mars frowned. He fiercely wanted to debate the topic of who needed who but refrained from doing so. His self–preserving ambitions would take precedence for the time being. Demo would be stepping on eggshells to survive his time with this pompous devil.

"Of course I want to know. Who wouldn't? If I'm a part of this sick freak's motive to kill then I'd better know every detail. I'm not going to get jerked around, and you'd better not be wasting my very valuable time," Mars grunted.

"You leave that part to me. We'll know soon enough. I just needed you to be here."

Mars smiled like a snake. Something about Demo using Mar's own tactics had delightfully excited him.

"You smug little rat. Should have known better, knowing where you come from."

Demo let the comment glance off his Mars proof armor.

"What took so long? I've been here for hours. Why did you even bother giving me a time?" asked Demo harshly.

Mars shrugged his shoulders haphazardly.

"Men like me don't *give a time* that matters to those who don't. I'm here now. Besides, do you know how hard it is to break away from my laundry list of commitments? Every lawyer in this city is constantly trying to get in my good graces. The only reason I'm in, is because of the little murder scheme you swear I'm a part of," Mars said, adjusting a pearly white button on his elaborate sports jacket.

"The only scheme was bringing you in. The rest is factual."

Mars rolled his eyes.

"Facts don't matter in things like this, Demo. This is politics. And where exactly are we anyways? If I'm not mistaken, this is Judge Ridding's apartment building."

Demo managed a mischievous smile.

"Oh, no, no way…I'm not going to be seen with you here. This guy has published more books than I can count. He's an icon in the law scene, and I don't want him to see me with the amateur Sherlock."

Demo's smile faded. Mars's was insufferable. His selfish banter never seemed to end.

"Just do it. If I'm right, both your lives could be in danger. I'm looking for connections to the dots hanging around. If this involves you, it could also involve him," said Demo sternly, exhibiting his growing annoyance.

"Fine, have it your way this time—it better be worth it—if you embarrass me I'll make sure you never make it into another courtroom again."

Mars reluctantly pressed an electronic call button before being promptly answered by a sweet, older woman's voice.

"Who is it?"

Mars cleared his throat, smoothed his hair back, and assumed his pompous demeanor once again. Demo was surprised at how fast Mars could slip back and forth between his many faces.

"Mars Baloducci, ma'am. I was just in the neighborhood and thought I'd stop by and see Judge Ridding."

There was a pause, then a loud crack as the solid gate came loose, swinging slightly open.

"Come on in, he could use the company. Please shut the gate behind you if you'd be so kind. I'll let him know you're on your way up."

Mars smiled, showing his insanely white teeth. Demo couldn't believe that Jacky actually had someone who rivaled her unblemished, porcelain diamonds. Mars reacted quickly, swinging the gate open and pointing inside.

"Let's not keep him waiting."

Demo obliged by stepping through the gate to an inner courtyard. It was amazing what walls could hide. From the outside the building had looked like nothing more than a lifeless mausoleum harboring the rich from any wayward passerby of lesser economic means. But beyond the golden gate was a little slice of city heaven. Plants, fountains, and pristinely decorated effigies sprang up at every corner. Little granite benches dotted the space to help those overwhelmed victims of such lavish excessiveness take a break from it all and recover. Demo shook his head slowly. With so much suffering on the streets it just seemed wrong to him.

I wonder what the rent on this place is...

Mars, however, obviously didn't agree. A certain gleam in his eye exhibited a man who was stepping into his own personal idea of paradise. Judge Ridding was far more important than Demo had realized. Suddenly he was regretting his decision to plead his case before this audience, just to end up in what most likely would be a den of rapacious vipers. Once past the outside garden area, they arrived at the front of the building. Here they were met by the staff. The doors opened without command, and once they stepped inside the true decadence of the palace continued. There must have been enough granite to start a quarry, with some to spare. Golden trim raced along the walls like vines from a jungle. Demo was completely lost.

"What floor, sir?" asked a well-suited staff member.

Demo paused, not knowing what to say. The atmosphere was drowning him alive.

"Forgive my friend—he's new in town—we'll be taking the lift to

Judge Ridding's suite, please."

The man nodded, keeping an eye on Demo at all times. It was apparent that he stuck out like the black sheep that he was.

As they stepped into the elevator, Demo began rehearsing the poorly put together story in his head. He knew it was a long shot, but it was all he had and time was now of the essence. Watching Mr. Ridding's practiced employee push the button for the suite floor, he took a deep breath. This could work; after all the judge and Mars could potentially be in serious danger. The only real lie he had to propagate was his underlying motive to inspect every individual with scrutiny. Anyone could be guilty at this point.

Mars had not known any of the details but how could he? He wasn't the one digging in the trenches for evidence. He only used what was found. Mars had a way of pulling diamonds from the filth. Demo had to be very abstruse in his descriptions of most of what he knew, but he had hit heavy on the details knowing what Mars and the judge would want. The blood legacy murders were becoming a legendary saga of good versus evil; anyone who could be involved in the case would instantly be thrown into the books of history. If the recent murders were indeed part of it then Mars and the judge would be only another chapter.

Demo endured countless barrages of incredulous comments and remarks that Mars could not resist throwing his way. His ego needed to take this chance, no matter how idiotic the prospect. So despite their disdain for each other, they had teamed up. Demo needed Mars and the judge to help make a connection, and Mars and the judge needed Demo to solidify their place in the ongoing investigation. At least this is how it seemed to Demo. It was no doubt a long stretch to assume that either of these two men of prominence would actually heed his warnings. But if he could gain anything from his visit that would help him in assuming the right role, he had to take the chance; even if his plan looked primed to fail.

The elevator door dinged, and the doors slowly opened, only to be met by more doors. *Doors, doors and more doors, this is how the wealthy and powerful live,* thought Demo upon seeing yet another testament to decorative grandiosity.

"Just let me do the introductions. The last thing I need is for you to stick your thrift store shoes in your mouth."

Demo smiled. In a way, Mars was incorrigibly predictable. His flare was superfluous and boring. But it seemed to work, in a career where first impressions could land you massive deals.

"Man likes his privacy," said Demo, smiling.

Mars pursed his lips and furrowed his brow. He appeared to be stretching his face muscles. *What a clown*, Demo thought. Mars knocked on the door nervously. This surprised Demo. Mars intimidated by another living, breathing human? This would be a show to remember. The door opened slowly to reveal the revered judge's warm face.

"Mars Baloducci—it's good to see you—come on in," said the judge.

"I can't tell you how much this means to be in your beautiful home, Judge Ridding. I was in the neighborhood and just couldn't resist stopping by," schmoozed Mars.

"And you," the judge said, looking at Demo, "I don't believe we've ever met. What might your name be?"

Demo froze. He was nonchalantly letting his eyes wander around the room, sucking in information as they went. It was hard for him to turn the detective off.

"I'm Demotreus Ward. I live just on the other side of town."

Demo briefly looked the judge over; an older man, perhaps in his late forties or early fifties. He had a stern yet welcoming look to him. He was wearing a wool sweater from an earlier year. It had some Greek letters on it, no doubt from an old fraternal order of some sort. *Remnants of the past*, Demo thought. The judge's face was covered with a well–groomed beard that attached to a nice thick wavy mess of curly hair. The hair was slicked back behind his head and firmly fixed in place. Demo was becoming more and more self–conscious. The judge smiled before putting out his hand.

"Well, it's nice to meet you, Demitrius…or, *how* do you say it correctly?"

Demo shook his head.

"Don't bother, just call me Demo. Pretty much everyone I know does."

The judge's smile faded slightly.

"I see. Well, Demo, you can call me Lyle, Lyle Ridding. I've seen much of your work pass through the courthouse, but sadly haven't seen you."

Demo shrugged his shoulders.

"Not really my scene. I prefer to be in open space."

It was clear that Lyle's renouncement of titles bothered Mars who thrived on animosity between ranks. He needed to say something.

"He's sort of a detective. And I must apologize that he's placed me in a rather awkward position. I must also confess that it's part of the reason I decided to stop by," Mars said gingerly.

Demo cringed. Mars was lying. He had no idea that Demo was bringing him to Lyle's suite. Demo had spent all the time tracking it down—Mars had merely shown up—but his lies were as smooth as silk.

Lyle's eyes remained on Demo. It was as if he were trying to pick him apart right on the spot. But with a smile, he returned to playing the gracious host.

"Well, come inside, come inside. Let's get to know each other better. The fall season has really started to pick up, hasn't it?"

Mars gave the judge a chummy smile that was so utterly fake a mannequin would have been offended.

"But it's nice and toasty in here. Is that floor ebony? It looks amazing."

Lyle smiled. Running one of his hands through his hair he responded.

"It's Macassar ebony, actually. You've got a good eye for indulgent detail, Mr. Baloducci."

Mars's fabricated smile grew even larger.

"Only details that divulge mutual passions…"

"Can I get you boys anything to drink?" Lyle asked as he stepped away from the duo.

Demo immediately put up a hand.

"Not for me; at least not anymore. Just a glass of water would be fi—"

Mars plopped out his order without letting Demo finish his. "I'll take a brandy on ice if you've got it."

Lyle smiled as he ushered them toward a luxurious looking couch.

"A man after my own heart.

Please, take a seat, and I'll go fetch you boys some drinks. Make yourself at home."

Demo thought the words to be mildly hilarious. *Home*, he thought. *This place is no more a home than a museum.* His mind meandered around the room, trying to take it all in. It was like siphoning glue through a straw. The thick layers of items placed in nitpicky order showed signs of a very well organized person. Each item had its place, every knickknack, every piece of furniture. Pictures of family, vacations, and summer homes joined the fray, making an appearance behind expertly blended mood lighting. *How do these people even have lives?* Demo thought, lingering on what appeared to be a jewel encrusted chessboard where the game was one move away from a well thought out checkmate. The only outspoken detail seemed to be the absence of a father or mother in any picture frame. But at Lyle's age it was dismissible, as there's only so much space on a wall, after all. Demo continued on while Mars relished the moment like a boy finally getting to see inside his dad's secret clubhouse.

"What a place, right? Of course to you it might as well be the Taj Mahal since you have no real sense of discernible taste. With all the scum rising up in this town, I'll get the big ticket that's waiting for me, no doubt. The *Baloducci* suite has a nice ring to it."

Demo endured Mars's self–indulgent banter until Lyle reappeared with the drinks they had ordered. Mars put his placating mask back on in record speed.

"Thank you so much, sir. It really is an honor sharing a drink with you."

Lyle smiled at Mars before serving Demo his water; at least what *Lyle* considered water. Demo's mouth dropped slightly open when he looked into the glass; it was filled with not only water but leaves, lemon, and a slab of cucumber. He had no idea what to do with it. *I asked for water, not a vegetable and fruit orgy.* Demo smiled and brought the cup to his mouth to take a sip. *Good night! That's the best water I've ever had.* Demo quickly downed the glass, forgetting all etiquette with a loud slurp. Mars looked repulsed as he gingerly sipped on his own liquid concoction.

"Mmmm…is that Mendis coconut I taste?" asked Mars, breaking the awkward moment.

Lyle smiled politely.

"You really do have a nose for these things, Mr. Baloducci."

"Please call me Mars. I insist. All my friends do."

Suddenly Lyle's smile faded to a frown.

"Let's talk about less pleasant topics now. Your presence here seems quite alarming, if you don't mind me saying so."

Mars practically vomited out his liquid gold at such a drastic and sudden turn in their otherwise phony conversation. But he recovered quickly. Placing the glass down carefully onto an elaborate coaster, he responded.

"Well, to be honest, it's the reason why I've brought Demo with me. He's the guy taking this thing apart. I just happened to be in the right place at the right time."

Lyle sat down slowly. He, too, had conjured up some liquid majesty from somewhere and was now sipping at it steadily. He nodded his head as if agreeing, and placed one of his legs over the other to assume a more relaxed pose.

"I'm more than happy to hear it then. I assumed that Mr. Ward's presence here was far more than mere happenstance."

Demo felt the empty weight of the glass in his hand. He regretted drinking it so fast—when would he ever get another glass of water like this one? His brain sparked into action to give the answer he had rehearsed so poorly with Mars.

"I believe that the recent murders…" he began.

Lyle injected his own curiosity into the mix.

"Murders? Plural? More than one? I've only heard of the courthouse murder, which could still be a suicide, mind you. You're proposing a serious idea, Demotreus."

Demo paused in his thought process, shocked that Lyle had pronounced his name properly. *He must have a very acute attention to detail that extends far beyond his lavish collectables*, he decided.

"My apologies, it wasn't meant to come out that way. I'm still a little flustered from it all. It's just come really fast and all at once. Trying to say the right words can be challenging."

Lyle's eyes seemed to recede slightly into his head. But Demo continued.

"It's really just by chance that I'm even involved in this mess, but I firmly believe that what I found has a direct connection to you both; that is, you and Mars."

This comment shook Lyle out of his comfortable posture. He was now sitting on the edge of his seat.

"I was there, at the courthouse, by accident when the murder or suicide happened. I got a front and center view of the man before he passed on."

Demo paused and looked down at the shimmering bottom of his empty glass. He was omitting so many things, but all that mattered is what Lyle needed to hear. Demo's world was a million shades of grey. If explaining it to Mars over the phone had been difficult, the task at hand seemed even more daunting.

"But what bothered me the most is the *way* he died. As I'm sure you're aware, he blindfolded himself before collapsing on the steps. I'm sure he was poisoned, which we'll soon know for sure. But what bothers me is *why?*"

Lyle appeared slightly flustered as Demo continued.

"All that trouble to drag him there just to die on the court steps. It was symbolic; more than just a suicide. This man wanted to be *seen*. He wanted the world to *know* something."

Demo paused, whirling his glass around in small circles before coming to a stop.

"I believe he was sending a message. And one of you might be the next victim."

Lyle calmly sat back and let what Demo just said sink in.

"So…you're telling me that this was no straightforward suicide or murder? Do you have any evidence of this? Pardon me for saying so, but that mostly sounds like conjecture."

Demo pushed the argument back, using his most recent find.

"I found tracks down at the harbor. I was going to hail a taxi after I'd been at the original scene of interest, but I had a wild hunch and followed it down to the docks. I saw a particular dock that seemed perfect for what I was looking for, and sure enough I found tire tracks leading to the river. I believe there's more than one person involved."

Demo was captivated by his ability to rehearse such a story with so much conviction. Lyle, however, wasn't as impressed.

"So that's what this is all about? You're worried that there's another killer on the loose who's coming after us? Mr. Ward, I'm sorry but that sounds beyond ludicrous."

Mars sat there dumbstruck. It appeared that something had just clicked in his head.

"You, Mars, or anyone else this individual deems worthy of the cause. That's why I had to get to you first. There's no telling how deep this goes," Demo stated, still resolute on the matter.

Lyle took another sip of his liquid courage. He was piecing things together as he went. His ice cubes clanged against their crystalline hold when he suddenly jutted forward.

"Mr. Ward, I appreciate the concern, I do, but you have to see the conflict of interest here. I'm a judge. I can't have my potential trials being convoluted with hearsay. From what I've gathered you don't have any solid evidence. Those tracks at the dock could have been from anybody. And I certainly don't think that the authorities on this case would revel in knowing you're currently withholding potential evidence. Even more uncertain is the legality of you nosing around on this case. These are some serious claims."

Demo made his move.

"I saw what I saw and my rationale seems sound enough. I'd strongly advise taking some major precautions as it would be in both of your interests to do so. And I've *told* the proper authorities about the tracks, but *they* aren't seeing what *I'm* seeing. They're swamped by all that's happened lately, and don't see how any of this could possibly effect you *both*. But I beg to differ. The more I step into this, the more I'm realizing that every angle, no matter how absurd, must be looked at. You were both symbols in what would have been a very important case. Be you symbols of justice or symbols for corruption, I don't know, but symbols nonetheless. It's been my experience that you only toy with the real victims for so long before finally ending the show. I just couldn't live with myself if I didn't at least warn you both. And I wanted you both here just in case something connected you two. It could be anything; from a ruling gone bad to the wrong guy going down. Whatever it is, I think you should examine those possibilities just to make sure."

Mars took a gulping swig of his drink.

"With all due respect, I have never had a single one of my clients even *whisper* Judge Ridding's name in a negative light. I keep an extremely professional atmosphere that is well guarded and safe for all parties and interests."

Lyle remained silent. It was apparent that he was scanning through his mind, looking for anything that would connect him to Mars or the recent events. Demo appreciated his silence. It meant that this hadn't all been for nothing. As Lyle continued, Demo watched intently assessing his every reaction.

"Look, Mr. Ward, this is highly inappropriate. And to be honest, I'm just not finding any connection. In fact, all I've really seen here today is a bunch of scare tactics. I've sat on countless murder cases and have never had a problem. It's not my place to bend the rules, only to enforce them. I'm sure I would have noticed if I saw any hint that I was tied to any of this. I just don't think Mars and I share anything that would merit such heinous acts."

Mars furrowed his brow angrily.

"Sir, I do apologize. Had I known Mr. Ward would take it this far, I never would have agreed to *any* of this. I certainly hope this isn't some ill attempt to panhandle us into a business proposition, Mr. Ward; you being a sort of detective and all. Using scare tactics such as this to do so would be most shameful."

Demo watched Mars closely. He wanted to see the sliver of doubt that could point to a possible connection that Mars desperately didn't want to talk about. With the same interest, he glanced at Lyle. Both men appeared steadfast in their confidence. Demo appeared to be up against a wall.

"Look, I apologize. I just started putting things together and the feeling was too much to shake. I wanted to make sure you both knew, just in case I'm on to something. I'm sorry for my methods. I know they must seem strange."

Lyle shook his head carefully.

"Fine. I'll be cautious and look into anyone I may or may not have deeply offended. If I come up with anything I'll be sure to let the proper authorities know."

Mars looked content enough with the response. Demo's face told a different story. Ditching his effort at speaking in abstract ideas, he made a bold statement.

"I believe that man had a connection with the blood legacy murders. This thing could go back decades."

Lyle's eyes faded. His demeanor shifted to one of serious introspection. But the comment was dismissed and a forced smile returned.

"I'll be the judge of that, no pun intended. Now if you please, I'd like for you boys to leave. This was a lot to take in and I'm going to need some time. But I really do appreciate your concern, Mr. Ward. And I appreciate you bringing Mr. Baloducci with you. I wish you the best in your ongoing work."

Mars nodded and headed for the door after laying a thick layer of accolades in Lyle's lap. It was clear that Demo's comment had upset Mars greatly. He didn't want to hear that the cases could be linked. A connection like that could leave a soulless lawyer like him dead in a gutter. How many guilty men had he let walk free? This was a serious conflict of interest. Mars's eyes snapped onto Demo, signaling to him that it was time to go. Demo, however, had one last thing to say.

"Checkmate."

Lyle's complexion went blank. He was completely caught off guard and his posture tensed.

"Checkmate—on the board over there. *Looks* like some seriously unfinished business, but the game is really already over."

Lyle smiled. Demo's comment seemed to amuse him, if only marginally.

"Mr. Ward, in my line of work you learn that there's *always* another move."

Demo contemplated the comment with a slight bit of interest, but threw it aside for the moment when something else suddenly hit him.

"Thanks again for the water and letting us into your home. I know you're a *very* busy man."

Lyle's warm face returned, ushering in a spring–like feel to the room to replace the cold, bitter topic of their discussion.

"It's my pleasure. We'll have to do it again, Mr. Ward—or *Demo*, if I may."

Demo strained out a smile. But in his mind he wasn't smiling at all. He was realizing something he had clumsily overlooked.

"The blood; it's always about the blood, isn't it Bobby?" Demo mumbled carefully outside the hearing of the other two men in the room.

There was something he needed to know but didn't know how to find out. But he had to try. If he didn't, his mind would implode and refuse to turn off. He joined Mars and promptly left the Judge's suite. In the elevator, Mars returned to his usual, charming self.

"I thought you said we were in *danger*; not that we're part of an infamous unsolved murder spree. You babble like an idiot and act as if you actually have some hard evidence. I'm trying to listen to a guy who says my life is in danger, but that's hard to do if I think I'm only getting pseudo facts about a freak show."

Mars continued with his verbal onslaught all the way outside. But as they walked, Demo's smile grew wider and wider. He needed to pay a visit to one Kevin Randall. His stomach let out a gaseous moan at the thought of what he needed to do; track down what could have been either a *victim* or a *murderer.* Either path could lead to an unwanted ending, but it was the only path that made sense at the moment. As Mars mouthed his final string of tightly sewn threats, Demo called a cab. It came as no surprise that Mars didn't offer him a ride; he didn't want to taint his otherwise flawless car. With a screech of rubber against asphalt, Mars left Demo to his own devices, alone and vulnerable.

CHAPTER FIVE

Down the Rabbit Hole

Demo regretted scaring Lyle and Mars so much. *Do I really know what I'm doing here?* he thought, still questioning his rash—and perhaps folly—decision. Where he overachieved with his well-crafted, insightful intuition, he more than trumped with his nonsensical logic. It was an obvious testament to Bob Cat's importance on the team. He was the brute, logical brick that smashed through people's windows. Their relationship was often oil and water, but somehow they were a pair of inseparable opposites. Demo thought back on how they had first met, what seemed like eons ago.

Bob Cat was a soon to be convicted killer conceived by the violence of the street; a man who had in truth only been in the wrong place at the wrong time. It would have been so easy to just join in on the *clean up the streets* hype; to raise a drink at the bar, chumming up to celebrate another victory in the race to take just one more rat out of society. But for Demo, Bob Cat's case was special. It required a special thought process. It required someone to understand Bob Cat, and then turn the whole case upside down. Had Demo neglected the details and not stuck to his gut feeling, Bob Cat would have just been *Bob Cathy Briar, death row inmate.* Suddenly, the familiar sound of a highly accelerated car stopping on a dime woke him from his daydream. His cab had arrived.

Demo ducked inside his ride and breathed in the deep history of it all; noxious layers of coated ash from an almanac of cigarettes, smoked throughout time, seats sloppily altered by sweaty backs. It was as comforting a scene as Demo could get. He gave the cabby the directions to the spot where he had left his car. His efforts, he now realized, were laughable at best. If the killer had been following him, the judge's house was a shoe in for the place he'd end up. The driver sped off, leaving the lavish world of Club Ridding behind. Remnants of the ambrosial water still lingered in the back of his throat. He looked on, waiting for his stop to come. And come it did, but just as fast it disappeared in the rear view mirror. Confused, he slapped the glass separating him from the driver.

"Hey! You missed my drop off!"

The driver said nothing. Instead, he kicked the accelerator. Demo looked through the glass at a scruffy-faced man with a look of real contempt. *I'm dead*, Demo thought, as he realized the missed drop off was intentional. He suddenly felt woozy.

"Where are you taking me?"

Demo began to kick, doing his best to mimic an out of control child fighting for freedom from the back seat, but the old cab held its own. He wasn't going anywhere. Giving one final kick of frustration, he wondered if he could pry open the doors and make a stuntman–like exit. He wasn't surprised in the least when he found the doors adequately locked. He looked down at the floorboard, feeling a breach of despair begging to leach away what little courage he had left. He didn't want to die like this. Maybe he'd been wrong when Bob Cat had told him it was connected to the mob and he had stubbornly disagreed. It would make sense to have the mob take him out like this. Cab drivers were like apparitions; they easily slip in and out of one's mind without leaving a trace. Hire the driver to pick up the target and drop him off. From that point on the real horror would begin. They would undoubtedly try and make an example out of him. He decided he would reassume his child–like temper tantrum to make their *example making* of him that much harder. The driver would be in for the fight of his life.

Demo watched as the driver carefully maneuvered his way through the city, doing his best to avoid any unwanted attention. This wasn't his first time. The thought of a seasoned mobster cab driver sent icy chills down Demo's spine. Suddenly, the driver pulled into a dark alley that was heavily shadowed, empty, and ripe for villainous activity. His body would more than likely be found in a nearby dumpster; or at least what was left of it.

The car abruptly stopped and the driver got out, slamming the door viciously. He pulled out a phone, and mumbling into it, gave off the clear impression that he was taking orders. He snapped his phone shut, apparently satisfied he knew what was wanted of him, and approached the car door. Demo prepared himself. In his mind he had already rehearsed every angle of what was about to transpire; a flurry of kicks from his long gangly legs, leading to an incapacitating barrage of fists. He had seen Bob Cat do it many times, so why couldn't he? When his captor opened the door, Demo attacked. The door swung open with such speed that it recoiled and slammed back into his legs. The impact sent acute, sharp pain coursing through his body. He had hit nothing but thin air. The door had behaved like any tangible object subject to the basic rules of physics. It ended up bringing the fight right back at him. But where was the man? Demo grimaced, still feeling the pain of his wasted aggression. That was until he saw the sleek silhouette of something he wished he would have remembered to keep on him—a gun. Well, a pistol to be exact. Crap. The driver was armed and he was not. His mighty kicks had been wasted on air due to a well-seasoned driver who had calmly stepped back and watched the door bounce off of Demo's flailing legs. Demo reluctantly exited the car, the pistol keenly aimed at him. The man motioned to a door a few feet from the car, which looked to blend almost perfectly with the wall itself, aged magnificently with the splotchy stains of forgotten years. With every choice being forced by a chamber with a bullet, Demo didn't hesitate to follow directions. Demo approached the door and immediately noticed the obvious.

"There's no handle. How am I supposed to get in?"

The man ignored him. He was intently focused on his watch. After a few ticks of the second hand, he nodded then got back in his car. Demo couldn't believe his eyes. *What sort of sick game is this?* he thought, forgetting his rather precarious situation. Dwelling on the details would have to wait; with a crack the mystery door opened, and out stepped a pair of well–dressed thugs. Demo quickly sized them up and raised the white flag.

"Just do what you've got to do and let's get this over with," said Demo quietly, putting his hands out as if waiting to be handcuffed.

The rough looking pair looked at each other and shrugged as the taller one pulled a black cotton bag from his back pocket. Demo's eyes rolled to the back of his head. How much more predictable could the mob be? Maybe they'd tell him he's gonna be *sleeping with the fishes* which would delight anyone with a mob–style death fantasy; unfortunately, he wasn't one of them. *Sleep with the fishes, what a clever saying. I wonder where it comes from?* Over his head came the shroud of darkness, blocking out what little light there was. The inside of the bag smelled surprisingly clean. It even had a soft feel to it, which seemed a little out of place in a kidnapping. The force of the men, however, was anything but soft. They moved him along like two giant ogres leading him to a boiling pot. Demo began hoping for a quick death. The mob had a history of drawing things out in the most unpleasant way. As he was drug down the alley, he heard another car pull up, its squealing tires echoing off the walls. A picture quickly formed in Demo's mind.

He imagined the car tracks at the dock on the day of their creation and the car that might have made them. But in this case, the kind of car didn't really matter since the killer had no real connection to it. But what *did* matter was the *how* and *why*. He thought he'd covered the *why* pretty well, but the *how* was still a spark of electricity firing his cerebral circuits. Luckily, the answer to *how* didn't take long to manifest—after all, it's what he would have done—a nice solid weight to the gas pedal, sending the evidence to the bottom of the river. But there was the question that really began occupying his mind with growing protest; why *him*? Why had the killer bothered to leave a parking ticket on his car with the license plate number of a car belonging to the late Kevin Randall? Or had Kevin Randall done it himself before dying? And why had Kevin purchased that particular year and model? Who *was* Kevin Randall, and what connection did he have to Demo? He needed to find out, what *made* Kevin Randall, *Kevin Randall?* Only then could he truly assimilate the killer or victim. Only then could he start filling the gaping potholes in his cognitive freeway. *I'm going to find you and make you pay*, he thought to himself, feeling a renewed sense of being.

He had been so caught up in his mind's vortex that he barely noticed the abrupt stop. Apparently, they had arrived. Demo sniffed the air for anything telling; burnt rubber, generic cologne, and leather. His curiosity surged for just a moment as he tilted his head to try and catch a glimpse of his new comrade's faces. They responded by aggressively lowering his head for him.

A door swung open and the chill of the impending autumn crept over him like an army of ice ants. He was snatched out of the car by four, maybe five hands that drug him away as if he only weighed a few pounds. He stretched out his toes, trying to scrape them along as they went. Maybe he could leave a trail that he could follow back when he finally escaped. His optimism was making him sick—he knew better—this was the end of the road. Now more than ever he wished Bob Cat would have stuck around. He and Jacky were the only two real connections he had. He was too far gone for most regular people; a noxious mix of guilt, motivation, depression, and seemingly aimless intuition. Who would stick around for that? Life just seemed easier when he stuck to the few friends he had and remained single. His gift (or what some considered his mental illness) was the only thing that got him out of bed every day.

Suddenly the air turned from uncomfortably cool to a more tolerable temperature. *Have we gone inside somewhere?* He didn't remember hearing nor feeling the presence of a door. But judging by the change in air, they were most certainly in space with heat. He dwelled on this fact for a moment and realized something he was now quite certain of; this was no mob job. Suddenly, he was shoved from behind, which sent him reeling to the floor. Sometime during the altercation, his mask had been hastily removed and light poured into his eyes, momentarily blinding him.

Sitting on the floor, Demo worked hard to regain his composure. His body felt like a rickety old shack being held together by a few rusty nails. He really needed to start working out if he was going to endure pummeling like this.

"Wait here," mumbled a creepy voice moments before a loud slam echoed through the room.

Damn it, Demo, you went through at least two doors!

Demo shook his head violently, feeling pathetically incapable.

How am I supposed to be a world class detective when my head is so busy I can't even retrace my own steps?

The ill sentiment was rapidly replaced by wonder. Where *was* he? What was this place? The room blazed in eye–burning white. Once his vision returned, he saw a plain, stainless–steel table with a pair of chairs opposite each other in the center of the room. On the table sat a single plastic cup filled with what he assumed was water. The intense glare was coming from blindingly white walls, which gazed down at him like four mad scientists staring at the rat they would soon be dissecting. This was definitely *not* the mob.

Wiping himself off, he stood up and plopped down into one of the two chairs. He tried to spin the chair but found it locked in place. His eyes then found the glass of water. If this ended up being an interrogation, would he want the water now, later, or never? Was it even water, or was it some concoction meant to loosen his lips? What did he know? Whoever brought him here had probably wasted their time. As Lyle and Mars had so adamantly reminded him, he didn't have any hard evidence; only feelings, ideas, and scenarios that played out in his mind like a Hollywood movie. *I can always ask for more water.*

Demo grabbed the cup of whatever and gulped it down. He grimaced. Lyle's water had ruined him. With a rush of air and a slam, he was suddenly in the company of the last person he had expected to see.

"Demotreus Ward, you know how long it took me to finally say that, right? You've got a mighty weird name, son."

Demo couldn't believe what he was seeing. He had to shake his head, close his eyes, and blink hard a few times before it sank in. It was Roslin Tanner, who unceremoniously scooted the remaining empty chair closer to the table. He was adorned with his usual mysterious government man suit and persona. His eyes fixated on Demo, letting him know that something important must be going on. As usual, Demo was so caught up in the mess that was his mind, he could only respond with chatter.

"They make these cups so small. It's literally like two, maybe three sips, then all you have left is an empty cup. This water sucks anyway."

Roslin's eyes flashed a brief but obvious concern. He was undoubtedly wondering just how out of it Demo really was. He made an attempt to speak, but was caught off guard by another oddly timed comment.

"The name—*my* name—came from my dad. He drank too much. And he and my mom didn't really see eye to eye on much of anything. Amazing how two people like that can still procreate…I'd think there should be a law or something. They were on the verge of splitting up when I was still just a bun in the oven…or so I was told. Mom was on another one of her drinking binge roller coasters before I started kicking inside her belly. Things went south during the delivery, and the only emergency contact was my father. Old drunk shows up after the dust settles and signs the birth certificate with one of his proud Greek names. Did I mention my old man is Greek? Only he's a south paw and a drunk, more art than form. Misspells it then walks. Mom was too apathetic and selfish to care, so bang, the name stuck due to a rare form of pure laziness."

Roslin leaned back in his chair and smiled. This was more information than Demo normally would bother giving. And surprisingly, at least to his knowledge, it was all true. Oh, that the bleeding hearts of the world would unite to pat him on the back for not changing his name. But the same apathy had prevailed somewhere in Demo's own genetic makeup inherited from his parents; apathy towards anything his brain deemed a pointless detail, and therefore worthless to him. Holidays, schedules, and an encyclopedia of people kept his apathy alive and well. He could easily wear the title of bum in everything but his one true passion, so he didn't mind his name being odd. After all, what's in a name?

"I see. Well that answers a few questions I wasn't going ask. I don't suppose you know why you're here, do you?"

Demo paused. Assuming that this was a test, he knew that Roslin would be showing him off like the freak show that he was.

"Well, some things are more obvious than others. For starters, we're somewhere comfortable and safe, but where you're still required to dress professionally. This means a government facility. But not just *any* government facility; one that comes with all the hush–hush and secrecy conspiracy theorists love. This was obvious from the well–rehearsed kidnapping. The first driver was obviously one of your guys by the way he took orders over the phone and avoided speaking with me directly; not a mob boy. Judging by his car and how he so nonchalantly took me from A–to–B, I'd say he's quite seasoned at being an undercover agent. Also, he brandished a nice gun that I'm now assuming had its safety on or was completely empty. Took me a minute to realize it was the same kind of gun I'd seen attached to some of your men's hips; I'd get more creative with that if I were you. The other two goons were just hired muscle. Pay at the docks hasn't been so good, I suppose. Then there was the blindfold. Did you guys seriously just pull that out of the dryer? It was softer than my sheets. Why bother if you're just going to kill me? Then there's the fact that I wasn't bound, which meant it was someone that knew me, or at least *of* me; they'd know I wasn't going to put up much of a fight. And judging by the short distance we drove, we've got to be somewhere near downtown. And finally, seeing the way you smiled during the story of my name, which was true by the way, showed me that you're not hostile, at least not now. Also, judging by the way you're behaving, you feel assured that you're in the driver's seat. This means the only reason I'm here is to help you with something, as I'm one hundred percent positive you aren't here to give me anything. And considering recent events, I'll bet this conversation won't get much further than these walls."

Roslin's smile faded but then returned. A lot of what Demo had just spouted off must be true. But with the smile returned, it didn't matter. Roslin was still very much in control.

"The only thing I don't understand is why *me*, and why *here*? I'm no government errand boy. I'm not even on the payroll. You've got layers of people who can investigate, interrogate, and get things done just as well as I can, so again, why me?"

Roslin stood up, screeching his chair back a few feet. Demo itched nervously.

"Would you like some more water? We keep the good stuff downstairs."

Demo didn't nod. He stared at the white walls and wondered if anyone was staring back. Reluctantly, he stood up. He knew it wasn't as much an invite as it was a direct order to get moving. From the wall of white cracked the gap of a door slowly opening. Stepping outside, Demo was taken back. It wasn't anything like he'd imagined. It was more like the hallway from a science fiction movie, an overly lit hallway stretching on and on, dotted with entrances, doorways, and other connecting hallways at every turn. White paint, white floors and white just about everything else. Demo glanced down at his scuffed up dress shoes. The contrast was remarkable. He was an out of place dirt clod in a clean room. Roslin stepped ahead of him, assuring his alpha status.

"Follow me and leave all the questions for later."

As the pair walked, other people could be seen scurrying around—all finely dressed and walking with intent and purpose—each on some sort of government payroll that didn't exist on paper. *Who are these people?* Demo's thoughts drifted slightly off course as he walked. He nearly plowed in to a very busy–bodied woman. Regaining his composure, he looked into the eyes of an odd looking gentleman, wearing a very peculiar hat, who walked down the hall looking completely out of place, much like himself. The man looked back into Demo's eyes and a connection was made; he too was caught in something deep. *Who was that guy?*

Snapping back to the present moment, he realized that Roslin was far out pacing him. He sped up just as Roslin made an abrupt stop. Demo scraped his heels on the floor in an effort to stop himself, and ended up just inches away from Roslin's back. Roslin turned around, which sent Demo reeling backwards. He flailed his about wildly in an attempt to regain his balance. Roslin's eyes caught only the spinning arms of a man who looked borderline insane.

"In here. And please don't touch anything."

Demo did as he was told, his face red as a turnip due to his embarrassing lack of motor skills. His shame quickly faded to wonder with every step they took. Roslin flashed credentials, entered codes, and scanned his fingers through a series of doors that looked to be space age. Once past the last door, true scientific magnificence could be seen; an array of wires and lights weaving in and out of the walls and connected to various monitors. Clear panels buzzing quietly gleamed with information. But it all seemed to come together at a glass window. Without thinking, Demo stepped forward. On the other side of the glass was another room. It was also brilliant white, with a large gurney looking device in its middle. It seemed that every inch of the room was well lit up and alive. Wires fed into the gurney from the bottom before plummeting into the floor. Even through the glass, the room purred with fierce power. It truly was mind–blowing. Just as Demo was about to speak, someone else entered the room; a portly man with thick, wide–brimmed glasses and oily, matted, brown hair. He wore a sweat stained t–shirt with some famous Sci–Fi characters from the movies printed on it. It was apparent that his motor skills would be right on par with Demo's. He bumped into a desk as he became intently focused on Demo.

"Mr. Ward, I'd like you to meet Julius Orson."

Demo nodded but didn't move. He didn't understand what was going on. Julius seized the moment by grabbing Demo's limp hand.

"You can call me *Jo*—everyone here does—at least the people I see."

Demo slithered his hand free from Jo's grasp. He forced a smile.

"I'm sorry; I still don't understand why I'm here. I'd really like to get home."

His remark made both Roslin and Jo smile. This made Demo feel completely uneasy.

"Let's just consider this your second home, shall we?" suggested Roslin sarcastically.

"Look, I've really enjoyed the whole Sci–fi top–secret thing, but I've got nothing to offer. I'm sure this is about the recent murders and my nosing around, but you've really got the wrong guy."

Roslin turned up his nose at Demo's comment. It was obvious that he wanted things to go more smoothly than they were.

"Mr. Ward, do you know what we do here?"

Demo's stopped, realizing that he had absolutely no clue where he was or what was going on. His silence beckoned the answers.

"These theatrics have put me in a rather precarious situation. I'm not going to play coy on this one, so let's just cut to the chase. Should you wish to go further, I cannot stress enough the importance of confidentiality. The work we do here is of significant importance."

"What work are we talking about?"

Roslin smiled a very impish smile.

"We've been watching you for some time now. More importantly, *I've* been watching you. You've got a real skill for solving the unsolvable. I'll admit your methods are far from textbook, but they seem to get the job done. You possess a gift for understanding the psyches of less than reputable people. You're a—"

Demo interrupted Roslin on the spot.

"A *freak*—a freak that ignores details and evidence and almost always goes with what I *imagine* happened—what *I* would have done in their shoes."

Roslin's smile drooped slightly. His eyes sent out the vibe of a man desperately trying to maintain his eloquence.

"You're unique, is what I was *going* to say—much like what we've got going on here—it's *very* unique, wouldn't you agree?"

Demo ignored the rhetorical question. He couldn't handle the suspense any longer. His curiosity had already beaten all logic into submission, and he was tired of all the games.

"Just spill it. I know you guys must have followed me to Judge Ridding's apartment. And that wasn't an isolated incident. I have the right to know why people like you are spying on me. I deserve at least that much if I'm going to go down this rabbit hole."

Jo stepped in but was shooed away by a stern look from Roslin who accepted Demo's remark gladly.

"Listen, Mr. Ward, I probably should remind you of the seriousness of joining in on our little project here…"

Demo probed again.

"Just what kind of project *is* this?"

Roslin looked over Demo's shoulder before elevating his gaze toward the ceiling.

"A project meant to save lives."

Demo's posture relaxed from big, tense adult to small, inquisitive child. He had to know more.

"I could tell you all of the stipulations I agreed to just so I could talk to you about this, but something tells me you wouldn't care."

Demo nodded, puckering his lips.

"I'll just get the most obvious out of the way—we believe this is tied to the old blood legacy murders. Many man hours have been put into solving these cases since so many of the targeted individuals are people of some prominence; judges, police officers, lawyers, and now high ranking government officials."

There was suddenly a wondrous twinkle in Demo's eyes. Roslin's last phrase had put so many doubts to rest.

"So, the latest murders are part of the blood legacy murders. I *knew* it. They had the calling card of the same brilliant, artistic, and sadistic mind," said Demo with a smile.

The smile obviously upset Roslin who apparently found nothing about this subject to smile about.

"Mr. Ward, those people are dead. This isn't a game. Real people are getting hurt."

Demo hung his head, letting the moment of elation pass. He felt immensely guilty for the happiness he'd felt about such a dreary subject.

"I'm sorry. It's the freak in me slipping out. I can't help myself sometimes. I just can't believe after so many murders there haven't been any real leads. It takes a sick sort of brilliance to achieve that kind of status. Even though sick and distorted, it still takes a dazzling mind."

Roslin glanced at Jo, who nodded before disappearing from sight. He then slowly turned towards Demo.

"That's not entirely true. Mr. Ward, you should follow me."

Demo did as he was told. There was no stopping the train now. Roslin had given him so much info in so little time that he wondered what else this secretive government world might hold. Going down a spiral set of stairs, there was no way to be prepared for what was in front of him.

The once lonely gurney was now accompanied by another gurney of almost identical design. It was now obvious that the gurney–like devices were anything but. They had been converted to what looked like dentist chairs, and were covered with a white porcelain gloss that emitted a glowing aura. The wires from the floor ran up into the base of each one, disappearing into a futuristic chassis. On top of the chairs were lighted panels located at critical points along the human body. Near the top where the head would rest, were a million different flat probes with small metal nodes running from their centers down into the jungle of wires. Demo wanted to ask what it was, but realized that his presence alone would force an explanation. When he looked over the second chair, his heart sank. Even though it was the same design, it held a human body. The man's face was completely blank as if stuck in a suspended state. He was tightly fastened to the chair with his eyes wide open and gazing into the empty void of the room. Demo tried to take a step back when he was met by the very firm torso of Roslin, blocking his only exit.

"Mr. Ward, I'd like to introduce you to someone; Spencer Vulcan, or as most of us have come to know him, *the bloody Vulcan.*"

Demo's heart threatened to race out of his chest. None of this seemed remotely real. How could it be? It had to be a nightmare. Despite his best efforts, he couldn't shake this murky reality. He was afraid that this time he'd gotten himself in *way* too deep.

"While Spencer may currently appear harmless, it would be an understatement to say he's one of the most prolific killers of our time. After years of work, we were finally able to capture Spencer and bring him here. Due to the special cases that he's been tied to, he's part of the ongoing work here. We had hoped that with Spencer's capture, the blood legacy had ended. But we were wrong. It appears he wasn't alone. But we can't interrogate Spencer, as you can see; unfortunately, he slipped into a coma. We're not sure when or if he'll ever wake up. So until that happens it remains our job to find anything we can to help solve these murders and end them once and for all."

Demo grimaced. If his act was the dog and pony show then Roslin had just brought the whole circus.

"That's all dandy and what not, but how the hell are you supposed to get anything out of a man in a coma? I can't help you anymore than the next guy. He's basically just a rotting vegetable; a vegetable whose mind I can't possibly crack."

Roslin snapped his fingers before pointing one of them directly at Demo's head.

"Precisely," he said poignantly.

Jo suddenly reappeared from somewhere behind them. In his hands rested a glowing tablet, tracking vital signs and streams of data.

"He's active; been active for about five minutes," Jo panted, motioning for Roslin to take a look at the numbers flashing across the screen.

"Perfect. Let's not waste this opportunity. A picture's s worth a thousand words, as they say."

Roslin ushered Demo to Jo's side. It looked like the explanation Demo desired was finally on its way.

"Mr. Ward, what if I was to tell you that we have a way, a *real* way, for you to finally do easily what you have always had to work so hard to do; truly get inside the mind of a killer."

Demo shrugged his shoulders.

"I'd say I've also got a talking spider that leaves me clues scribbled in a web every morning before I head out to a job."

Roslin nodded at Jo to fill in the gaps.

"Imagine your mind for a second. Okay…when you did that, you activated the part of your brain that stores information. It becomes electrically charged, putting out an emission pattern. Now, imagine dreaming while you're sleeping; your dreams are amplifications or augmentations of an alternate reality that you create in your head.

These dreams open up super highways of electrical patterns. These highways stream limitless amounts of information back and forth at lightning speeds, creating everything you see, smell, hear, and touch in a world that you constructed, detail by detail. It's nothing short of miraculous. And you still have your daytime consciousness intact. You don't wake up and suddenly become a different person, or assimilate the dream. You still have a measure of control, some cognizance that allows you to separate the two worlds. The only difference is, in one world you can be anything you want without boundaries, and in the other—"

Demo added his own interpretation,

"You're a bum, kidnapped detective whose *head* is starting to explode!"

Jo nodded. He brought the data filled tablet into Demo's eye line. Demo saw the outline of what must be the brain activity in Spencer's mind. Spasms of electricity pulsed like a human heart.

"We've tapped into those highways and kept them open so someone else can drive through them. We can literally assimilate into a world created by someone else's subconscious; the drive of a lifetime, I say."

Demo's head felt insanely dizzy. This was all coming way too fast. He still couldn't believe what he was hearing. He shook his head forcefully, shooing out the hazy moths of doubt. He had to try and understand what was going on here.

"And what does any of *this*, have to do with *me*?" asked Demo firmly.

Jo looked at Roslin, who gave a tiny nod.

"Well, Mr. Ward…*you* are the *driver*."

Demo's head began to spin again. Had he understood correctly? Was he really hearing what he was hearing? Did they really expect him to sit down in a wired–up chair, spill his brains into that *psycho*, and then just go on his merry way?

"So you're telling me that with all these gadgets, you guys have somehow tapped into Mr. Bloody Vulcan's head? Is that even legal? And why not use this somewhere else, like the military? It seems like something that requires a lot of training and responsibility. I mean, is that thing even *real?*"

Jo let out a chuckle that he tried unsuccessfully to muffle. Roslin quickly interjected with the correct response.

"I know this all seems pretty crazy. Believe me; I had a hard time with it myself when it landed on my desk. But this technology works. We've achieved things we couldn't even dream of with our old methods. This technology has helped save lives that would have otherwise been lost; helped bring to justice those that deserved it."

Demo sneered in disgust.

"You're playing god. *No one* reserves the right to unlock the only real safe we have. Where's the humanity in that?"

Roslin's face flustered.

"Mr. Ward, this isn't about playing god; this is about getting results. This program has been a significant investment. Sometimes we have to sacrifice the few for the greater good."

"The only greater good I see here is for those with privilege and power. What about your everyday murders? What about the *common* people who endure horrible things? This will just cause an even greater divide," argued Demo angrily.

Roslin threw his hands in the air, letting his professional armor fall away for just a moment. It was evident that Demo's attitude was extremely frustrating to this man who almost always got his way.

"I'm not the one who decides those matters, but I am the one who makes sure they get taken care of. Although your incredulous attitude is admirable, it's poorly placed. Remember, we brought you here. If we didn't think you could honestly be a benefit to this program, we never would have bothered."

Roslin produced a small computer memory stick, and moved his hand calmly towards Demo.

"If you choose to help us, I can give you more tools than you've ever had before. This could be the career opportunity of a lifetime. And as a bonus, you might help solve one of the most extensive murder investigations of our time. You would be saving lives, Mr. Ward. That's what this is really about. It's far bigger than the both of us."

Demo glared at the small device in Roslin's hands. He already knew what it contained; all the evidence that the feds had gathered on the blood legacy murders. A literal treasure trove of digitized data that he could use to further comprehend the sick freak he was pursuing. But to take the stick meant to take on the project; a project that so far had not been named and only loosely explained. If he was going to do this, he had a few demands of his own.

"If I do this, I get my own team. I'm not going to cuddle up with a bunch of book smart agents looking for their next promotion. I need real people with real understanding. I'll want Bob Cat. Lastly, I'll need my space. I can't be expected to understand these sickos if I'm constantly being tailed and watched."

Roslin unconsciously put his free hand to his head as he listened, covering one of his eyes. His reluctance to give in to Demo's demands was on full display. But he knew that if Demo was requesting that one of the only two human connections he valued be by his side, there was no room to budge. Roslin looked over at Jo and nodded. Jo nodded back and vanished from the room.

"It's done. I'll still be placing you all under careful surveillance, despite your protests. From there, we'll see how things go. And remember— you will all be held responsible for anything and everything that happens here. If you fail to follow our guidelines the consequences could be devastating."

For a moment Demo was taken back. Just how much did they know about him? Why was Roslin so comfortable agreeing to his demands? What exactly *were* the potential consequences he was talking about? Doubting that an agency that hides this kind of technology so easily couldn't make him pay if he made a mistake would be dangerous. Now he wished more than ever that it really *had* just been a mob job. The only real question left was just how far down the rabbit–hole would this take him? Just how sick and twisted could the mind of a notorious killer be? What dark secrets waited inside that monster?

"Why haven't you done this already? I mean, sure, I've got a useful skillset for this, but how do you know it's safe? You say you've used it, but judging by the way you brought me here, I have my doubts. What if you hook my brain up to that whacko and I end up *looking* like him? Can you assure me something like *that* won't happen?"

Roslin put on a sanguine smile.

"You have my word."

Demo warily grabbed the device from Roslin's hand. Although in reality it was as light as a feather, in his mind it might as well have weighed a ton. Was he really going to do this? A part of him wanted to face the music of knowing too much and walk away. Roslin could really put the heat on him, no doubt. But if it was all true—if he could actually get *inside* a killer's mind, especially one like the Bloody Vulcan—then wasn't it worth a chance? After all, he *was* trying to save lives.

"I'll find you when I'm ready. It will take me some time to think this through and understand just what I've got myself into."

Roslin's eyes shimmered with a serpent–like guile. Demo was his new puppet, and he couldn't have been more pleased.

"Mr. Ward, you have no idea what you've just gotten yourself into. Welcome to project Fathom."

CHAPTER SIX

Wandering Duck

Walking away from the facility Demo was sure he felt sicker than he would have had he been told he had a malignant tumor; at least with a tumor, he'd know what to expect. And worse, he'd thrown Bob Cat into the mix. His naïve choice of words wrapped themselves around his heart like a boa constrictor. Maybe Bob Cat was right; maybe this was too deep, even for a freak like him.

Fishing around in his pocket, he toyed with the small electronic piece of memory resting there. He knew it was too late now. His curiosity and obsession with saving lives had damned him. He truly felt like a dead man walking. But if he was going to go down, he'd go down with a fight. He needed to see what the stick of memory had to offer. He chose to walk all the way home, which ended up being way farther than he had expected. He wasn't afraid. After all, he was more than likely being tailed. Although Roslin had agreed to some of his terms, he knew better than to trust Demo out in the open with sensitive information. As he walked he pulled out his cellphone; still no missed calls from Bob Cat. *Bobby, what is going on with you?* Things were getting stranger by the minute. Smoke and mirrors sat fixated at every point in Demo's mind. *What is real? What is actually happening?*

Climbing the stairs to his apartment, he let current reality drift by him like a ghost. Occasionally someone he thought he knew would ask how he was doing or throw a generic one–liner his way. But he was like a lightning bolt looking for ground to strike. He came to a pause in front of his door. He stuck his hand out and turned the grimy doorknob. Surprisingly, it opened without a key. *Damn it, Demo, you forgot to lock your door again!* He shook his head, dismayed by his stupidity. *Why can't I remember these things?*

As he stepped into his tiny apartment, the smell of a decaying lifestyle hit his nostrils—rotten food, dirty laundry, an aroma spawned by pure laziness—but for better or worse, it was home. He felt his stomach grumble but ignored it. He had more important matters occupying his already busy mind. In a zombie–like trance, he looked at his old computer; smudges, crumbs, and coffee stains coated the surface of almost every exposed inch of it. *I'm a complete slob.* He made a silent affirmation to change his ways, knowing he wouldn't remember or care about it in just a matter of minutes. Probing his finger around the case, he finally found the power button. With a sticky push, power began to flow into the worn down machine. While he waited for it to boot, he looked around, wondering if anyone had been in his apartment to scrutinize his lifestyle. It didn't matter; anything of real importance was parked safely in his brain. His home was really only where he existed on the temporal plane; a place to do the inconvenient things his body demanded he do.

The screen flickered on, signaling that it was ready for his input. Demo started to insert the stick into its new master when suddenly his pocket vibrated. Placing the stick back into his pocket, he pulled out his phone. His eyes unhinged from their sockets. *Finally! Bob Cat.* Demo tried to think of what to say. He had direly missed having Bob Cat around. He'd even been kidnapped embarrassingly easily by men who were probably on their lunch break. Answering he said the only thing that came to mind.

"The blood, you were right about the blood, Bobby. They're coming for you now. I'm so sorry."

Bob Cat remained silent a moment leaving only a static purr to fill the gap.

After what seemed an eternity, he finally spoke, "Demo, *what* are you talking about? I need you to stop, okay? Just stop. I don't need this right now; I need you to listen."

Demo's eyes darkened. Bob Cat's tone sounded eerie and foreign to him. This wasn't the Bob Cat he knew.

"I've been thinking a lot lately, and we do need to talk. There's been a lot going on, and a lot has changed. I've got a lot to get off my chest…"

Bob Cat paused. Demo waited for him to continue, but instead Bob Cat pivoted the conversation sending it down another path. Within seconds, Bob Cat's voice returned.

"Demo, that was Jacky on the other line. She's blasting off about something that just went down at the precinct. She wants us both down there *now.*"

Demo still couldn't find the right words. He was still trying to wrap his head around Bob Cat's obviously upset state of mind.

"I'm sorry, Bobby. I know that this is a lot to take in with everything that's going on. I didn't want it to be like this. I didn't want things to get out of control."

"But it is Demo. Just get down there."

Again, Demo was left hanging; this time signaled by the monotonous chime of an empty connection. His journey into the blood legacy murders would have to wait. Real life was dragging him back again.

Demo walked out his door, leaving his festering swamp of curiosity behind. Why couldn't his brain just shut off for once and let him focus on one thing at a time? He was so caught up in his own personal maelstrom he had forgotten to lock his door, yet again. His absentmindedness towards all things normal people did was his literal calling card. His pace quickened. He wasn't just motivated by the prospect of new evidence to dissect and then piece back together; he wanted to see Bob Cat. He wanted to tell him everything. He wanted a human being to share in his madness, even if just for a moment.

His journey to the precinct was largely forgotten. He wasn't paying attention to anything in the tangible world—instead he was anticipating, analyzing—digging inside himself to find his hidden corruption. His heart raced and memories from his past pelted his emotions like a hurricane. Assuming that kind of darkness would certainly take its toll on Demo's already perturbed soul. This killer was not your garden variety sicko. He cringed when he thought of the killer. Inside he felt the icy shards of doubt encasing his heart. They had told him what had happened all those years ago was an accident; that it wasn't his fault. So why did he still feel so much pain? Why did he feel the filth of sin caked so heavily on him? He struggled to breathe. *I'm so sorry, Mike. I'm so, so sorry.*

The cab stopped at the steps of the precinct. Demo looked out of the window at a whirlwind of commotion. The media had smelled the fresh carrion and were already pecking for scraps. Clearly, something horrible had happened. As Demo exited the cab he was met by a wall of eyes, every pair cutting into him and assuming the worst. Questions exploded like mortar shells dropping from the sky all around him. He found himself completely paralyzed; this was hell.

"Demo, Demo, get inside!"

He recognized the voice instantly. It was Jacky. Suddenly the world became far smaller and more manageable. His twisted family was calling him home. Without hesitation, he plowed his gangly body into the amassed crowd. It surprised him just how aggressive he could be when pushed. But he hated every second of it. Once he saw the very distraught Jacky, he pushed the scavengers aside like a great crashing wave into the blue wall of uniforms. Jacky looked like death itself. Her eyes were puffy, red, and filled with a noxious mixture of rage and sadness.

"To hell with those vultures! Can't they *ever* just leave things alone? How are we supposed to get a handle on things when the media is spamming a pile of lies to people?"

Demo looked around. The precinct looked like the scene he had left at the warehouse, with people bustling around, noses down. He felt a sudden acute swell of nausea. *Has the monster killed again?* It relieved him greatly to see another face he needed to see; Bob Cat.

"One day they'll get what they want and really see up close how sick these freaks really are. And I can't blooming wait," Bob Cat sneered as he stepped into their tiny circle.

Demo gave Bob Cat an enthusiastic smile. Bob Cat remained somber and indifferent.

"Bobby, I'm really glad to see you. There's a lot I want to talk to you about…well, both of you, actually."

Jacky waved one of her hands in the air, shaking her head.

"Demo, not…not right now, *okay*? I didn't bring you here to chat. In fact, I'm going to wind up taking a severe lashing for sneaking you both in. But this is *my* house. If Roslin wants to shove his hand into the hive, then I'm gonna sting back. I'm the queen bee here; everyone would be wise not to forget it."

Jacky hesitated to continue. She nervously ran one of her hands through her ponytailed hair.

"Whoever this is has put out a new breadcrumb for us to follow."

"But nobody's dead, right? Nobody's been hurt?" interjected Demo.

Jacky looked annoyed, but also relieved to answer.

"No, Demo. Thankfully, not this time."

Demo visibly let loose the wound up coil of tension his body had become, but felt more confused than ever. "Then why is everyone so spun up? This still looks like an evidence scrap to me."

Jacky nodded.

"I just needed you to see something. It won't stay with us long, if even a molecule of it appears to be connected…"

Demo looked over her shoulder as if ushering her to move on. Bob Cat's cologne reminded him of what had really enticed him to come in the first place. He looked over to see Bob Cat looking blankly on.

"You went back to the old stuff. I guess it's not my place to ask why."

Bob Cat looked at Demo through a sliver of one eye.

"Let's get this over with. I don't want to be around this any longer than I have to."

Demo wasn't surprised by Bob Cat's resistance to answer him. Judging by his behavior, it was obvious. His attempt to rekindle his relationship with Jacky had been dampened. Bob Cat had been cut out from his once–upon–a–time idea of marriage. Things had changed. Bob Cat had changed. Up ahead, Jacky's heels clacked as they followed her. They arrived at a wooden door, slightly ajar. Jacky pried her fingers into the gap before giving one last command.

"I need you to see this for what it is, Demo. Don't convolute this with everything else that's been going on. We need to be sure."

He didn't know what to say. He never thought of himself as someone who convoluted his gut instincts. But he obliged by nodding. The door opened and Jacky did what she always did by shooing the current occupants out. They scattered like cockroaches caught in the light, and soon the room was primed for inspection. Demo stepped inside just as Jacky pointed to a metal table.

"This showed up mysteriously in a box outside our door. Brains say they can't trace just how or when it arrived. Whoever left it has been watching us for quite some time to know how to pull this off. Some sick freak came *this* close to my house! I'm going to put one right between his eyes!"

The tone of Jacky's voice said it all. She was done playing nice. She was ready to do whatever it took to eliminate the depraved demon targeting her office; *even* if that meant breaking protocol and being completely subordinate to her superiors.

Demo could see clearly now what she had been pointing to. On the table sat a small doll—a very *peculiar* doll—a doll he was quite sure he'd never seen before. It was a boy doll with big oblong blue eyes. It was dressed in suspenders with a matching cap. These details were interesting, but shadowed in comparison to its most dominant detail; crimson red blood had been poured carefully over the doll's body. It left horrific dripped patterns on the otherwise playful toy. Demo's mind suddenly snapped two pieces of the puzzle together. Jacky started to give him further details, but he promptly cut her off.

"No fingerprints, no tracking, innocuous box, and no one saw anything," Demo stated, glancing at Jacky.

She clicked her heels together and let out a sigh.

"Demo, I *hate* it when you do that! For once, can I just finish a damn sentence? I'm supposed to be the one who gives *you* the facts. I'm the one in charge!"

Bob Cat quietly smirked.

"A woman who likes to take charge; where's the whip, Master?"

Jacky hissed at Bob Cat, who was acting more like himself for the first time since they'd met up.

"Shut up! And *you*! What else do you know? You always know *something* so *what* is it? And don't drag it out with some inane buildup!"

Demo shrugged but responded swiftly.

"The blood … well, Bobby was really the one who reminded me of it. It's always about the blood."

Bob Cat grinned stupidly at Jacky.

"And you said I never do anything."

She ignored him.

"So what about the blood? I've got a team analyzing it as we speak."

Demo shook his head.

"Not just *this* blood. The guy at the courthouse who died on the steps was *also* covered in blood. It took me a while to realize that it wasn't *his*. So why would you bathe in someone else's blood? And whose blood *was* it? That question tormented me until we found the bodies in the walk–in freezer, and I saw the witness whose eyes had been—for lack of a better word—*removed*. He'd also been completely exsanguinated. That's a lot of blood to handle. The blood has some quasi–religious meaning in the killer's mind. There are some deep layers to this that I'm still struggling to understand. But unless I can peel those layers back and expose this sick freak, he'll always be a step ahead of us. He *wants* us to see. He *wants* us to follow. He's sending us a very clear message that we just aren't grasping."

Jacky sat silently for a moment before giving Demo an extremely hard–nosed look of impatience.

"Demo, I didn't bring you in here to speculate. We've got bodies popping up all over the city like daisies including dead officers; *MY* officers!? I don't just sit back and let that happen, and I'm *damn* sure not going to let it go. I've got the Feds breathing down my back, and all we've got is this blood–soaked doll. So spare me the conjecture and just tell me what the hell's going on."

Demo glanced at Bob Cat, looking for some kind of back–up—it didn't come—he avoided Demo's stare like an ashamed child. Demo's mind was whirling like a tornado. Pieces of evidence, clues, facts, and gut instinct assumptions appeared on a loop. It was a forced zenith in his decision making that he wasn't completely comfortable with. But Jacky meant business, so he had to at least try.

"The man at the courthouse talked about belief; the eyeless victim staring at the wall was obviously symbolic of something. The artistry of the frozen crime scene was—"

Jack covered her eyes with one of her hands.

"Demo, don't!"

Demo nodded. He needed to mute the aspects of the case that reminded Jacky of her agonizing loss. His mind kept racing, but his lips remained sealed. He had to traverse the path to reach the destination. It was the only way his twisted intellect would do things.

"Eyes of beauty."

Bob Cat stepped closer to Demo, looking as if he'd seen a ghost.

"What are you talking about now, Demo? Just words from a demented mind?"

Jacky silenced Bob Cat with a razor sharp look of rage. Demo took a deep breath.

"The suspect wanted us to see those words, to see the blind angel he created. *Angels*…that's what *we* call them…"

Jacky's eyes were beginning to sting. Demo could tell that she didn't want him to continue, but also knew that he had to. He stepped closer to the tainted doll.

"Someone here is in a lot of danger. I suggest getting everyone's families under police protection pronto."

Jacky let out a muffled sob that she quickly replaced with a boiling rage.

"Demo, Bobby—do whatever it takes, do you hear me? I want this bastard *dead!* Your involvement is off the record as far as I'm concerned. I'll light this city on fire if I have to; *anything* to flush this rat out!"

Jacky's eyes glowed red. Demo knew that she wanted her space now without her having to say it. Nobody was going to see her human side, not even him or Bob Cat. As she spoke, Bob Cat dropped his head to his chest, looking completely deflated. Everything happening was taking its toll.

"Demo, do you have everything you need? Have you seen enough?" Jacky asked, absentmindedly staring off to further signal to them that she was done.

Demo perused his thoughts. His arm began itching nervously, as if a tiny flea circus had taken up residence there. He needed to catalog what he had seen today; every detail of it right down to the blood patterns on the doll. Odds are he would never see it again. Once satisfied, he nodded.

"Good. You guys need to go. I'm sure word is out by now and Roslin and his dogs will be barking at our doorstep any minute. Go out the back. Martinez will make sure you find it."

Bob Cat opened his mouth to say something. His eyes betrayed a slight sense of endearment towards Jacky in her softened state, but words escaped him. He closed his mouth and turned to leave.

Bob Cat called to him, "You coming, Demo? You said you've seen enough."

Demo blinked his eyes, mimicking the shutters of an old fashioned camera. He hoped he was right about the symbolism. He also hoped that his quick response would make a difference. The few threads of sanity he had left were beginning to strain under the pressure. But it was time to go. Without saying another word, he followed Bob Cat out the door. It was shutting quickly, so Demo had to make an awkward lunge to make it out. Clumsily he staggered into the hallway, knocking into a few unsuspecting uniformed officers.

"I'm sorry, the door was shutting," he explained bashfully.

Bob Cat let out a grunt and without turning his head blurted out, "Still the same old klutz, eh Demo? You need a hand, hotshot?"

Demo tried to force a smile but couldn't. He knew this moment of normalcy with Bob Cat would be fleeting. Soon things would digress back into the whirling cesspool of stress this case had become. It was then that an acute point of clarity emerged from his mind like an alligator from a swamp—he had forgotten to warn Bob Cat—his prideful critical thinking hadn't saved him from neglecting his friend's safety. *Damn it!* Demo looked up to say something to him when he realized that Bob Cat had left him far behind. He frowned.

"Demo, Jacky told me to walk you guys out. Looks like Bob Cat's already long gone—in *more* ways than one."

He looked over to see a stern-faced Martinez scowling at him. Who knew how much stress *he* was under, what with all that was happening…Jacky was relying on him now more than ever. Demo dropped his head slightly. Martinez had really nailed it.

"Bobby's going through some stuff. He just needs a little space."

Martinez looked at the floor. It was apparent he was waging some sort of internal warfare, contemplating the unspeakably disgusting things he'd had to take in. He was on the verge of purging.

"Demo, tell me just *one* thing; there's just *one* thing I've got to know. Can you *catch* this guy? I mean, do you *really* think you can bring whoever this is down? Those two cops were my friends—friends and family—that's what this is *really* about. I can't sleep at night worrying about 'em. I'll do anything to make this right."

Demo seized the opportunity. He could feel Martinez's real fear coming to light. He was a good cop; he could sense that things had escalated and that innocent people's lives were at stake; even worse, *children's* lives. The doll had shaken him to his core, touching something deep and primal in him. Demo knew he had to seize the moment before it was gone.

"The victim at the courthouse—all the blood—I need to know whose it was, Martinez. If I'm right, it's the same blood that's on that doll. Am I?"

Martinez nodded affirmatively and pointed down the hall.

"Demo, you know the way out. Shut the door tight when you leave; Ted the security guy's out grabbing lunch so no one's watching it right now. People have a nasty habit of leaving the doors unlocked back there. If you do, I'll tell Jacky you guys did what you were told without putting up a fight."

Demo smiled slightly. It appeared he still had some friends who were willing to help when they could.

"Thanks, Martinez."

Martinez cocked his head and smiled crookedly.

"You can thank me once we've buried this monster six feet under. Now, *go*."

Not wanting to press his luck, Demo jogged clumsily away. His gangly body looked like a cheap–suited scarecrow running through fields dotted here and there with human bodies and shiny objects. He wanted to catch up to Bob Cat before he got out of the building. When he reached the hallway leading to the back door, he was completely let down. Bob Cat was already gone. Demo swallowed a lump down his throat that seemed to burst inside him like a water balloon leaking sadness. *Is our partnership over? Has it really come to this?* Demo let the feeling pass. He knew he had more important things to do and little time to do them. Instinctively, he followed his memory back to a room he hadn't visited in what seemed like a lifetime. He glanced around to make sure he was alone. Alone he was, except for the tiny blinking eye on the mechanical, panning camera at the end of the hall. Demo stared at it as if expecting someone to pop out and stop him. Then something odd happened; the blinking light on the camera faded and suddenly the camera was still. Immediately his eyes snapped to the evidence room. There, the normally locked door was slightly ajar.

"Thanks, Martinez," he mumbled aloud.

Like a fox in a hen house, he burst through the door and began his hunt. The room was filled with folders, bags, and boxes that held every kind of evidence imaginable. He *had* to find it. He'd seen it before; he just needed to locate the right one. He hoped beyond hope that Roslin and his crew hadn't taken it away already. But if he knew Jacky, she'd fought tooth and nail to hold onto whatever she could, for as long as she could. Yanking open drawer after drawer, his efforts were finally realized when he found the folder that contained the crime scene photos evidence list from the courthouse. And there it was; the record containing the juicy little tidbit of information he was so yearning to devour.

KEVIN BARTON RANDALL

He scanned down the page, feeling even more panicked when he heard a noise in the hallway. He needed to commit it to memory right *now*. He scanned each detail of the info in front of him, but one thing stuck out more prevalently than the rest; the address. Now he knew just where he needed to go, which left only one more question. It showed up just below the address—the license, year, make and model of a car—more specifically, a 1972 Cadillac DeVille. Tossing the folder back on the desk, he looked for the accompanying evidence drawer. He found it quickly, locked tight. *They can't remember to lock the other drawers but can remember to lock this stupid drawer?*

Demo let out a moan of frustration. The sound of footsteps in the hallway seemed to be coming closer. He needed to do something, and fast. Glancing around the room he looked for a way to get into the drawer. Usually a spare set of keys were kept hidden away, just in case. He racked his brain but came up empty. He attempted to assimilate the mindset of the men and women who routinely worked in these kinds of places. No doubt, the monotony had led them to keeping most drawers open for easy access. This probably meant that a missing pair of keys was often in hot dispute. If this was the case, then the spare set had to be somewhere easy for them to remember. *Under a desk, hidden in some jar?* That's when it hit him. Running back to some of the drawers he had ripped open just moments before, he searched through them until he came to a folder simply labeled with the letter K. He smiled as he slithered his fingers down to the bottom, bringing the spare keys out.

Like a well–trained burglar, he slid a key into the locked drawer and slid it open. *Voila! The blood! I found the blood, Bobby.* Demo identified the plastic jar with ease, its insides carrying the DNA rich leftovers of the horrific courthouse scene. He spun it around looking for a name or identifier, and there it was—

CARMINE BURKE

Demo let out the breath he's been holding. The blood wasn't Kevin Randal's. But what shocked him the most was that Jacky had lied to him. She had said the blood was still in the works, yet here it was. Why didn't she want him to know? Why keep something like that from him? She must be connected, but in what way he couldn't fathom. Suddenly, a conversation from the hallway caught him off–guard. How long had he been inside? Dropping the folder back into the drawer, he locked it back up and then placed the keys back into their uninspired hiding place.

Nervously, he cracked the door open to look for the source of the noise. He saw there was an ongoing conversation between two police officers walking down the hall and slowly back towards the main belly of the building. Demo tried his best to sneak the door open slowly. It let out a faint creak as he went. Panicking, he pressed the door more quickly hoping to mute the noise all together. But as always, his mind was ahead of his body. The door moved far faster than he had imagined and gravity took him the rest of the way. He plunged through the door and into the hallway, unceremoniously falling to the ground. The commotion alerted the two policemen who turned around to see Demo lying pathetically in the middle of the hallway.

"Hey! What are you doing? How did you get in here?"

Demo looked up and blurted out the most ignorant thing he could have.

"I was looking for the bathroom and got lost. Just trying to find my way out."

One of the officers squinted at him before shaking his head.

"I know *you*! You ran into me earlier! You got a real problem with walking and talking, don't you? Get out of here and don't touch anything, you weird crackpot!"

The officer rolled his eyes before pointing.

"And use the back door; you know…the one in the *back*."

Demo smiled, trying to look as coy as possible.

"You've got it, Sir. I apologize. I'm leaving right now."

Demo looked up at a camera that was now actively panning and blinking. Looks like Ted's back from lunch. I hope he didn't see any of this. Jacky would rip my head off.

He jumped up and practically sprinted out the back door under the scrutinizing eyes of both officers, who now seemed to find his mere presence ultimately unbearable. Once out the door he headed directly into the shaded light of the back alleyway behind the precinct. It was telling how fast the feeling of safety and comfort he had felt in the building was quickly replaced by an eerie sense of fear. *I'm a wandering duck out here. Or is it sitting duck?* Just more of the stupid thoughts that often plagued his mind in a useless fashion. Nothing compared to his hatred of alleyways—alleyways in crowded cities—he might as well be drowning. He tried to keep walking, but was immediately cut off by a hand and a damp rag slammed strategically over his mouth. The world spun wildly around him as he fell limp into the assailant's arms like a baby into the arms of a parent. Demo now found himself helplessly in the clutches of yet another unknown quantity. It appeared the wandering duck had wandered too far. His life could very well soon be over.

CHAPTER SEVEN

Real Imagination

Demo woke up to the smell of cologne. The scent strummed his memory like a guitar playing a familiar tune. It was an unforgettable scent. Shaking his head to clear the cobwebs, he looked around. Miraculously, he found himself free to roam around. The haziness in his head, however, deterred his ambitions of moving. He felt like a broken receptor that was only picking up static. Rubbing his nose, he could smell the faint remnants of chemicals. He closed his eyes trying to get it together. A part of him wanted to puke his guts out from the forced nap he had taken. Seeing the perfectly white walls, along with the familiar jaunt he'd just taken, he gave in willingly. His insides heaved, blemishing the otherwise perfect floor. The foul odor rose into his nostrils, but he was proud of it. His timing couldn't have been better.

"Damn it. Demo! What's *wrong* with you?"

Demo opened his eyes to see Roslin moving towards him. This came as no surprise; in fact, it was expected. Roslin was now his new big brother, always watching. Demo smiled, proud of interrupting Roslin's otherwise impeccably organized life.

"Sorry. Didn't know I had it in me."

His smile grew wider upon seeing the reaction his play on words had. Roslin's look of disgust grew, becoming even more pronounced. Suddenly a third voice interjected.

"Well…you always had a way with words. Always acting the maggot, aren't ya?"

Demo's smile faded, suddenly placing the familiar cologne. With an unexpected burst of energy, he flew out of the chair and spun around. There he was met by the flinty eyes of Bob Cat. For once, Demo's normal freak response was quiet. His response came both calmly and directed.

"How did *you* get here?"

Bob Cat snorted angrily before looking directly at Roslin.

"Why don't you ask the horse's arse yourself? I'd like to know as well."

Roslin stood his ground firmly, glancing over Bob Cat's shoulder and shaking his head disappointedly at two large men standing guard at the door. Each man showed signs of having been caught in what must have been a vicious brawl.

"Did I do that?" Demo asked, pointing at the men at the door.

Roslin let out a laugh that was strangely accompanied by a snicker from Bob Cat.

"You can thank your friend here for that. I grabbed *you* myself; thought it'd be easier that way."

Demo grimaced. He really was a weak, pathetic fool. He was feeling more and more like a small kid on the playground surrounded by bullies.

"Well, they deserved it. And I ought to finish the job right now with you. You've got no right bringing me here."

Bob Cat's stance turned aggressive but Roslin was quick to remind him of his place.

"Oh, what are you going to do, Mr. Briar? Have it out right here like we're in one of your trashy bars? I think not. And besides, having you here wasn't even in our plan. You can thank your accomplice for that."

Bob Cat snapped his head towards Demo who was completely caught off guard.

"What is he talking about, Demo? These freaks read me bedtime stories and dragged me here because *you* told them to?"

Demo didn't know what to say. He couldn't formulate lies quickly enough to make any real sense. He could only tell the severely unwanted truth.

"It was my idea."

Bob Cat let out a slew of curse words that were expertly tied together to form a noose around Demo's neck. Demo took it willingly. He knew dragging Bob Cat even further into the case unwillingly might have been an enormous mistake. But he didn't have anyone else. The only other person he had a real connection to was Jacky, and for reasons quite obvious, she could never know. Once Bob Cat's temper subsided he looked at Roslin with burning embers for eyes.

"And so you agreed to this?"

Roslin rolled his eyes. He was becoming more aggravated the longer they wasted on emotion.

"Look—as far as I'm concerned you're now officially a loose end. But what we're doing here is far more important than your sense of outrage. I don't care why he brought you here; all I care about are the results. I put my neck out on this one and don't want it being hacked off because of the incompetency of you two idiots! I don't have time to keep explaining myself!"

Demo looked at Roslin, who was literally foaming at the mouth. He knew they were in no real position to argue.

"I suppose they've already explained to you what this is, Bobby?"

Bob Cat shrugged and looked away.

"They've spewed out more crap than a bull on laxatives, but I'm sure they've done their best."

Demo nodded his head.

"Then you've got to understand what they—what *we* are trying to do. This thing is huge."

Bob Cat swung at the air making everyone in the room tense.

"This is what I was talking about, Demo. We shouldn't be in this. We shouldn't be nosing around where we don't belong."

Demo slumped against the wall.

"It's too late for that, Bobby. We're a part of it whether we like it or not."

Bob Cat paced in a tiny circle before snatching a chair off the floor and heaving it forcefully into a nearby wall. The impact sent tiny parts of it flying through the air.

"Haven't we done enough? Case after case we solve, and we get no respect from anyone. But *now* suddenly they care? What a bunch of shite in a bucket!"

Roslin had heard enough and was about to step in when Demo surprisingly waved him off.

"We gotta do this, Bobby. Not for us but for all those people out there. This *isn't* going to stop. More innocent people are going to die."

Bob Cat walked over to a wall and braced himself against it, staring at the floor. His lips were moving but nothing was coming out. He knew he was caught in a predicament of duty. Self–preservation and needs versus the greater good; or at least what they were being *told* was the greater good. Why was everything so very, very grey? Minutes passed, intensifying the silence, before Bob Cat finally surrendered.

"Well, let's see it then. The damn machine…let's see it."

Roslin let out the long breath he had apparently been holding in.

"I thought you'd never ask."

He showed Bob Cat the way. Demo had already been through this particular orientation. When they arrived in the lower room, they were met by the pale complexion of Jo.

"Sir, he's really been kicking into overdrive. I think if we hurry we'll have a solid window."

Jo paused when he saw Bob Cat and Demo. He almost went cross–eyed. He adjusted his thick glasses and flicked his fingers across his nose.

"Another one? Soon we'll be throwing birthday parties."

Demo glanced at Bob Cat, worried his aggressive nature would set back in. Instead, he saw Bob Cat staring in shock. All the sci–fi wizardry of the room was sweeping him into another plane of thought. It wasn't until he noticed the body that he came back around.

"And *who* the hell is *that*? Are we just visiting a morgue today?"

Demo looked sternly at Roslin.

"I thought you explained everything?"

Roslin shrugged.

"I believe I explained what we're doing here, but it's possible I missed a few details."

This time Demo snapped out of his normally complacent self.

"Just how *many* did you miss?"

Roslin turned his back.

"I don't need to defend myself. I do what I do because it needs to be done. I'm not going to spend another second on this discussion. We're already pressed for time. That's why we had to do what we did to get you here. I shouldn't need to remind you that you're already a part of this. As sick and twisted as this is, we're going to be a family from here on out. Is that clear?"

The mention of the word family stung Demo like a snakebite spreading rapidly to his heart. He *had* a family; his own twisted family. And now, because of everything going on, Jacky was slowly being pushed out. Bob Cat was quick to turn Demo's thoughts into words.

"No. This…this right here is *no* family of mine. This is just *wrong*."

Roslin furrowed his brow, letting his chiseled expression finish the argument.

"Right or wrong, it's going to happen."

Jo broke the tense fog that enveloped the room with a statement that reminded them of why they were there in the first place.

"I suggest we get someone linked up now or we'll miss our chance."

Roslin let up on his aggressive argument and nodded.

"Do it. Hook Mr. Ward up. Give him the rundown. I'll be watching, as will Mr. Briar from up top should anything happen. Now, if you would please follow me, Mr. Briar. You're both in for quite the show."

Bob Cat reluctantly followed behind Roslin as he made his way from the room. The entire time Bob Cat kept his eyes on the still body of Spencer, the bloody Vulcan. As they walked, Bob Cat's gruff voice could be heard as he continued drilling Roslin for answers. Demo, however, was left alone with one of the most awkward people, aside from himself, he had ever met.

"You ready for the ride man? This thing is gonna blow your mind."

Demo looked at the obviously excited super nerd that called himself Jo. His own eccentric demeanor had truly met its match.

"Tell me what I need to know."

Jo let out a yelp of excitement, as if he'd just been given a new toy; a toy he couldn't wait to shove a firecracker into so he could stand back and watch it explode.

"The machine is what it's all about. It's truly amazing, and has made all this possible. I mean, the technology in this thing is out of this world, man. And I mean literally out of the ballpark."

Demo sighed.

"I already got the sales pitch. Again, what do I need to know?"

Jo's mouth quivered, confused by the lack of interest in the finer details of his precious gadget.

"Fine, have it your way. I guess to you it's just an everyday machine that sucks your brain into his...no big deal," Jo said sarcastically, pointing at Spencer.

"You'll literally be inside the mind of a prolific serial killer!" He could barely hold back his deranged excitement. It was apparent that he had been cut off from mainstream society for quite some time. Jo calmed down and answered Demo's question.

"A few things...this isn't your average road–trip unless you're used to traveling on a limitless highway with billions and billions of other cars. To get you in there, we've got to share the road. I'll be rerouting your brain to temporarily merge with his. The machine will be your on ramp!"

Demo rolled his eyes.

"I don't need any more of your highway metaphors. Just give it to me straight."

Jo smirked.

"Okay, if you insist. You and Spencer will be sharing brain activity. The two of you will be joined within his psyche. Once there you'll be fully immersed in whatever Spencer remembers. Double consciousness in one subconscious; it's freaking brilliant! It's like cake with layer upon layer of sweet, tasty icing!"

Demo cringed. His mind had already gift wrapped a question for Jo to open.

"Wouldn't sharing the space eventually push one of us out? Seems like that would be an exhausting process."

Jo smiled, gleaming ear to ear.

"Not just one, but potentially both. You *both* could end up as mindless bobble heads. That's why we limit the time. We estimate that you have about a half an hour before things get ugly. And I do mean they get *ugly*. Should Spencer's mind begin to fall apart under the stress, who knows where you'll end up?"

"Wait—what exactly do you mean, *end up*? What exactly are we talking about here?"

Jo let out a long sigh of frustration.

"That's *why* I was giving you the highway analogy! One would *think* you would have *appreciated* that. If Spencer's mind crashes while you two are still hooked up, you'll be stuck in his brain. It's like breaking down on the highway without knowing where you are. The only way we'd ever find you again is if Spencer took us to you—which he couldn't because he'll be an official addition to the food pyramid in the vegetable group."

Demo's eyes widened. What the hell had he gotten himself into?

"That sounds ridiculously dangerous. Why aren't there countermeasures or a fail-safe? It sounds like you'd be gambling with your life every time you use that thing."

Jo practically danced in place.

"Exactly! The adventure of a life time, and you're the lucky guy who gets to do it! I wish I could—I really do—but they won't let me for some odd reason."

Demo couldn't believe what he was hearing. Was this guy for real or had Demo already lost his mind and this was all just his imagination. Demo paused, watching Jo rally and begin to prep the machine just to the side of where Spencer lay. He looked down at Spencer and saw his blank expression which showed no signs of pain or struggle. It belied the truth of the horrible nightmares that could only be understood from inside—or, for lack of a better word, *fathomed* from inside.

"Oh, and one more thing—I'm so silly, I almost forgot—when you're in Mr. Vulcan's mind, you want to make sure you don't stand out. The mind will act the same way your body would if it was attacked by a foreign body. If he singles you out he could easily trap you in his brain forever."

If the world wasn't already spiraling madly out of control for Demo, it most assuredly was now.

"So, are you saying he could be actively pursuing me, even inside his mind? Are you *insane*? This sounds like suicide! How am I supposed to work inside his mind, *and* avoid being found out, all at the same time?"

Jo let out a childlike giggle.

"Well, that's going to take some real imagination, isn't it, Mr. Ward?"

Demo wanted to throw up again. How could he talk so lightly about something so absolutely serious? It was like dancing around a stick of lit dynamite.

"It takes a lot more than just some *real imagination* to fly under the radar of a killer's warped mind, don't you think?"

Jo clapped his hands like a seal begging for a fish.

"Why do you think we brought you here? You wouldn't be here unless you were some sort of freak—just like me—just like all of us here!"

Demo watched Jo smile at what he obviously thought was their newly discovered comradery. He knew this wouldn't end well. His heart was clawing its way free from his chest in an attempt to commit mutiny. It went against everything logical, but if it meant stopping a madman then it had to be done. The gangly, awkward, uncoordinated superhero in him had arrived.

"Let's get started."

Jo jumped into place.

"I thought you'd never ask! Please, if you could take a seat next to Mr. Vulcan."

Demo did as he was told, although sitting next to Spencer made him instantly nauseated. This was the last place he wanted to be—in *any* reality. The cold steel worsened the experience even more. It was like a thousand tiny, ice cold arms were reaching up to grab him and not let go. While he waited, Jo attached an array of wires to his vital areas, arms and legs.

"We'll be able to monitor your heart rate as well as your other vital signs. In the event of an emergency, we'll begin the shutdown process and pull your consciousness back out of Mr. Vulcan here. It takes a minute or two to do so, so we need to be Jonny on the spot with the problems early. Luckily we have some of the best of the best to help with that."

"And who do *you* consider the best of the best?" asked Demo incredulously.

"I am," Jo grinned manically.

Without warning, Demo's chair flattened out. As it reclined his body stretched out until it came to rest in a sleeping position that matched Spencer's, whose cadaver–like body brought up what he thought was an extremely relevant question.

"Jo, what happens if I die inside his mind; you know, in his *subconscious*?"

Jo paused for a moment, taking his concentration away from the whirlwind of his preparations. His eyes darted side to side, his lips tightly pursed.

"I have no idea, honestly. I'd imagine it would be rather unpleasant. The mind is one hell of a convincer, and if it truly believes your dead, then my best bet is that you'd go along with it. I never really thought of that one. Just try to stay out of any falling dreams because you could actually hit bottom."

Demo's insides churned as if attempting an uprising to get him out of the ghastly predicament he had gotten himself into. But it was too late now. Suddenly, there was a purr of power all around him sending all the hairs on his arms straight into the air. A surge of energy streamed through his body, growing ever greater by the second. It was like nothing he had ever felt before. It frightened him to the core.

"Jo! Jo! What's happening? I feel like I'm ready to explode! What are you doing?"

Jo rushed back to the table. Staring down at Demo's sprawled out body, he winked.

"When I said this was going to blow your mind, I meant it quite literally. In a minute, that's exactly what we're going to do. I'm so jealous right now! Power overwhelming, am I right? Oh, you probably don't even get the reference. Enjoy the ride, Mr. Ward! See you when you come back to reality!"

Demo wanted to scream as the surging power washed over him like a tidal wave. It was as if his body had harnessed a thunderbolt he could no longer contain. Then, in an instant, all of the power surging through his body bolted directly to his head. A massive wave of energy blasted Demo's mind, sending him into a dizzying world of light mixed with darkness. Everything faded into a chaotic vortex far from the reaches of Demo's familiar reality. Streaming pieces of fragmented memory swirled around him like a tornado, each on a loop showing important times in his life. A great deal of pain broke through the infinite fathoms of his mind. Slowly, a distant but free feeling hit him like a boulder rolling a thousand miles an hour. He swore he could sense himself leaving one place and entering another as if caught midflight on a spaceship; completely weightless and unhinged. This feeling permeated his being and grew until it consumed him whole. Suddenly, the whirlwind returned, sucking him into its perfect chaos once more. This time he was again surrounded by pieces of light filled with memory, only these fragments weren't his own. Unfamiliar voices, smells, and sights flooded the vortex, dragging him ever further into its madness. Just when he thought he couldn't survive another second more, it came to an abrupt stop. Everything slowed down and became convoluted. The distorted images began to form the world around him. Nothing had prepared him for this. Nothing could have.

CHAPTER EIGHT

Boogie Nights

"Yo, watch it, man! You 'bout took my head off!"

Demo shook his head, trying to flush out the fuzzy balls of confusion in the attic of his mind while someone rubbed his shoulder as they passed by. His eyes slowly adjusted, and what he saw before him was beyond belief; a far reaching city filled with old styled buildings, neon signs, and cars that looked more like boats with wheels than actual automobiles. There was something very strange, but at the same time very familiar about it all.

"Far out threads, man."

Demo glanced over to see a, tall, skinny woman blow past him on extremely old fashioned roller skates. Her tight, bell–bottom jeans flashed a brilliant yellow that contrasted starkly against her bloused, long sleeved purple shirt and turquoise necklace. Looking past her, this new world continued to unfold. It was filled with afros, men with long hair, floral shirts, funky headbands, and a color scheme reminiscent of his great–grandmother's living room. *Where am I? Or better yet, when am I?*

Suddenly a large group of people stormed the streets, chanting loudly.

"One more step, one more day, we ain't gonna stop till we get our pay!"

"Equal opportunity for all races!"

"Down with the man! Down with the plan!"

The group was mostly made up of African American men and women, with a few Caucasians mixing in on the outskirts. They held picket signs with lively messages and drawings. Some depicted a strange, big–nosed man in various comical scenarios. Demo didn't know what to make of it. *Who wasn't getting paid? What races were they talking about? Who was the man, and what plan did he have?* These questions came to Demo's mind, betraying his lack of knowledge about relevant history. He wanted to reach out and ask someone what was going on. This was becoming more and more preposterous by the second. *How am I supposed to work in this? How am I supposed to find Spencer in a massive city from yesteryear?* His thoughts were interrupted by a young boy who bumped into his side, sending a stack of newspapers scattering all over the ground.

"Hey, watch it, mister!"

Demo spun around to see the boy desperately trying to pick up all of the newspapers he had been carrying. Without thinking, he began to help as people passed them like cars on a freeway.

"I'm sorry. I didn't see you there. Here, let me help you pick those up."

The boy frowned.

"Now I'm gonna be late. I sure hope they don't get too angry."

Demo forced a smile.

"I'm sure you'll be fine. Just tell them you ran into some guy on the street."

The small boy shook his head no, ignoring Demo's comment completely. This made Demo feel horrible for ruining the young boy's day. As they finished picking up the papers, the boy looked at Demo queerly as he scanned him over carefully.

"You sure have a groovy looking suit, mister."

Demo looked down at his worn, old suit realizing just how out of place it must look. What was old to him was still futuristic to the boy, whoever he was.

"I work at the bank. I'm new."

This made the boy crack a tiny smile. Then without warning, he was gone, disappearing into the flowing river of bodies.

"You're welcome," Demo mumbled aloud.

A hand grabbed his shoulder.

"Sir, is everything okay? Was that boy bothering you? Been a lot of petty thefts of late."

Demo turned to see two officers standing behind him. Each had a wonderfully groomed mustache that jutted out from the sides of their faces. Their uniforms looked more like historical relics than law enforcement garb. Behind them sat their giant, boxy car, parked tightly against the curb. Demo tried to respond but found himself stumbling over his words. *Why am I always running into pairs of cops?*

"Down with the man, you filthy pigs!"

It came so fast there was no time to react; a sugary shower of soda thrown by someone now running away as fast as they could. The two cops gave chase, leaving Demo alone with his mouth wide open. This place pulsed with tension and excitement. Figuring Spencer out was going to be the challenge of a lifetime. Time ... just how long he'd been here was a mystery; he hadn't been paying attention. Glancing down at his arm, he realized he didn't have a watch. Yet one more thing he wished he had learned to keep on him. But he had a much bigger problem right now. He was drawing a lot of attention to himself. This was evident by the confused stares he was getting *I better get some new "threads", ASAP.*

Ducking into an alley off the main street, he tried to think up some sort of plan. He needed something, anything, to keep him from sticking out. He had seen what most men were wearing, and as ridiculous as they looked, he needed to assimilate, but how? He instinctively reached into his back pocket looking for money when he realized he only had a credit card, the only thing he ever carried. He had a gut feeling that his modern payment method wouldn't be accepted at any store in this time period, let alone in Spencer's head. *Spencer's head—* that's where he was—he *had* to remember this. Everything around him was constructed from either memory or pure imagination. He needed to play by Spencer's rules to find him and finish the job.

Thinking it over carefully, he came to an almost obscene conclusion, one that would require him to digress to an almost childlike state. He couldn't control Spencer's world, but perhaps he could control his own. He needed to believe in it; not just see it. He needed to convince his own subconscious that it was as real as the world he had come from. He needed to use Spencer's rules to bend his own reality. It had to be subtle. He closed his eyes and envisioned one of the men on the street. *Bell bottoms, kooky shoes, a tie-dyed t-shirt, and hair...* It was the hair he struggled to imagine so he latched on to the last image he had. He needed to fully immerse himself, to leave the Demo he knew behind and become someone different, someone groovy. It was a struggle, but he finally felt at peace with it. Opening his eyes, he couldn't believe what he saw. His raggedy, futuristic business suit had been replaced by a wonderful arrangement of hipster color. A bright white, collared shirt left open sent a thrill of sensation cascading down his chest. Looking down, he saw his fashion montage included faded brown pants with flared bottoms. A nice leather belt with shoes to match, and a thick mustache affirmed his new place in the Fathom society. He was rather pleased with himself and his ability to adapt so quickly in order to blend. Taking a deep breath, he stepped back into the street.

"That's one cool cat," said a man to one of his friends, seeing Demo for the first time.

"You sure are one far out dude. Like, totally digging your look," said another.

Demo was shocked. He had done his best to blend in but was still receiving far too much attention. *What's their problem?* he wondered. *I don't have time for this.*

Ignoring his fan club, he walked down the street away from them, his hands deeply buried in his pockets, his eyes darting back and forth. *I must look like a complete stiff, if stiff is even the right word.*

"Hey, don't I know you from somewhere?"

Demo's nerves rang him like a boxer taking hits. Had he already been picked out? Was he going to be stuck in this memory of a city forever? He traced the voice to a beautiful woman standing outside of a shop filled with t–shirts and knick–knacks of every kind. Her long blonde hair went well past her waist. Her vibrant blue eyes scanned Demo carefully, looking more befuddled by the second. Demo did what he always did and responded incorrectly.

"I'm a new bank…I mean, a bank, I'm new at. I'm new."

The woman cracked a smile.

"I've never seen any banker dressed like that."

Demo cringed. He fought the urge to switch back to his more familiar and comfortable clothing. He had to stay in character, no matter what.

"Oh, I mean I'm on my *way* to the bank. That's right…I like, totally am, like on my way to the coin house. Gotta keep working for the man, you know."

The woman tilted her head, grimacing slightly.

"You're not from around here, are you?"

Demo, why do you suck so much?

"Just visiting from out of town, on a…on a business trip."

His new friend laughed out loud.

"Just how *far* out of town are we talking here?"

Demo shrugged.

"Like, way far out there."

The woman winked at him. Instantly, his insides turned to Jell–O.

"You can say that again," she said, glancing over his shoulder.

"But between you and me, I'd stay clear of any banks around this neck of the woods. Word on the street is the local gangs are planning something big. I'd just chill out somewhere safe if I were you. It's been really weird around here lately. Wouldn't be taking any strolls at night, if you know what I mean."

Demo's jiggling gut solidified and was replaced by a stack of bricks on his chest. It was getting late.

"*Gangs?* What exactly are you talking about?"

The woman waved both of her hands in the air as if trying to put out a fire.

"Chill out, man, chill out. Like, it's no big deal. I've probably said too much already. Just keep your head on straight and I'll catch you on the flip, alright? It was nice meeting you and all."

Now it was Demo's turn to grimace. *Catch me on the flip?* What's wrong with these people?

She, pointed him away from her general location, obviously hoping to lose him. He complied by walking away. He decided to dwell on Spencer, rather than her sudden dismissal. He hadn't had the proper time to analyze him thoroughly anyway. The circuitry that contained the facts he was after had yet to be opened. He had to wing it. He knew enough about the blood legacy murders to know that miscreants from all walks of life shared certain virtues with this killer. It was very likely that Spencer got his start the way many murderers do; as a hired gun or mercenary. *Or worse.* Thinking about it made him sick. He knew he had to put himself in the last place he wanted to be; with the dark devils in the city's underworld.

First, he had to find the right place, find the right degenerate, and then hope that Spencer would show up too. It was a long shot, but time was of the essence in both worlds and it was the best he had.

Walking down the street, the odd sense of familiarity was replaced with his own thoughtful recollections. He *knew* this city. It had changed drastically, but a few things had thankfully remained more or less the same; the historic courthouse, some of the towering skyscrapers, and a few of the restaurants suddenly gave him the warm fuzzies. *This* was *home*. Demo shook his head at such a ridiculous idea. How could this feel like home when he was sitting inside of someone else's head in a time he had forgotten? He needed to be very careful, less he forget his place in this.

"*The Godfather*… Have you seen *The Godfather*?" a man carelessly asked his friend as Demo passed a street–side coffee house.

"Not yet, but I'm going to. I'd be stupid not to check that out."

The Godfather? Demo stopped by the coffee shop for a moment to listen in.

"I'm heading down to 5th Street—maybe we should all meet up there—who knows what might happen?"

The other man nodded while drinking his coffee.

"You got it, man. Somebody's gonna be sleeping with the fishes tonight."

Both men laughed as one of them got up, said goodbye, and left. Demo couldn't believe what he was hearing. *Somebody's gonna be sleeping with the fishes tonight? Could they be planning a hit? How could they talk about it so openly?* But this could be a potential lead. He needed a direction, and now maybe he had it. It wasn't like him to try and tail someone, that was Bob Cat's realm, but it needed to be done. He was searching for a needle in a *stack* of needles, so he had to take some risks.

At first it was extremely difficult for him to follow the man and go unnoticed. He was trying his best to fly under the radar, but he kept getting stared at by just about everyone he passed. *What's their problem?* He mixed spurts of sprinting like an idiot to catch up to his quarry who was playing it cool in an effort to dissolve back into the scene. The man he followed kept up a steady pace; he definitely knew where he was going. Demo had to admit that he had probably walked these streets many times before in the future. Or *was* it the future? Just how exactly could he describe it?

His cluttered brain clamored on until the man made an abrupt stop at an alleyway. Without hesitation, he disappeared from the sidewalk and was out of sight. Demo panicked. He had just lost visuals of his target, and what was worse, it was into another dark lane. *I hate alleys so much!* Forgetting to blend in he bolted forward, trying to catch up to the mysterious man. He clumsily carved a path through the people, upsetting them as he went. He needed to find this *Godfather* and start asking some questions. His time must be running shorter by the second. Time … was that even relevant when you were sitting inside somebody else's head? Was his new notion of time just a figment of his or Spencer's imagination? He couldn't get caught up in a hamster wheel of thought. He needed to focus. Scraping his shoulder as he went, he twisted around the corner and into the alley.

As always, it was dark and filled with shadows. *Why can't they ever put lights in these things?* Although he knew that this was somehow all a dream, the sting on his scuffed up shoulder felt all too real. If that could manifest, he'd hate to see what a heated piece of lead between the eyes could do. But his biggest problem was the man he was following; he was nowhere to be found. The alleyway didn't have any doors that he could see and was innocuously filled with the inventory of all alleyways; garbage, rats, and dumpsters. Looking around, he didn't see any fire escapes or ladders. *Lax on all the codes back then, I see.* This led him to conclude that the man he was looking for must be inside. Demo shivered at the prospect. Even in what was nothing but a memory, the fear was real; but he had to do it. For all he knew, he'd be ripped back into reality any minute. *Reality—* what a funny word that was to him now, especially since everything around him seemed as real as real gets—even the dingy odor of the aged infrastructure played into the fantasy.

Taking a deep breath, he moved further into the alley. His arm began to itch, a useless indicator of his level of stress. For once he ignored it, doing his best to look like he knew what he was doing. His leather shoes scraped against the ground, dragging loose pieces of garbage with them. Looking at the trash, something caught his eye; a flimsy, stained piece of paper that had almost floated away. On it were various advertisements, articles, and a bold headline on top:

FIVE MEN ARRESTED AT DNC HQ. IS THE WATERGATE LEAKING?

Demo paused. _Watergate…I know the name, but not much of the real story behind it._ He wished now that he'd paid more attention to all the contrived education he'd received. Reaching down, he diligently searched for the date the paper was published. Strangely enough, he found nothing. Flipping it over, he found something even more surprising; a jumble of nonsensical words and blank space. _What the hell is happening?_ Demo's train of thought was suddenly derailed by a pair of voices.

Ducking behind one of the dumpsters, he peeked around the corner like a child spying on his parents. Had he been seen?

"You got the stuff?" someone said from the shadows.

His voice rang a bell. If Demo had heard it right, it was the voice of the man from the coffee house.

A second person answered, "Chill cat, chill; of course I do. Like always, on time, and delivered with pleasure."

Two shadows shook hands in the dark, sliding a small plastic bag from one to the other.

"I'll catch you on the flip side, brother. Let's keep this whole thing ice cold, as always."

"Right on, man; I can dig it."

Demo watched as one of the mysterious men disappeared into the darkness and headed off into another adjoining alley. This was his chance. He needed to act quickly. Preparing to move, the adrenaline rang in his ears. It was normally Bob Cat's job to wring people out.

He knew, in reality, he didn't resemble a wringer in the slightest. But maybe with the right modifications, he could at least represent some authority. He tried to conjure up the costume that would make the most sense. His wild thought process kept leading him to old movies that reminded him of the world he was temporarily stuck in. He dug deep and came up with the best he could do; a concoction of modern day policeman mixed with a Burt Reynolds in Boogie Nights. *Or am I thinking of a different movie? No, Boogie Nights is exactly what this is like.* With the right amount of thought, he pulled the outfit from Spencer's mind and onto himself. He felt powerful for just a moment before again realizing that this wasn't his world, and he had absolutely no control over it. His little tricks were purely survival tactics now. He stepped out saying the only thing that came to mind.

"Hold it right there, Cat! Officer Hooker, *freeze!*"

The man froze in place, his jaw dropping to his chest. Immediately, Demo felt completely idiotic. Where had *that* come from? Decades of reruns suddenly coming together to utterly humiliate him? He needed to say something, as he realized his stupid mistake. He had forgotten a gun. He just asked a man with probable ties to the underworld to hold still, and he had no gun to persuade him to comply. *Can I even conjure a gun? Probably not the best idea.* The anti–climactic moment came as expected; the man took off running. Demo let out an enormous sigh of frustration.

Why do you have to run?

Demo began chasing the man through the darkness of the narrow passage. The clacking footsteps of shoes against pavement echoed off the faceless walls. He tried to imagine himself as a skilled Olympic sprinter, but it just wasn't happening. They ran on, occasionally knocking over well–balanced piles of garbage that would topple to the ground leaving cluttered piles marking their path. Demo gasped for air, continuing past his comfort zone. It was strange to feel so exhausted in what was supposed to be nothing but a dream, but the burning and churning of his lungs made it real enough.

"Stop! I just need to talk to you!" huffed Demo, pleading with the man who was increasing the distance between them.

Demo watched the man dart around another corner when a sick, sinking feeling settled in his gut. He was on the verge of losing him. What could he possibly do now? The man would soon be out of sight and he'd have nothing to work with. Then it hit him. This might be Spencer's world, but he still commanded his own consciousness. He could use Spencer's rules to become whatever he could fathom. *Fathom* was truly a poignant name for such an incredible device. But it didn't grant him god status; if Spencer singled him out, he'd be nothing more than a prisoner on an eternal death row. But he had to try—he had to believe—it was time for his skills to be put on full display.

"Alright, let's play this game."

The rules were being set by the world around him. Conjuring up minor changes in appearance was one thing, but he didn't want to press his luck by making waves. He wasn't an expert on the topic of mind–sharing but had a hunch that suddenly turning himself into a fire hydrant would have him pegged in a heartbeat. This meant that, at least for the time being, there wouldn't be any superhero antics forthcoming. He was very much just a regular Joe walking down the street. So what could he use here? As his pace continued to decline he had a sudden insight. *I know these streets. I know the nooks and crannies. I've spent years in this place. Well…years in its future.* As the man was reeling out of sight, Demo thought about what he had seen so far. He was looking for landmarks, things that drew a map for him to follow. A smile took over his face as he turned and headed back the other way. He had a plan now and was going to catch his mystery man.

Leaving the alley, he glanced over at a nearby parked car to catch a glimpse of his reflection. So many things were suddenly making sense. The man that stared back at him *was* him, but outfitted in a horrible mesh of bad fashion and police uniform, topped off by a giant afro. *You've got to be kidding me.* When he changed his imagined hair style from sloppy spaghetti to groovy chick magnet, he must have fixated on the afro he had seen earlier. Now he was a Caucasian male dressed like a drag queen cop with a beautiful globe of hair. It's a wonder he hadn't been arrested already for escaping the loony bin. Looking around, he realized it was too late to change. People were already staring at him. He couldn't risk this. His gangly legs carried him as fast as they could toward his final destination. It was also an alleyway, but one that cut through to the last place he'd seen his prey running. He also knew that between the man and his salvation were various obstacles that made progress extremely slow. He knew that the man wouldn't risk back–pedaling for fear of running into his ever diligent pursuer. His odds of catching up seemed pretty good; then again, the man was more than likely just a shred of imaginative consciousness created by Spencer to populate his bustling mind, and who could disappear at any moment.

But he had to trust his instincts. The man would be there.

After passing what seemed to be miles of blank, confused stares, he darted into an alley that he hadn't visited in ages. The densely packed buildings created a maze that made traversing them difficult. Darting the wrong way due to panic would be a horrible decision. Fortunately, years of chasing bad guys and sneaking around had familiarized him with the sprawling gauntlet. He made his way down the snaking path trying to avoid another dumpster. As he jogged around it, a homeless man awoke from his daytime slumber.

"I ain't squatting. I'm just taking a nap!"

Demo looked at the pile of rags and dust that were barely discernible as a man.

"Squat all you want. I couldn't care less. Just take it somewhere else. I need this dumpster."

The man let out a heavy sigh, making it known that he wasn't happy. But Demo was a man in uniform…*sort* of. Once the man moved on, Demo pushed the dumpster with his weight. It moved, and he rolled his eyes upwards in gratitude, finally having a bit of luck in his otherwise luckless endeavor. Now, he waited. Rolling the dumpster to the end of the alley where it connected to another part of the maze, he peeked around the corner. He almost jumped out of his clothes in excitement. There was the hunted man, scaling a fence. Once over it, his mad dash resumed. The pounding of sneaker on pavement echoed loudly. Demo's timing had to be right for once. If he missed, there was no plan B—or was it plan C now? Demo's mind wandered for an instant before something brought him back.

"I forgot my things!"

It was the homeless man. He stood inches from Demo's back. *Could your timing seriously be worse?* Demo's face tightened in disgust. This was the last thing he needed right now. Soon his prey would blast past and maybe never be found again.

"It's a big, black plastic bag, and I'm not leaving without it!"

Demo wanted to scream. Instead, he flung open the top of the dumpster and quickly looked inside. At the bottom was the black bag the homeless man wanted. Like the klutz that he was, he attempted to reach inside. He shifted his weight to one foot as he stretched, reaching for the bag. He had forgotten how easily the dumpster had moved. His weight propelled both he and the dumpster haphazardly forward. A loud crash and a brief moment of commotion ensued before he was able to assess the situation.

Demo patted down his quirky clothing, trying to free himself from the filth that he'd fallen into. He looked around and saw an enormous mess of toppled boxes, piles of trash, and right there, in the dead center of it all, the mystery man who appeared to be struggling to come to. Demo hastily put all the clues he had gathered together. If this was Spencer's dream, then the *Godfather* might be Spencer himself. Right now, he had to work on this tough guy; he had to become Bob Cathy Briar. Swallowing a glob of nervousness, he pounced on the man and grabbed him by the collar.

"I heard you at the coffee shop. I saw you in the alley. I know what you were planning to do. I need you to take me to this *Godfather*! And I need to see what that other guy gave you! Nobody's going to be sleeping with the fishes tonight! You hear me? *Nobody*!"

The man's eyes grew as wide as a full moon in a clear night sky. He looked completely capsized in a sea of confusion. Demo, however, did his best to remain stern despite his ridiculous appearance.

"Tell me what I need to know! I don't have time for this. *Please*!"

Demo pulled back a fist. Had he just said please? Demo, you idiot! Bobby never says please!

The shock on the man's face finally wore thin and he began to respond.

"I don't know what you're talking about, man. I wasn't doing anything, dude…like, I was just going for a walk."

Demo snapped back.

"I saw you take something from your buddy. Give it to me or things are going to get very weird."

Weird? Why did I just say that? What the hell is wrong with me?

The man looked bewildered.

"Weird? Man, I don't know what you're on, but fine; just take it and leave me alone!"

He shoved a small plastic bag at Demo, who made one more demand.

"The *Godfather*, where can I find him? I need to know *now*, or *else!*"

Demo did his best to look insane but came off more like a goofy–eyed nerd. But whatever he did, worked.

"Down on 5th by the deli. You can't miss it. Now please, man, just leave me alone! You're a freaking nut case!"

Demo released him, feeling content about his interrogation skills. The man squirmed free and bolted as fast as he could. Without hesitation, Demo stood up and began running in the direction of the street the man had given him. He blasted past the homeless guy who was rummaging through the dumpster like a raccoon. In his mind, a timer was just about to start beeping. Half an hour to do all that he had just done didn't seem possible. Who knows when he would ever have the chance to access the same memory or dream again? He had to make the most of it. As he continued on, things around him seemed slightly different than before. Smaller points of detail seemed to be missing. Sounds were more generic, smells were starting to fade, and the resolution of things was becoming more and more shaky. It was as if the world around him was being deleted. But he didn't have time to contemplate this new strangeness; he needed to get to that address.

When he finally arrived at his destination, his sides were burning madly. He was heaving for breath but had made record time. What he saw made tears come to his eyes. He had sought out the *Godfather*, and the *Godfather* he found. There, written on a marquee, were the times the *Godfather* was playing. Inside the box office sat a young man who was staring at Demo's circus garb. Demo slapped his hand against his forehead forcefully. How could he have been so *stupid?* Was he *really* this ignorant? In all the hustle and bustle to catch his suspect, he'd never stopped to think about it clearly. The *Godfather* was a damn *movie. It's a movie! A stupid, stupid movie!* He felt like throwing up. All his work and effort had led him to nothing. Pulling the bag the man had unwillingly given him from his pocket, he opened it up and took a whiff. *Grade A, 100% marijuana—the good, old stuff that smelled like skunk.* Great. He'd stopped an imaginary man from going to the movies high on cannabis. He hung his head as low as low could go. This case was a nightmare. Despite his woes, he had the eerie feeling that he was being watched. Glancing around, he didn't see a soul. In fact, he'd been so caught up in his personal dilemma he'd neglected to see that the once packed streets were now almost completely barren. Sheer terror suddenly gripped him. What was happening? Then, out of the corner of his eye, he saw a dark, shadowy figure disappear behind a building. They must have been watching him the whole time.

"Who's there? What's going on?"

No response came. But what did come, was earth shattering; and nothing Demo could have imagined prepared him for it. The details of the buildings began to fade, and with it, the words on the theatre. The young man in the building completely vanished. Within a few more pounding heartbeats, the world began to rip itself apart, disappearing into a massive storm of electricity and space. Demo could feel himself shrink from the horrific terror that now gripped him ever tighter. The only thing he could think of was to run. Turning sharply, he ran, feeling a torrent of chaos nipping at his heels like the very hounds of hell. Pieces of the world flashed around him deconstructing into nothingness. The street he was running on heaved itself skyward, throwing him down with great force. Had Spencer finally come? Landing on the almost liquid ground, he hit with a rippling thud. Sharp bolts of pain racked his body rendering him utterly immobile. His heart was ready to explode. He would soon be forever a prisoner in the mind of a killer. If something was going to happen to save him, it had to happen now. And then it came. Despite the unmitigated pandemonium all around him, a new sensation took precedence. A great churning ball of energy was growing in his head until it could grow no more. Right at the precipice of unbearable pain it released, sending the energy out through his body. Now, the process that had brought him here in the first place was running in reverse. As the world around him collapsed, he could only hope that he'd made it in time.

CHAPTER NINE

Tora Tora

"Mr. Ward, Mr. Ward, can you hear me?"

The words echoed through his head, the world around him a hazy jungle of sound and motion. Demo tried to shake it off but found his body as unmovable as a corpse. Was he the newest edition to Roslin's vegetable garden? He tried to remember what had happened, but was struggling. His mind was stuck in warm–up mode, still trying to get its engine properly revved up.

"I'll kill you right now if you've hurt him!"

Demo's ears perked up at the tone and influx of a mad Irish American he knew very well. His eyes wandered the room blankly, trying to find something of interest to lock on to. *What happened to me?*

"Back off, Mr. Briar; I'm *warning* you!"

Slowly but surely he came to. He was piecing his fragmented mind back together and what he remembered infuriated him to no end. What had he seen and so narrowly escaped; a thunderous wall of churning death that had nearly ripped his soul from his body? And who was the man in the shadows? Was it Spencer? Was some part of Spencer toying with him? Had he really been discovered so easily? He had questions that needed to be answered.

Feeling the blood return to his limbs, he weakly sat up.

"Hey! He's back online!"

Demo glanced over to see an ecstatic Jo bobbing up and down like a jack–in–the–box.

"Mr. Ward, can you hear me? Do you know where you are?"

Demo winced. The new inquiry was from Roslin who was standing a few feet away. Looking over at the chiseled statue of human discipline that he was, Demo frowned. He didn't know why, but a part of him wanted to choke the life out of Roslin, regardless of the consequences.

"Course he can hear you, you blooming idiot! He just had his brains sucked out, and you want to pillow talk?"

Demo smiled. Bob Cat had a way with words that mimicked a nubby piece of silk fabric rubbing against you; both pleasant and painful at the same time.

"I told you once, Mr. Briar, to watch your tone with me. Don't make me remind you again."

Demo's smile faded. It was his turn to assume the spotlight. None of these men had any idea what he had just gone through.

"What *was* that?" probed Demo.

His comment shook the other members of the group. It was Jo who jumped in to explain.

"You're home! You're back in the lab!"

The simplicity of the answer aggravated an already wound up Demo.

"*I* know *that*! I'm talking about in *there*! One second I'm tailing a guy and then suddenly the world turns all Mount Vesuvius on me and blows up!"

Roslin immediately looked away, mumbling a literal word puzzle of profanities. He looked at Jo menacingly, who cowered like a misbehaved dog.

"Whoops! My little bad! I might have left out one teeny tiny little detail."

With inhuman speed, Demo sprang up and grabbed him by the neck.

"You're *little bad* almost tore me into a million pieces! You need to start explaining *now*!"

Jo was taken aback, as was everyone else, by Demo's sudden burst of aggression. It wasn't like him to behave that way. Even Bob Cat swallowed a massive lump in his throat brought on by the electrifying display Demo had just put on. What was even stranger was Demo's upper hand. Jo's lack of interpersonal skills affected him physically; he was squirming like a worm.

"Look, I forgot, okay? I'm sorry there's like a million things we aren't sure of! So don't go all nuts on me! Besides, you came out just fine!"

Demo's head pulsed at Jo's obvious lack of concern for human life. Was he really just an experiment to them?

"Both of you calm down; we don't have time for this!" Roslin's voice thundered with power reminding everyone in the room just who carried the bigger stick.

"He's got a right to know, you moron! Because of *your* little toy, he was almost left a permanent couch potato!"

The tension in the room was palpable. Something needed to happen. It was Roslin who took the first steps towards a more civilized approach.

"Our apology for that small oversight but what is done is done. When attempting things of this nature there's always an inherent risk. There's a lot we still don't know."

Roslin glanced at Jo compelling him to divulge what he knew.

"The *fade*... you probably saw what I call *the fade*."

As he spoke, Demo slowly eased his grip on this epitome to poor hygiene.

"What do you mean *the fade*? You can't just throw that out there assuming we'll understand."

Jo nodded at Demo's response as if expecting it.

"I know, I know, it's just that it's still a crazy theory. You see, the mind creates these worlds, populates them, and fills them with life, but it also tends to take them down, the further away from the epicenter one gets."

Epic Center? What is he talking about?

"Don't give me any earthquake lessons; just tell me what you mean."

Jo put one of his hands on his now tender neck. He had arrived at a new found respect towards Demo that even his scattered brilliance had to give caution to.

"*The fade* is when your consciousness drifts too far out of line with his.

Your electrical patterns are dwelling in two different locations, and *one* of those is in the sleepy part of Mr. Vulcan's brain. It's like with any subconscious train of thought. You dwell on something only so long before moving on to something else. It's just that in this case, the *something* else is located *somewhere* else, and thus the brain stops supporting the old status quo, resulting in your Mount Vesuvius experience."

Demo blinked his eyes slowly. Taking in everything Jo had just said felt like trying to swallow a very large pill without water.

"Wait—so what you're telling me, if I'm getting this right, is that the world I was in was suddenly being deconstructed? That Spencer had somehow moved on to something else?"

Jo snapped his fingers while continuing to rub his neck with the other hand.

"Not necessarily on to something else, but too far away from the memory of that specific location for it to remain solid. If you wander significantly away from the center of activity, the epicenter as I said before, you may hit the dormant parts of his brain. These areas would then become unsupported by his subconscious, and *boom*, game over."

Demo wanted to dry heave. Had he really came so close to becoming a permanent residence of the bloody Vulcan neighborhood? That was definitely not his idea of a utopian existence.

"So how am I supposed to know when I'm getting close to this thing you call *the fade*? Just guess and hope for the best?"

Jo let out a small giggle, amused by Demo's simple question.

"Details…it's in the details, no doubt. Try conjuring up a room in your head. Try filling it in with everything a room usually has in it. You'll find it's quite difficult to hold on to. Now try imagining a whole *world*; your brain has to not only create it, but sustain it. It's a freaking miracle that it works at all, but like all things, it has its limits. As the imagined world changes or the focal point moves, the details outside of the effective radius become more and more unstable until…"

Demo shook his head.

"…the fade."

Jo practically gleamed at his accurate response.

"Winner, winner, chicken dinner!"

Demo glanced at Spencer who lay there as quiet as a sleeping baby. His mind still had other issues to resolve.

"And what about my abilities? While I was in there, I changed things as well."

This comment made Jo put both hands in the air and wave them about frantically.

"No! No! You *don't* want to *do* that! You'll be conjuring up elements into a subconscious that's creating them, *controlling* them!"

Bob Cat practically spat on the ground while giving immediate feedback.

"*Conjuring? Elements?* Are we playing some kind of dungeons and dragons shite now? Allow me to grab my staff."

Demo smiled mischievously.

"But I did conjure up stuff. I changed my clothes and altered my appearance. Or at least I believed that I had, and it seemed to work."

Hearing his own words made him bite into his cheek slightly. His definition of *worked* was slightly skewed. He'd been lucky not to have been flagged in the first five minutes. He was going to need some serious practice.

"You did? That's amazing! The implications of that are mind boggling. I've got to go crunch some numbers and—"

Roslin stomped his foot in a very Jacky–like way.

"Jo! Focus! We need to understand every detail if we're going to get anywhere."

"Sorry, just a very exciting find. I never fathomed that something like this could occur; one person's consciousness creating visuals inside another person's consciousness. Talk about a brain teaser! My thoughts are as follows; what you did must have created a wave or rift in Mr. Vulcan's plane of cognizance. But it must have been minor, since he didn't perceive anything as out of the norm. Had it been, well, I doubt we'd be having this conversation."

Bob Cat mumbled a line of profanities before attempting to clarify his inadequacy at understanding the language of Jo.

"And what's that all supposed to mean? Could you repeat it for those of us who didn't graduate from the intergalactic university?"

Jo grimaced as if he had just sucked on a lemon at Bob Cat's remark.

"It's like the ocean, okay? Now picture it filled with sharks swimming lazily around until something stirs the water *just* right. If you create too many waves, you're as good as dinner."

This comment resonated with Bob Cat, who suddenly exchanged his agitated state for one of genuine concern.

"You're telling me that Demo could have been torn to bits by that mangy animal?"

Jo shrugged.

"Who knows what could have happened? It would ultimately be up to Spencer. Hate to see what he'd do if he wasn't in the mood for company.

Suddenly Demo's mind lit up. So many things were suddenly coming back to him in high definition and clarity. His horribly conjured–up disguise had brought him a lot of unwanted attention. But those changes had been minor. So the question is, just how far could he go?

"And what about weapons or anything else I might fathom?"

Jo closed his eyes and let out a cat like purr. Just hearing the project and machine's name pleased him greatly.

"I don't know. This is entirely new to me. Conjuring things too dramatic could drop a boulder in the pond. But I could be wrong. Maybe the proper isolation of those synapses would in fact negate the effect as long as it's properly done and managed. Oh, wow! So many possibilities! Exciting, right?"

Demo stared blankly at this truly mad scientist. It was no wonder he'd ended up in the *no–longer–so–secret* secret building as Roslin's babbling sidekick. Roslin frowned at them both as he brought his phone to his ear. After spouting off a few grumbles of understanding, he alerted the rest of the crew.

"We've got a problem. Intelligence has found something and we need to get on it immediately."

Every man in the room took a deep breath. The nightmare would continue. There would be no respite.

"What is it? What's going on?" asked Bob Cat intensely.

Roslin responded swiftly.

"Bodies we believe to be linked to the case have been found. Apparently, it's something we have got to see to believe."

Demo's eyes watered. He remembered the deranged man's last words: *Now I believe.* That's what he'd said before he died. It was a statement that was religious and intimate; it pointed to a belief that would have taken time to harden into the malevolence that had manifested on the courthouse doorsteps that day. But just what, exactly, had that man believed in?

"Then let the blues take it on and pass the information. We can't be playing errand boy on top of everything else."

Roslin frowned. Something he'd heard in the stream of information had put a dagger in him.

"We've got to go *now*. We've got ground to cover."

Demo knew what that meant. In his head he was screaming, *more death! More innocent lives being lost to a sick, twisted game!* Roslin ushered them out of the room, leaving a still twinkle–eyed Jo behind to crunch numbers and fine–tune his assumptions. As they left, Bob Cat began to tear into the fabric of Roslin's demeanor. The two were truly a pair of immovable objects. Neither would back down from their stance. Demo, meanwhile, was lost in a sea of thoughts that swirled around him. Even the glaring white walls of the facility seemed fuzzy and out of focus. He was trying to find something to grasp on to, some needle in a haystack to pull him free from his gut–wrenching doubt. He'd always found some thought process he could use to understand what he needed to. But this was pure chaos. The targets were all over the place, but the murders themselves were impeccably executed. The symbolism was there, but the meanings still foggy. Why be obvious when you can hide the more sinister? This darkness was dragging up memories he'd worked very hard to forget.

As Roslin practically pushed him into an unmarked car, one memory stuck out above the rest: it was of the cold, dead body of an old friend; a friend who had been at the wrong place at the wrong time. Demo's pain felt like a noose tightening around his neck. With each passing second it became harder and harder to breathe. *What is this case doing to me?*

"Mr. Ward, are you listening to me?"

Demo shook his head sharply chasing the blustery clouds of thought away.

"Sorry. I was just remembering something."

It was Roslin's voice that had beckoned him back from the darkness, which was odd since Roslin was rarely the bringer of anything light.

"That's exactly what I was asking you to do! For crying out loud! Have I been talking to a wall?"

"Lay off him. He's been through more than you know about, and a 'ell a lot more than some suit and tie could handle."

Roslin smacked the dashboard of the car that they were sitting in. His prolonged exposure to Bob Cat affected him like radiation poisoning.

"I don't *care* what's happened in the past; none of us should! I *need* to know what's happening *now*. We're on our way to a new crime scene, when neither of you have given me any real direction from the last one!"

"Tell me, Mr. Ward, what did you see? Did you get anything from Spencer? I need to hear *everything*, and you better not hold anything back!"

Demo thought over the event carefully, like an artist proofing a painting before calling it finished. It was the inherent *lack* of details that bothered him most. Besides the ambience and obvious time difference, he had found nothing of any real relevance. His Spencer bounty hunting skills needed some polishing.

"The Godfather…I found *The Godfather*."

Roslin relaxed his pose, befuddled by such an acute singularity.

"The *Godfather*? *Who* or what is the *Godfather*?"

Demo put his head into his hands resisting the urge to punch something.

"A *movie*. It's a dirty, stickin', rotten movie. I chased a lead, scrummed down a guy with a bag of weed, all to end up at the opening night of the damn *Godfather*."

Roslin sat back in his seat, releasing the gust of air he'd been unconsciously holding. It appeared his rage had peaked and now he was lost in a sea of it. Things seemed to be turning for the worst.

"Demo, are you telling me that *all* you found was an old *movie*? Am I *hearing* you right?"

Demo nodded at Bob Cat's question—he had heard him right—but there were a few more details that might salvage a scrap of usefulness from this situation.

"I was in the city; *our* city, but in another time. I saw a lot of things that I need to research, things that I believe to have historical importance. I doubt I found Spencer, but with some time I think I can take apart the world and time he created. That'll help me understand his mindset, and hopefully lead me to his trail."

Roslin took a deep breath. Trying to contain himself was an obvious struggle for him. Demo watched him closely. *What happens when Roslin snaps?*

"Fine, fine, that's fine. So you know for a fact it was the same city? Beyond a shadow of a doubt?"

"I walked the very streets I've walked a hundred times. Things looked different but they *felt* the same. It was the same city; *my* city."

Roslin looked at the driver then at the odometer. He whispered something across the seat before turning back around.

"Well, let's hope you get another opportunity. I fear things will become much, much worse every second this goes on."

Demo did what he always did best; he ignored everyone else. He was deep in meditation trying to connect the dots from Fathom to the real world. Roslin was correct that things would continue to escalate until resolved. He needed to accelerate the process.

Hours that seemed more like days passed before the unmarked car arrived at its intended location. It looked like an old, abandoned homestead. The buildings were all beautifully aged, creating feelings of nostalgia. But one building stuck out more than the rest; an old barn. It was a deep, rustic color and was comprised of antiquated wood boards fastened together by old rusty nails, which appeared to be the only thing holding it together. On the near wall was a flimsy, double door that had been shut tight for years; at least until now. It was the door that had drawn attention to the barn. It had been moved, the oxidized lock broken. Special Agents were scattered around the property, scrapping for evidence. But the once quiet barn held something dark inside—something that wanted to get out, to be heard—the silence had come to an end.

As he exited the car any attempt to converse with Demo was deflected and ignored. He was honing in on the barn. As he paced forward, Roslin intercepted everyone in Demo's path, waving them off forcefully. It was amazing how much of Jacky's attitude seemed to dwell in this man. But that was a history to revel in another time. As he entered the rickety building, he saw a board resting by the door bearing the words, *Tora Tora. Tora Tora…that doesn't ring any bells.* Another interesting but subtle detail was the condition of the wood; it was obviously much newer than the rest.

The inside of the barn was much like the outside. Old pieces of farm equipment sat deteriorating into the ground like plastic toys slowly melting in the sun. But at the back of the barn was something truly maniacal in every regard. It was fashioned from the same aged steel that dotted the interior. Its execution was meticulously wrought. Long, rusty poles were carefully connected to a circular center piece. Wires, cables, and other odds and ends were used to construct an evil effigy of the scales of justice. But the weight plates held the real horror. On one end was a pile of ashes and bones; on the other, a decaying body dressed ceremoniously in judicial garb. The scale sat in perfect balance. The scene compelled Demo to purge his insides out. It was truly deranged.

"This is sick. What a sick freak!" grumbled Bob Cat, turning away.

Roslin's pace slowed until he came to a complete stop, his eyes fixated on the corpse dressed like a judge. It sat motionless, eyes stuck wide open. The odor of acrid air pelted against him. He averted his eyes in anger and disgust. Demo observed Roslin's reaction carefully. One thing was obvious now—this particular scene of well-crafted brutality had come too close to home—for Roslin, this was personal.

"Tora, tora; *what* does that mean? Is that some sort of historical saying? I seem to remember it in possible reference to a war or conflict," Demo mumbled.

Roslin kept his gaze locked on the corpse in front of him. He obviously couldn't yet muster up the will to converse.

Bob Cat jumped in to soften Roslin's silence, "What are you saying, Demo? You need to speak English."

"It's written on a board outside. I find it oddly out of place. Why would something like that be at the entrance to this nightmare? When was it put there?"

Roslin slowly turned. His demeanor showed the great signs of wear and tear that had ripped a gaping hole in his ever-resolute disposition.

"We've got a room full of dead bodies, and you want to know what a damn piece of wood on the door means?"

Demo shook his head.

"It's not a *want*. I *need* to know. It's the little things that matter the most."

Roslin clenched his fist tightly turning it almost bone white. He began to speak but was abruptly cut off.

"I'm sorry for your loss. No doubt the one up there dressed like the man of justice is a friend of yours. Based on the symbolism we've been left so far, I'll guess he was an actual judge and has been missing for quite some time. I'd also assume that this, this *sickness*, has a direct connection to the other murders. My only question is *how*? How did this come to light and how did you find this place?"

Roslin turned away, his eyes falling back on what was once his friend.

"He told us."

"What do you mean, *"He told us?"* *You're* telling me that you *knew* about this, and you *still* let it happen?" Bob Cat spit angrily.

"We *didn't* know… at least not until *now*. All we had to go off of was a misdirected piece of mail that ended up at one of our buildings. How were we supposed to know it actually *meant* something?"

Bob Cat threw a bare knuckled punch into a flimsy piece of wood that collapsed under the force. The commotion shook the room to a standstill. All eyes now rested on him.

"It's your blooming *job* to follow up on *anything* that might stop something like this before it happens!"

Roslin shook his head.

"It had no relevance until now; in light of all our other cases, of which you have no idea, we thought it was pretty minor. Once we realized this was escalating, we rechecked everything—and I do mean *everything*. That's how we ended up here. Don't you think I regret not acting sooner? That man up there was one of my old friends and now he's dead. The only consolation is that his missing person's case has finally been solved."

Demo closed his eyes, still feeling sick to his stomach from his initial scan of this macabre scene.

"It wouldn't have mattered. They were already dead. The killer wouldn't have clued you in until their work was complete."

Roslin stared down each idle officer, sending them scurrying back to work. Demo approached the grotesque tableau gingerly. He didn't want to accidentally miss anything or disturb the scene. Before him was hell incarnate; a pile of burned human remains on one side, and a slain judge on the other. He needed space to think…he needed space to become what he needed to be.

"I need some time alone in here."

Bob Cat looked sternly at Roslin expecting another fight for power. But it never came. To everyone's surprise, he bowed out and gave Demo exactly what he had asked for. Bob Cat assumed his usual position in a shadowy corner of the room and waited for the magic to happen.

Demo went back to the door. He already knew what was outside but wanted to see if any bread crumbs had been idly left behind. But inside, he knew better. The killer had been scrupulous. As he walked into the room, he could feel the same darkness he had felt in the walk–in freezer at the warehouse. It slowly began to ooze over him like putrid tar.

"I'm so proud of this…and *yet*…something *needs* to be balanced."

Demo continued mumbling his thoughts as he went. The fact that this had been a forced entry begged the answer to a few questions.

"Why here? And why would you go through all this trouble?"

He moved closer to the remnants of what had undoubtedly been a horrific murder. The smell of burnt flesh was overwhelmingly acrid. That mixed with the smell of decay emanating from the other body were almost too much to bear. But he knew he had to continue, to fight through it. Looking up at the expertly put together pieces of metal that comprised the large scale, he was taken aback by the craftsmanship. How such crude elements could be reworked with such artistry spoke of real talent. He moved on to the piles of ash and bone. He was sure the ash had been created earlier and at some other location that had yet to be found. *Why bother burning them? What made them so special?* The thought raced through his head like a speeding car. *This was personal.* Sucking in a large gulp of air, he did the next thing that made sense.

Bob Cat turned away, contorting his face in disgust, as Demo plunged one of his hands deep into the ash. The sensation of charred bone fragments slipping through his fingers was absolutely appalling. Gritty remains of a once vibrant life tumbled over his hand like sand on the beach. His mind was giving orders driven by questions he wanted answers to. He was coming to his wit's end when suddenly he felt a smooth stone rub against his hand. With all the caution he could muster, he slowly brought it into the light; a diamond. A diamond had been intentionally placed in the ash. Demo nearly fainted. The monster that had done this was becoming more complex in his thinking. A numb feeling was dragging Demo's soul down to the very depths of what he thought was humanly possible. But he still had one more body to inspect. An older man was curled up in the fetal position, his attire reeking of rotting carcass. A white wig completed the satire of the outfit, with a gavel to boot. Demo couldn't take any more. The smell and visuals were too much.

"Okay, I have to get out of here. I need—I just need to leave."

Bob Cat nodded his head before opening the door. He cleared a path for Demo, who ran past a sea of onlookers to a nearby bush, where he heaved up what little he had left inside. The pain brought him back to the stark reality of what had happened here. But at least he had gained some ground. In fact, he was now positive of at least one thing; the killer wasn't alone. The clues swirled around him like a carousel out of control. *What does it all mean? What are you trying to tell me?*

"Mr. Ward, what did you find?" demanded Roslin, coming into view.

Demo paused, still feeling the nausea pulsing in his gut. He produced the diamond. Roslin took a few steps forward allowing the diamond to fall into his outstretched hand.

"What's this?"

Demo shook his head to clear it. He needed to be Demo again.

"Purity, innocence, perfection…many adjectives apply, but those are the ones that come to my mind."

Roslin stared deeply into the sparkling rock.

"I need more than that. I need something I can *use*."

Demo's ears began to ring. He didn't want to explain what he thought about what he'd just seen. He didn't want the rot to enter him. But he knew he had a job to do, and do it he would.

"This location is relevant. The pile of ash with the diamond represents fire and pressure creating perfection. What's a diamond but ash under pressure? The scale is an obvious reference to justice. The meticulous design made with elements found here, points to the intimate connection the murdered man dressed as a judge has to this place; we can assume he's the owner. It also divulges the killer's intent. He wanted this to *matter* to his victim. But making that happen would take time and careful planning. The symbolism would need to be preserved. The pile of ash was left for a far more sinister reason. Burning those victims, whoever they were, freed the killer's deranged mind from their tainted image. What better cleanser than fire? This was almost an act of love—twisted, sadistic love—the kind of love one would only share with someone he loved the most. The ashes were members of his family. A family ripped apart by some sort of sin, brought back together by the purity of fire. I have no doubt in my mind that the man decaying inside shared a connection with the slaughtered family. His death was deserved in the killer's mind. The scales of justice had finally been balanced."

Roslin stared at the ground in disgust. He, too, was connected to this case on more than just a professional level. Demo pressed on.

"There's more to this that I'm starting to see. This isn't someone that's doing things on his own. This has the ring of a teacher and pupil partnership. It's more complicated than I originally foresaw. We're dealing with two perpetrators."

Bob Cat's head sunk deeply into his chest. The darkness was beginning to break them all down.

"I know this is a horrible time to bring this back up, but I have to. I just remembered what the words on the board that hung on the door meant. But first, before I tell you, I need to know something else."

Demo locked onto Roslin. "The letter; what did it say when you opened it?"

Suddenly, Roslin looked as if he'd just seen death itself. His eyes darted nervously back and forth.

"Tora, Tora"…

Demo closed his eyes. The killer had again proven his worth as a talented adversary of the most despicable kind.

"Surprise, Surprise…" Demo said quietly.

CHAPTER TEN

Bush Zombie

Repugnant, gruesome, vile, utterly shameless—Demo tried to describe the pure evil he felt was now a part of him. He sat slumped in the car as they drove along the seemingly aimless back country roads heading home. Everyone was silent as no one had the will to make small talk, or worse, attempt to dig deeper into what they'd just seen. The only sound was made by the tires moving swiftly over the pavement, which produced a therapeutic hum. So much to try and decipher; so many lives lost. Carefully crafted murders, some decades old, raged forward in time like a river that couldn't be dammed. In a sick way, Demo found the murderer's steadfastness admirable. Staying with something so long was a feat few people could match. But at the same time, he hated them—him, her—it didn't really matter. Whoever it was, they plagued his very existence. Why couldn't the world be kinder, be a thing of beauty? Why did reality have to be so ugly much of the time? Demo raised his head and saw Bob Cat staring blankly out the window. If jaded had a look, that had to be it.

"So, is it just you now, Bobby? I mean, at home?"

Bob Cat squirmed a little in his seat.

"What's it matter? Ain't a damned thing I can do about it now…'haps its better this way. They deserved better 'an me, anyways."

Demo's insides clenched. Someone in his twisted little family was hurting and he was unable to fix it. What crushed him most was watching someone whose emotions were usually a block of ice, suddenly begin to melt.

"I'll get these guys, Bobby—I'll get 'em and make 'em pay—I *promise* you that."

Bob Cat glanced at Demo and managed a slight smile of gratitude for his good intention.

"You really are as thick as sod, aren't ya? I sure can pick 'em."

Demo smiled back in solidarity. In a strange way, both men were realizing that their small gang was all each of them had. Forgetting to be cordial, Demo turned his attention to Roslin, who also looked as distant as a far off planet. It was disquieting to see the burden of regret, anger, and remorse each of them was carrying. The amalgamation of their emotion was welding them together like the twisted metal they had just left behind.

"I need to know more about the victims back there. It's obvious you know a lot more than you're telling. If we're going to make this work, we can't hide anything from each other."

Roslin let the comment go unanswered long enough that it appeared to have crashed and burned. Demo finally spoke up. He knew he was right; everything had to be out on the table if this case was going to get solved.

"He was an old friend. Someone I knew long before I got involved in any of this. We served in the military together for a while before we went our separate ways. Beyond that, it's been the occasional email or Christmas card. I have no idea why he would have any involvement in this or why someone felt that he deserved to die that way."

Demo put his hands into the air.

"*Deserved*…that's the key here. Why go through all the theatrics? Why drag us along? Why single out these people? The motive is still convoluted to me. I need to get inside Spencer's head again. I need to get back to the Fathom."

Roslin nodded his head.

"It's about time you stopped kicking and screaming. We'll get you back in, but you've got to start producing results. These little jaunts aren't cheap."

Out of nowhere, Bob Cat smacked Demo's shoulder, leaving it tender and sore.

"Bobby, I've got something for us to get done on the outside. But first I need to refine my skills. I need more involvement with Spencer. I need to grasp the way he perceives reality. If he was awake this would be a lot easier, but he's not so I've just got to take the plunge."

Bob Cat resumed staring out the window. It was apparent that something was troubling him deeply.

"And what if a storm brews up again and sucks you in for keeps this time? You're risking more than most would be willing to on such an unsure thing."

Demo's brow furrowed slightly in recognition of the truth.

"Well, it's a chance I've got to take. Otherwise, out here, they'll always be a step ahead."

Bob Cat snorted in retort.

"Bunch of blooming fools—that's what we are—a bunch of blooming fools…"

Demo rummaged around in his pockets before finding what he was looking for. Trying his best to avoid being seen by Roslin or the driver, he palmed it to Bob Cat.

"Cloak and dagger?" he whispered, surprised by the sudden gift.

"It has everything we know about the blood legacy murders on it; at least that's what I've been told. If this falls into the wrong hands a lot of people could be out in the open."

Bob Cat shook his head.

"No, no, no! I'm not babysitting something this heavy. I can barely keep track of my pack of gum, let alone this."

Demo didn't back down.

"Do it, please, Bobby. I'm too easy a target. They'd *expect* me to have it. Just hold on to it until I need it."

Bobby stuffed the electronic device into his pocket, letting out a gruff stream of air.

Demo glanced up at the rearview mirror just in time to see the driver staring back at him. The driver quickly diverted his eyes back onto the road. Something was definitely off about the way he had been watching them. But he was one of Roslin's men; if he was involved, then anyone could be, right up to the very top.

The remainder of the drive was largely uneventful. Only the occasional muffled sound would slip through the awkward cement of silence that had been poured inside the car. But once they arrived at the facility, Demo came alive. He exited the car, on his own for a change. He walked swiftly to the unmarked door on the side of the massive facility and waited. He was fighting the doubt and fear that nipped at him like a stray dog. But he felt that he was making progress, even if only by inches. Spencer must know who the killers are. He must know what's motivating them. After all, Spencer had been part of the original scheme. But now he was the bastard stepchild of an ongoing case. No more connections to the outside world; for all intents and purposes he was as good as dead. But he was their only edge. Demo was dedicated to beating them using Spencer's own imagination against the maniacal game being played out in Demo's reality.

Bob Cat frowned as he grudgingly stuck a new piece of gum in between his clenched teeth. It seemed that at least for the moment things were more or less normal, whatever *that* was. After Roslin made a quick phone call the door opened and Demo entered the building. Like a small boy on Christmas morning, he raced through the halls on route to the room that potentially held the gift of answers. He only got so far before the security people in charge of the mysterious building held him back.

"Always with the doors in this place…doors, doors and more doors. How does anyone get anything done around here?"

His question was answered by a man carrying a sleek, black pistol. He eyeballed Demo looking for any sign of his credentials.

"Step away from *my* door, Sir. Step away or I *will* shoot you."

Demo gazed up at the ceiling. Why was reality always so difficult? So much red tape, so many opinions…

"He's with me!" screamed Roslin, stomping down the hall towards them. "Put your gun down!"

The man looked at Demo then at Roslin then back at Demo. It was obvious Demo's presence was an unwelcome one.

"I came in through the secret door; you know the one outside."

The security guard shook his head and sheathed his weapon.

"Idiot..." he mumbled as he walked away.

The doors finally opened and the group marched in. They were met by the usual awkwardness of Jo, who practically tap–danced at the announcement there would be another venture into Fathom. The room had already been prepped. This secret government organization was very efficient, even if despicable. It was no wonder a man like Roslin called the shots.

"Jo, report?" asked Roslin sternly.

Jo smiled and opened his arms like a ballerina dancer.

"Fully active and already streaming some exotic visuals, if I do say so myself. I can't wait to—"

Roslin put a hand up almost instinctively to stop him.

"Just get my guy inside. We need to escalate this. You can nerd out later."

Jo gave him a sharp frown of disapproval, but he did what he was told. Demo did most of the prep work for him this time. For all of the device's complexities, lying down on a table and getting your brains sucked out seemed fairly easy.

Lights, camera, action...

Demo braced himself for what he knew would be another mindboggling ordeal. But despite his best efforts, he still felt like he was getting utterly ripped from his body in the same way as before. This time he had to focus and be quick. He had to adapt. He had to think on his feet. And most importantly, not get caught. As the streaming fragments of light slowed around him and the aloof feeling faded, he found himself in his new world.

Immediately, an almost drowning humidity swept over him like exhaust from a car. An intense wave of heat pelted against his body A river of sweat flowed into his eyes making them sting viciously. When the world finally came into full view, he was completely taken aback by what he faced; jungle, and lots of it. He faced a seemingly endless wall of vegetation like nothing he'd ever seen before; contorted branches, roots, and thick underbrush. Looking around, he realized that he was completely alone.

"Spencer, where are you? What is this place?"

As he began his search, the quiet of the jungle was replaced by a wide array of animal sounds, each cleverly camouflaged just out of view. Demo pushed on, already feeling lethargic from the intense combo of humidity and heat. He had never experienced anything like it. Taking a break, he rested an arm against a tree. Wiping a stream of sweat from his brow, he attempted to map the area out. Nothing but green surrounded him, with the exception of a narrow path cut out of the jungle floor over the years by a small, trickling stream. Apart from the extreme nature of the climate, it was actually quite beautiful here. Taking a long look up the stream he immediately saw something that didn't belong—or, maybe it *did*—it was up to him to find out. A sharp edge covered in vines stuck out into a clearing that was just a football field or two away. It certainly had to be something that hadn't grown here. This helped animate Demo's quest. Anything out of place could be immediately flagged as territory that Spencer might be dwelling in. The trick would be to find him without being noticed.

Plodding up stream, his worn out dress shoes sucked up water like sponges, making them heavier and heavier. Once again, his neoteric style was proving to be a major hindrance. But what *did* people wear in the jungle? His exposure to safari attire had been limited to a few contemporary movies and television shows. He didn't have the slightest idea what he should be wearing. And if he got it wrong he'd be a sitting odd duck for Spencer and his jungle expedition would no doubt meet an untimely and messy end. He needed to find someone created in Spencer's mind. He could learn how to play the part from them and then move forward. Stretching his skinny legs, he began edging closer to what was looking like some sort of building. As he got closer a revolting smell struck his nose. It immediately reminded him of the rotting body in the barn, only amplified tenfold.

What the hell am I walking into?

It continued to intensify until he finally reached the edge he was looking for. He bent at the waist and vomited until all that was left were dry heaves. Grabbing at his knees, he finally gained the courage to look up.

The sharp edge he had seen protruding from the walls of green had indeed been part of a building—a shack to be more precise—one of many sitting in the small clearing. Each crudely constructed shanty appeared to be barely standing up against the choking might of the jungle. But it was what surrounded the buildings that had pressed his gag reflex into overdrive; *bodies*. Dead, rotting, bodies were strewn all around and staged in various positions. Flies hovered over them like tiny little helicopters. Blood was splattered everywhere. The scene couldn't be more appalling. The attire of the fallen men made it clear that they were some sort of military, but of what origin, he wasn't sure.

What happened here?

Fearing the worst, he knew he had to do something. The clock was against him and he still hadn't located Spencer. But what could he do? Making a panicked, nonsensical decision, he decided to move in closer. He needed to check the bodies and then continue following the trail. The thought of being sucked up by *the fade* sent shivers down his sweaty back. It was this greater fear that made his fear of the unknown ahead the lesser evil. Stepping out into the clearing, he took one long, deep breath. The foul odor permeated the air like thick smog. It was an odor he'd never forget. As he stepped closer he saw a lightening flash of movement from the corner of his eye.

What was that? I am so done with this place already. So, so done...

He stared at one of the shacks nearest him where he thought he'd seen the blur of motion. Focusing all his energy on the situation at hand, his nerves were literally strumming his insides like a twelve string guitar. Was anyone watching him? Was he really alone? Swallowing the boulder of fear in his throat, he stepped towards the shanty as quietly as possible. His sloshing shoes made the only discernable sound between him and the visually loud environment. Something moved again. Moving calmly, he inched his way forward his heart jumping in and out of his throat with each step. What had he just seen? Nearing the edge of the shack he saw one of the rotting corpses baking in the sun. It almost seemed to sizzle in the heat. Staying focused on the corpse, he saw it again; a quick, jerking movement that seemed to come from the body.

Are they still alive?

The suspense was too much. He had to take the chance. He peeked around the corner and blurted out,

"Hey, are you still alive?"

Demo dropped his head, realizing how stupid his question was.

Sure, ask the corpse if it's still alive. The corpse was indeed a corpse. It appeared to be a male riddled with bullet holes and burn marks, and well beyond saving. The movement had come from the stubbornness of a bird trying desperately to unhinge the remains of one of his eyeballs. Demo's head spun around in a dizzying whirl of disgust. He'd had his fill of gore; of blood and guts. He had just plain had enough. Cutting loose his frustration, he let out an unearthly scream.

"Is *anyone* here *alive*? Is *anyone* here even *real*?"

Suddenly his attention was seized by a flutter of movement. The corpse jerked upright and began to take on a repulsive life of its own. Demo watched in horror as one by one each rotting carcass rose skyward raining pieces of decayed flesh onto everything. Demo's heart stopped. He had asked for life, and life had answered by raising the dead.

"You've *got* to be *kidding* me!"

The skeletal soldiers fell hard back to earth and sniffed the air, zeroing in on their target; Demo's time was up. With a blood–curdling howl, the army of undead sprinted after him. It was a well–known fact that Demo lacked the physique or prowess of *any* kind of athlete, but *especially* a runner. Luckily, within the endless possibilities of Spencer's mind, Demo's gangly legs moved faster than they ever had. He raced back towards the tiny stream with tears in his eyes. He suddenly missed the cold streets of the big city more than he thought he could. He'd even take the soul–sucking *fade* at this point. The idea of being devoured, piece by piece, by a rotting horde was nightmarish. Feeling them gaining ground, he glanced behind him. There his eyes met the empty faces of the ravenous, reanimated corpses, which reminded him to run faster. Despite his legs feeling like a campfire dosed in gasoline he had to dig deep and find something. He didn't want to end up losing the game to a bunch of malodorous mold balls with legs.

"Bush zombies! Bush zombies from *hell*! I *hate* this place!"

Bush zombies seemed an adequate name for the cannibalistic hounds snapping at his heels. This was a nightmare he was just trying to survive. Just when he felt he could go no further, his battered dress shoes gave out from under him. It appeared that a moss covered rock would seal his fate in one slip.

I forgot to change! Why can't I remember these things?

With a painful thud he hit the ground. He cowered into a ball, the pattering feet of zombies growing closer. In mere seconds they would dig their rotten, yellowed teeth into his scrawny body and devour him. The fear he felt was all consuming. As badly as he wanted to break free from the nightmare's ghastly grasp, he just couldn't seem to shake it. It was too real; so real that every heartbeat vibrated in Demo's chest like a pounding drum. He had only come into Spencer's world twice, and it looked like it was one too many. His life would end soon. Then suddenly his growing despair was thrashed off of him by an incredibly loud burst of noise and energy.

The sudden eruption roused him back to his senses. It came again and again like the deafening splatter of giant rain drops against a tin roof; it was the sound of bullets; bullets that were flying through the air to meet the rancid army head on. Chunks of rotten flesh and body parts flew through the air as the zombie horde let out howls of agony. Demo raised his head up from his cowardly position to see the source of his redemption. A small group of men armed to the teeth; dressed to literally kill. One of the men approached Demo without hesitation.

"You alright, Sir? You need to get up and get out of here. This place is crawling with the infested."

Demo didn't know what to say. In none of his preparation did he expect such a baptism by fire.

"Sir? Can you hear me? We've got to go, *now!*"

The crackle of the gunfire raged around him while he slowly rose to his feet. The soldier looked at him strangely. In all the commotion he had forgotten to put on the right attire. But it would have to wait. A more pressing issue was still falling on them; *zombies*. Flesh hungry zombies with super–human speed. This was enough motivation to get him moving again. When he was back on his feet, the soldier pointed towards the stream.

"Head *that* way! Viet Cong are dug in deep and the undead don't care what side you're on! Now *go!*"

Demo couldn't believe what he was hearing, but as the soldier finished speaking, he affirmed the seriousness of the situation by firing a round just over Demo's shoulder, nailing a zombie directly between the eyes. It was *definitely* time to go.

As he ran for his life (again!) the battle raged on around him. A swarm of flesh eaters rapidly trekking through the jungle ripped any soldier they caught unaware limb from limb. This was an absolute hell hole, and he couldn't seem to find his way out. Demo's mouth gaped wide open as he sucked heavy breaths of air in and out. His eyes bulged from their sockets like two balloons primed to burst. He had never run so hard or fast in his entire life. He knew he had to survive long enough for Jo to pull him free.

Splashing through a pool of water, he looked behind him to check the status of the ongoing chaos. Guns, soldiers, zombies—the perfect theater of death in the jungle—Spencer's mind was as lethal as it was deranged. It seemed as if imminent doom was upon him, when again Demo saw something sticking out that didn't belong. He recognized what it was instantly. A very large cement building with barred windows, sandbagged bunkers, barbed wire, and all the other makings of the perfect evil fortress from the most nefarious of dreams. Looking around, it seemed his only choice. Without thinking further, he ran straight into the open field between the exposed edifice and the jungle gorge. Stepping carefully over some barbed wire, a heinous hiss erupted from somewhere just outside his peripheral vision. Looking over cautiously, his heart sunk. A stray zombie was heading straight for him. The zombie's left arm was completely absent but his hunger was obviously and insatiably intact. Demo knew that no one would be saving him this time. He was very much on his own.

Darting like a gazelle through the obstacles in his way, he felt the adrenaline in his body surge like an open fire hydrant. The sound of the zombie hunting him was getting closer by the second. He had to do something desperate. There was no way he was going to hold his own against Spencer's super–zombies. Looking back at the building he saw his only saving grace dangling from a blown out window: a long braid of sheered cable. Little sparks erupted from its end, showing signs it was a potential hazard. But compared to what was behind him, it was worth a shot flat out. He veered towards the cable as he did his best to dodge the terrain of warfare that set just the right mood for heart attack levels of enjoyment. Giant holes blown cleanly into the ground slowed his progress, along with the occasional burning tank or crashed airplane. His poor progress was weakening his chance for survival. A wisp of air from behind reminded him how close the zombie was. It attempted to grab Demo by the neck and drag him towards its gnashing jaws. The moment chased all logic from Demo's mind. He dove over an exposed bunker, landing with an excruciating thud against the packed ground. With cat like reflexes, he jumped up in time to see the zombie follow him right down the same path. Before he could scream, everything turned to smoke with a deafening noise. Demo was thrown back several feet by the sudden explosion. Rotting zombie showered him with gooey clods. A loud hum filled his ears as he tried to regain his composure and assess the situation properly. His zombie stalker was no more. An unexploded mine had ended Demo's nightmare. An unexploded mine that he had almost run directly into.

"This is ridiculous!"

Demo looked at the disgusting layer of fleshy chunks that covered his already ugly suit. He knew deep down that it was all a figment of Spencer's psyche but the experience was realistically repugnant. His moment of logical reprieve was unfortunately over; additional members of the horror army were quickly catching up, each fleshy, bloody body tensed and ready for action.

"I'm never doing this again!" Demo screamed inside his head.

Like a pack of lions ready to chow, they were moving in. He had to get up the cable fast or become an all–you–can–eat zombie smorgasbord. Their red, murdering eyes told the whole story. They had one thought on their minds, and it wasn't to play nice. This time Demo wasted no time purging his curiosity of their whereabouts—he only had one thing in mind—getting up that cable and into the cement fortress. It was his only option. If Spencer was to be found anywhere, it would be here. And right now anything seemed better than being outside.

As he approached the severed lines of cable he briefly paused; was he really going to climb this? The putrid, rotting fog drifting under his nostrils told him he was. Grabbing hold, he heaved himself upward, doing his best to avoid the loose end with electrical potential.

"I really, really need to start working out!"

Hand–over–hand, he climbed up the wall like a kid at the playground. He was quickly realizing he hadn't used these muscles in far too long. But he kept moving with all the purpose of a creature fighting for its life. When he was just a short distance up he felt familiar wisps of air graze against his pant legs. He looked down and saw a large group of animated corpses thrashing wildly just below him as he climbed. He wanted to puke. He'd only seen things like this in the movies, yet here he was living it out, scene by terrifying scene. This reminded him that almost no one ever survived those movies, which reinvigorated his climb. His arms quaked from exertion, but his renewed effort proved to be his saving grace; with one last burst of energy he collapsed just inside an opening in the building. Lying on his back panting, he tried to recover the strength to keep going.

I know this isn't real…I know this isn't real…Get up, you idiot! Get up!"

Getting slowly back up on his feet, he glanced down at the mindless horde whose lack of climbing skills had temporarily interrupted their hunt. He angrily kicked some loose debris onto their heads.

"I *hate* this other place!

His scream echoed off the insides of the cavernous building. Although he thought he was safe for the time being, it suddenly seemed quite odd to him that he would be. Could he really be alone? The only safe harbor in the jungle was vacant? *This can't be right*, Demo thought… *Where was everyone?* He decided the only thing he could do was just keep going. He really didn't have any other option. If Roslin found out that all he'd accomplished was to avoid becoming a flesh buffet, he'd wish he had stayed there anyway. The room was decorated like a typical horror movie set. Empty gurneys smothered in blood, bullet holes dotting the walls, torn and dirty clothing strewn about, and mysterious jars whose contents left too much to the imagination.

What is this place?

He paced around the room looking for an exit, another avenue of escape from this nightmare. Down a hallway off of the room he was in, Demo saw a pair of double wide doors. Approaching the door to the left, he turned the knob, but got nothing. He tried throwing his weight against the giant metal door, but again came up empty. It was locked tight. Beginning to feel desperate, he tried the other door with the same results. Both doors were impassable. He wasn't going anywhere. He let out a groan of frustration.

"Of *course*! Why *wouldn't* they be locked? Maybe I should just ask for a key!"

As he ranted, something caught his eye. A subtle reddish glow called him back to the main room. His hope was shakily renewed. A control panel he had missed when he rolled in hung on the wall, held up by a few pieces of wire.

Red means no, green means go!

Maybe it was a long shot, but the button that glowed red might open the doors that stood between him and freedom. His ears pricked; he could have sworn he just heard something. Demo was suddenly ready to move.

"I'll take door number one *or* two, thank you very much!"

He looked over the dials and switches on the exposed control board.

"Which switch do I push? Who comes up with these stupid things?"

He took a deep breath. Panicking now would do him no good. He needed to stay calm and do his best to logically weigh the choices. That's what he *should* have done. But instead he started at the top and flicked every single switch, from top to bottom, as fast as he could. Sparks flew, lights flickered on then off, and a few blood covered monitors flickered, sending a buzz through the air. With each flick of a switch his heart jumped into his throat. With the last flicked switch, the red light turned green, and a loud clack of gears moving boomed through the room. Surprisingly, both doors squeaked open. He let out a long sigh of relief. He had done it. He had survived the jungle, land mines, and the zombie army. Maybe things were finally looking up. He was tempted to crack a smile until he heard something move again. His tiny reserve of courage shattered into even more miniscule fragments. Behind the door the mysterious sound became amplified by the motor–like growl of what sounded like something quite large. The growl became growls, escalating Demo's already dismal outlook even further. As he watched in horror, the door began to pulsate with the force of the creatures behind it realizing their freedom was near. He backed away from the control board, keeping his eyes locked on the door. Inch by inch it pushed further and further open until he could see a collection of dark, glowing eyes fixated firmly on him. He backed up hurriedly, letting out a yelp when he knocked into something behind him. The something fell against his back then plopping onto the floor with a squishy thud. Fearfully, Demo turned to see the body he'd disturbed; a body that had been torn to bits. Beside it lay a giant dog collar. Glancing upwards he saw the last thing he wanted to see; a tattered sign that read:

KENNEL LAB

His head practically unscrewed itself from his body. The mysterious jars of chemicals, the tell–tale signs of death in every corner, the growls and glowing eyes…

Let me guess…mutant zombie dogs.

Mutant zombie dogs that were undoubtedly just as hungry as their disgusting counterparts stuck outside.

"Spencer, when I find you, I'm going to kill you!"

Just as he finished his guttural cry of anguish, the door finally opened enough for a gigantic, snapping head covered in bloody fur and stiches to push its way out. A true hound from hell, whose deep yellow, bloodshot eyes traced every movement he made. It was time to run for his life again. Wasting no time, he sprinted for the other door. From behind him ferocious howls echoed off the walls deafening him. He hit the door but struggled to get it to move.

These doors are massive!

They had obviously been made to hold things in including the horrific monsters that were bearing down on him now. With a sudden burst of adrenaline, his arms tugged on the door wildly trying to get the stubborn door to budge. When it finally opened just enough for his scrawny body to slip through, he felt a rush of elation. Scraping his chest as he pushed himself through the small opening, he finally slipped past it just in time for it to be slammed shut by the unearthly force of growling mutant animals heaving against it. He ran as fast as he could away from them, looking around with renewed disgust at his continuing nightmare. His new path was littered with more testimonies to depravity. As he made his way through this maze of death, a loud crack brought his attention back towards the door he had so narrowly squeezed through. The door was moving yet again but this time in the opposite, undesired, direction. In utter amazement he looked on as one large paw slid into view prying at the door, tugging at it backwards.

"Oh why not…? Problem solving dogs from hell. It makes perfect sense."

With one massive heave the door opened to the awaiting pack of hounds. They took advantage of the new opportunity by leaping into the hall gnashing their jaws at the air. Large elastic strands of putrid drool streamed from their frothy mouths smearing the ground. They were going to gnaw on his bones one way or another.

The chase resumed with Demo's distance advantage diminishing by the second. He could hear objects being flung wildly into the air as the massive beasts ripped through the halls behind him. All he could do was keep running as fast as his already completely exhausted legs would let him. Spinning recklessly around a corner, he crashed into a shelf holding operating room instruments, which fell to the floor clacking loudly. A scalpel sliced his shoulder on the way down, leaking blood down his arm. His adrenaline kicked into high gear. He ran past every horrific design element with lightning speed. He needed to continue to distance himself from the pack of ravenous dogs, but his hopes were smashed when he realized his getaway was about to come to an abrupt end.

He could barely believe what he was seeing. An airplane that had crashed into the hallway was creating a formidable wall. Looking behind him, he knew that death was imminent if he didn't at least try to find a way past this. Jumping up and down with all his might, he tried to grab onto anything that he could pull himself up on and away from the madness approaching. But with each effort he fell back down, sliding off of the plane's smooth metallic surface.

"I'm not going to die like this! I'm not going to let you win!"

Demo made one last valiant effort but plummeted ungracefully back to the ground. Sharp bolts of pain rang through his body. He had failed. He put his head into his hands. He hadn't imagined it ending like this. Just when it seemed his life was beyond saving, a beckoning call ripped him back into action.

"Grab my hand! Hurry! Just *do* it!"

Demo looked up to see another soldier looking worse for wear, but it didn't take much prodding to get him to do what he was told. Draining his reserves one more time, he leapt into the air. His hand slid down the soldier's arm and was miraculously caught in midair. With the strength of a superhero he dragged Demo up the side of the plane and away from the roar of Lucifer's hounds.

"Keep moving! We've got another one!"

Demo fell backwards onto the ground. He now realized that they were a level up. The plane had burst through and opened up the bottom floor to one just above, segmenting the two areas apart. Catching a glimpse of what was below sent chills through his body like a million icy needles. The mutated zombie dogs were jumping into the air and snapping their jaws madly. They were within inches of reaching the top. Without warning, the now all too familiar sound of gunfire erupted. Waves of bullets pelted the pack of dogs, ripping pieces of flesh off their body like a blender. Howls of pain filled the air as the dogs that still could backed away from the giant aircraft.

"I'm almost out! I need more ammo!"

Demo looked around and saw a small group of soldiers sitting amongst the rubble. Each man's face was almost completely covered in ash and debris. All of them looked incredibly jaded and a bit distant. But they moved with precision and purpose. Another magazine was quickly loaded into his savior's gun, who continued his hot lead assault. Demo's heart sank deep into his churning guts. This was too much to take in. A hand landed firmly on his shoulder as he was trying to clear his head, and its owner began asking him questions.

"Who *are* you and *what* are you doing here? Don't you know this is ground zero? You're dressed like some stupid civilian! You've got no business being here!"

Demo looked blankly back at the man whose stale, cigarette–laced breath was making him sick. But he needed to respond and start playing the game. He needed to start taking control.

"I'm with the network. Crash landed just miles from here. You want to tell me what's going on here?"

The man looked befuddled, but Demo used every fiber of his being to look confident and sure of himself. He didn't lose eye contact for even a moment. But then someone else answered his question.

"Whole place is gone to hell. War went south and the Viet Cong got desperate. You can thank them for the break out of infection. I hope they all die!"

Demo gasped. The divide between reality and fiction was getting closer. But all that mattered was that this was real to Spencer, so he needed to believe it too.

"We've got no comms, no patch outs, and we're being overrun at every previous stronghold. Whole place is in chaos but *you*, a *reporter*, made it through? Pardon my BS meter."

Demo shook his head.

"You have no idea what it took for me to get here. But now I just want to get the hell out of here."

The man nodded. Even he couldn't argue with that desire.

"We've sent a small team out looking for a radio uplink. They should be back any second. Till then I suggest you pick up a gun and shoot anything that's not singing the national anthem."

Demo nodded in agreement. The man shoved a large assault rifle into his delicate hands.

"I don't know how to use this. I've only got experience with small arms; pistols or whatever."

The man rolled his eyes before pointing down the length of the airplane where the other soldier was still firing the occasional round into the hallway.

"You think a little pea shooter's gonna stop them? If so, then by all means, be my guest."

The man stepped away and began spouting off orders to the others. Suddenly, a man holding his side and breathing heavily shuffled into view. His presence obviously aggravated the man in charge.

"Private Vulcan! Where in Satan's backyard have you been? We've been stuck here for hours!"

Demo's insides churned violently. Had he really just found Spencer? And not just found him, but was now sitting a mere two feet away from him? Catching Spencer's eye, time seemed to momentarily freeze. What stood before him was a sleek, well-trained killing machine. Everything about him was calculated and cold. His posture showed his casual insubordination. He couldn't hide that he was a stick of dynamite with a very short fuse, and he very obviously didn't care. As his boss continued to verbally attack him for his lack of concern for others, he gazed at Demo curiously.

"And where's the rest of the group? Where's Dicky and Smalls?"

The question took Spencer's attention off of Demo. He snarled back at his superior officer in response.

"They've been taken care of. I did what I had to do."

The man grabbed Spencer by the collar.

"Just what the hell is *that* supposed to mean?"

Spencer shoved the man off and backed up.

"Dicky's *gone*—ripped limb from limb—and Smalls got bit. So, like I said, I did what I had to do."

The soldier slammed Spencer into one of the nearby walls.

"You've got a real problem with taking orders, *don't* you? I'm gonna make sure they hang your stinking carcass from a tree when we get back! I'll see you *court martialed* for the crap you've pulled out here!"

Spencer let slip a wicked smile that seemed to darken the room even more.

"I did what was right. And I won't be hanging from any tree anytime soon, you can count on that. And who's this guy?"

The gruff looking man released his grip on Spencer.

"He's with the network. Crash landed a few miles from here. Moron is lucky to be alive. Stupid media can't keep their filthy hands out of anything."

Spencer looked at Demo incredulously.

"*What* network? Ain't any networks who would know about this."

Demo felt himself begin to fall apart. Spencer was every bit as cold and scary as he'd imagined he'd be. Demo knew he had to come out on top of this and leave no evidence behind. This is the very last place he'd want to be stuck for the rest of his diminishing consciousness.

"*WAR* network; you won't hear of us anytime soon. Let's just say we get paid to be in places like this. What we do with the information is up to our discretion."

Spencer looked Demo over top to bottom before shaking his head in disbelief.

"You look like a fruit basket to me. Do all the idiots there dress like you?"

Demo knew he had to supplant this. He needed to make Spencer believe that he had conjured him there; that Spencer himself had thought up this idiotic scenario.

"We don't get out much. We let the *doing what needs to be done* get done by better men than us. You guys do what's right."

Demo's cleverly crafted words seemed to appease the dark ego that was closely inspecting him. Spencer's smile widened. He enjoyed being praised for a job well done. He liked the validation that what he was doing was what needed to be done. These key points were duly noted in Demo's mind. He opened up the floodgates in his own mind to take in every little detail, every shred of character that he could steal from Spencer's mind unnoticed. He was cut short by a massive explosion. All the men in the room were thrown against the walls, each one landing with a sickening thud. Rays of sunlight rushed into the room through a newly opened and massive hole in the side of the building.

"Those idiots are blasting the facility with us still inside!" someone screamed hoarsely from beneath the debris.

But it was what came crawling *through* the hole that brought the men who *could* stand back to their feet. Waves of the undead clawed their way up the pile of newly formed rubble that led conveniently to them. The men began screaming as they fired furiously at the nearing horde of flesh hungry zombies. This time there was no escape. One of the men nearest the hole was pulled into the mass of rotting flesh screaming as he was chewed apart. Demo wanted to run but found his legs completely useless. The blast had temporarily crippled him. Panicking, he searched for Spencer but he was nowhere to be found. A rot–faced zombie was footsteps from reaching Demo. It lunged forward just as a hurricane of sparks filled the space. Waves of electricity pulsed through Demo before everything went dark.

CHAPTER ELEVEN

Flaming Feline

A tiny pin of light grew in time with Demo's heartbeat. Each thump in his chest sounded like a distant echo floating through infinite space and time. As the bright glow expanded so did his perception of reality. A rush of air whooshed past him as he hit the ground.

"Demo, Demo, can you hear me? Are you alright?"

Demo looked around and saw the perfectly white floor he had grown to loathe. How could anything be so clean, so untouched? Suddenly he slammed his hands over his ears and let out a loud guttural scream. Jumping to his feet, he ran directly into an unsuspecting Jo, who fell backwards against the force into a nearby wall. Demo lashed out at him like a maniac out of control.

"They're everywhere! They're killing everyone!"

Jo looked desperately at Roslin for some sort of aid. Roslin obliged by grabbing Demo from behind with the help of Bob Cat. They dragged him back and away from the trembling Jo.

"Get him away from me! He's gone totally mad!"

Demo's eyes watered. His energy suddenly escaped him and he fell limply back into the two men's arms. He felt as if every nerve in his body had been strung out and cut with jagged scissors. Walking carefully backwards while holding Demo's relaxed body, Roslin and Bob Cat placed him cautiously down in a chair near a table. They watched as Demo struggled to regain his bearings. He dropped his head into his hands, resting his elbows on the glossy table.

"I feel sick."

Roslin looked at Jo who just shrugged.

"You doing alright there, Demo?" Bob Cat asked him, putting a hand on his shoulder.

He shook his head and beads of sweat raced down his face. He stuck his hand out beckoning in silence for something to appease him. Roslin was a step ahead. Placing a large plastic cup into Demo's hands, he watched as he snatched it up and gulped it down.

"That's still some good water. And this time it's in a bigger cup."

Roslin remained motionless but responded.

"I pulled some strings."

Demo sat back in his chair allowing their scrutiny to fall squarely on his face. He was clear enough to know that they had business to attend to. Glancing at Jo (who immediately cowered), he began to regurgitate everything he'd seen. He watched Bob Cat's face contort when he talked about the mutated zombie dogs from hell. Large canines had a way of putting Bob Cat on edge anyway; this sounded like his worst nightmare. But it was the climax of the story that made Roslin's ears perk up.

"So you met him? You finally met Spencer?"

Demo nodded, realizing that Roslin had cut off his enthusiastic life and death story.

"Finally, after all this work…"

It appeared that for once Demo had done right by Roslin who was pacing around the room and mumbling under his breath.

"Unbelievable! I mean, seriously freaking unbelievable! Jo blurted out. "This is like uber levels of synapse cohabitation! Total mind freak right now!"

He was bouncing up and down on his heels and looked as gleeful as a kid in a candy store.

"Would you two please shut up? Did you forget that he's a human being and not a piece of your shatty lab equipment?" grumbled Bob Cat.

"He's right…one thing at a time, and at the right pace. Last thing we need to do right now is burn our only bridge." Roslin answered. Bob Cat raised his eye brows in surprise.

Demo rolled out of his chair and threw up. He watched weakly as the spotless floor became tainted by another spewing stream of vomit.

"Damn it, Demo! We just had this place cleaned! Do you have *any* idea how hard it is to hire people for a facility that doesn't exist?"

Demo just stared. The gears in his head were spinning round and round. There was something he wanted to do.

"I need a break. I need some time to piece this all together. I'm getting closer, but now I need to tie that world into this one."

Roslin glanced at Jo who looked at the floor.

"I don't think that time is something we have the luxury of extending to you right now."

Demo shot Roslin a stern look of disapproval.

"*You* want to try that thing out and see what *you* can do? By all means, be my guest. But something tells me that isn't exactly part of your plan. So, once again, I need some time."

Roslin spun a half circle throwing his hands in the air. The human aspects of investigations were always cumbersome and inefficient. For a man as robotic as Roslin Tanner, this was proving to be difficult to deal with. Bob Cat reaffirmed the request by placing his wide frame between Demo and Roslin's frustration.

"The boy needs a break. I suggest you give it to him."

Roslin wrung his hands in frustration.

"Fine, have it your way. But if anyone dies while you're taking your little siesta, it's on *you!*"

Demo got out of his chair, giving Bob Cat a look that said to let it go. Still feeling exhausted by his mind trip, he headed for the exit.

"If I'm right, we're already dead. We just don't know it yet."

The comment shook Roslin from his self–indulgence and back into the crude reality that they were all at risk. Wearing a somber mask, he quietly escorted them out.

On the way home it became apparent that they were being followed. The standard, unmarked car manned by two large men in shades stayed closely behind Demo and Bob Cat.

Could these guys be any more obvious?

They were Roslin's guys, Demo was sure. Roslin was becoming more and more of a threat. A man so bent on attaining success could be capable of being very destructive; especially if something got in his way.

"Where we heading, Demo? I mean, seeing as I've got nowhere to be…"

Demo gazed out the window. He knew that Bob Cat was trying to assume his habitually cool self but that on the inside he was a veritable squall of emotions.

"I need to eat. All this puking my guts out has left me starved."

Bob Cat smiled and instinctively reached for his gum, only to find an empty packet. Bob Cat was nervous.

"I know a place; we'll stop by and grab something."

Demo nodded without speaking. He had begun to actively think things through. Spencer had told him a lot without saying much of anything. The world he had created was a partial truth mixed with an imaginative, sadistic boldness. But what had struck him most was Spencer's demeanor. An uncaring, uncontrollable, insubordinate, self–justifying jerk—but a jerk that enjoyed praise—praise that could only come from someone even more sinister. Spencer was the puppet; the puppet master was still to be found. It had become clear to Demo that even with the absence of Spencer (due to his forced gurney vacation), the man behind the curtain was still pulling the strings. The question that made his heart shriek with terror was whether the master was now teaching someone new. He needed to put an end to this soon before the blood legacy was out of their control completely.

When they pulled up to the drive–thru window, Bob Cat ordered half the menu along with a horse trough of soda. When he looked at Demo for some input on the situation, he only received a vacant stare in return.

"I hate it when you do this crap. I never know what's going on in that noggin of yours."

Bob Cat went ahead and ordered for Demo, his usual plain chicken sandwich with fries, and a half–and–half mixture of coke and Dr. Pepper. At the pick–up window Demo had an epiphany. Maybe he was doing this all wrong. Maybe chasing the killer directly was a horrible idea. Playing the killer's game on his terms was a poor plan. This murderer was good; perhaps *too* good. But his apprentice, the active hands staging his theatric scenes of horror? They would be a chink in his armor.

"Sir, did you want cocky sauce with that?"

Demo shook his head. He glanced over at the older woman handing them their bagged food with cigarette smoke stained hands. A rash near her ring finger that had been rubbed raw made him glad she wasn't the cook.

The degrading nature of the job was etched in her face. Demo was fixated on her. As usual, his answer was inappropriate and off topic.

"You should quit this job. Seriously…just do it. No one should ever have to ask people if they want cocky sauce. Oh, and that guy's no good. You deserve better."

The woman's eyes grew into two full moons. She thrust her arm out of the drive–thru window dropping a bag into Bob Cat's lap. Her lower lip quivered as if she might cry. But to their amazement she began to nod.

"You're right. You're right! I've been slaving away here for years while my old man sits at home watching football. Says he can't find no work! Well, I've got a job for him! Thanks for the advice. I think I'll take it!"

Demo ignored the woman as he rummaged around in the bag for his sandwich. She handed a bewildered Bob Cat their drinks and slammed the window shut without another word. As they drove off Bob Cat just shook his head.

"They put the damn sauce on it! I didn't want any sauce! Why can't I ever remember to ask for no sauce?"

Bob Cat looked at Demo and then at the bag of food between them, then back at Demo who was pouting.

"Mind telling me what that was all about? You practically had that lady singing for you and I know you've never even met."

Demo wiped off the sauce on his chicken sandwich with a napkin.

"Well…there was the obvious, and then there was the rash on her ring finger."

Bob Cat blinked slowly.

"Okay…I'm not following." Demo swallowed a fry.

"The rash was from playing with her ring. Up and down it must have gone a thousand times…she was thinking about whoever gave it to her and didn't know if she should stay or go."

"So, you got all of that from truck–stop Jenny's ring?"

Demo shrugged, biting off a chunk of his now sauce barren sandwich. Once he finished chewing, he answered nonchalantly, "Nah, mostly I just guessed." He shoved another French fry into his mouth.

Bob Cat's rolled his eyes dramatically.

"You really are a lunatic. You better not be playing your little guessing game with any of this other shite."

Demo smiled.

"Let's head to my place. We've got decades of murder cases to look through."

Bob Cat nodded and stepped on the gas.

The pair made their way to Demo's rundown apartment with no further small talk. When they arrived, Bob Cat saw that the door had been carelessly left open. Sadly, it didn't surprise him. Inside was a festering mess that could have easily been on the verge of spawning new life.

"Oh, for the love of mercy! Would you at least get a maid!" grumbled Bob Cat, pinching his nose.

"Sorry. I don't really think about that kind of stuff…you know how it is."

Shaking his head, Bob Cat scrummaged around the wasteland of a kitchen until he produced a broom and a mop.

"You do yours and I'll do mine."

Feeling slightly guilty, Demo grinned sheepishly.

"I'll make it up to you, Bobby. I promise."

"You can make it up to me by ending this nightmare."

Demo slumped into his computer chair.

"You got that memory stick?"

Bob Cat rummaged through his pockets and then tossed it at Demo's head.

"Hey! Be careful! This thing is extremely important!"

Bob Cat chuckled.

"Seems like a waste of time to me. What you gonna find on there that you don't already know?"

Leaving Bob Cat to his cleaning frenzy, Demo powered on his dusty machine. Inserting the device into the computer, he was hit with an informational bad dream—decades of terror and murder, case after case, all seemingly unconnected—an athlete, a broadcaster, a city bus driver, the governor's son, ad nauseam. He looked over every detail, stretching his mind to try to find a link; purpose, sanctification, purity, sacrifice, justice; justice being the common thread that seemed to tie the filthy grime of malicious theatrics together. And what would fuel someone to continue for so long? What kind of world had created this monster?

Demo leaned back in his dingy chair, which squeaked helplessly under his weight. He rubbed the back of his neck, feeling the intense fatigue from having no sleep and so little to eat. He glanced over at Bob Cat who was curled up on the couch, snoring away. He envied him his ability to shut his brain off and be somewhat normal. That particular talent had eluded Demo his entire life. Looking around the room he could see the absolute precedent he was setting for his pathetic home life. He really needed to get out and try being human again. Something suddenly caught his eye; a small flimsy picture frame that sat front and center on his coffee table.

That's not mine…

Standing up timidly, he soft stepped over and picked it up. A much younger, livelier version of him stared back, dressed proudly head to toe in the Academy's best. Next to him, the harrowing image of a friend long lost was sarcastically smiling back. The day was as fresh to him as the day of it happened. The years hadn't taken the sting out at all.

Why would you leave this? Why bring this memory back?

Demo's once safe harbor, however chaotic it was too others, now felt lost at sea. Someone had been inside his house; someone who'd had free run of his place and left a photograph that screamed for his attention. He needed to keep moving.

"Bobby…Bobby, wake up!"

Demo stood over the dozing sack of man and shook him roughly.

"Bobby, I need you to get up *now!*"

Bob Cat grumbled a stew of vocabulary sludge before begrudgingly opening his eyes.

"Demo, what *is* it? It's the middle of the blooming night."

Demo paced back and forth, still holding the flimsily framed picture in one of his hands.

"It's Mike, Bobby. The killer knows about Mike. He knows about me, and he probably knows about you. He's probably watching every move we make!"

Bob Cat snapped into a more stable position.

"Slow it down, Demo. You've got your quills up. Now, tell me again what you're trying to say?"

Demo flung the photo onto Bob Cat's lap. Bob Cat inspected it carefully.

"That's *you*? You look like you're ten years old! And that's Mike? But what's he got to do with anything? He's…well, *dead.*"

Demo shook his head wildly.

"I don't know. This guy is messing with us. He's obviously spent a lifetime perfecting his craft and is using it now to dissect us. I can't keep up with this sick freak. Every time I feel like I'm getting closer, he digs out another chunk of me."

Bob Cat stood up angrily, firmly grasping the photo.

"Then maybe it's time *we* start doing the digging. Maybe it's time *we* start breaking some rules. If they aren't gonna play nice, why should we?"

Demo paused. Staring down at his mildew infested carpet he knew what they needed to do. He had planned on trying to do it the right way, but now the stakes were too high. This killer was eloquent, calculated, and demented. And judging by the information that had been force–fed into Demo's mind, it was obvious to him that the murdering wasn't going to stop.

"Smash n' grab."

Bob Cat looked befuddled at Demo's outlandish comment.

"Smash and *what?*"

"Smash n' *grab*; that's what they call it, isn't it? We head over to Kevin Randall's apartment, break in, take what we need, and then get the hell out. Otherwise, we're never gonna get into that place—you know all about the red tape— and don't forget the Mar's effect."

Bob Cat snorted in anger.

"That weasel in a suit. I'd love to catch him alone in a dark alley with a dumpster his size."

"Easy, Bobby—that's what they want us to do—they want us to keep being who they know us to be. They expect you to bruise someone up and for me to keep playing nice with Roslin and his goons. We need to disrupt the flow; we need to not be us."

Bob Cat bobbed his head up and down as he agreed with each sentence line–by–line.

"Hell, that sounds mighty good to me. I'd prefer breaking the rules anyway. 'Bout time you took the short leash off me."

"Let's go visit and see what turns up. I'll be looking for a lot more than just evidence of murder there, so I'll need time to focus. And as we both know, prowling around a crime scene at night can get a little sketchy."

Bob Cat thumped the side of his hip.

"I can erase any sketchy real quick with a few rounds in the right place."

Demo smiled mischievously; they were back in action.

"Only one problem, Bobby…how do we get out of here without being noticed? Last I checked those guys never clock out."

Bob Cat let out a devilish smile of his own.

"That apartment next to yours still vacant after that old hag finally croaked?"

"Yes, it is. Why?"

"Don't you worry about that if there's one thing I excel at, it's creating a proper distraction." said Bob Cat.

They went down the fire escape ladder, doing their best to distance themselves from the smoldering building. Plumes of smoke poured from the side of the apartment building and streamed into the night air. Promptly the entire area erupted in commotion; fire alarms, screams of panic, and screeching fire trucks filled the air.

"Bobby, I thought you said it was just going to be a little Boy Scout fire?"

Bob Cat shrugged and reached for another rung of the rusty ladder that was leading them down to a dark alley.

"It was a couple metal trash cans filled with garbage, carefully stoked. It'll be fine…those guys are professionals."

"But what about my apartment? It looks like it's getting out of control. What about my stuff?"

Bob Cat looked at Demo with disappointment.

"Demo, your stuff is garbage. Besides, it'd take more than a fire to clean your nasty place out."

Demo wanted to cry. Why he had agreed to use Bob Cat's tactics was now well beyond any logic he could muster.

"That poor old lady…It was vacant, right?"

Bob Cat rolled his eyes.

"For the love of sweet mercy, would you just let it go? The place was vacant! I checked and all I saw was an old litter box."

"I think that was the super's cat! I vaguely remember him saying something about using that place to keep the odor out of his room."

Both men soberly looked up at the ever growing clouds of smoke. Bob Cat drew a cross over his heart with one of his free hands.

"Oh, mercy…that's gonna be one flaming feline…"

As they approached the bottom, they let go of the rusty scaffolding from an uncomfortable height. They landed forcefully, both getting the wind knocked out of them.

"In case of fire, stop, drop, and—"

"*Roll…*" grunted Demo.

"If the fire don't kill you, that stupid thing will," he continued, looking back up from whence they'd come.

"We need to move. These guys are good and it won't take them long to realize that nobody's home."

Bob Cat nodded and they sped down the dark alley.

"You got a direction we can nab a cab?"

"I did a reverse look up on that Kevin Randall guy, but found almost nothing. He preferred working in the dark. Hey, I know someone who will be tickled to hear from us."

Bob Cat stopped dead.

"Oh no, Demo, we ain't gonna call her at this hour. Are you out of your blooming mind? She'll hang the both of us by our man parts just for even mentioning this."

Demo shrugged.

"We don't have any other choice. Besides, you always had a way with Jacky. If anything, she'll be happy to know we're being completely insubordinate to Roslin."

Bob Cat spat on the ground.

"I should have taken my chances back there in the room with the flaming feline."

But it had to be done. Stealthily, they moved through the shadows before hailing a cab a few blocks away. Once inside, Demo motioned for Bob Cat to keep quiet. The last thing he wanted was for Bob Cat to say the wrong thing at the wrong time. Jacky and Bob Cat got along together like an arsonist in a room full of dynamite.

"What, you don't think I can handle myself?"

Demo shushed Bob Cat again. The phone rang only once before being picked up. The immediate response caught Demo, who was caught in a stupor of thought, completely off guard. Jacky, however, was as razor sharp as ever.

"Demo, is that really you? You've got real nerve calling me at this hour after going who knows how long without saying a word!"

The phone slowly distanced itself from Demo's ear as the yelling grew stronger in fervor. A literal dictionary of curse words and life ending threats came out of the phone's speaker. Demo glanced at Bob Cat who looked as smug as ever.

"Man, do I love a woman who can sweet talk," he whispered just loud enough for Jacky to pause.

"Is Bobby with you? I've been through hell and high water these past few days and you two idiots are having a slumber party and making prank phone calls? Tell me where you are so I can have Martinez shoot you both!"

Taking a deep breath, Demo attempted to calm the storm in the only way he knew how; blatant honesty.

"That's what I was going to tell you. We're still working the case. We're going to break–in and look over Mr. Randal's apartment. Thing is, and this is funny, really…we don't know where he lives."

Bob Cat slapped the back of Demo's head.

"What's *wrong* with you? She's the last person on earth you should be spouting off to and there you go all willy–nilly."

"Jacky, I'm sorry, but this thing is bigger than we thought. Playing by the rules isn't getting us anywhere and we need to kick this up a notch. We need to get into that house one way or another. You can say it was all our idea and that you had no involvement. As far as I'm concerned, this phone call never happened."

"You're damn skippy it never happened! This is all on *you* two idiots, and I'll swear that right up to the firing squad! And another thing, just where have you been? Word on the street is your Roslin's favorite new toy, Demo. So, what exactly is going on there?"

Bob Cat started to answer her but was cut briskly off by Demo, who slowly swung his head back and forth. This served as a quick reminder of what they had sworn they wouldn't do. And besides, their deal with the devil had serious implications if they shared information. The consequences could be dire. So they sat silently for an awkward minute to let the soon–to–come lies percolate. Lying was never Demo's strength, but it came quite naturally to his partner.

"I got a divorce, Jacky. I've been wallowing around like a pig for a while and drinking away my sorrows. Demo's been keeping an eye on me while we followed some leads. It's mostly my fault."

"I'm sorry, Bobby. I didn't know it was that bad. You should have told me sooner."

Bob Cat stared at the back of the seat in front of him.

"Doesn't matter…you'll listen to Demo if you know what's good for you."

"So…let me get this straight…you want me to give you the address, so you can break in and take what you think you need to solve the case? And on top of that, you want me to do it even *after* you divulged your idiotic plan to me? Have you guys been drinking?"

Demo shook his head and Bob Cat let out a muffled chuckle under his breath. Jacky went silent. Demo was about to ask her if she was still there when she spoke.

"Look, boys…I haven't been exactly honest with you. Under normal circumstances, I wouldn't utter a word but I think you have a right to know. We've already solved the case."

Demo practically dropped his phone He ran back outside. Bob Cat followed behind him and pointed at the cab driver.

"Hey, *you*—don't go anywhere—we're not done here."

Demo began pacing wildly while he whispered into his phone.

"What do you mean *solved?* There's more to this thing! There is *no way* it's been solved."

Demo listened intently. He could hear Jacky taking several long, drawn–out breaths; she was preparing him for the letdown.

"It's done, Demo. We found prints, we found a motive, and so this one is heading to the books."

Demo slammed the phone against his side. He couldn't believe what he was hearing.

"*What* motive, Jacky? *What* are you talking about?"

A heavy sigh came before the answer.

"We tested the blood and swept the scenes for prints and everything came back positive for Randall. The blood belonged to the soon to be witness and the prints were those of Mr. Kevin Randall. And on his kitchen table he left a letter incriminating himself further. He even explained how he did it, right down to the finest detail. It's just a pity he's dead. I would have loved to watch him hang; just another pathetic copycat trying to find a place in history."

Demo's insides churned—this was wrong; *very* wrong—could they possibly *believe* that this had all been a one–man show.

"Jacky, he was just a pawn. He's not the one you want! That guy was taking orders. He was just the fall man. You've got to trust me; this thing isn't over! You're doing *exactly* what he wants us to. He *wants* us to believe! He *wants* us to play his game!"

"Damn it, Demo! I don't work like you do. I follow *rules*; real rules in the real world. I can't just go off of your hunches. I need solid evidence. Don't you think I've stewed over this a thousand times? I've lost more sleep over this thing than all of you combined. But the facts are the facts. And this guy was practically dripping evidence from every pore. The witch hunt is over, Demo. There's nothing I can do about it."

Anger welled up in Demo's gut. He didn't want to hear any more. He knew that this was exactly what *he* would have done if he were a master puppeteer.

"Just get me to his place, Jacky. I *know* he wasn't working alone. He can't be. If I get there and can't find a molecule to support my theory, then fine, expunge me from your memory and let's be done with this. We can all pretend it's over and hope for the best. But I'm not going to let one more person die while I'm still on this!"

"Tell me then, Demo, how do you *know*? What do you have that you're keeping from me? What are you hiding? This isn't how it used to be with us."

Demo hung his head. His twisted family was falling apart. All this secrecy came at a price. He was going to lose Jacky.

"Nothing, Jacky…I'm…I'm not hiding anything."

He knew it was obvious that he was lying. *So* obvious in fact, that even though she didn't let on, he knew he'd cut Jacky deeply; the image of her looking away, trying to hide her pain and tears, streamed dead center in his mind.

"Consider this your last favor. As far as I'm concerned, we're done. I'm not going to put myself on the line for someone who lies to me point blank."

Demo's heart was breaking. That was the last thing he'd wanted to hear, and yet he knew it was coming. You can only dance with the devil so long before becoming his partner. They had officially lost Jacky.

The phone clicked off. Bob Cat walked up and put his arm carefully around Demo's back.

"She'll understand, buddy. It's better this way; she doesn't need this on her plate."

Demo's phone buzzed with a message from Jacky. She had come through with her end of the deal.

"Bobby, I don't know what's better anymore. I feel like I'm losing myself to this. I don't know what I'm becoming."

Bob Cat slowly nodded his head before heading back to the cab.

"It's like you said, we're in too deep now. Way I figure it, I'm either going to die trying, or die fighting. But I ain't letting up on this bastard."

Demo felt himself sink. This case was an absolute nightmare.

"Let's hurry things up. Roslin's boys won't be blind to us much longer."

Not one to argue, Demo let himself into the cab behind him.

The address was nothing special. No evil mansion, no lone house in the woods, just a plain apartment in the slummy part of town. As the cab pulled up, a few drifters scattered this way and that like roaches caught in the light. This was the stomping ground of addicts, homeless people, and characters that could make the devil cringe. Going up the seemingly endless flight of stairs, one thing stuck to Demo; the building's age. It was lacking almost every modern convenience conceivable. Stomping up the stairs they finally reached the thirteenth floor.

"Thirteenth floor…lucky us," said Bob Cat sarcastically.

Demo examined the text message carefully.

"It says *13E*…gotta be somewhere at the end of the hall."

Bob Cat instinctively pulled out his pistol and held it at the ready.

"Never know what might pop out in one of these places."

Walking down the hallway, weird smells and noises set the mood. Who knew what travesties hid behind these doors? But for now they only had time to hunt one monster and one was plenty. Finding the right door, Demo foolishly turned the knob.

"Locked…"

"Of course it's locked, Demo; not everyone leaves their doors wide open."

Bob Cat approached the door then meticulously scanned the hallway looking for any signs of life. Quietly, he removed the yellow tape that had been placed over the door along with the warnings of tampering with a crime scene. Then with the force of a bull dozer he plowed into the scrappy obstacle. With a loud thud and a crack, it broke open flinging a small brass lock to the floor.

"Now, that felt good!" he exclaimed.

Demo looked down the hall, expecting someone to come rushing out because of the random eruption of noise. But apparently, at least in this neighborhood, it took a lot more to get people out of bed.

"Let's go, Bobby."

Demo's scarecrow–like body was shadowed by the wide mountain that was Bob Cat. Together, they were a living, breathing example of yin and yang in action. As they crept slowly forward into the dark apartment, Demo found a light switch and flicked it on. Immediately, the entirety of the tiny apartment lit up. Both men gasped.

"This place is so…*clean*. It's organized…well put together."

Bob Cat gnawed on his cheek nervously.

"You're right, Demo. I ain't seen a place this put together since Roslin's fun house."

They split up to more quickly inspect the place. Generic books, unopened junk mail, and a mundane collection of movies—nothing about this apartment stuck out in any way—in fact, it was so normal it was freaky.

"It's like this guy crash landed in the ghetto from some other planet. Why would he choose to live *here*?"

"Maybe he's been sucked dry and had to start over. I can feel for him there," said Bob Cat, picking up a family photo.

"That's strange. Look at this picture."

Demo approached Bob Cat cautiously. He was still leery of someone popping in on them.

"Doesn't this look a little off? Here's this guy with his wife and kids… only the wife looks out of place."

Taking the photo from Bob Cat, Demo scanned it for any telling details. It looked like the ideal family, sitting on a soft bed of grass in front of a very quaint home. But the woman was definitely out of place; at least her photo was. The shading, the lighting, and even the choice of clothes were odd.

"It's like he photo shopped her in. Why would the freak do something like that?" asked Bob Cat.

Demo paused as an acidic bubble rose up through his throat and burst. He had just been hit with an extreme case of acid reflux generated by sudden anxiety.

"Bobby, you remember the barn? You remember that horrible machine with the dead judge and ashes?"

Bob Cat's complexion blanched.

"You're not telling me that…"

Demo nodded.

"I think we found the connection we were looking for. A family torn apart by some perceived evil—in this case, I'm assuming his late wife— purified by flame. This sick freak kept on living the lie that everything was fine, right up to the point of photo shopping another woman into his family photo. Putting her there made it complete; made *him* complete. I think I'm going to be sick."

Bob Cat put the photo down gently.

"Those poor kids…"

They continued to look for anything that Jackie's team, or anyone else for that matter, might have missed. They had done a marvelous job of scrubbing the man's house down for any shred of evidence. It was no wonder Jacky had told him that the case was as good as over. So, why would a man so meticulous, leave so much behind? To Demo's mind there was only one answer; he was told to. The man was being guided down the dark path and it had consumed him and his family. And the lamp that lit his way was held by evil manifest in its purest form. The same evil that Demo was now sure had guided Spencer all those years. But what was the connection? What was this man's connection to not only the mysterious puppeteer, but to the murdered mobster? What did Kevin Randall know that made him worthy of such a dark crusade? Demo needed to find more answers. He needed something tangible to help make his point. But the room just wasn't helping him.

"I'm not seeing anything out of the ordinary, aside from that photograph, Demo. This place is a desolate desert."

Demo agreed silently, feeling frustration swell up inside of him.

This can't be it! You're not the man in charge; you're a peon. You make mistakes, you deserve to be punished.

"That's it! He was being punished!"

Bob Cat's face scrunched tightly in confusion.

"Please, catch the rest of us up?"

"Sorry, it just occurred to me. The man was being punished that day on the courthouse steps. He said that he *didn't believe* and *had been warned*. His cruel master must have had enough. So the question is *why* was he punished?"

Bob Cat grinned.

"Because he's a hole in a donkey's backside?"

"No, Bobby, you gotta be serious. In this man's head whoever was manipulating him was like a god. He followed him without question. But he was torn; torn between the love for his false god and the love of—"

Bob Cat finished for him.

"His family."

Both men sat silently for a moment to let it sink in.

"That explains the symbolism left in the ashes and all the effort he put in. His family wasn't part of the plan. But wait…that's not right—her photo's gone, her image removed—No, that's not fitting."

Bob Cat looked on while Demo searched his mind, trying desperately to think of something he might have missed.

"The children…the *children* weren't part of the plan. He'd taken it too far and relinquished his entire family rather than the single perpetrator who deserved it, the doer of wicked deeds. He'd disobeyed his master, and for doing so would never see the light of another day. That's got to be it!"

A look of befuddlement washed over Bob Cat's face. Sometimes Demo's rants made him feel crazy.

"What does it all mean then? What are you rambling about?"

Taking a deep breath, Demo continued.

"The last time I was inside Spencer's mind and finally found him, he was a brutal, calculated killer. He had all the telltale signs of a four star psychopath. But he also thirsts for praise, for appreciation of his abilities. You take a man like that, and pair him with an equally devious mastermind, and you've created the legacy of murder we all know. But Spencer went missing—turned up on the wrong side of town—and now he's Roslin's pet hamster. So now the puppet master needs a new set of hands to carry out his work. He goes looking and turns up this sicko. Only this nutbag still had a shred of humanity left that he just couldn't let go of. He then disobeys his master by going rogue, and performs his own version of crazy. And that ends that. The puppeteer has to move on. He lets it all fall on his damned ex-pupil, and he disappears back into society like nothing ever happened. No doubt he's already started looking for his next protégé."

Bob Cat looked sick to his stomach.

"Demo, this is heavy. You sure this guy didn't do it all by himself just to get attention?"

Demo placed a finger on each of his temples before humming aloud. He was trying to concentrate on the flashing pieces of puzzle that were snapping together to give him a clearer picture. The incurable sickness he contracted by assimilating the killer's persona into his own was telling him so.

"I know it, Bobby. You've just got to trust me. This is exactly what happened every other time to his victims in the decades past. The cops always think it's a copycat or coincidence and move on. But this time things have changed."

"How so?"

"Now they have me on their side."

Demo dropped to the floor without warning and began crawling around like a diseased dog. Bob Cat sat silently in place watching Demo do what he does.

"If I'm the pupil, I'm going to make mistakes. I need my selfish indulgences. I need my space. I'm organized, motivated, and rearing to go. I'm an ideal candidate for this apprenticeship, but I'm still learning. I'm going to hide things for my own pleasure."

Demo shimmied around the floor feeling it carefully with his hands. It looked like complete lunacy until he yelped with joy.

"And Dingo was his name–O."

Bob Cat approached him from behind carefully examining what Demo had found.

"I don't see anything; just the floor, a wall, and a cabinet. But you know it's Bingo, right?"

Demo ran his hands over the seemingly smooth surface.

"Who's Bingo?"

"Never mind…what did you find? I'm tired of being in this crap hole."

Demo stood up and pried his fingers into the small crack behind the large cabinet.

"Help me pry this thing off the wall."

Bob Cat disappeared from sight.

"Hey! Bobby, come and help me!"

"Move!" Bob Cat yelled, wielding a solid metal shovel.

He stuffed it forcefully between the cabinet and the wall. A loud series of squeaks screamed at them as nail by nail the cabinet broke away from the wall.

"I hope you know what you're doing…this ain't exactly easy," huffed Bob Cat, still pushing on the shovel.

"Trust me. The signs are all there. This thing has been moved many times before."

With one last crack the cabinet came free from the wall. Bob Cat jumped back as it plummeted to the floor with a massive thud.

"Sure hope these people think Santa Claus is paying an early visit. I'd have blown our heads off by now."

Behind the cabinet was a disgusting collage of stains, each with its own distinct color and odor. But there was also a board; a board that had been purposefully placed to cover a hole that was just big enough for a full grown man to crawl through.

"If you'd be so kind…"

Bob Cat obligingly ripped the board free with one strong pull.

Taking a breath, Demo plunged his head through the newly exposed opening.

"It's pretty dark, but I can see some pipes and there's enough space for me to climb down."

Demo shot a hand into his pocket and brought out his cell phone. Swaying it back and forth for light, he plotted a route and began jerking his body through the hole.

"You sure you got this, Demo? You never were the physical one."

"I've got it, Bobby. I've climbed on worse things than some old pipes."

Demo's words proved to be poorly chosen; the second his weight landed the pipe gave and he tumbled into the dark.

"Demo!" screamed Bob Cat, sticking his head further inside the hole.

A moment passed followed by another, but then a tiny gleam of light started moving about. Demo rubbed the back of his head while taking deep gulps of dusty, stale air.

"That was a lot easier in my mind."

"What's did you say?"

"Nothing…I must have slipped."

Demo's pride had been discreetly obliterated. His more adventurous self would just have to wait for the Fathom. Looking around the space he had fallen into, he discovered something horrendous; a shrine made out of evidence had been carefully erected beneath the floor of the deceased zealot. Newspaper articles documenting the missing persons, maps of locations, photographs, and schedules were marked with lines and arrows pointing this way and that; but one stood out above the rest. Right dead center was an article that hit Demo squarely in the gut:

Recently arrested Carmine Burke, believed to have ties to the mob, has agreed to a plea bargain on behalf of the party of interest. Mr. Burke claims that the information he can provide will lead to the capture of the infamous blood legacy murders killer. Mr. Burke is being transported to a safe house as part of the witness protection program.

Words of hate scrawled in pen filled the article with tiny arrows pointing towards a photo that had been carefully glued on. Demo assumed it was of the man written about in the article. But even more interesting, was the fact that the photo wasn't alone. Next to it was a photo of a beautiful woman whose eyes had been meticulously gouged out. More hateful words surrounded it:

LIAR, CHEATER, WHORE, SLUT

Demo sat back. It was beginning to make sense. The only problem was that it all pointed to Kevin Randall. Randall's wife was no doubt involved with Carmine, hence the lewd language. The dead Judge had been involved with Randall's divorce, his loss. Carmine was involved with the dark underworld. But who would have leaked anything to Carmine? Who would have been so careless in an otherwise perfect scheme?

"You clever, clever psycho…"

Closing his eyes, he looked through his internal files—the witness, the judge, the mobsters and the cops protecting them, artistry of the most heinous nature, dastardly deeds committed in poetic overtures—this was unreal.

"You say something, Demo?"

Demo wondered how long the man had spent sitting right where he was sitting now. How many hours had he stewed away in the darkness before letting it consume him whole?

"Did you find something? I'm getting awful lonely up here in Mr. Whackadoodle's apartment."

Demo placed one of his hands over his face. The bitter cold reminded him where he was.

"Bobby, I'll need some help getting out of here. I think I hit the jackpot. It seems that Mr. Kevin Randall was far more human than I'd expected."

The bunt end of the shovel dangled down into the dim light of Demo's cell phone.

"Grab this and I'll fish ya out."

Demo grabbed the shovel handle and held onto it tightly. Using his other free hand, he grasped at the pipes, trying to push himself up with Bob Cat's aid. At the top he wriggled like a fish on a hook to get back through the hole in the wall.

"You didn't bring anything back with you? What was the point of this then? If you just wanted me to smash through a wall, there were a lot of places much closer than this."

Shaking his head, Demo let loose of the shovel.

"We've got to put it all back. Back together as well as we can."

Bob Cat's head practically spun off his body.

"Why? Who cares? We just torched a place and you're worried about cleaning up?"

Demo nodded with animation.

"Exactly! That's exactly the point! No one can know we were here. No one can know what we know. We do things wrong, we break the rules, but nobody knows it but us. You and Jacky are the only two people I trust. As far as I'm concerned, anyone else is a potential accomplice; or even the murderer himself. Also, we need to talk about your distraction methods because I'm almost positive we're both officially fugitives now."

Bob Cat snorted loudly.

"Better to be in prison than out here anyways. And I think you've forgotten the door… So what's our next move? Wait around to see if he shows back up?"

Snapping his fingers, Demo began walking towards the door.

"I need to get back to Spencer. I need to use the Fathom again. He's got the missing keys to some doors I need to unlock. But now that I've affirmed an idea that I had there, I'll be ready for him. And you're right about the door; let's hope no one notices it's been opened. I'm sure there's got to be a looter or two around here they can blame."

"You really are some special kind of freak, Demo. Never cease to amaze."

The men smiled but only for a fraction of a second. An abrupt noise from somewhere outside the door opened their adrenaline valves.

"What was that?" whispered Demo, looking out into the hallway.

"A peeping Tom looking for trouble is my guess. Here, take my gun; who knows what I'll do if I have it? Besides, I need to relieve some stress."

Leaving his gun with a stupefied Demo, Bob Cat immediately sprang into action. Demo wasted no time trying to follow. They ran out through the busted door, sweeping across the small apartment with purpose. If someone had been eavesdropping on them they needed to know who and why. Stepping into the apartment building hallway, they saw the silhouette of man darting around the corner heading for the stairs.

"Oh, no, you don't! Time to give someone the beating of a lifetime," grumbled Bob Cat, picking up an almost illogical amount of speed for his size.

As they continued in their pursuit of the man, it became increasingly apparent that Demo's actual endurance was far less admirable than he'd imagined. His lungs felt like firecrackers were being exploding inside him with each breath. But he needed to keep up. He knew that Bob Cat had a way of letting himself come unglued. Keeping his focus on Bob Cat's back, he thought about all the possibilities as to who they might be chasing. It was a game against time to decide who it was before Bob Cat snatched him up by the neck and showed Demo that he'd been correct.

Suddenly, Bob Cat disappeared down a flight of rusted stairs. The pounding of feet against metal echoed off of the aged cement walls. Demo's lackluster speed meant he was losing distance. Bob Cat, however, was narrowing the gap between him and the man in the shadows quickly. It was astounding just how quick Bob Cat could move if given the right motivation. Even considering the years of nasty fast food, soda, and cigarettes the man could still shake a leg.

Groaning and moaning, Demo finally reached the bottom of the stairs. Briefly, he looked back up and realized they had gone all the way back down to the ground level. Being someone who normally never burns more calories than his shoe size, this was an astronomical feat. But he had to keep moving. He'd lost sight of Bob Cat and the last thing he needed was to be caught alone without his muscle. Swallowing a mixture of sweat and acid, he pressed on. As he burst into the alley he could see that Bob Cat was almost completely on top of the once fleeing man. Demo winced as he imagined the pain Bob Cat was about to inflict on the poor guy. A wall of bricks made of man falling on top of you couldn't be pleasant.

The sound of two men scuffling back and forth filled the otherwise silent corridor. Bob Cat was fully pressing his advantage. The other man let out tiny squeaks of pain and desperation while getting pounded by Bob Cat's hammer like fists.

"I said *stop*, for the last blooming time!"

Bob Cat was now firmly on top of the man in question, his mountainous frame pinning the man down with ease. Without thinking, Demo pointed the gun at the man on the ground, but not before fumbling around nervously while trying to get his fingers in the right place. Bob Cat blushed in embarrassment. Demo tried to recover by using one of the brashest tones he could muster.

"You heard the man! Stop or I'll shoot!"

The man stopped his worm–like wriggling as he was told. Approaching slowly, Demo put the gun down and replaced it with his mobile phone. Using it to illuminate the man's face, their heartbeats both accelerated.

"Mars? Mars, what in the world are *you* doing here?"

On seeing who had just assaulted him, his expression went from terrified to obnoxious and proud.

"I should be asking *you* two morons the same! Now would ya get this stinking guerilla off of me, please?"

Demo nodded at Bob Cat who reluctantly pushed off, making sure to dig his knee deep into Mar's torso as he stood up.

"Are you sure we can't just kill him and put him in the trash where he belongs?"

Mar's face shifted ever slightly at the alarming threat. After taking a bruising from Bob Cat, he no longer doubted his angry statements. But Mars was Mars, so he did what he always did best; threaten legal action.

"I'm going to have you both locked up for life! I'll put you in so deep you'll *never* get out! You're both dead! You hear me? Dead!"

Demo shook his head at the ridiculous temper tantrum he was witnessing. But an elephant–sized question remained; just what *was* Mars doing here?

"Dead or not, you've got some explaining to do!" exclaimed Bob Cat, scooping to pick his gun up off the ground and place it back in its holster.

Mars looked around and came to the conclusion that another foot race was beyond reason. He was alone and vulnerable. Being the snake that he was, he needed to figure out how to slither away.

"I said start explaining!" Bob Cat growled, placing one of his hands firmly on Mars' shoulder.

Mars slapped it away before pointlessly attempting to clean himself up.

"You know, that was a five–thousand dollar suit you just ruined. What's that, like three times your yearly salary?"

Bob Cat glared at him menacingly.

"Fine, fine have it your way! You two will be behind bars anyway, so what's it matter?" Smoothing a large chunk of his pampered hair back into place, he continued.

"You two pinheads honestly think you're the only ones keeping tabs on things? I'm just ensuring my own legacy in this…nothing more than that."

Demo scratched at his arm feeling the hairs suddenly stand up straight into the air. His lies were compelling, but still lies. The truth was obvious to Demo, who took a vicious stab at Mars.

"You filthy little liar! You're tampering with the crime scene! You've been mucking up the case by altering the details!"

Mars straightened his back and moved his neck tightly back and forth as if adjusting a tie.

"Tampering is a little harsh. I prefer, keeping things in order so the right man wins."

"And *you'd* be the right man?" spat Bob Cat in a thunderous voice.

Mars took a few steps backward exposing the impending doom he now feared.

"I don't have to answer any of your questions. I'm not the idiot who broke down a crime scene door. Would it kill you to learn how to pick a lock?"

Bob Cat snarled like a tiger and stepped closer to Mars, sending him sprawling back into a cold, brick wall.

"Ya know, I usually don't like to get my hands filthy by dealing with rats like you, but tonight I might make an exception."

The situation was gravitating towards going from bad to worse. Demo had to do something.

"Shut up, both of you! And don't move. I need some quiet time."

Both men looked at Demo with complete confusion. Had they really just heard what they thought they'd heard?

"We can't do anything to him and he can't do anything to us."

Bob Cat and Mars turned their attention to Demo.

"To hell I can't. I'll snap his scrawny neck!"

"Like to see you try, big boy!"

Demo clapped his hands together to get their attention back on being grown–ups.

"That's it! You two are geniuses!"

They glanced at each other in confusion.

"What are you looning off about, Demo?" probed Bob Cat.

"Don't you see? This whole process has rules, just like any other game. And it's because of those rules that our killer did what he did. The kids, the man at the courthouse, the witness, and all the other victims are part of it. But you can't kill just *anyone*; there are rules, order, commandments. He's playing god."

Mars and Bob Cat looked like two deer caught in the headlights. Demo's insanity was becoming too weird for them to deal with.

"I'll explain later. We need to move fast. As far as I'm concerned we're all active players of this game now, and I'd hate to find out what happens when our turn is up."

Mars looked like he had just swallowed a rotten egg whole. Was Demo really telling the truth or just ranting again?

"There's one thing I know for sure. None of what we saw or did tonight better get out. If it does, it could mean an early exit for us."

Bob Cat nodded, but Mars appeared more reluctant.

"And what if I talk? What if I decide to put the heater on blast? What could I possibly have to do with any of this? Why would anyone want to hurt me? And besides, they've already solved the case. I was just visiting to keep certain things in order."

Demo looked right through Mars with a piercing stare.

"That's not for you to decide. Anyone could be at risk. I feel like I'm getting closer which means he's going to become more desperate. I'd hate to see what he'd do. So if you really think this case is cleaned up and closed, then by all means, go blow your horn. But if I'm right, you'll be dead in a week."

Mars looked at the sky. He was resiliently fighting the urge to be his usual fractious self. But deep down inside he was a self–preserving coward; a coward who realized that Demo or Bob Cat could very likely be dead in a week as well, and he could escape somewhere deep into the Bahamas. As a trickle of blood seeped out of his nose, he was starkly reminded of his own mortality.

"Fine, I'll keep our little visit here hush hush and play nice, for *now*. But if you two dogs can't find the right trail and it goes cold, then I'm making no promises. Nobody attacks me the way you did. Nobody! And let's remember who *really* runs the courthouse around here."

Bob Cat had had enough.

"Get out of here, you slimy maggot, before I change my mind!"

Mars sprinted away from them and headed down the dark alleyway and out of sight.

"You believe any of that shite he just spewed through his teeth?"

Demo shook his head.

"There's no way of knowing what's true with that man. For all we know he could be in on it. Our best hope is that we scared him enough to fear for his own life. But we've got work to do. If I'm right, this is going to be the quiet before the storm. There's someone I need to talk to. Someone that could help me better understand this mess. I just hope he doesn't turn us in."

Bob Cat stared at the ground. Warily, he asked only one question.

"Who do you have in mind?"

Demo closed his eyes, doing his best to retrace his way back to the location where they had first met. It was the complete opposite of where he stood now.

"Lyle Ridding."

CHAPTER TWELVE

Prank Call

The air was bitter cold, arresting the nerves in their bodies, as they looked up at a daunting castle–like edifice. Each was imagining their own version of how things might pan out. Demo was shaking violently, both from the frigid air and his nerves, which were getting the better of him. He really hadn't had time to plan this out. It had come so abruptly.

"So this is his place? You weren't kidding; he's a complete arse."

Demo looked over at Bob Cat, still not sure what to say or do.

"Well, what's your plan? We got here and you said you wanted to talk to him, so what now?"

Gazing up at the heavy, wrought iron gate in front of them, Demo put out a quivering finger and pressed the call button. A moment or two passed before the familiar, warm tone of a woman came out.

"Hello; what can I do for you two gentlemen?"

Demo tried to speak but instead let out a long wheeze. He was the worst person on earth when it came to human interaction. Bob Cat, however, was more than happy to oblige.

"Here to see the judge. Got some questions we hope he might answer. We're detectives."

The speaker went silent. It was obvious the woman was checking their request with the judge. Both men held their breath, worried they might be snatched off the street by Roslin's goons any minute. They were both pleasantly surprised by the clank of the massive gate opening.

"Please close the gate behind you if you would be so kind."

They quickly dashed through the gate into the courtyard and then shut it behind them. Bob Cat threw an envious fit when he saw the opulence.

"These little pricks, hiding in here like kings, can't even share a nickel!"

"Easy, Bobby…he's one of those pricks we need right now. Save your economic disparity speech for later."

Bob Cat shook his head, showing obvious signs of disgust.

"To me, a guy like this is no better than Mars; people getting paid to play god. How many innocent men and women have they put behind bars for a little kickback?"

Putting his hands in the air and waving them awkwardly downward, Demo did his best to calm the tired, upset Bob Cat.

"I know, Bobby, I know how you feel, but for now let's pretend he's just any chump from the streets."

"A chump who lives in a multimillion dollar estate on top of the clouds… Ole' boy can suck eggs for all I care."

Going through the same routine as before, Demo did his best to dodge the extremely concerned looks he was meriting by being so obviously out of place. And to make matters worse, he'd brought Bob Cat, whose fashion sense leaned more toward barbarian than upper–class citizen. But it didn't matter; all that mattered was they were in. Perhaps he had made an impression on the prominent judge after all.

When the elevator finally reached the top, and after enduring a constant barrage of Bob Cat's anti–elitist rhetoric, Demo tapped on the elaborately carved doors. They opened slowly but steady, and soon they saw the amiable face of the judge. He was immaculately dressed, as always, and received them immediately with his usual offer of refreshments.

"Boys, come on in. Can I interest either of you in a coffee, or a hot chocolate perhaps, on this brisk early morning?"

Demo glanced at Bob Cat, who looked like a corpse that had just dragged itself free from the grave. But he was a far cry from looking like royalty himself. He just hoped the judge would sense their urgency. He needed to hear a few things that only a judge might grasp and he needed to hear it firsthand.

"Just water for me, thanks," answered Demo timidly.

"I'll take a hot chocolate and a shot of vodka if you've got it."

Lyle looked slightly confused, but not one to argue, he receded into the depths of his luxurious home.

"You sure this is smart? This guy's safer than the president, for crying out loud. He practically lives in Fort Knox."

Demo put a hand up to shush him.

"This guy can get to anyone; he's proven that. Besides, this is the only judge I have any real connection to. He's our only option at this point."

Lyle returned and gently placed a silver tray in front of Demo and Bob Cat. They both forced a smile in thanks.

"So, what brings you two gentlemen here so early in the morning?"

Demo began to respond, but was rudely interrupted by a loud belch from Bob Cat. Demo's face turned to an immediate red like an old fashioned thermometer ready to pop.

"Apologies for the inconvenience but we just couldn't wait. I promise this will be the last time I bother you, Sir."

Lyle's smile softened as he sat down across from them on an opulent leather couch.

"It's fine. I'm sure you're just trying to do your job. Who am I to get in the way? I must apologize for my brashness when we first met; I was just a bit shocked. Things of this nature can often taint an otherwise fruitful relationship."

Demo nodded harmoniously along with the wonderfully crafted message Lyle was giving.

"I agree. I'd like to start over; start fresh. And more importantly, I'd like to ask you some questions, if you don't mind."

The judge looked up at a large wooden clock then back down at the sitting duo.

"I've got a little time. I don't see why not."

Taking a deep breath, Demo tried to tame the roaring lions of chaos that urged him to just ramble, he needed to be articulate for once.

"How does it feel?"

Well, there goes being articulate.

Lyle shifted in his seat. The comment had definitely caught him off–guard. But he was more familiar with Demo's unfinished roller coaster of a mind than he had been before.

"How does *what* feel, my boy? You'll have to be clearer, I'm afraid."

Getting a look of pure annoyance from Bob Cat, Demo shook his head, trying to organize the clutter into proper streams of conversation.

"Sorry, I jumped ahead there. You're a judge; a rather well known judge at that. So you've probably dealt with every kind of case there is. I can only imagine what walks through those courtroom doors every day."

Pausing, Demo thought of the smug looking Mars walking in to defend some creep, smiling about all the lying he'd done that day.

And all of them rely on you to pass fair judgment. You really are like a gatekeeper in many ways, Judge. But one wonders the toll it takes on you to have to play god…all those mixed emotions. So, I guess that's what I was trying to get at by asking you how it feels."

Lyle sat back in his chair and gazed into the air, apparently pondering Demo's words carefully.

"Well, to be honest, it is hard. It's a hard thing to do when you don't actually know what happened. And so many things can get mishandled in a courtroom. I guess I simply try to follow the law as best I can."

Demo looked displeased by Lyle's response.

"Yes, but how does it *feel* when you drop the gavel and finally sentence someone?"

This made Lyle shift his position, but his resolve remained steadfastly intact.

"Powerful, I suppose, to be quite honest. To know that you hold the key to someone's future can be quite consuming. But it's a power controlled by rules; rules that allow me to use that power to extend the hand of justice. Without rules it would be chaos, but any judge could tell you that. I guess I'm not quite sure what you want from me."

"And what if a judge was to break those rules; to allow their personal convictions to supersede all? What would that merit in response?"

Squinting his eyes to the point they were almost shut, Lyle responded slowly.

"I'd imagine that the judge in question would be subject to the very same rules of punishment; a punishment to fit the crime, if you will."

Lyle smiled warmly before standing up. Calmly, he walked over and relieved both Demo and Bob Cat of their empty glasses. Demo kept his gaze straight ahead. He was trying to get any piece of new info he could.

"And what if you accidentally punish the wrong person? What if the wrong judgment is passed down?"

Lyle stopped on route to his kitchen. Demo's words had definitely hit home.

"I can assure you that it will never happen on my watch. I didn't get to where I am today by taking short cuts. I treat each case as if a member of my own family was on trial."

Demo took the opportunity to dive a bit deeper.

"Family? I've never really heard you talk about your family. I'd love to hear about them."

There was a brief silence as Lyle disappeared into the kitchen then reappeared.

"For me, Mr. Ward, it's always been about family."

Lyle paused, taking a deep breath of air.

"I've got a typical family with two wonderful children who are both doing well in their pursuits. I couldn't be happier."

It was wrong to probe, but Demo didn't care anymore. Every minute he wasted allowed the killer to gain ground.

"And your wife, does she live here with you?"

Lyle bowed his head slightly and responded tenderly.

"She's gone."

Demo was taken aback. It appeared everyone shouldered a burden in some way.

"I'm so sorry. I didn't mean to—"

"It's fine. It's good to be honest and try to heal…it's a process, you know. She died some years ago from cancer. The most nefarious of diseases; there was nothing we could do."

"I'm sure she was a fighter," chimed in Bob Cat.

Demo watched as Lyle tried to fight back a sudden rush of emotion.

"Well, I'm sure both she and your parents are proud of what you've been able to accomplish."

With the mention of his parents, Lyle's posture instinctively changed to a more aggressive one. But in the blink of an eye, he returned to his normal self.

"I apologize for my behavior. It's just the reality of things. I have been, for all intents and purposes, an orphan most of my life."

The air in the room seemed to thin as Demo and Bob Cat gasped in unison. This was something neither of them had expected. It made Lyle's success even more amazing; an orphan boy who rose to fame and respect.

"Well, I'm impressed. Most could only dream of attaining your level of success, Sir. I know our courts are truly blessed to have you," Demo stated dryly, trying to be sincere.

His comment brought another warm smile from of Lyle who then kindly began to usher them to the door. As they walked, Demo noticed the chess board pieces in the same exact position as before.

"Have you had any luck finding anything that could potential lead back to you?"

Lyle suddenly frowned.

"Well, word on the street is that the latest crimes have been solved and are being dealt with. This gives me a well needed respite. I've been having trouble sleeping lately; scary times these are. But there is just one thing…"

Demo snapped his head back to get a direct line to Lyle.

"What's that?"

Lyle looked slightly disturbed.

"The other night I was watching the news as is my habit, when the phone rang. Now *that* isn't out of the norm, but who was on the other line upset me."

"Who was it?" asked Bob Cat, taking a sudden interest.

"You see, that's the problem. It was just silent. I cordially asked several times who was calling only to get nothing in response. After a minute or two, I hung up the phone and returned to my routine. The question that still bothers me is who knows my number? I'm a judge so I rarely give it out.

"Prank call maybe?" suggested Demo without conviction.

They shook hands and said their good–byes. To most people this visit would seem frivolous, but to him it had been essential. Taking the snippets of emotion Lyle had shared with him would help Demo share the mindset of the killer, and it centered on the law and on justice and its execution; a true god unto himself. He felt that he was getting closer than ever before. But he needed to understand one more thing to seal the deal; Spencer the Bloody Vulcan.

CHAPTER THIRTEEN

Dungeons and Dragons

Heading back out through the courtyard, both men were swallowing large clumps of doubt. They were now more alone than ever, their freakish little family torn apart by deceit, lies, and murder. The world was so complicated now, so full of questions. They were an inseparable part of the monster this case had become; a case that everyone thought was solved; a case with a willing sacrifice to take the fall and disappear into death. Demo stared down at his beat up shoes. He had done more walking and running lately than he had done in his entire life before. And he still wasn't done.

"So, that was weird. I'm all for group therapy, but what was the point of wasting the time to see that jerk?"

Demo knew what to say, he just didn't know how to say it.

"Bobby, anything seem off to you about that guy? Anything you'd consider a little weird?"

Bob Cat plastered on a cheesy grin.

"Besides…*everything*? The guys a complete rutabaga, a fruit basket stuck in his mighty castle. Just another elite looking down on us rats."

"But he *was* very nice."

Bob Cat curled one of his lips and nodded.

"Yeah, he was a nice old man. I might be being a little harsh. Best hot chocolate I've had, well, I don't really drink hot chocolate."

Demo began to say something but stopped when something caught his eye. Letting out an audible sigh, his head flopped onto his chest.

"You call a cab, Bobby?"

Bob Cat, bewildered, turned to see what Demo was looking at.

"Oh for Pete's sake, you've got to be joking! Can't we get a break from these guys?"

As Bob Cat continued his anger filled rant, two large men approached. Demo looked them over and instantly recognized them as Roslin's men.

I didn't know Bobby had brothers.

One of the men gestured towards the unmarked car that sat humming nearby. Judging by their faces, they'd been out all night, undoubtedly flipping over every stone in the city looking for them. Both of them stunk of smoke and ash. Demo immediately caved, realizing he had no chance against the great walls of Roslin. Bob Cat was far more disorderly, waving his hand in front of his nose.

"You two again? Been out camping, I see. What's the matter? Didn't take enough lighter fluid?"

One of the men furrowed his brow and tensed his massive body.

"You'd like another go at me, Princess? Pride still a little hurt from our last dance?"

The man stepped forward but was abruptly blocked by the massive arm of his companion.

"Bobby, let's just get this over with. I'm tired, completely gross, and more than likely homeless."

Bob Cat kicked at the ground in protest, but did as he was told.

"Fine, have it your way. But I'm not gonna listen to any of that country shite you two muscle heads listened to last time! I'd rather be shot than sit through that again."

They climbed into the cozy government car. The driver zipped recklessly through the streets, blasting the country radio station that Bob Cat so adored. It was obvious that they were desperately trying to cover up the fact that they'd lost Bob Cat and Demo for an entire night, with no idea where they'd been.

When they pulled up to the secret door that was no longer so secret, they walked up to it and waited before entering. They were met by a steaming hot Roslin who was practically bursting at the seams.

"Just where in this forsaken city have you two idiots been? I get notified your apartment building is on fire, next thing I know you've gone missing, and now you show up smelling like something the dog dragged in!"

Demo and Bob Cat both hung their heads like two children being scolded. Roslin used every vulgarity he could think of to verbally lash out at them. Demo let out a tiny smirk that caught Bob Cat's attention before he quickly dismissed it by shaking his head. It was amazing how much the whirlwind that was Roslin reminded him of Jacky. It was no wonder the two had a history; at least Demo suspected they did.

"So why come back? Why leave us, burn down a building, and then walk back in like nothing happened?"

Demo took charge. There was something surging inside of him that needed to get out, and this mindless banter wasn't helping.

"We've got work to do. I've got the angle, I've the mindset; all I need now is Spencer. One way or another I'm going to break him and solve this damn case!"

Roslin and Bob Cat were stunned. This sort of brash behavior was remarkably unusual for Demo. Demo blew past Roslin and headed towards the lab. Roslin glanced at Bob Cat who shrugged.

"Don't say a word, you idiot! You're not helping anything!"

"What happened to being a professional?" Bob Cat chuckled.

"Remind me to have Jo suck your brain into a hamster when we're done."

"Tisk, tisk…where are the big government man's manners?"

The two continued to argue until they met up with a very impatient Demo.

"Can I get an access card or something? This is really getting old."

Roslin closed his eyes and took a deep breath. He was fighting off the urge to shoot them and call it a work place accident. Not giving Demo the satisfaction of a retort, he quickly escorted them inside. Jo bounced into the room like a spring bunny. Roslin waved a hand in the air.

"Not now! Do we have a window?"

Jo looked sad and excited at the same time. His wit was almost completely bulletproof. It would not be deterred by the storm cloud Roslin had brought in with him.

"Your timing couldn't be better! He's in deep cycle and streaming. His wave patterns are incredible! I mean, it's like the fourth of July in there, man!"

Roslin looked at Demo and threw out his hands.

"Well, you wanted Spencer. And by the way, do either of you have any idea how much it's going to cost me to cover up the burned down apartment? Do you have any idea how hard it is to cover up something like that so late at night?"

Demo ignored Roslin and headed for the table. Bob Cat took his stance next to Roslin and put an arm on his shoulder.

"You've had a rough night. Maybe you should just take a day off."

Roslin shoved Bob Cat's arm off of his shoulder before dusting it off.

"A man like me doesn't take breaks. You touch me again and I'll blast that arm off."

Bob Cat gave him a mischievous grin. They were finally beginning to understand each other. In the meantime, Demo had sat down on the futuristic table. Tapping his foot he watched as Jo finally caught his eye and scurried off and away. Laying himself down slowly, he examined his memory in an attempt to perform a subconscious information shakedown. He had to be ready. He couldn't be caught off guard again. Suddenly, a flurry of lights began to swarm him like a hive of killer bees. Reality disappeared and a new world came into view, enveloping his consciousness in its entirety.

Demo stayed still. He was dumbstruck by what had taken shape around him; clouds, waterfalls, and a vast expanse of heavenly sky. For a brief moment, his heart slowed its vigorous pace.

Goodbye jungle zombies.

His heart picked up the slack as his situation become clearer. He wasn't just *seeing* clouds; he was physically *standing* on one. This sent off an alarm that made his nerves tingle head to toe. He suddenly felt overwhelmed.

What is this place? How am I doing this?

Closing his eyes, he tried to get a handle on the confusing reality he was stuck in. This was Spencer's world and it worked by Spencer's rules. He needed to forget what he thought of as possible.

"Okay, let's do this..."

Taking a step forward he watched as his foot disappeared into a foggy mist of clouds before coming to rest. Not believing what he had just done, he repeated the process until fully satisfied. Looking like a child splashing in puddles, he continued, taking more and more steps of courage, which then illuminated his inner imagination front and center.

"This is awesome!"

Demo danced around on top of the cloud, still not believing it was possible. Such a heavenly manifestation was greatly appreciated compared to the horrific rotting zombies and gigantic mutant dogs. But his joy was cut short by his honed and targeted mind, which was quick to remind him that all good things come to an end. He had a job to do. Kicking a small tuft of cloud just ahead of his foot, he watched as it evaporated into thin air. Then something came into view that widened his eyes into saucers; an enormous castle off in the distance. Its massive walls were etched from pure fantasy, and were only trumped by the atmosphere scraping towers towering steadfastly above them. It was a mythological symbol of man's might against an unforgiving world.

Spencer's got to be in there.

Demo had one obvious problem; how to get there. He paced around on his mysteriously solid parcel of nimbus until his sense of hearing came to his aid. A roaring sound reminded him of the oddity he'd momentarily overlooked; waterfalls. Waterfalls that poured out from the clouds like open faucets. But there was something unique about them. Normally water flows *down*—that's a given—but here physics had been set aside. The water was not only flowing down, but upwards and sideways too. The streams of bubbly water connected the clouds together like pearls on a necklace.

You've got to be kidding me…

Glancing back up at the distant castle, he knew what he had to do. But actually *doing* it was another thing entirely. Just a few steps away his own carefully constructed waterfall rose from nothingness. Its crystal clear liquid glimmered magnificently against the deeply contrasted sky and clouds. The flowing water was his only hope of getting from one place to the next. But on either side of the watery path was impending doom; a never–ending fall into the empty void of Spencer's mind. Demo suddenly gasped for air when he realized he'd forgotten to breath. Fighting against his own will, he approached the roaring, vertically climbing waterfall. He plunged one of his hands deep into the rapid movement.

Ice cold shivers shot out from his hand and into his body. But that played second string to the immense power of the water itself. It felt more like a vacuum than a jetting stream. It was difficult to keep the rest of his body out of the water as it seemed to beckon him closer with its overwhelming force. He knew if he was going to do this it would be all or nothing. Taking a step back, he silently recited a makeshift prayer. If he was wrong, he'd be sucked high into the heavens both out of sight and out of mind, literally. Taking a long drag of air, he heaved himself forward into the roaring waves.

Instantly, his entire body was overcome by the intensely brisk water. But it was the force that took his breath away; every last particle of it. With the speed and velocity of a bullet, he was ripped from his cloud and into the suspended waterfall. The extraordinary amount of power that now gripped him was remarkable. He felt completely helpless and weightless. The adrenaline rush was unreal; this really was the ride of a lifetime. This enticing idea was forcefully countered by his ego; was this going to be the ride of the *end* of his lifetime? Just as it seemed that his body might be aimlessly thrown to the mercy of the sky, he was spat out onto another puffy cloud. He let out a scream of sheer terror as he clawed at puffy gobs of cotton candy and wildly tried to hang on.

This place is going to kill me!

Shockingly, his efforts were rewarded. Somehow his momentum shifted forward and he found himself on his back gasping for air. Staring up at the endless universe filled with clouds, waterfalls, and stars he attempted to regain his composure. He hadn't counted. He was sure he had at least a couple dozen more suicidal escapades ahead in order to reach his final destination; the enormous castle carved from his imagination. Icy cold water drained from his pant legs when he stood up. He mumbled some vulgarities, realizing how much pain he was being forced to endure at Spencer's hand.

I'm going to kill you when I find you, Spencer!

He had to plot his path. He needed to ride the right waterfalls to the right clouds. This notion was easier conceived than realized. Racking his brain, he took a hypothetical pencil and connected the clouds like one would connect the dots. Once he felt at least partially satisfied, he began to take the plunge over and over again. With each leap into the hovering waterways, his heart would stop for a moment. At times, an extremity might find its way free of the rushing current and grasp at air. He just hoped he didn't have a heart attack. He pressed on; he needed to move quickly. The last thing he wanted to happen was to be caught out on a cloud with nothing to show for himself. Roslin would kill him for sure. He took another plunge then took a moment to get realigned. His thoughts were suddenly interrupted by a clap of monstrous thunder.

Demo bolted upright. He was now at least three–fourths of the way to the gargantuan castle, but things were taking a most unwelcome turn for the worst; the most nightmarish of worsts. Like a fantasy battle of man against beast, the hidden chaos could now be both seen and heard. Flames dotted the landscape of the mythical castle and the cries of both men and women fleeing for their lives filled the sky. And above it all roared a great shadow—an age old harbinger of death—a dragon. Demo's eyes lit up with both fear and wonder as the expansive creature weaved its way carefully in and out of the clouds before plummeting itself down towards the castle, spewing flames as it went. The vile serpent in the sky was sowing pure havoc. Demo glanced behind him; maybe he could sit this one out. Maybe he'd wait for a kinder piece of Spencer's mind to come around before attempting to dive any further into this unhinged madness. But something inside him knew that wasn't an option. He was, after all, dealing with a complete psychopath. Scratching nervously at his arm, he went head first into what would turn out to be his last few dives before total madness.

Spewing from the last pillar of water, he hit the massive cloud that was home to the gated city with a surprising thud. A sharp sting in his shoulder reminded him that things were still very dangerously real here. Demo could now hear the screams and pleas for mercy on full volume. Standing up, he saw a massive gate that had been torn to bits by cataclysmic claws. Inside pure insanity was unfolding. People were running wildly, some trying to put out fires, others fleeing for their lives. Among them were armor–clad soldiers firing waves of arrows into the sky in an attempt to slay the beast.

Demo caught the eye of a warrior who gave him notice with a very bewildered look. But this exchange was ended by a stream of fire that turned the man to ash. Demo scrambled through the gate and into a dark space between buildings. The smell of smoldering flesh stung his nostrils. A fire ball sent a rickety building crashing to the ground. Things were falling apart around Demo very quickly.

Cautiously, he edged back out towards the open. He practically had to force his heart back down his throat. Peeking around the corner, he searched the sky for the deathly lizard. It must have been satisfied for the time being; the sky was still. Walking into the open, he marveled at the mythically styled architecture that Spencer had dreamt up.

This city must have been beautiful before all of this.

Cautiously, he made his way through the streets, trying at all costs to avoid the inhabitants. They were a sad sight to see. Even though deep down inside he knew that these men, women, and children were all being fathomed up by Spencer's mind, their heartbreaking sorrow was real. He had just made his way around a small, partially scorched fruit stand when the dragon returned. It swooped by with a monstrous force that almost rattled Demo's bones right out of his body. Its serpent–like eyes scanned the city for its next potential target. With a massive flap of its expansive wings, it took aim and let loose all hell on a nearby building.

Demo's legs quivered like jelly as pieces of burning shrapnel burst into the air leaving thick trails of smoke behind them. It took cat–like agility to dodge the fiery rain of debris. He desperately tucked, rolled, and crawled to stay out of sight of the murderous monstrosity. Demo watched the dragon flap its massive wings as it ascended back into the sky.

Spencer, where the hell are you?

Now running for his life through the mythical city, he gave up his intention of obscurity. His thoughts were solely focused on finding Spencer. Demo, recalled the old stories he was told as a child about man versus beast.

A knight…Spencer must be a knight!

The idea seemed plausible given the current fairy tale he'd found himself in. So…where would a knight hang out?

He wants to be seen. He wants glory.

Darting around the city and dodging the hellfire as hordes of soldiers fought valiantly against it, he made astounding discovery. There, dead center of town, were the massive towers that he'd seen from outside.

"Watch thy self, you peasant!"

Demo was thrown to the ground by a force from behind him. He quickly rolled over grunting loudly, and looked for his assailant. What he saw drew from him the only words he could think of.

"Great. My knight in shining armor," he mumbled loudly.

And a knight it was. A strong–willed, courageous, and valiant knight (from the looks of him, at least) riding his trusty steed into the palace ahead. This fellow was equipped with all the fixings of any mythical adventurer's dream. Demo needed to follow him. He was almost positive the man under the armor was Spencer. What kind of knight would Spencer imagine himself to be? Demo knew the answer was a *violent one*. Springing to his feet, he gave chase to the clacking of hooves. As he sprinted behind the knight into the massive palace, he felt the ground shake beneath him.

"This can't be *the fade*; not now!"

To his relief, it was instead the result of the war waging outside. The massive granite and marble walls were being shaken by the horrendous onslaught being unleashed by the dragon. It would only be a matter of time before the castle succumbed.

"Onward steed, we ride to victory!"

Looking ahead, Demo saw the noble rider he was following gallop up a gigantic flight of stairs.

He's heading to the towers. That crazy idiot is going to fight that thing from a tower!

A thunderous roar reverberated through the entirety of the great palace, the large pieces of disembodied rock crashing down from the ceiling reminding Demo that time was short. A bowling ball sized chunk struck the knight and horse who were working their way upward. The force threw the man from his animal and onto the stairs. He landed with a metallic crash. The horse was no more.

"Vile flying beast! I will revenge mine house then relinquish thee forever!"

Demo's head rang like a brass bell. It took him a second to finally come to. He saw that he had some serious ground to make up. The ever gallant knight was pressing forth. His heroics just wouldn't stop.

"This guy doesn't know when to quit!"

Demo tried to take a mental photo but came up short. The man's articulately crafted helmet gave nothing away. Feeling exhausted, Demo called out to him hoping to slow his momentum.

"Hey, buddy! Slow down, would ya?"

The knight paid him no mind. Demo kept the chase up the massive stairs and straight into impending doom. He wanted to puke. Was he really going to see this through? Would he get anything from it? Even his incredibly complex mind was having trouble putting things into perspective. Another thunderous roar echoed through the great edifice. He didn't care. He had to keep moving.

They climbed the spiraling staircase higher and higher into the tower. Just when he thought he couldn't take a single step more, he arrived at the top. The tower was barely being held together. A large portion had been viciously ripped away by a maelstrom of fire from above. It left him fully exposed and much higher in the sky than he preferred to be. Standing on an exposed plank of wood, defying all odds and logic, was the knight. He raised his gleaming sword into the air while pounding his shield against his chest.

"Have at thee, vile worm!"

Demo cringed at the theatrics coming from his mouth.

What a closet nerd.

It didn't take long for the climax of the story to be reached. The dragon had heard Spencer's call and was coming at him fast. Its snake–like scales slithered through the sky weaving in and out of the nightmarish plumes of smoke and clouds. In the blink of an eye it was upon them. Swooping in at knight, it unleashed hell. A pillar of fire fell around him as he raised his shield in defense. He heaved his sword skyward seeking the heart of the fire–breathing beast. It found its mark on one of the monster's legs leaving a long gash. It roared into the sky only to circle back to retest the courage of man. Letting out an ear–splitting scream, it approached like a flaming missile. But just as it was about to unleash another firestorm, it was struck by a massive object midflight.

A large boulder had smashed into the beast's massive chest. The soldiers below had finally found their mark. With a deafening screech of pain, the sky serpent fell into the tower, missing Demo and the knight by mere inches. Piles of rubble buried the monster, and a hush followed the settling dust.

Thank goodness that's over. If I ever see another castle I swear I'll burn it down myself!

The momentary respite came to an abrupt end. With a demonic howl, the reawakened beast shook off the debris and rose from the ashes with full force.

"No man can kill me!" it hissed through rows of serrated teeth.

Demo let out a whimper. He suspected this wasn't going to end well. It was possible that Spencer's monster could only be relinquished by Spencer himself. This reinforced Demo's idea that the knight must be him.

"A thousand curses, death lizard! I will ease your suffered existence!"

Demo was a bit shocked by the eloquence of the knight's words Spencer was more articulate than he'd assumed.

The knight ploughed head first into the beast swinging his trusty blade.

"Now you die, monster!"

Demo watched as amidst the pillars of smoke and fire the pair began the fight of a lifetime. The knight dodged each attack from the dragon with expert precision. He struck the beasts arm, spilling a crimson river of blood onto the ground. The battle was unimaginably entertaining but also petrifying. The knight swung around again, creating a swirling cloud of smoke and fire. He held his sword with both hands thrust high above his head, and slammed it down with all his might into the dragon's neck. A blood curdling scream filled the air and then it went eerily silent.

Demo waited. His heart was practically exploding from his chest. What just happened? Did the knight win? Was the dragon dead? Miraculously, just moments later Demo saw the battered silhouette of the knight walking away from the abject destruction.

He did it…that crazy psychopath really did it.

Demo stood up, resisting the urge to clap. The knight strode confidently into the light covered in blood and ash, with wounds on every inch of exposed flesh. He raised his sword defiantly into the sky.

"I have vanquished the demon! Let the entire kingdom be—"

The knight's words were cut off by a wall of fire. It completely consumed him in mere seconds, leaving behind nothing but a charbroiled corpse in an armored oven. Demo gasped with the realization that he had been wrong; completely and utterly wrong. While it was true that Spencer wanted to be recognized, Demo had overlooked a deeper truth—Spencer had a love for destruction, suffering, and power, not heroics—Spencer was the dragon.

Oh…that's not good!

Demo's mouth fell open in a pant. His fear was suddenly at an all-time high. Through the churning clouds of smoke he stared into the dreadful, soul-snatching eyes of the gigantic creature. He desperately kicked off his shoes and ripped at his clothing in an attempt to alter his appearance in any way possible. He couldn't be caught so obviously out of place. Straining against his mind, he imagined his rags turning to armor.

"Fool! No mortal can destroy me! Now lay rest with your weak brethren!"

Demo turned hard looking for a way out. There were only two options; run past the dragon and back down the stairs, or die. The choice was pretty clear to Demo. He wasn't sure, but he figured that even Bob Cat would opt for the stairs. Just as he prepared to make a dash for it, the dragon roared.

"*You* there! You are not of this place! What unseemly garb doth thou wear?"

Demo stood as still as a statue. He knew running was pointless. He was left with convincing the beast that he not only *belonged* here, but that he also deserved to *live*. That was probably going to be a stretch. Keeping his eyes focused on the monster, he carefully stepped over to where the slain knight lay and picked up his still smoking sword. The burning sword seared his flesh. It was almost unbearable to hold but he had to play his part. It was his only hope.

"I am Merlon, great sorcerer and sage! I come seeking an audience with you, Lord Dragon man!" He bowed deeply.

Is it Merlon or Merlan, both sound wrong? Dragon man? Really, Demo? That's the best you could do?

The giant reptile actually looked a bit surprised by the sudden pronouncement. He looked Demo over slowly and carefully. It was becoming obvious that Spencer's mind was suspicious of him, and if he didn't do something soon the charade would be over. With no other option coming to mind, he did the only logical thing he could think of. Throwing the sword in the air, he pointed and ran as hard as he could, shouting as he went.

"Look over there! Me thinks mine eyes doth see a great gryphon!"

A gryphon? Where did that come from? Dragons probably eat gryphons for breakfast!

Shockingly, the ruse seemed to work. For just a moment, Spencer's focus shifted away from him, giving him a brief shot at escape. He ran with all the fervor of a well-practiced coward down the seemingly endless flight of stairs. Despite the horrific events that had just transpired, he felt at least mildly safe now that he'd distanced himself a bit. Granted, the building might collapse on his head as he descended, but even that was better than being outside with dragon Spencer. As his heavy breathing echoed off the cavernous walls, he became aware that he wasn't alone. A second echo followed his. Slowing just enough, he glimpsed up and behind him; what he saw turned his courage to putty.

A mammoth sized man wearing an executioner's mask was suddenly hot on his heels. His bulging muscles pulsated with each thundering step he took. And if that wasn't already enough, he was wielding an axe twice the size of Demo's head. Demo had hoped to find Spencer and he had done just that. He should watch what he wishes for.

Could this get any worse?

"Sage, I do not take kindly to your tricks! Don't you know that I am all powerful? I have neither bounds nor limits! Dragon or executioner, it's all the same to me!"

Demo knew this might be his only opportunity to get what he came for. He would have to interrogating the blood thirsty psychopath while running for his life.

"You are great, both winged or man! I am but a small, lowly wizard who now sees my deceit and knows he must be punished!"

Demo knew from experience that his clever words could prod Spencer in the direction he wanted him to go. That was his new challenge; to outwit Spencer by outrunning his axe.

"Step closer so I can end this game!" growled Spencer as he gained ground on Demo.

"But what of your master, does he approve of such barbarity?"

Nicely done on that one…

There was a pause and Spencer's executioner slowed for just a moment. He was apparently considering this new question, but soon shrugged it off.

"What I do with my power concerns no one! Now stop slowing your inevitable demise!"

Spencer swung his axe at Demo, missing him, but just barely. It crashed into the wall behind Demo with a sickening thud that sent pieces of rubble flying.

"But what of justice? What of rules? Do you care nothing for these things?"

I hope that works…

Again, the giant man took a short pause; Demo's tactics seemed to be working.

"*Justice?* What does a stupid mage know of such things? It's not your place to demand justice!"

Down and down they continued, Demo managing to stay a step ahead. He ran past the massive entrance hall and down the dimly lit stairs into…a dungeon.

Great…the full gambit, dungeons and dragons!

"Justice must be earned! I am the executioner of justice!"

Demo listened intently. His mind was dissecting each word. He was pulling more of Spencer out with every exchange. But he had a problem; the stairs had to run out sooner or later. And when they did, Spencer's axe would have his head rolling.

"But I've done nothing wrong! I stand unaccused! What form of justice is this?"

Spencer let out a howl of frustration.

"Stop with your games! I grow tired of you! I don't need to answer to those rules! Not here! Here, I am in charge; I make the rules! And I decree that you do not deserve to live!"

Demo picked up his pace but was suddenly stopped short. He had finally reached the bottom of the hellish stairs only to find…nothing; nothing but a large piece of floating rubble that led nowhere. His time had just run out.

"At last, you coward! Nowhere to run, no words to save you! I will gut you for wasting my time!"

Demo looked over the edge. What he wouldn't give right now to manifest a pair of wings and fly out of this asylum. But with Spencer's consciousness nipping at his heels, he knew that he'd be marked and shut down, forever the wizard Merlon stuck in Spencer's mind. This left but him only one option; he'd have to jump. The mere thought of it made him cold with fear. Taking one last look behind him, he took what he hoped wasn't his final step. As he did, executioner's axe grazed his neck leaving a trail of blood droplets falling behind him.

"Farewell, you cowering whore!" Spencer screamed over the edge.

Demo's arms flailed through the air as he tried desperately to grab ahold of something. But there was nothing. No magical cloud of puffy white to save him, no watery escape route he could take. He wondered what it would be like to be trapped in a never–ending fall. Or would he just become nothing; erased, eradicated from existence, leaving a hollow self behind in the real world? The rushing surges of air reminded him that he'd soon find out. He watched as a sudden electrical storm rushed at him at light speed. He tried to remain conscious but found himself rapidly losing his grasp. He closed his eyes as the prison of *the fade* began to wrap itself around his consciousness. His mind went blank as time passed through both thought and reality. It finally had come to an end.

CHAPTER FOURTEEN

Ice Tomb

Blinding fragments of light began to slice their way through Demo's thick blanket of darkness. Each beam blended into one column of light that then illuminated the hazy images taking shape around him.

As Demo came fully back to consciousness, he let out a piercing scream of terror. He shot off the table, ripping off wires as he fell to the floor. It happened so fast that no one in the room had time to react.

"Somebody grab him! He's gonna knock himself clean out!"

Demo struggled to focus on the person yelling he believed to be Bob Cat. But then the weightless terror of falling to his demise took over his being once more. Screaming madly, he squirmed around on the floor, still unable to bring himself completely back to reality.

"Get a grip on yourself, Mr. Ward! I don't want to have to sedate you!" barked Roslin, nearing Demo's seemingly possessed body.

"Back off, you blooming idiot! Ain't nobody gonna shoot him up! Give the man some space!"

While Bob Cat and Roslin quarreled, things slowly began to clear up for Demo. He felt as if his brain had been put through a meat grinder. He needed to pull it all together, but he was busy vehemently fighting off the urge to puke his guts out. Pushing himself onto his knees, he finally gave in to the feelings begging to be purged onto the pristine white floor. The resounding sound of Demo's breakfast hitting the tile made Bob Cat and Roslin's argument come to a screeching halt. Demo awaited the usual retribution for ruining Roslin's perfect world, but it surprisingly never came. Instead, Roslin's fiery arrow landed on a different target.

"Dammit, Jo, I told you to get a bucket next time!"

Jo stood shaking in place near one of the exit doors, dangling a bucket from one of his scrawny hands. His terrified eyes were fixed on Demo.

"I didn't want to get choked again by that psycho!" he pleaded in his own defense.

Roslin rolled his eyes and shook his head.

"When this is all over with, I'm going to blow this building up with you inside."

"Why wait? I'd be more than happy to oblige you right now. 'Case you didn't notice, I'm pretty good at destroying things," snorted Bob Cat sarcastically.

Demo stood up, having regained his composure, just as Roslin opted out of Bob Cat's generous offer choosing instead to walk away mumbling.

"I hate, hate, hate that man…I really hate him…"

Bob Cat's snicker was quickly replaced by a serious look of concern.

"You alright, Demo? You looked like you were a goner."

Demo wiped the cold sweat from his forehead and looked at Bob Cat dead on.

"You have *no* idea."

"Please tell me that I didn't risk my neck just so you could ruin my floors again? Can you at least tell me that? If not, I'm ready to pull the plug on this!"

Roslin's temper divulged his inner feelings of frustration. It was clear he was harboring sincere regret.

"Dungeons and dragons…" Demo said softly under his breath.

"Say what?" asked Roslin.

Jo scurried excitedly to Demo's side.

"Did you say *D* and *D*, as in *Dungeons* and *Dragons*? That's crazy, man! I'd *die* to get a chance to fight a dragon and save a damsel! Total brain fizz right now!"

All three of the other men responded in almost perfect synchronicity.

"Shut up, Jo!"

Stung by their rejection, Jo retreated to the exit, cowering like a disciplined dog. Roslin took a couple of deep mantra breaths before continuing.

"Okay…let's just calm down and see what our dear Mr. Ward has to say, alright?"

Demo nodded. He had gotten better at dealing with Roslin and his expectations.

"I'm now positive that these new murders were done by a team; but a professional team with distinctive roles. I was plunged deeply into what Spencer's mind is capable with each manifestation. I noticed a recurring theme. His role is the destroyer; the soldier or executioner to meter out what his warped mind sees as justice. But by himself he's just a loose cannon. He needed guidance—he needed direction—he needed a *God*."

His audience was visually taken aback by Demo's declaration.

"What do you mean, *God?*" asked Bob Cat intensely.

Demo licked his dry lips. He wished he had some water.

"I mean *God* in every sense of the word. Spencer operates without rules, but he still craves praise. The piece of garbage can't live without it. So, you find someone highly narcissistic with the intelligence to rein Spencer in, and you've got an unbeatable combo. The only trick would have been how to make Spencer align himself willingly. That would've been tricky. How do you organize chaos? The puppet master, the man that really runs the show, works deep in the shadows. That's where he prefers to be, watching his masterpiece evolve with every killing. He was the head of his very own religion; and was Spencer's God. If we're going to stop them, we've got to find the monster in the shadows."

They each took a moment to reflect on what Demo had said, but it was Roslin who finally broke the silence with a surprisingly Jacky–like response.

"I hate to burst your fairy tale bubble, but according to people in the know, they've already got this thing in the can. If I was to go along with this, I'd have to believe that all of the evidence is misleading, and that all of the man hours, put in by not only me but all of my people, was completely wasted? Is *that* what you're *telling* me? That I'd go against every sensible fiber of my being to cover your tracks, *just* in case you're actually going to solve this case *correctly?*

Demo felt a familiar itch crawling up his arm, but fought the terrible urge to scratch it. He was on to something big and he knew it. He wasn't about to walk away now. He was going to win.

"That's *exactly* what I'm telling you."

Roslin turned away rubbing his chin roughly. He stomped one foot on the ground confidently before turning back.

"Then tell me what you need. I'm all in. One way or another, this thing ends for good."

Demo glanced at Bob Cat, whose tongue was apparently tied tightly in shock, his eyes glazed with amazement at what he'd just witnessed.

Demo looked back at Roslin, feeling brave. "I need to be alone. There's something I need to do and I can't do it with anyone around."

Roslin swallowed his anger. It took everything he had not to lash out in frustration at Demo's never–ending list of wants. But Demo pressed on.

"That means you too, Bobby. Whoever this is has an incredible skill set; the best I've ever seen. He probably knows we're here. He has more than likely been having us watched for quite some time; maybe even before *we* knew we were involved."

Roslin quaffed at Demo's remark.

"I highly doubt that. We're the best at what we do, and nobody gets in or out of here without us knowing about it. *Nobody.*"

Demo shook his head as he stared at the ground.

"I wish I could believe that, but this man doesn't use normal tactics— he uses the human soul—as far as I'm concerned he could have gotten to anyone."

Demo turned to see Roslin pause midair with one finger pointing directly at him, but he wisely decided to keep whatever he was going to say to himself.

"I've got to go soon. I'm sensing that this maniac is planning something bigger than just murdering one or two people at a time. If I'm right, he wants to set something up intended to be the climax of his damned existence; a literal sacrifice for the world's unwillingness to listen. A lot of lives could be at stake."

Demo began to walk steadily for the exit. He was a man on a mission. What he did needed to be done, despite the sting he felt at having to treat Bob Cat with such disregard. He had assimilated enough of the personas of mad men to feel the dark clutches of evil slowly trying to encase his heart. Was he losing himself? Was he in too deep? Taking one brief look back at the men he was leaving behind, he saw a very disappointed Bob Cat refusing to look back at him. But Demo needed to be convincing; he couldn't give in to his own humanity.

First, Demo decided to go to the last place he really wanted to go; home. He was letting his more sensible self take the wheel and drive him to an unproductive slumber so his body and brain could recover. He knew more than anything, he needed some rest.

Once there, the familiar smells of his unkempt ode to laziness hit him with a deep nostalgia. Mixed with the now partially scorched wall from their idiotic escape, it reminded him how far down he had gone. It was far from perfect, but in the storm he was enduring, was a moment of reprieve. Ripping at some caution tape that had been placed outside his door he entered then sat on his bed. He blacked out from pure exhaustion within a few beats of his heart. Collapsing like a ragdoll that had been played with one too many times, he fell into a deep sleep.

The night was filled with heartbreaking remembrances that tortured his soul; a convolution of real events mixed with the summoned up nightmares of Spencer the Bloody Vulcan's mind. Demo's mind was spinning wildly out of control until suddenly there was one point of absolute clarity; the dead, still body of his late partner, Mike. Demo felt his eyes sting as if hot acid was being poured directly into them.

Mike, no!

But his greatest fears were being relived. Mike had been shot. Not only had he been shot, but multiple times. His dead body was slumped on a couch in a room that was in complete disarray. Demo wanted to puke. He glanced down at his trembling feet at a small pile of empty beer cans. He had been drinking and the last thing he remembered was the vicious argument they had gotten into. His heart ached; he already knew what would happen next. He needed to escape this vivid nightmare; he needed to release himself from the prison he had built, brick by brick, by years of self–torment.

Demo woke up suddenly. Still feeling overwhelmingly sick to his stomach, he wallowed around on his dingy sheets. The images were fresh yet brought with them an age old pain. Doing his best to meditate himself back to sanity, he mumbled out loud.

"I'm sorry, Mike. I'm truly sorry."

It took what seemed like hours to finally feel completely assured that Roslin and Bob Cat had both come through on his request. A tinge of remorse still edged his emotions. Everything about this case changed the way he operated, how they operated. Trust now sat on a knife's edge for all of them. One wrong decision could send his carefully constructed house of cards tumbling down into nothingness. He was behaving erratically, this he knew, but it was intentional. In his mind the only way to deal with such perfectly orchestrated chaos was to lose himself in it—let all logic go and nurture the madness within—he could only pray that he wouldn't lose himself completely.

Standing at the edge of the docks he felt the brisk air rush in and out of his lungs, leaving a frosty chill behind. It was much colder outside than it had been earlier. He recalled the first time he had come here and all the horror he'd experienced. But that's why he was here. He came to the one place that was still an open question mark. The site of the mysterious disappearing car, or at least he maintained as much.

Scuffling his feet so as not to slip, he looked at the now ice covered tracks that were barely visible. This had to be the spot; at least that's what his brain was telling him. It felt sadistically right—all that pride and power— except for one big screw up. He stood facing the river, realizing that he more than likely wasn't alone. An ominous presence lurked in the shadows of the massive warehouses, just out of sight.

Sitting in the shadows like always, sneaking, hiding…

He stood motionless, but his brain was a superhighway with bumper to bumper traffic; sparks of information sped all trying to snap the million pieces of the puzzle together. An illogical trove of clues created in Spencer's mind had to be turned into a tangible understanding of a spree of heinous acts.

What is the message you are sending? What do you want me to know?

He was so caught up in his unspoken debate with himself that his fully exposed back was an easy target. It took just the blink of an eye for the small amount of force that hit him to take an immediate effect. Even halfway through his gravitationally inspired descent, Demo's mind remained foolishly oblivious to what had just transpired. It wasn't until the harrowing rush of air against his face ripped him free from his thinking that he let out a scream of panic. He was falling. But it was *where* he was falling that sent him into a new level of terror. He was falling into the river. Within seconds, his gangly body hit a newly formed, thin layer of ice. Immediately it gave way under his weight letting out a horrific crack. Millions of razor sharp, icy needles buried deep into his flesh. He was now fighting for his life in the frozen jaws of death.

As he kicked his legs madly, his hands desperately searched for an opening in the ice layer. The current beneath his feet was ripping him away, streaming him into the river's dark fathoms. The air in his lungs was being compressed out of him with each passing heartbeat. Sheer terror now gripped his every thought.

I don't want to die down here! I don't want to die in this ice tomb!

He felt himself begin to fade. The cold was taking a serious toll on his energy level, like a watery vampire sucking each chilled drop of life out of him. The probing hands rapidly turned to pounding fists. His head felt like a sinking boulder that he could no longer fight to keep up. Something needed to happen and happen fast. Watching as the cloudy layer that imprisoned him started to slip further away he knew his life was coming to an end. He would more than likely never be found. His body ripped into a million pieces in its icy tomb.

I'm sorry, Bobby…

As his life essence flowed out of him, he was suddenly jolted by a forceful burst of energy, followed by a beam of light that broke through the murky water. It was almost angelic in its presentation. But it was short lived. From above a strong arm plunged into the icy grips of the river to save his life.

Demo felt a strong tug begin to pull him upward. He felt completely weightless and detached. All of his feeling had, for at least the time being, frozen over. But with a few more mighty yanks on his collar he was swept onto a solid piece of cement. He peered up to see who his guardian angel was but instead was met by a foggy haze.

"I've got you, Demo! Man, hold on!"

The cloud refused to clear from his vision. That didn't matter much though, since Demo's body was twitching from an uncontrollable shake. He had been under too long, and his body was beginning to shut down. Doing his best to open his almost completely numbed lips, he mumbled out his plea for life.

"I'm so damn cold…"

Again he felt weightless as his mysterious savior picked him up and carried him up some stairs and into a parked car. Demo listened as the person fumbled with their keys until finally the engine clicked over with a quiet purr. With great relief, saving waves of heated grace burst from the car's heater, blasting full throttle at Demo's frozen limbs.

"You've got to get those clothes off, and I need to get you to a hospital!"

Demo rolled his head; although still in tremendous pain, he could at least see clearly again. The voice had been suspect but the face solidified for him that his rescuer was Martinez. He watched as Martinez helped him get his coat off before tossing it into the back seat of his parked car.

"No, no, I'm fine. I don't want to go to the hospital."

He looked at Demo, dumbfounded.

"I don't care what you think! You almost *died* out there! Just what the hell were you *doing* out there, man?"

Demo shrugged.

"Looking around…no big deal…"

Martinez shook his head with a deeply frustrated look tattooed on his face.

"Looking around for what? What would bring you out here?"

Demo looked down at his sloshy, ice–buckets for shoes. He slipped one off and watched a snow cone full of slush plop onto the car's floorboard where it melted away into nothing. He was about to answer the question when something else began to itch in the back of his mind; a question that *he* wanted answered. Still shivering wildly, he looked as sternly as he could at Martinez.

"A better question is what are *you* doing here?"

Martinez shifted in his seat. It was obvious that he wasn't used to being the one under question.

"I was in the area and heard a splash in the river, so I rushed in to check it out."

Demo took on a harsher tone.

"Cut the crap, Martinez! This is the murder scene of a cop! It's freezing out and we both know this is the last place anyone's gonna be hanging around!"

Martinez was shocked. He had known Demo professionally for quite some time now and it wasn't like him to be so dark and ferocious. Martinez looked away appearing surprisingly distant and disconnected.

"Martinez, *tell* me! I'm *not* messing around!"

Suddenly Martinez erupted.

"Because Jacky told me to; she told me to tail you! You've got her all worked up and worried so she asked if I'd be willing to keep an eye on you, so I did! Don't pin this on me! I just saved your damn life, man!"

Demo slumped back into the car seat to ponder.

Who pushed me? How long have they been watching me?

"Ok, I'm sorry, you're right. I've just been through a lot lately and needed some space. I came out here to look for something."

Martinez stared at Demo incredulously.

"Well, did you find it?"

Demo nodded.

"I think so."

Martinez put his foot on the gas.

"I'm taking you in. You look like death and I'm not about to leave you out here in the cold."

Demo nodded again but then caught Martinez's eye. He was trying to will Martinez into understanding something.

"I can't be taken in, Martinez. Don't take me back to Jacky."

"But that's my job! That's what I'm supposed to do! I ain't gonna lose my job over this, Demo. You know me better than to ask me to do that!"

Demo gazed out the window and sighed.

"I'm asking you as a friend."

Martinez pounded on the steering wheel with a tightly clenched fist.

"Martinez, just drive me to the courthouse. I'll be fine from there. We can pretend this whole thing never happened. Please; you can't take me in; I'm begging you. A whole lot of lives may depend on this; *please?*"

Martinez looked beside himself. He was a man of honor who strictly adhered to a certain code of conduct. Now he was caught between loyalties and he was steaming with frustration.

"Fine, fine! I'll take you to the courthouse and drop you off! But I'm telling you, man…if Jacky finds out, it'll be my badge. I ain't supposed to be doing this stuff, dude. I ain't gonna bail you out again."

Demo nodded, and then muted the conversation by turning his full concentration on what passed outside the frosty car window. Despite his freezing extremities, a surprising warmth surged up within him. He was closer to solving this case than he'd ever been, at least so he thought. His dark journey was coming full circle.

When Martinez pulled up to the courthouse, he looked nervously around, making sure they hadn't been seen.

"Okay, we're here. You can sit up and get out."

Demo did as he was told and slid out of the car like a snake. Martinez sped away leaving a shivering Demo standing directly on the courthouse steps. His mind was swinging around from one thought to another like a deranged monkey. Slowly, he slipped off his pants, unbuttoned and removed his shirt, and then kicked off his shoes. He felt the intense cold gnawing into his flesh like a school of piranha. Kneeling at the steps of the courthouse, he put his hands up high in the air.

Okay, god…do you see me now?

Raising himself up slowly, he sluggishly walked over to the only phone booth he knew of. Crammed himself inside of it, and took a deep breath.

So what now? What's your next move?

Pulling out his soaked wallet, he fished around for a credit card. With his nerves on edge he clumsily swiped it and dialed a number from memory. Taking in the moment in its entirety, he waited for an answer. It finally came and so did his only words.

"It's me."

CHAPTER FIFTEEN

GhostNapped

The drive back to the now enigmatic building of mystery was routine now. When he had gotten into the car he knew he would have some explaining to do. In a short time he had successfully pinned himself against the wall. He had alienated his allies, been baited out by his enemies, and felt himself slipping every day he remained on the case. Looking over at Bob Cat, he knew he had cut him deeply. Bob Cat had just lost everything, and now he was on shaky ground in a relationship with someone he thought he could trust explicitly… and that someone was Demo.

Demo didn't know how to repair relationships; he only knew how to destroy them. But he at least had to attempt to bring their friendship back from the cruddy hole he had dumped it in.

"I had that dream again…the one where I kill Mike."

Bob Cat remained silent, staring ahead as he drove.

"I had to lie to them to come and get you. That seems to be all we do now is lie. We lie to each other and we lie to ourselves. Jacky's gone, my family's gone, and now I'm picking you up naked at a phone booth. Just one lie after another."

Demo cringed at the pain that spilled out along with Bob Cat's words.

"I'm sorry, Bobby, it's just the way it had to be."

Bob Cat whipped out a cigarette and took a long drag off its poisonous end. Demo thought to ask the obvious question, but stopped himself. He knew why he was smoking again. Bobby didn't care anymore. As they arrived at Roslin's secret, fun house neither looked each other in the eye. Demo still felt the almost uncontrollable urge to shiver. His clothes had for the most part dried, but his confidence was still drowning in an ocean of doubt. Could he really beat this thing? Would winning mean losing everything he held dear?

"I'm so sick of this shite," mumbled Bob Cat trailing off and flicking his used up cigarette into the alley.

Once inside the building, Roslin was on top of them like the apex predator that he was.

"What happened to you? I give you some leash and you come back half frozen to death?"

Demo glanced up to see a surprising look of concern plastered across Roslin's normally indifferent face. Also of interest was the blue and black shiner he was sporting.

Had Roslin and Bob Cat finally had it out?

"Rough date?" asked Demo, keeping an eye on Bob Cat's reaction.

Surprisingly, Bob Cat looked just as surprised as he was.

Who had Roslin been tangling with?

"Forget the eye; we've got more important things to talk about. Where have you been? And don't dodge me. I deserve some answers here!"

"He broke him."

Both Bob Cat and Roslin looked at Demo when he spoke. They were fully accustomed to Demo's nonsensical ways of doing things, so they stayed silent and waited.

"He broke Spencer just like he broke Kevin Randall. He broke them down in order to rebuild them the way he wanted them. Every murder through the years a work of art, carefully crafted and executed; but his hands were always clean. He needed a new zealot, one worthy of him, someone he could lord over, dig into their lives and manipulate to the point of insanity."

Roslin interjected.

"What you're describing is brainwashing. So are we up against an entire cult that this madman has put together?"

Demo shook his head.

"There's no way he'd risk that; too many ideas, opinions, too many loose ends to oversee. With one blind follower at a time he can create intimacy, becoming almost like a father figure."

Demo's words trailed off.

Was it possible? Could there be a connection?

"I need to go back in time; at least back in what Spencer perceives in his mind as the past. I have a feeling that whatever I missed the first time is waiting for me there. I've been going about this all wrong. I've been treating Spencer and Kevin Randall as cold, calculated killers, which they are, don't get me wrong. But they're *also* victims. They've been deceived just as much as we have. They've been turned into rabid dogs released by their master's call."

Bob Cat grumbled.

"Just what does all that blooming nonsense have to do with us? Or *anyone* for that matter?"

Demo shrugged, shaking his head.

"I'm not sure. But something is happening right under our noses and we just aren't seeing it. Someone pushed me off the dock trying to silence me, but failed. I must be getting close. The pressure's mounting. Something will have to give soon."

Roslin grimaced.

"I thought you'd eventually bring that up," he said, looking discouraged.

"What do you mean?" Demo asked.

"We found the missing car…or at least what was left of it."

Resisting the urge to throw a declarative fist pump into the air, Demo calmly pressed further.

"*And?*"

"Typical in every way—generic car, bought with cash, no discernible records as of yet, and no real history—we're in the process of scrubbing it as we speak."

So you are human…

"And what do you suppose they're gonna find in that old tuna can? If this guy's as good as Demo says they'll come up empty."

Demo imposed himself into their conversation.

"But there *was* a car! Don't you see? There was a car and he disposed of it in a hurry! This is great news!"

Both Roslin and Bob Cat both looked at him warily. Roslin thought to question Demo's seemingly premature joy but were promptly cut off.

"I need to speak with Jo right now! I need to get myself back into Spencer's mind, but this time at the right time and place."

Demo darted off, leaving them behind. Roslin closed his eyes and let out a sigh of sour air. Beneath his breath he was reciting a stream of four–letter poetry as he motioned for Bob Cat to follow.

Once they had made it through the extensive security protocols, Demo went straight for Jo. When Jo saw that Demo was making a straight trajectory for him, he tried to avoid him for fear of being strangled. By the time Bob Cat and Roslin reached the control room they found a rather peculiar game of cat and mouse being enacted.

"Get this freak away from me, man! I've got data to go over and he busts in here like he owns the place!"

Roslin put his face directly into his palm. For all of Jo's strengths being brave was definitely not on that list.

"Demo, please back off of Mr. Orson."

Demo paused in his pursuit of Jo, feeling largely unmoved by the commanding decree from Roslin.

"I was just trying to tell him to get me back inside Spencer's head. I don't know what his problem is!"

Jo scoffed at his remark while adjusting his now crooked glasses.

"You're my problem, man! You give me the heebie–jeebies!"

Demo's shoulders slumped. He hated having his progress slowed. How was he supposed to get anything done?

"Both of you just calm down; and for once, Mr. Ward, please speak in a language that we can *all* understand!"

Demo bit his tongue; to his amazement he was on the verge of a verbal onslaught of his own.

What's happening to me?

"The first time I went in, I ended up in the city. I need to get back there. And it's imperative that I do it soon."

Roslin looked at the befuddled Jo, who rolled his eyes in protest.

"Okay. I'll check Spencer's trace patterns and see if anything lines up with the data log from Demo's first trip; but don't let him follow me! Last thing I need is some pyscho looking over my shoulder!"

Bob Cat grinned.

"Just one big happy family…"

"Shut up, you. You never help the situation," retorted Roslin, straightening his immaculate suit.

The group fell into a momentarily silence, each of them piecing together their own conclusions. It only took a few minutes for the ecstatic Jo to burst back into the room.

"The print pattern's a match! The synaptic mold fit almost perfectly with the correlated data from your first trip. This table's a hot ride, man!"

All three of the men looked at Jo with long faces drawn out by pure exhaustion. Being accustomed to the look, Jo iterated his point further.

"It looks like he's in the same state of mind. Now is as good as ever to try."

"Well, why didn't you just say so?" snapped Bob Cat sarcastically.

"Let's do this then. I don't want to waste any more time."

Demo hurriedly sat down in Fathom. He tried to prepare himself mentally as best he could. Who knew what darkness he was getting into? He put his curiosity on temporary hold as the familiar waves of energy surged through him like a roaring river, out of reality as he knew it into the world of the Fathom.

"Yo, watch it, man! You 'bout took my head off!"

Demo shook his head trying to flush the fuzz balls of confusion he'd picked up on the way in

Wait, I know this…

"Far out threads, man."

Demo's pause in thought was broken by a déjà vu in full clarity. He stood quietly and tried to recall every step of his first journey. A woman on roller skates flew by him swinging a flashy turquoise necklace around her neck as she passed. Then he heard the thunderous chants of the group he remembered from what seemed like ages ago.

It's all the same. At least so far it's all the same. That means the boy should be—

"Hey, watch it mister!"

Demo already knew what was going to happen since he'd seen it before. But he needed to react genuinely. He still wasn't sure where Spencer's manifestation was dwelling.

"I'm sorry. I didn't see you there. Here let me help you pick those up."

The boy frowned.

"Now I'm gonna be late. I sure hope they don't get too angry."

Demo frowned. For some reason he felt inclined to address the situation with a bit more bravado.

"Who are *they*? What will you be late for?"

The boy looked like he was in complete shock, but his tense face eased and he returned to his endeavor.

"That's none of your business. Not anyone's place to be asking who and what. I shouldn't be talking to strangers."

Demo watched as the boy gathered his things and sped away. As he left he shot Demo an incredulous look of concern.

"You sure have a groovy looking suit, mister," mumbled Demo underneath his breath.

Demo felt his nerves humming inside of him like a beehive. He needed a direction; he needed to move quickly; a hand rested on his shoulder from behind.

"Sir, is everything okay? Was that boy bothering you? Been a lot of petty theft as of late…"

Demo realized what he had to do. But doing it horrified him. Taking a long–legged stride he began to run away from the dumbstruck policeman.

"Sir, sir, are you okay?"

Glancing behind, he'd turned just in time to see a well–aimed soda bomb hit the police officers dead on. In an instant they were off in hot pursuit of the hate mongering protestor. Demo kept his momentum forward. He needed to find her, the woman from before. She knew things about this world that he did not. As he approached her novelty stand, his wit sparked into motion.

When his eyes met hers he was taken aback by her beauty. It was amazing that a manifested apparition of Spencer's mind was able to ignite a little flame of romantic feeling in an alternate reality.

"Hey, you look like you could use a break. Those are some far out—"

Demo interrupted her mid–sentence to try and hurry things along.

"Threads, am I right? I'm not from around here, and I come from way, way out there."

The slender torso of the woman moved slightly backwards, putting some distance between her and the human oddity that stood before her.

"Yeah…that's what I was going to say."

The woman was being defensive making Demo realize how brash he'd been. Taking a deep breath first, he continued.

"I'm sorry; I'm just a little stressed out what with all the commotion around here. Been hearing some serious allegation about the gang crime 'round here. I didn't mean to spook you out like that."

His comment seemed to briefly relax both of them a little. Dropping her shoulders, she nodded her head.

"It's fine. I can't blame you for feeling that way. I'd close up shop and leave if I could, but I just can't pull enough green."

Demo took a step carefully forward, watching her body language closely.

"I've got to be honest; I'm not really from here at all. In fact, none of this seems real to me. But I've lost a friend and can't seem to find him. I'm worried that he got caught up with the wrong crowd and now can't find a way out. He's the reason I'm here. I really, really don't want him ending up being just another statistic, ya know?"

The woman suddenly darted back into her shop and out of sight. Demo visually deflated.

Well there goes that option. I guess I could always chase the Godfather again.

Just as he was about to forsake his resolve and leave, a slender hand jutted into view. It hesitantly beckoned him to come closer. Sliding into the quirky shop, he was snatched up by his collar and found himself face–to–face with the gorgeous woman.

"Look, buddy. You'd do well not to go poking around like that in public. When people disappear here, it's probably for a good reason. Don't try to raise the dead."

Demo closed his eyes, trying to calm himself as his ears rang with an orchestra–like fervor of rushing blood. He couldn't lose this lead.

"He's a good friend. He'd do the same for me."

To his surprise, the grip on his collar loosened up enough for him to squirm away. Staring into her two brilliant, blue eyes, which were assessing him carefully, an answer finally came.

"Head to the docks and hit up the old warehouses. That's where all the bad people do their business. But don't tell anybody I told you so. To be honest, you probably won't last five minutes out there. Nobody does."

Demo nodded as if agreeing. But in reality he was screaming from the inside out. Just what was he getting himself into? Stepping back out into the fathomed world of old, he remembered why she would say that.

He moved with great purpose and courage. Ignoring suspicious glances, his pace remained unbroken. So many things were coming woefully together. So many things that had been overlooked, misunderstood, and left behind. If he was going to get this right, he'd have to face them all again.

Arriving at the docks, he was completely in awe at how different the area was back then. The aged buildings of his reality had been replaced by their much younger selves; proud, ambitious edifices of a time now forgotten. But the ambiance in the area was unchanged. It was dimly lit, out of the way, and for all intents and purposes, a murderer's playground. What better place for evil creatures to gather, plot, plan, and execute? It had easy access to the endless sprawl of the city, criminal anonymity hidden within fabricated businesses, and the wide mouth of the river to dispose of any dangerous evidence. This had to be the place.

As he searched the buildings for the so–called fishery, he couldn't help but whirl with the realization of where he was. He was standing in the fresh, untainted tomb of the unfortunate victims of his own, true reality. He recalled the cop car ride that had taken his breath away. He recalled the grotesque scene of violence that had taken some of Jacky's few and proud away. It was now far more organized; cleaned up. The loose objects that had been scattered at the scene were now laboriously placed in neat order outside of the massive doors leading into the warehouse. It seemed that the attention to detail in this place was in high resolution. But it was what he saw next that rewarded his efforts; a large metal sign that read *"Fish Co."*

As he approached the building, something caught his eye that shook him to his very core—an old yet surprisingly new car—old in the sense of his memory of it in his reality, but new in every other aspect. He approached it gingerly, knowing he had seen one just like it that had contained one of the now deceased zealots who followed the puppet master. The flashbacks of that day ran full view through his brain, reminding him what he was fighting for.

Cadillac DeVille…you kept this car…why?

The automobile sat just a hundred yards or so from the looming warehouse. It appeared to be empty, but not long. It was apparent that the driver had left the car only moments before his arrival. He needed to find his courage. Stepping just a bit closer to the car he saw something he had seen before but in a much more macabre way. A small doll with a blue hat and blue suspenders sat in the back seat. It, unlike the one of recent memory, was in pristine condition. This brought his thoughts back to the woman with blue eyes.

She had divulged the area by Spencer's perception of it. It was a long shot but in Demo's mind, this would be the epicenter of activity. Strangely enough, it was eerily quiet. But he knew better than to trust his insights here. The warehouse had to be the place. It would contain the key to the end of this madness. Turning his attention away from the car, he pressed on toward the beginning of the end. But his progress was suddenly thrown backwards by an immense force. It muffled his screams for help with an ice cold hand pressed harshly onto his face. Demo tried to fight back but found he was completely helpless. The phantom of the night would be having his way with him one way or another.

He watched as the warehouse and car slipped further from view. Then without warning, he was tossed to the ground. The impact jolted his body with pain. He gasped madly for air, teetering on the edge of consciousness. He tried to stand when the feeling of cold steel pressed firmly against his head froze him with terror. Next he heard a warped, almost inhuman voice.

"Get up and move."

Not one to argue with a dark demon manifested within a killer's mind, Demo got up. The man herded him around like a lost calf. With each step the man's pistol dug deeper into Demo's back as he barked orders at him. The man pushed him farther away from what Demo had assumed was the epicenter of activity in Spencer's mind; so far, in fact, that the familiar details had begun to fade. Store signs and street signs were lost to him. This gave him insight into a very obvious fact; this man was not a part of the nightmarish apparition. So who was he then? What was he going to do with Demo?

"Down there."

Demo looked where the man was pointing. It was down a flight of stairs leading into a dark tunnel. He tried to catch a glimpse of the man's face but was distracted by the whirlwind of *the fade* that was just a stone's throw away. Its raging sparks crackled and thundered showing off all of its destructive power and force. Another shove of the gun barrel into his back forced him to move.

Reaching the bottom, he saw the dank emptiness of the tunnel. If there was ever a better place to be forgotten, he hadn't seen it.

"Sit!"

The stern words came from Demo's captor. He did what he was told, plopping down on the murky, sewage covered floor. His nostrils filled with a horrid stench. The man stayed, but kept himself in the shadows, doing his best to remain unseen. He was like a ghost, a nightmarish ghoul that plagued his mind like a cancer.

Great. I've been ghost–napped.

Demo watched as the mysterious man paced back and forth, letting out a telethon's worth of jumbled words. It was almost as if he was struggling to contain himself.

"Why are you here?"

Demo couldn't muster any words. The man's voice was chilling. It was as if many people resided in that one tortured body. Demo's heart pounded against his chest as if trying to burst free. But he had to finish this. He had to press the demon further.

"I was going to ask you the same thing."

The comment made the man shiver. One of his hands shot into view for just a moment. It was pale, worn, and skeletal. It shook wildly as the man tried to regroup.

"Did they send you?" he demanded, pointing his pistol into the maelstrom outside.

Demo didn't speak; he only nodded, hoping he could buy time.

"Dammit, they never stop! It never stops!"

The man's words came out tinged with fear, remorse, and pain, and then he went silent. When it seemed that the silence would go on forever, he stepped from the shadows into view. Demo gasped in horror. The man was a walking corpse. He wore the attire reminiscent of none other than Roslin Tanner. But inside was a man barely grasping to life. His eyes sunk back into jutting sockets. His hair was matted, long, and unkempt. He was a collage of deterioration in the process of fading away forever. Suddenly the man tightly grabbed a hold of his own fist that held the gun and struggled with himself.

"I'll kill you, you little rat fink!"

The threat spewed from the man's mouth forcefully. It made Demo cringe. Was he talking to him?

"I can't … I can't keep doing this."

Demo's curiosity could be held at bay no longer.

"Doing *what*? What is *wrong* with you? Who *are* you?"

The man let out a tiny fissure of a grin very briefly before reassuming his chaotic persona.

"Who am I? Who am I? Who am I?"

Demo watched as the man paced back and forth, grasping at his head and occasionally letting out bursts of anger.

"I'll slice that heart free, Anthony! Come on, let me find you!"

Demo then did something unthinkable. Standing back up, he grabbed the struggling man and shook him.

"Get a grip on yourself! Fight this!"

He watched as the man's stormy eyes calmed. Then, without warning, he collapsed. With a loud clack, the gun bounced into the churning water outside. Immediately, Demo pounced on him, doing his best to keep the man cognizant.

"Stay with me, buddy! Stay with me!"

Feeling hopeless, he did the only thing that seemed logical; rearing his arm back, he let it loose and slapped the man across the face. The man let out another guttural scream before finally appearing to calm down a bit. He glanced up to catch Demo's eyes.

"I'm sorry … it's been a long time … a very, very long time."

Demo was shocked by when the once convoluted mesh of voices melded into just one.

"I'm Anthony, Anthony Dredge, an agent with those who sent you here."

Demo's eyes bulged open. Had he just heard that right? The implications of the statement being true were grave, and completely ridiculous.

"What did you just say?"

The man shook his head.

"Still lying like always…*damn* you, Roslin."

Demo gasped, "You know Roslin?"

The man took a deep breath then shakily got to his feet, doing his best to dust off all the filth he had accumulated.

"Know him? I was one of his golden boys. Piece of work had me caught up saving lives for the greater good; doesn't surprise me in the least that he's got a new errand boy. That man will do anything to get results. I suppose that's why he is who he is and I'm here."

Demo shook his head, and then shook it again. An enormous amount of information had just poured out even though so little had been said. He now had a novel's worth of questions to ask. But he also knew his time was short. He had to be concise, articulate, and to the point; no easy feat for Demo.

"Yeah, I hate that guy too."

The man cracked another miniscule smile that quickly faded. His hands began to shake violently but he did his best to control them.

"It comes and goes. I won't be able to maintain this much longer."

The man closed his eyes tightly. He appeared to be in an excruciating amount of pain.

"I guess I better explain a few things. I'm Agent Anthony Dredge, or at least what's left of him. I was part of the Fathom project to help solve the blood legacy murders. I was deployed; hell, I don't even remember when I was deployed anymore. All I remember is being found, tortured, and then forgotten. I've been rotting away here ever since. I'm sure Roslin's had my body disposed of along with any other traces of my existence."

Demo slouched against the wall. He felt deeply betrayed. He had been so preoccupied, so focused on the obvious evil candidates that those nearest to him had been swept under the rug. He was a fool for ever trusting such a secretive man and organization.

"Why wouldn't he tell me? Why would he lie about this?"

The man let out an almost inhuman–like cackle in response.

"Isn't it obvious? Would you have come? How do you think they came up with all their little rules? You're standing next to their first test rat."

Demo frowned, trying to hide his boiling feelings of anger, betrayal, and revenge.

"What's happening to you?"

The man placed one of his hands in full view. He looked at its pulsating veins now vividly visible beneath his paling flesh.

"I'm losing myself. After Spencer caught me here, it became my prison. He tortured me for a while until it bored him enough to let me take a back seat. I became a permanent resident of this damned memory in this damned place, reliving the same moments over and over again, with no end in sight. Each day, another piece of me chips away and becomes part of him. His filth seeps out of me now; unhinged, uncontrollable. I can't imagine a worse hell."

Demo's heart sank. Anthony Dredge had truly suffered greatly at the hands of the powers that be. Suffered greatly, and been rewarded with a decaying purgatory with no escape. But then something occurred to him that hadn't before.

"I saw you. You were watching me the first time I came here. You were the man standing in the shadows, weren't you?"

Anthony nodded, now starting to look feeble and mad again.

"When you've been here as long as I have, you don't miss a thing."

There was a brief pause. It was clear Anthony was beginning to lose the battle with Spencer's vicious, unyielding subconscious.

"I'll gut ya like a fish, Anthony!"

Demo put a naïve hand out in an ill attempt to comfort the suffering man. But the battle he was waging came from within. He began to speak but was cut off by a declaration from Anthony.

"That's why I brought you here. This is the edge of this world. Spencer's focus never looks at the edge. I've been surviving like a rat in the shadows all this time; trying, hoping, that Spencer will forget he's locked me away in this hell. Hoping that someday I can finally just be blissfully erased."

Anthony put his head in his hands and quivered. His behavior was becoming increasingly erratic.

"Filthy bastard! Coward! You're a coward, Anthony!"

Anthony swung one of his free hands madly in the air, striking aimlessly. He was fading fast, and so was Demo's time. He needed to ask the right questions and he needed to do it now.

"Anthony, I need you to tell me something, okay? Did you find Spencer here? Who is Spencer in this world?"

Anthony twitched violently. His body looked like it was possessed by a demon; but a demon with a name.

"Anthony, I don't have much time! You've got to tell me where Spencer is! Did you find him here? What do you know? I know this is the place; this must be where it all started!"

His lunatic behavior was escalating. Anthony smacked his hands against his head repeatedly, mumbling a slew of gibberish. His eyes were completely untamed, uncontrolled, and malicious. He lunged at the unexpected Demo, grabbing him by the neck. Demo was surprised how strong the possessed Anthony was. They clashed together, rolling around in the repugnant sewage water that filled the tunnel.

"Anthony, *stop!*" pleaded Demo, through the vice–like grip around his neck.

He flung his hands recklessly about as he tried to devise a counter offensive. But overtaking the insane, almost inhuman movement of Anthony was proving to be problematic. He had to do something soon; Anthony was squeezing the life out of him. Demo's focus right now was just to survive. But Anthony's attack would not cease. He seemed to be growing stronger the longer they fought. Demo had to do something or risk being forever entombed inside Spencer's warped mind.

Glancing around, he found a transparent beacon of hope: an empty beer bottle. Its label was long gone along with most of its more intricate features. Even its shapely outline appeared fuzzy and faded. But all it had to do was manifest correctly against the head of Anthony.

Demo abated his attack against Anthony, and focused his effort at the abandoned bottle. He could see the dark cloud beginning to pour in from the sides of his peripheral vision; he was passing out. His finger crept along the ground one grimy inch after another. His vision was now completely clouded. All around him was the warm blanket of unconsciousness begging him to let go. But from somewhere deep inside he found one last fragment of awareness. Amidst Anthony's demonic like banter, he let out a painful scream of agony, stretching his arm beyond its limits. Suddenly, the smooth neck of the bottle was in his grasp, as he swung it upwards and released it against the head of a monstrous Anthony.

"Let go of me!!!" Demo shrieked with exertion

Anthony fell back against the wall, and then slowly slid to the ground, hand firmly against his forehead. A stream of crimson red blood spewed out from between the cracks of his fingers. Demo rolled onto his back, gasping for air desperately. Seconds passed slowly as the two struggled to regain their composure. It was Anthony who spoke first.

"I'm so sorry for all of this. I'm sorry for bringing you here. I can't keep him out anymore; he's becoming too strong."

Demo coughed out a glob of blood that spattered onto his shabby suit. He slowly rose into a seated position. He wanted to speak, but Anthony had more to say.

"It's been such a long time—so long since I've felt anything real—this is all I know now."

Anthony let his hand drop to his side. He walked over to the entrance to the murky tunnel and stared into the raging tornado of the fade.

"It's funny…when I first came here I thought I knew everything there was to know about evil. I'd seen so much of it back there. I spent my life searching for it. A lifetime of following my own intuition, tracking dead–ends…and the whole time he was right under my nose. I must have run into him a thousand times. But naivety has a way of hiding those things. I was a damn fool for not seeing it. Now it's too late."

Anthony dropped his head into his hands. His soul was obviously bursting with regret. His pain was almost palpable. Demo's mind cranked away, realizing that he too had used a phrase much akin to what Anthony had just said. Suddenly his gut filled with a sickening goo that percolated its way up into his throat, threatening to spew its acidic contents into his mouth. His mind stopped at one conclusion he had previously neglected to see. Now that it had come into view, it was more than he thought he could bear. But Anthony had spoken clearly; there would be no mistaking it any longer. He was chilled to the bone by the next outburst from Anthony.

"You need to leave *now*. It's coming! Go! *Run!*"

Anthony's words shored up Demo's resolve. Anthony's legions of inner demons were returning, all speaking at once. Demo needed to run for his life. The fade was closing in on them. The waters beneath it churned madly before being sucked up into its blackened depths. The sight was beyond any nightmare Demo could have conjured up himself. He turned and saw Anthony clawing at his hair, ferociously losing control. He wanted to save him but knew deep down inside that Anthony was too far gone. If Demo was going to end this madness, he had to survive. Using every ounce of energy left inside of him, he sprinted towards the city while everything behind him was rapidly ripped apart. He only looked back once and saw Anthony gazing at him. Only something deep inside told him that Anthony was no longer alone. A single heartbeat later he felt the world around him breaking apart. Waves of current pulsated through him before everything went black.

CHAPTER SIXTEEN

Dark Horse

As light shattered his darkness, Demo's body shot straight forward. But it was out of neither shock nor surprise, but pure anger. He had collected his thoughts together into one vengeful conclusion; he would make Roslin pay for this. They had all been deceived by him, who had assured them a safety net that Demo now knew was gaping with massive holes. Lies, murder, and betrayal—a common recipe for evil—and it now appeared that no one was beyond using it as a means to an end. He leapt off the table and threw all of his weight into an unsuspecting Roslin. As they crumpled to the floor, the room burst into action.

"Get that crazy lunatic off of him! He's going to kill him!" Jo pitifully pleaded.

Demo's eyes darted violently back and forth as if still caught up in a dream. But the feeling of Roslin's neck struggling to breathe beneath his grip was real enough for him. There was a darkness surging in him that beckoned him to press forward, end it, and cleanse the world of one less deviant. This darkness gorged itself on his soul. A small part of Demo took pleasure in thinking about killing Roslin inside his own security blanket of a building. It would be poetic.

"Liar, liar, murderer!" Demo screamed frantically.

"Let go of me! Let go of me!" the choked words slipped from between Roslin's purple lips as he desperately tried to pry Demo off.

"*Demo*, get a hold of yourself!" screamed Bob Cat, grabbing him from behind.

Bob Cat's words stirred a deep feeling of sorrow in the utterly enraged Demo. As the sadness grew, his grip loosened from Roslin's windpipe. Taking his shot, Bob Cat's snatched Demo up into the air like a kite on a string. Demo's feet kicked wildly with unchecked fury.

"What the hell is wrong with him, man? He tried to kill Roslin!" Jo muttered, back–peddling out of the room.

Bob Cat continued to subdue Demo into complacency, throwing a menacing glance at Roslin who was struggling to get back up.

"What's he talking about? You've got some explaining to do!"

Roslin stood up defiantly, straightening himself back into his model of professionalism.

"I said, *what* is he talking about? Those aren't words my boy throws around lightly."

Roslin shook his head while looking away. Demo's sudden change in allegiance had him baffled. His head dropped to his chest.

"Is it even possible?" he whispered under his breath.

Bob Cat growled, "I *said*—"

Roslin sharply cut him off this time. "I *know* what you said! I know what he said! I know all of it! Don't you get it? I always know everything! I'll be damned if I take orders from some no name team of losers! It's best you remember your place, do *you* hear *me*?"

Bob Cat released Demo, who was standing on his own finally, but still barely keeping it together. He took an aggressive bound directly towards Roslin, who stood his ground firmly.

"I've had enough of you! You chose us, *remember*? If you think you've got all the answers then why even bother?"

Bob Cat looked coiled and ready to strike like a venomous serpent. But a pacifying hand landed on his shoulder and pulled him back. The hand belonged to Demo who was marching past Bob Cat on his way towards Roslin again.

"I'm his new test rat, haven't you heard? I'm a lot like his old one, Anthony Dredge."

At the mere mention of the name Roslin's demeanor changed from powerful and stoic to crumbling and shaken. Bob Cat turned his attention to Demo.

"Anthony Dredge? Who's that?"

Demo pointed one of his fingers directly at Roslin.

"Why don't you ask him? In fact, why don't we ask all of them; Jo,

Roslin, and this whole bogus organization? They've been telling one lie after another to cover up even more. This wasn't just about solving a case. This was about the Fathom program. It always has been. You lied about everything. It's already been tested on one of your own, Anthony Dredge. Now he's locked away forever inside that sick freak's head. I sure hope his loss was worth the price of admission!"

Roslin grabbed a chair and flung it against the wall where it splintered loudly into pieces.

"I did what I had to do! Anthony knew what the dangers were, and he still chose to follow through with it! You can't put this on me when I'm the only one standing between you and a really ugly world, a world you have no idea even exists. A world filled with such evil it'd make you drop down to your knees and beg for mercy! Did I know that Anthony was still inside? Did I know that you'd find him? Does it really matter? Think of the possibilities a machine like this has to offer! This thing is bigger than you, me, or even Anthony!"

Bob Cat spat out some vicious comments in return.

"You dirty bastard! You had us testing out your new toy? What about all the innocent men and woman who've been victimized? We just gonna chalk them up, too?"

"I don't need to justify progress! Without this machine even more innocent people would die! So what if one or two of us becomes collateral? This was *never* about us; it was about saving lives! Do I wish things could've been different? Of course! Do I wish Agent Anthony Dredge was still with us today? That goes without saying! But I'll be *damned* if I let all the progress we've made this far fall apart over your weak sentimentality!"

Demo closed his eyes and recalled Anthony's tortured words. He had paid the ultimate price for his hope; the hope that he could help finally bring decades of bloodshed to an end. What did it matter who was to blame for what? If the ferocity of the master puppeteer couldn't be stopped, who knew what else would happen?

Bob Cat looked poised to launch a vicious assault against the arrogant Roslin, but was halted by Demo.

"Stop. He's right. He may be a dirty, lying jerk, but he's right. This is what he wants us to do. He wants us to fall apart, blame each other, turn on each other, and then waste our time while things are tidied up. We've all lied to each other. We intentionally kept each other in the dark. The sooner we accept that and get over it, the sooner we can get back to work and end this once and for all!"

Roslin looked at Bob Cat who stood only a few footsteps away now, panting heavily like a bear in case he had to swing into action. Roslin spoke up next.

"Anthony was a friend and a damn good agent. Losing him was like losing the son I never had. But he knew that it was for the greater good. Not a day goes by that I don't blame myself for the losses here. If I could make it all go away, I would. But I can't. I can't stop evil from being evil, any more than I can stop gravity from pulling me down. But I stand against it. I choose to fight back! So it looks like we've all got a choice to make now. If you want to walk away and pretend none of this ever happened, you know where the door is. But don't expect me to shed a tear for you."

Demo gave Bob Cat a look of concern, and then responded to Roslin's speech.

"He's going to do something big soon. He knows us and knows what we're up to. He'll stop at nothing now to finish his work. I've been so blind, so blind to the obvious. I need a night to put things together. I need to solve this before anyone else we care about dies in some disgusting display of self–indulgence. I'll also need you to have the Fathom ready for one last trip back to where I just came from. I don't care how long it takes; it's where I need to be."

Demo looked directly at Jo, who quivered and nodded his head.

"Stressing Spencer out like that with constant probing…I don't know if he can maintain. It's not like he's got a power cord I can just plug in. The man is, for the most part, human. We might just fry him *and* the machine if we drag this out too long. He's been accessed so many times."

Roslin interjected.

"He's right; constantly probing him like this could have unwanted long term results."

"Good thing he's already dead then," Demo stated, breaking from the group and beckoning Bob Cat to follow him. The two walked away, leaving a dumbstruck Roslin and Jo behind.

Are they going to let us walk? Are they going to let us do this?

Demo's head felt like a pound of cement was solidifying inside of it. But another part of him felt more at ease. He had proven his point. He had driven the nail as far in as possible. Now it just needed to bleed out Roslin's otherwise impervious, icy heart.

"Where we going, Demo?"

Demo shook his head to clear it, realizing he had been so deep in thought that he had made it from the secretive building to the alley behind it with no memory of making the trip.

"I need to run home and look over some things. Do you have paper and pen on you?"

Bob Cat obliged him by fishing around in his pockets. As he did so a long, slender cigarette plummeted onto the cold, concrete ground.

"I wish you'd stop."

"I wish I could," Bob Cat answered, frowning as he picked it back up.

"What is it that you want me to jot down? You know we've got technology on our phones for this crap, don't you? And you do remember we started a fire in that building, right?"

"Not anymore. Mine's fried, lost it in the river. Who knows what else I dropped back there. And at this point, I couldn't care less about my apartment. I just need to see it one last time. We'll be careful and sneak around like we always do."

Demo let out a sickening cough and a wheeze.

"Demo, you ain't looking so hot. Maybe take the night to rest on it."

"Can't rest, Bobby; I can't even sleep anymore. I don't know how much more of this I can take but there's no other option."

Demo grabbed the pen and paper from Bob Cat and jotted down a couple lines of info. His head felt like a thousand shards of glass were pressing into it. It was taking everything he had just to stay clear and focused, but he had to take this chance—his gut was telling him to—his gut also told him that if he was right, his days were numbered. It would all be coming to an end. Once finished, he carefully creased the note and slid it into one of Bob Cat's coat pockets.

"Don't you want me to read it?"

"Not now."

"Then when?"

"You'll know when."

Bob Cat's face looked like a maze of lines that formed then disappeared with each change of thought. But he went along with the charade… at least for now.

They arrived at Demo's house in a hazy plume of frost bitten air and exhaust. By the time they made it to the room they looked like they were on the verge of collapsing. Exhaustion, frustration, and a cesspool of mixed emotions were sapping their strength into submission. Demo walked over and picked up an old photo that had been tampered with.

"It really was my fault, Bobby. I've got to face that. I'm a killer. With a gun or by pure apathy, I'm a killer. Mike didn't deserve to die like that. He had so much going for him; a career, natural talent for saving lives, and a beautiful woman that loved him… I wiped all that out on that damned night."

Bob Cat threw his hands in the air.

"So *that's* why you've dragged us back up here? You want to take a trip down memory lane? What do you want me to blooming say? Yes Demo, it was all your fault you filthy piece of crap? Yes, Mike's dead because of you? That the world would be better off without you? You guys had something special. You were a great team and you did great things, but dammit, Demo, everybody's human! You've got to realize that and let it go!"

"But I'm not, Bobby! I'm not! I'm not human, I'm not special! All I am is lucky! That's all I've ever been; just one lucky break after another. Don't you get it, Bobby? This all started with Mike. I don't have some sort of super power. Nobody likes me and nobody wants me around.

I'm a freak; a freak on a chain that gets tugged on when they need me. I don't even know what I want anymore. Why bother saving the very people who lie, deceive, and belittle you? I'm just some dark horse that succeeds occasionally and then is forgotten. What do I even have after this? Am I really going to spend the rest of my life solving cases for pennies on the dollar? I've got nothing, Bobby. Nothing!"

Bob Cat looked saddened by Demo's remarks.

"You've got me and I've got you! And that's all we've got now! Jacky's gone, along with everybody else! But that arse hole Roslin is right! This isn't about us, Demo. This is about everybody else that's got someone or something to lose. It's being taken from them, ripped right out of their bloody hands. I've known you for years, but for all your faults, I can say this; you're a freak, yes! But a freak that's going to save lives, a freak that's going to give back to the people something they need—*hope*. You give them hope, Demo. You give *us* hope. Ain't nobody else can do what you do. You may be a freak, Demo, but you're also a bloody *hero*."

Demo felt his emotions humming like a power line. He had never thought of himself as a hero. That would be narcissistic in every way... at least so he thought. Maybe Bob Cat was partially right, but he was no hero, of that he was sure. Heroes didn't feel the way he felt; they don't fall apart inside. Heroes didn't let the people around them suffer so much. Heroes didn't have to lie to everyone, even themselves just to get by. But then again, maybe the world didn't need a hero right now. Maybe it needed a freak just like him. Demo started to say something when he was cut off by the buzz of the cellphone in Bob Cat's pocket. He snatched it out and spoke. His eyes bulged in disbelief. Reluctantly he handed the phone to Demo who was completely bewildered.

"It's for you. It's Mars."

"Mars?" questioned Demo, not believing what he had heard.

Demo placed the phone cautiously up to his ear. He was met by an emotional outcry from a very distraught Mars.

"Demo, is that you? You've got to get over to Judge Ridding's apartment! Something's wrong, something's very wrong!"

Demo gasped. There were so many things he wanted to ask but he could hear by his tone there wasn't time.

"I'm going there now! Please hurry. I'm worried about him! I tried to call the local police and they just said they'd look into it! What does that even mean? He could be in serious trouble!"

Mars is worried about Lyle?

The phone went dead.

"What's *that* idiot want?" probed Bob Cat.

"We need to go to Lyle's apartment. Mars is worried something's happened to him."

They rushed out of the apartment lightning fast. If Mars was this disturbed there was a reason. With screeching tires they sped off in the direction of the other side of the city.

When they arrived at the humongous luxury complex, they were immediately pounced on by a very agitated Mars.

"Where have you been? I've been waiting here forever! We've got to hurry!"

Bob Cat grasped Mars by the shoulder and shook him.

"Try and make some stinking sense! Just what the hell are you so wound up about?"

Mars looked pale and exhausted but completely wound up.

"The judge called to advise me on some things but while we were talking he suddenly stopped and said he thought someone was in his house. Next I just hear yelling and fighting. I don't know what's going on! What was I supposed to do?"

"Have you tried to get in?" asked Demo.

"No, I didn't know if I should! What if I went in and he was…"

"Don't jump to conclusions. One thing at a time, okay? Let's just get in there and see what's going on." Demo said trying to interject some calm into the situation.

Mars is a complete wreck. This is serious.

They hit the buzzer for the door.

"Well, hello gentlemen, may I—"

"We need to see Lyle and it's urgent that we see him now!" Mars screamed, losing his cool again.

"Please, ma'am, we need to make sure he's okay," added Demo quickly, looking at Mars with thinly veiled disapproval.

"I can assure you, gentlemen, Judge Ridding is doing just fine. He's up in the loft enjoying his evening tea."

"To hell with his tea! The man could be dead!" bellowed Bob Cat, letting his own frustration loose.

A long pause followed. For a minute it looked as if they weren't getting in. But then the security door snapped open. They rushed into the building and elevator in comedic fashion. Their adrenaline was running high. Would they get there in time? Or would they find another murder scene?

Mars began pounding furiously on the judge's loft door.

"Lyle, are you okay? What's going on?"

"Move aside!" growled Bob Cat lowering his shoulder.

With one football tackle aimed squarely at their obstacle, Bob Cat busted through the magnificent wooden door, sending fragmented splinters into the air. Once inside, they found what they feared most; a scene of pure chaos. Pieces of furniture were flipped over in the center of the opulent room. Broken glass mixed with thick blood splattered the floor. Following the trail through the apartment, they found the judge. He sat limply tied tightly into a chair. His mouth was gagged shut and his hands and feet were carefully bound.

"He's dead! Somebody's killed the judge! I'm calling the police!" screamed Mars running from the room.

Bob Cat stepped up to the judge and felt his wrist.

"He's alive. He's got a pulse."

Demo worked to bring Lyle back to consciousness. When he finally came to, he let out a shriek of pure terror.

"No, please don't! Please don't hurt me anymore! I don't know anything!"

Demo placed his hands on Lyle's shoulders pressing down on them firmly to assure him he was safe.

"It's okay, Lyle. It's okay, it's Demo; the police are on their way."

Lyle's eyes rolled from the back of his head.

"Oh, thank you! Thank you so much! He was going to kill me! He broke through the window and attacked me! If you hadn't have gotten here when you did, I don't know what else he would have done to me!"

Demo left the judge and sprinted to the bashed in window. The icy wind blew through it creating an eerie howl. Looking down, he saw that the fire escape ladder had been unfolded to the ground. A perfect entrance and get away from an otherwise impervious building.

"He must have used the fire ladder on the outside somehow! I don't know what he wanted from me! He was going to kill me!" Lyle was now sobbing uncontrollably.

Bob Cat joined Demo at the window, peering out of like a hawk.

"Wherever that guy went, he's long gone now. Good luck tracking that rat through the city streets."

Demo nodded. It was true. If the man had been able to plan the assault this well, he would have been meticulous in his escape, too. The only saving grace was that they had gotten there in time.

"You're gonna be alright, Judge Ridding. Help's on the way," Bob Cat assured him while he untied his limbs.

Lyle continued to gasp for breath. Tiny pieces of crimson stained glass riddled his body. A few well–placed cuts slashed here and there exposed the underlying muscle. They had made it in the nick of time.

Demo gazed back out into the icy streets of the city. As sirens echoed in the distance, something inside of him felt oddly disgusted; disgusted to the point of pure and absolute repugnancy. So many loose ends…

Turning to Bob Cat, who was still helping Lyle, he spoke the only two words he could think of.

"Dark horse…"

CHAPTER SEVENTEEN

Lamb to the Slaughter

Bob Cat spat at the floor. He watched as the saliva oozed its way between the filthy threads of carpet. He was contemplating his involvement, investment, and ultimately, his life.

"What were you babbling about back there anyways? *Dark horse?* What did that mean?"

He shook his head to clear it while he waited for Demo to answer him. The judge being carried away from his palazzo apartment by the police haunted him. They had come within a sliver of finding him dead. Now, standing in Demo's trodden down apartment, they were at another crossroad.

Demo was itching at his arm, pacing in small circles around in the middle of the room. He was completely out of his mind. His eyes were bouncing side to side as if watching a tennis match. He suddenly stopped, snapping his fingers pointedly.

"Dark horses is what we are, Bobby. Don't you see? We're the underdogs, losers, and rejects of society. But then suddenly we're called to the front of things; *why?* Why do we matter at all? Nobody knows us, nobody cares about us. We're an unexpected variable; a dark horse. Isn't that what they call it?"

Bob Cat looked amazed. It wasn't like Demo to actually get a phrase right.

"Yeah, yeah, that's actually right, for once. You actually said it right. But what are you talking about? You sound like a raving lunatic."

Demo looked annoyed but also apprehensive.

"Bobby, I need you to do something for me and you're not going to like it."

Bob Cat surveyed the room as if he already knew the answer.

"What, what is it you want from me now?"

"I'm going back, back inside the Fathom, one last time. But this time

I need more time. More time than Jo's going to give me. They don't want to risk losing their precious machine or human guinea pig. But if I don't get more time inside, I'll never find Spencer. It's Spencer who holds the last filthy piece I need to put any doubts to rest. My intuition is already there, but I have to be sure. Being wrong this time could cost me everything."

Snorting in anger, Bob Cat responded gruffly.

"I know what you're asking me and the answer is no! You heard what they said. You stay too long in there and both yours and that piece of shite Spencer's brains will be microwaved to a crisp. I'm not going to do that. You're not putting that on me!"

Demo grabbed him by the shoulders to hold him in place, and then looked him earnestly in the eyes.

"Bobby, you've got to. There's no other way. I know what I have to do now. I know how to find Spencer and end this! I can do it; you've just gotta trust me this one last time!"

"Demo, you could die in there."

"I know."

For a brief pause, there was an eerie silence. Demo's words hung somewhere between hope and sacrifice.

"I know, Bobby. I know I could die, but if not there then on the outside too. This is just how it has to be. I've got a feeling I can't shake. I've got to take a chance; it's now or never. I know I can't keep dragging myself through this evil and expect to come out clean on the other side. Last time…I promise."

Bob Cat let out a vicious snarl. He was not willing to agree that easily.

"So what is it? Who is it? Why can't you unlock your jaw for a minute and just let me in on this bloody mess? I can't work in the dark like this, Demo. You've got to let things go back to normal with us!"

"I can't do that now, Bobby. I can't let us go back to normal, not yet."

"I'll do this one last thing," Bob Cat reluctantly conceded, "But after that, it's over. Jacky was right to walk away from this. You're becoming a monster! This is consuming you whole!"

A complacent nod accompanied Demo's discouraged voice.

"I know, Bobby. I know."

Bob Cat walked to the door from where he scanned the room, looking at the fire damage, garbage, and utter disregard for cleanliness.

"This place really is a crap hole…you coming or not?"

Demo moved reluctantly, putting the old photo down gently.

I wish the fire would have just burned it all down.

On the ride back to the Fathom the two men sat in silence. There was nothing more to say. Their relationship had finally been strained past its breaking point. Bob Cathy Briar was just another name on a long list of people that had grown to loathe Demo's cursed existence. How much more could he possibly take?

At the entrance, they were both surprised to see Roslin standing outside with a group of what appeared to be agents of some kind. He looked like he'd been dragged through the very bowels of hell. On seeing Demo and Bob Cat's arrival, he directed his audience to move on. Among them was an odd looking man standing by Roslin and listening to him intently. Roslin put a hand on his shoulder and whispered something to him. The man nodded then got into one of the black, unmarked cars and drove off.

Who are those people?

Demo's mind just couldn't grasp everything that was being spewed at it day after day; secret organizations, scary machines, serial murder, and now another mystery squad.

Roslin ushered them over.

"It's about time you got back! I'm getting really tired of your games, Mr. Ward!"

Demo shrugged.

"Speaking of games, what was *that* all about?"

Roslin cringed at the question. His eyes twitched as he thought about his answer. He was going to lie.

"We had an incident. It doesn't concern this project, I promise you that."

Demo rolled his eyes. A promise at this point in their relationship might as well come with knife in the back. But he knew better than question him. Roslin would never tell him the truth.

"I need to get back into the Fathom. I'll need to have the same patterns matched as before. This is my last chance at this. I need everyone to play nice, just this once."

Glancing at Bob Cat, Demo caught a subtle nod of solidarity. It looked like Bob Cat would be following through with his part.

The group paraded through the usual routine until they arrived inside the room containing the Fathom. Jo met them with far more resistance than ever before.

"No, no, no. I'm not doing this! This is a bad idea! That section of Spencer's mind has been accessed too many times lately! And Fathom, don't even get me started on Fathom. We've pulled so much juice fueling your adventures that we could of lit up the city a hundred times over! I need some time to fix things, to cool things off, to let Spencer's mind reset."

"That's not an option. We don't have time to worry about your stupid machine or that maniac you keep alive for fun! Something big is going to happen. I know it! Now let's finish this once and for all!"

Jo threw his hands up in surrender and looked at Roslin in desperation, pleading with his eyes for Roslin to alter this suicidal course of direction.

Roslin's eyes narrowed to slits.

"Fine. We'll have Jo watch the controls and if anything gets too out of hand we'll shut it down. This means you'd have an indefinite amount of time. Jo could rip you out whenever he deems there's a risk to the program. Do you honestly think you can be effective in any way given these facts?"

Demo sat down in the Fathom without hesitation.

"Just turn the machine on."

His comment set Roslin off into a cavalcade of miffed gestures.

"And where exactly are you going?" Roslin asked Bob Cat, who had shadowed Jo into the control room.

"I want to watch the nerd play his video game. What's it to you?"

Roslin's eyes narrowed again. He was mildly suspicious of Bob Cat's sudden interest.

"Can we please just get this going?" Demo asked angrily.

Roslin shook his head.

"Jo, what's the read?"

Jo was orchestrating a plethora of commands on the super computer in the small room off of this one.

"I'm pulling it up now!"

Demo looked over at Spencer's still body. It had deteriorated to almost nothing of its former self. Decrepit and weak…yet there was still something deathly serious about him.

Long live Spencer the Bloody Vulcan.

"Take me where I need to go, you piece of filth! Take me back to the warehouse!"

Roslin looked slightly disturbed by Demo's comments to the unconscious Spencer.

"He can't hear you, Mr. Ward."

Demo shook his head.

"Oh, yes he can. He, just like me, wants this to be over."

Just then a thrilled declaration burst from the control room.

"I can't believe this! He's actually dwelling! He's dwelling in the same cognizant space as before!" Jo's elated response was quickly hushed to a whisper. "Why would he be doing that? I've never seen this before."

"Just turn it on! Let's finish this!"

Demo's eyes fell on Roslin. He didn't break his gaze until the sparks of energy swirling through his mind forced him to. In a brilliant burst of energy and light he was sucked back into Spencer's mind.

"Yo, watch it, man! You 'bout—"

The man's words were cut off by a clothesline arm thrust directly in front of him. Demo felt the man's throat smash directly into him. The force threw the man to the sidewalk.

"—'knocked my head off', yeah, I know."

Man, that felt good. But why?

The scene immediately burst into chaos. Some people screamed and ran, while others formed a small circle around the man who was now choking for air. Demo, however, was looking elsewhere. His eyes scanned back and forth like finely tuned radar zeroing in on its target.

"What's your problem, man?" screamed a slender woman on roller skates grabbing at her turquoise necklace.

That's when Demo saw him; every time he'd been right under his nose, stumbling along carrying his batch of newspapers. When his eyes met Demo's his mouth dropped open. Demo wasted no time reacting. Shoving himself through the crowd, he ran in hot pursuit of the small boy. The boy reacted by tossing his papers high in the air and fleeing with an astounding agility. As Demo's speed grew so did his rage. It wasn't like him to be violent, but after all he'd been through, he just didn't care anymore. If anyone stood in his way, he'd plow into them with no remorse. He wasn't about to let the boy slip out of sight.

The chase continued. If it wasn't for Demo's extraordinarily gangly body, he might have lost him a time or two. But he was fueled by a desire; a desire to finally rid himself of this hell. He watched as the boy darted into an alleyway. Demo followed closely, refusing to give in to his burning lungs.

"Oh, no you don't. Not this time!"

Following suit, he dove into the alleyway to see the fleeing boy shimmying up and over a fence. Demo let lose all the energy he had left. He reached for one of the boy's shaky feet just as he dropped down to the other side. He missed. Letting out a roar, he pounded on the chain link fence; he needed this to feel real.

"I'm going to find you!"

Demo watched the boy disappear out of view. Calmly, he turned and took a deep breath. His eyes watered with a salty sting. His emotions had truly become unchecked. He had just taken a massive risk, a risk beyond measure. But he had been right. Even inside Spencer's world, there was a mindset in his manifestations. Children still had a fear of adult authority figures.

But now came the tricky part. He knew where he needed to go. He knew how to get there. What he didn't know was what would be waiting for him. The thought of it made him sick. But it had to be done, even if he was a lamb headed to slaughter.

Let's finish this.

Demo retraced the route carefully, doing his best not to interact with any of the chaotic manifestations of Spencer's mind. Things had been rattled. Behaviors were now sporadic, unfocused, and unclear, roles diminished, details forgotten. If his goal was to upset the status quo, he had done so with flying colors. But jubilation had no place here. Soon things would escalate into another realm of perdition.

Walking past the parked Cadillac DeVille, he already knew what was inside it. Details of the real were hanging in his imagination like skeletons in a closet. At the entrance of the warehouse, he plunged his fingers into the massive door's crack and pulled. His heart raced around its cardiovascular racetrack. He knew that everything from this point on would be beyond belief.

Peering inside, all the memories of his nightmarish encounter there flashed before his eyes. It was beyond surreal to be doing what he was doing. This place represented so many things. But there was only one thing he really needed to see. History had a way of repeating itself for even the most genius of intellects. If he was right, the contents of this space would shatter his perception of how far the tentacles of evil could reach. He had to know.

Examining the room carefully, he was surprised how much could change by reversing time. The cluttered room of his reality was as clean and organized as ever in this reality. Everything was nicely organized and maintained. Then he saw it. It hadn't been diminished by time like everything else. Its stainless steel doors remained firmly shut. Demo approached it cautiously, doing his best to prepare himself for what he was about to see. As much anguish as it brought to his soul, he hoped he was right. Prying the two massive doors open, a fiendishly cold blast of air rushed out, revealing a blood chilling image.

Demo collapsed to his knees. He had been so blind. He had always believed they would never be capable of such heinous acts, such depravity. But the manifested evidence didn't lie. Tears filled his eyes and then froze to the outside of his face.

How could you do this?

The room was as before, only with newly deceased tenants that had been posed in a lovers embrace. Their last breaths had been undoubtedly been taken in sheer horror. There was more to this, of that he was sure. But he didn't need to see it. He didn't want to. The bodies were being prepped for disposal once they'd been properly appreciated. It hurt his soul to say it aloud.

"Mom and Dad…"

Just then he spotted something out of the corner of his eye. The boy had been watching Demo discover his bloody secrets. But Demo knew the child wasn't alone. He wasn't the one in charge, after all. Slowly turning around, he spoke boldly, feeling both a deep sadness and a burning rage.

"Spencer, it's time you stop running!"

The boy scoffed at Demo's remarks and disappeared into the shadows.

"There's no Spencer here. I'm Angel. I haven't done anything wrong!"

Demo tracked the path of his voice. He had to find the kid and his accomplice. He followed the boy's seemingly mindless banter up into the rafters above the warehouse floor.

"Dio, tell the bad man to go away! He's ruining it! He wants to hurt us!"

Demo saw a flash of the boy scurrying across a catwalk into an obscure corner, where he climbed a ladder hidden there with an intense fervor.

"Spencer, stop hiding from me! You know why I'm here!"

He swallowed a cantaloupe sized lump in his throat. Just how long would the play acting last before Spencer became Spencer the Bloody Vulcan again?

"It's over, Spencer! You've got nowhere to go!"

Demo stretched his legs out onto the catwalk where the boy had been. He raced forward into the unknown without the slightest idea of what might come next.

"Leave us alone!"

This time the plea was much closer. It came from a darkened corner hidden just out of view. Just as Demo was about to reach him, the boy darted into a storage room. It was shrouded in a shadowy blanket, making it the perfect spot to hide. He was standing in the doorway, his eyes filled with fear as if he'd seen a ghost. He held his hand to the dark shadows of the room.

Was this really Spencer the Bloody Vulcan? My, how things had changed.

"Make the bad man go away, Dio! I don't want him to hurt us!"

Demo stood there completely petrified.

Dio, who was Dio? Why does this feel so wrong?

He watched in horror as out from the shadows appeared yet another small boy. His childlike features belied his truly malicious intent. When he spoke he spoke brazenly with no fear whatsoever.

"You're not wanted here!"

The second boy stepped towards Demo, holding the other boy's hand tightly.

"We don't need you!"

Demo's mind spun into a flurry of pure madness. All of his worst fears had come to fruition. Surviving would be the challenge of his life.

"I know what you've done. I know what you've both done. I'm here to put an end to this!"

The demonic little boy spoke yet again, taking another bold step towards a now backpedaling Demo.

"We've done what was right! We've done what *is* right!"

Demo caught a glimpse of the first boy who was now being led by the other.

"Spencer, you can put a stop to this! You don't have to take his orders!"

"Shut up! Dio is my friend! Dio knows what's best for me!"

The boy called Dio was now within mere feet of Demo. His eyes looked ablaze with the very fires of hell. His intent was unmistakably evil.

"Spencer, he's not even real! Don't you understand? Don't you see? This isn't real! It's already happened! You don't have to relive this anymore! You don't have to be a prisoner!"

Demo watched as Spencer's eyes suddenly met his. There was something about the brief interaction that suddenly changed the flow of things. Demo refocused his attention on the maleficent child who was now within a step of him. The boy's eyes burned a blood thirsty red as he lunged.

"All wrong must be cleansed!" he screamed in an unearthly voice.

Demo fell backwards onto the catwalk, the child clasping tightly around his neck. The inhuman strength of the boy was astounding. Demo was being completely dominated. He fought hard to keep air flowing through his lungs. His attacker grunted like an animal trying to squeeze every ounce of life out of him. He needed to use the only weapon he had; the *truth*.

"He lied to you, Spencer! He used you! He's left you for dead and moved on!"

This comment made Spencer's childish apparition squirm in pain.

"No, shut up! He would never do that to me! He promised!"

Demo was struggling to speak while letting the life–giving oxygen flow into his lungs. He needed to move quickly or die.

"Think about it! Why am I here? Why did you have to trap Anthony? Do you honestly think I'd risk my life just to rot away in this hell? He's found another pupil, another *victim* to do his dirty work! You're nothing now, Spencer. *Nothing*!"

The young Spencer stood up straighter, his facial expression now more in keeping with the calculated killer he had become.

"Liar! I am his *everything*! I am justice, I am righteous, and I am his right hand executioner!"

Spencer's childlike voice had been replaced by that of an aged tyrant. Although his physical manifestation remained the same, his consciousness had called in the true monster. Demo was losing ground and found himself perilously close to the edge of the catwalk. He caught a glimpse of what lay below; a fall from this height would smash him to bits.

"I'm not lying! I saw the bodies for myself! I saw the scales of justice. I saw the eyes of beauty!"

At the mention of the phrase '*Eyes of Beauty*' Spencer's complexion changed drastically.

"Eyes of beauty, eyes that truly see…"

As Spencer trailed off, his other manifestation, the one Demo only knew as Dio, pressed on.

"Spencer, you can stop this once and for all! I can help you end this! I can release you from this hell!"

Spencer looked lost. Amidst the desperate pleas from Demo and the demonic growl of Dio, he was as calm as he'd ever been. Suddenly, the world around them began to vibrate wildly and images melted in an almost funhouse mirror way. Spencer and Demo grabbed madly at their heads. Bolts of searing pain gripped them both.

"What's happening? What are you doing to me?" bellowed Spencer, further shaking the tenuous fibers of reality.

Demo didn't know what to think. In horror he watched as pieces of Dio were ripped away and scattered into a million pieces.

"It's happening! Our minds are beginning to fall apart!"

Suddenly, the room was populated by every creature or thing ever conjured up by either man's vast imagination. Every nightmare, every dream, every triumph, every failure, all the suffering and the happiness began coursing through this reality like a hurricane. Every synapse fired off at random in a reflexive attempt to survival.

"Make it stop! Make it stop!" screamed Spencer in anguish.

But as Demo tried to speak, a memory slammed through his mind that took immediate precedence over all the others; the harrowing night his partner had died. In a flash of blinding light he was there again. In what felt like an out–of–body experience, he gazed on the bloody frames of his own history unraveling in cinematic fashion. He was sucked into the midst of it like a bad acid trip.

"Mike, Mike, what is this? What's happening?"

Demo got up from the couch, clenching its sides for support, the worn fibers squishing beneath his fingers. His head ached from a well–deserved hangover.

Why is this happening?

He looked down at his feet. There was the pistol he had long tried to forget. It had been fired multiple times, leaving the chamber empty, the smell of discharge still lingering in the air like a poisonous gas.

No, not again!

He reached down and picked it up. Why couldn't he remember anything? Why was he feeling so much pain? He was suddenly overcome with the intense urge to look across the room.

No, don't do it! Don't look; you know what's there!

But he couldn't stop himself. Giving in, he rested his eyes on the corpse of his partner.

No, no, please stop this! I can't, I can't do this!

He walked over and looked into the lifeless eyes staring blankly at the ceiling. Demo collapsed to his knees. He was overwhelmed by a deep remorse that soaked every molecule in his body with sadness.

"What have I done?"

Tears streamed down his face, his suffering continual. He wanted to change this; he wanted things to be different. He wasn't alone.

"You killed him? You killed one of your own?"

Demo turned to see Spencer; only in this manifestation, he was his familiar, adult deviant self. Demo winced at the sight of Spencer in his self–perceived form. His dastardly features were vile in every regard, a true dark soldier. Spencer walked up to the deceased body and hovered for a moment.

"So, now you know how it feels like to lose. You know how it feels to be wronged. Yet you were willing to take a life."

"Don't touch him! I didn't kill him! I didn't do this!" commanded Demo.

Spencer looked at him with dead eyes.

"He was always there for me. Just like your dead friend here was for you. He guided me, taught me, and cleansed me of all wrong. He showed me the truth that set my mind free. It's fitting that the one thing neither of us truly understood is what tore us apart."

Demo stood firmly in place. Something was about to happen. He had only one chance to use what he had learned from all of his hellish time with Spencer. One chance to pry Spencer's mind open and pull out anything he could to seal the deal. As much anger as it evoked, he had to give what Spencer thirsted for; *praise*.

"It wasn't your fault. He was using you all along. You did what was right. You were the angel the world needed."

Spencer glanced at Demo then continued.

"I suppose it's poetic, really love always is. Love of that vile woman! We could have had it all! We could have changed everything, together!

Made this world pure! They would have seen our work, our message! But she had to come along! He promised me she was worthy, cleansed, pure, one of us! But how could anyone have what we had? What we had was special, pure, untainted! Our work was beautiful."

Demo piped in.

"Was?"

Spencer shot a menacing look Demo's way. A wicked, nefarious grin crept across his face.

"Maybe that's why I slipped up. Maybe I wanted to be caught. If I can't have him then nobody can; he's *my* master, *my* teacher…*my* benevolent god! But he forsook our bond and remained free, tainting our masterpiece with the filth of lesser men! I'm glad she died. I'm glad she couldn't be saved! If I'm to suffer for my righteous acts, then so shall they all! I want them to suffer! I want them to die!"

The conversation was cut short as the same supernatural chariot that had swept them away returned. Reality twisted beyond all recognition. They felt themselves losing their souls. It was all coming to an end.

"*Who* couldn't be saved? *Who?*" demanded Demo as his hands suddenly stretched and contorted becoming part of the raging storm around him.

In complete horror he watched as the deformed shape of what was left of Spencer began to cackle like a lunatic. The world around them was collapsing one fragment at a time. Everything was passing into a haze, nothing feeling real anymore. A blinding light blotted out any remaining visuals, and then everything came to a magnificent end with a final burst of brilliance that faded quickly to complete darkness. The fates and futures of both men were dispersed into the infinite fathoms of space and time.

CHAPTER EIGHTEEN

Checkmate Suicide

Time can seem to have no beginning or end; just an arbitrary number of experiences that somehow translates into its passing. Time and space harmonizing together can create a plane of alternate existence that has no purpose, meaning, or direction; it just is. That's where Demo now found himself. All points of reality had been condensed into nothing. He was adrift in some new place, some other existence, out of reach of everything he knew. Lights flickered as they flew past him like lightning bugs in the night sky. Occasionally one would burst and the remnants of a past memory would erupt from it like an exploding firecracker, some were his, others were Spencer's. He wanted to rest. He was so, so tired. Maybe he had finally passed the threshold and lost himself completely. Maybe both he and Spencer were caught in a never ending wave of subconscious memories. Is this really how it would all end? He felt his load lighten as he began to fade away. Then, from somewhere far off in the endless void, an echo bounced off the walls in a foggy cloud of light. As it whizzed past Demo, he watched it weave through his fingers before disappearing back into the nothingness.

"Demo, get up! Demo, please get up!"

Demo? Who was Demo? This question seemed oddly complicated. He knew he was somebody, but *who?* It was shrouded in darkness. Was *he* Demo? He knew that name. It meant something to him somehow.

"Demo, don't die on me! Wake up *now*! I ain't gonna lose you!"

Another light filled cloud shot past his head. But then something seemed strange, a feeling that someone was near. He spun around to see a vaguely familiar face. It was someone he had known from some other place and time, only a much younger version. He floated up and grabbed a hold of Demo's shoulders tightly.

"They *need* you! They need you *now*! Wake up!"

Demo heard the man's words but struggled to understand them. The man was shaking Demo wildly.

"You've got to wake up! You've got to go back! Listen to me! It's Anthony, don't you remember anything?"

Demo's head began to wrench in pain.

What's happening to me?

From somewhere inside him a maniacal voice pummeled his thoughts with its presence.

"He's inside of me! I can't get him out!"

Anthony looked Demo in the eyes.

"You've got to fight him! Don't let him win! You can do this! Lock him away! It's your mind! You can control it!"

Demo thrashed violently with pain. So many thoughts, so many feelings, it was too much to deal with.

"I can't! I can't keep him out! He's too strong!"

"But you're stronger! Remember what you're fighting for! Remember why you came here!"

That's when all the pure moments from Demo's hardened life came to the forefront. All the love he had been given by Bob Cat and Jacky. He wasn't just fighting for himself; he was fighting for his family; his freakishly woven together family that had been ripped apart by the putrid forces of evil. Demo let out a guttural scream. He was trying to silence the voices clamoring in his head. He needed to get out.

Kicking frantically in the air, he began to push himself through the void. As he pushed on, images from his and Anthony's memory swirled around him. He was trying to find the source of the clamorous calls of his name. He was Demo, Demotreus Ward, freak, detective, and loner. He was remembering himself again. With all the effort he could muster he fought on. He paused for only a brief moment to look behind and see the almost opaque apparition of Anthony Dredge.

"Anthony, hurry! I can get you out!"

Anthony shook his head and raised one hand high and called to Demo.

"This is my out. I can finally be at peace. Thank you and goodbye!"

Demo's heart ached but he knew he had to keep going. Suddenly he was engulfed by a tunnel of light.

"Demo, get up! Demo, please get up! Say something, man! Come on!"

Demo's eyes rolled around in his head like a pair of loose marbles. He was coming to, but to what he wasn't sure. He felt himself go weightless as if being carried.

"I've got some of your damned fancy water! Come back for me, Demo!"

He could feel the sensation of something cold drizzling down his throat. His lethargic reaction to it forced his gag reflex. He spat out a cup's worth of water onto the floor. Seconds later, he heaved up every last bit of the sickness he was feeling inside. When he caught his breath, he looked up into the face of a very distraught Bob Cat.

"I thought I'd lost you! I thought you'd been sucked in!"

Demo smiled weakly at his friend. Bob Cat was a complete wreck, both emotionally and physically. The two had endured far more than either believed possible.

"I thought I'd lost myself."

Bob Cat unexpectedly threw his arms around Demo in a bear hug. He let loose a part of him he normally held back.

Flushing with embarrassment, he let go as quickly and croaked out, "We need to go."

Demo peered over at Spencer, now realizing he had escaped. What he saw was an empty shell of a man. He walked closer ignoring Bob Cat. He put his head close to Spencer's and stared deeply into his eyes. He wanted to make sure this was really over. Suddenly Spencer's hands shot up and grabbed Demo's throat, then twitched and fell limp. Demo staggered backwards barely managing to keep his balance. The sudden commotion sent Bob Cat into a frenzied panic.

"What the hell was *that*? I thought he was supposed to be a vegetable!"

Demo watched while the fearsome, bloodthirsty eyes of Spencer the Bloody Vulcan went dark. It was over. Both he and Anthony Dredge had finally been released from their damned prisons.

"It's over, Bobby. Spencer and Anthony are finally gone. Where are Roslin and Jo?"

Bob Cat smirked slightly before answering.

"Let's just say Roslin is taking a nap, and Jo's a little tied up with work."

Demo glanced around to see the incapacitated Roslin lying flat on the floor.

"You knocked him out cold!"

"I'd be lying if I didn't say it felt wonderful."

The two began their escape. Demo glanced into the control room where Jo was tied up with cables and gagged by his own dirty sock. He mumbled something indiscernible and was struggling against his restraints when Demo turned back to Bob Cat.

"There's one last thing we need to do here."

"Already ahead of you on that one…"

Bob Cat removed Jo from the control room with all the delicacy of a Sumo wrestler. Next he turned into a technology smashing wrecking ball. He crushed chairs into monitors and ripped cables free from the wall. Sparks rained down like an electric shower. The two friends worked valiantly to destroy as much of the Fathom machine as humanly possible. Once satisfied, they knew they better make a run for it. From the forsaken Fathom room, they sped through the building, slamming the highly secure doors behind them. Once in the hall, they casually walked as fast as they could get away with past all kinds of agents before practically falling out of the secret door that led to the alley. From there they ran for the car that they hoped would help them run for their lives.

Demo stared vacantly, trying to catch his breath while Bob Cat cranked the engine. He could still feel Spencer's presence inside of him. He had taken a piece of the monster with him into the real world. Now he would be tainted forever by the soul of a serial killer.

"There's something else we have to do."

Bob Cat slammed on the brakes before they had gone a block. He burned the tires viciously against the pavement, taking an abrupt turn into a back street. He slammed on the brakes again, shoved it into park, and got out. Demo followed, not knowing why they'd stopped.

"Bobby, what's going on?

"I'm ending this. Right here, right now. I'm done with this shite! I'm done with all of it!"

Demo raced around the car to Bob Cat's side. All of the feelings of torment, pain, and frustration that Bob Cat had stuffed down were pouring out like lava from a volcano.

"Bobby, you can't give up! We're so close to the finish line! I know what to do! Don't you see? We can finally be free of this nightmare!"

Bob Cat spat at the ground, and Demo grabbed him by the shoulder.

"Bobby, don't do this. Please!"

Then as if struck by a bullet, Demo fell backwards. His arms flailed through the air until he hit the pavement with a sickening thud. Bob Cat had hit him. Hit him right between the eyes.

"Consider that my resignation! We've been through a lot together, but I can't handle this! I'm not you! I don't understand anything that's going on! We've lost everything; our lives, our families, and Jacky..."

Bob Cat trailed off at the mention of Jacky and seemed to visually deflate.

"No, I've done my part. I can't play your sidekick any more. I'm out, Demo. This is goodbye."

A pulsating pain permeated Demo's body when he tried to get up from the ground.

"Bobby, please don't do this!"

"I already have."

Bob Cat turned his back on Demo. He was suffering, but remained firm in his decision. Tossing a crumpled up piece of paper at Demo, he got back in his car and drove off.

Demo got back on his wobbly feet. Tears pooled just behind his eyes, straining to burst free. He'd just lost the only person left in his despicable life that mattered to him. He was finally completely alone. All of his life he'd been an outcast freak. Only a few brave souls had ever attempted to endure his excessive behavior. Despite all of his efforts, he just could never manage to be the one thing he wanted most of all—*normal.* A burning desire rose up in him. He knew his next role would ultimately end his life; but it was a role that desperately needed to be played out. Opening the crinkled paper that Bobby had thrown at him, he read it carefully. Then he walked out to the street and hailed a taxi. Not allowing the driver to speak first, he asked him for some paper and a pen. The cabbie looked annoyed but gave him what he had asked for. Demo scribbled something down then told the driver to wait and began jogging back to the building he had just escaped. Once there he wedged the note into the crack in the door and walked back to the cab. He barked out some directions as he got into the back seat. This was the end of the line.

Arriving at Lyle's apartment building he rehearsed all the formalities to get inside to the elevator. The ride up the elevator was uneventful as usual. People of means always seemed to live in the most boring of places. Once it stopped, he stepped out and raised a hand to knock on the door when it opened quietly by itself. Standing in the doorway was the judge. His warm face greeted Demo appreciatively.

"Well, hello, my boy, it's good to see you! I can't thank you enough for what you did for me! I can't begin to repay such an enormous debt. You saved my life! Can I get you anything?"

Demo ignored him. He looked down on the familiar scene; an immaculately clean home, fine furniture, exquisite décor, and an elaborate chess board. The chess board…something still intrigued him about it. The pieces had again been meticulously placed in a way that ensured that the same side would inevitably lose.

"Can I sit?"

"Of course, of course, by all means, make yourself at home!" Lyle answered graciously.

Demo sat down, still silent. He was completely lost in his process, a process that only he understood.

"You'll have to excuse all of the security at the entrance. I don't feel safe anymore. To be honest, I've been completely beside myself."

"Why do you think he wanted to kill you…the man who broke into your home?"

The judge sat down in his own cushy chair.

"I don't know…I suppose he must have had a vendetta against justice. I'm sure many people have wanted to kill me, but to actually *try*…'

He unconsciously brought his hand up to his heart. His wounds pulsated due to his excited state.

"Do you think he was connected to any of the other murders as of late?" Demo asked.

Lyle looked calmly at Demo and shrugged.

"It's a big city. There's evil hiding in every corner. It could have been any number of people."

Demo turned his gaze towards the newly repaired window. He recalled the blood covered bits of glass that had once been scattered about.

"They cleaned this up fast."

"I couldn't stand the sight of it. I had them work double time to scrap every last piece as evidence so that I could put this horrid encounter behind me."

Demo nodded, but remained staring out the window.

"I lost my family. Well, not my real family, but the only family I really have."

Lyle looked at him distraught.

"What could you mean by that?"

"It doesn't matter now. It's done."

"Well, sometimes in life people move on; *you* move on. Things are always changing. Sometimes they even change for the better."

Demo scratched at a dry patch of skin on his arm.

"I suppose you're right. I guess I just needed someone to talk to, is all."

Inexplicably, he got up out of his chair and headed towards the door.

"So soon? Have I said something to offend you?" questioned Lyle, standing up to meet him.

Demo walked calmly to the chessboard. He fumbled with the doomed pieces, putting the king directly in an inescapable checkmate, a suicidal move.

"You told me once that you were an orphan, correct?"

"Yes, abandoned years ago. All water under the bridge now."

Demo closed his eyes.

"It must have been hard to lose your wife after losing your own family. Always difficult when someone you love so dearly is taken away from you."

Demo didn't need to turn and look at Lyle; his sorrow was palpable.

"I need to get to a hospital. I'm not feeling too well. I thank you for your time and hospitality."

Demo left the room. He knew exactly what he needed to do. He was going to die, *finis temporis*, the end of times. A phrase that had been conjured up not by him, but by the darkness that now dwelt inside him.

Checkmate suicide.

CHAPTER NINETEEN

Killing God

Standing at the edge, a bone chilling breeze swept over Demo's body. He had never been to this side of town nor inside any of its aged buildings. He was standing in historical pieces of rubble that were being prepped for their ultimate destruction. In days, maybe weeks at most, it would all be gone, along with its memories and long ago forgotten purpose. The old hospital had been abandoned by time only to be rebuilt mere blocks away. It brought up feelings for Demo that only a place like this could. He glanced down at the flimsy paper he was holding tightly in his freezing hands. It had to be right. This had to be the place. The trick was finding the right room. Judging by the number, it was on the fifth floor; five floors up in an off limits, crumbling building. He didn't care anymore. Live or die, it was all chance.

Climbing to the fifth floor, he did his best to keep his failing composure. His heart was pounding with adrenaline. He never thought his end would come like this. He'd always hoped somehow he could die a fat, old, and happy man with little grandchildren running about. But he just wasn't that guy. Fate had dealt with him harshly. The old hospital creaked and moaned with the effects of time. Now it felt haunted. Room by room Demo made his way, carefully examining each door until he finally arrived at room *513*. There was nothing special about this room to him, but he knew to someone else it represented years of bottled–up feelings. To them, this was the gate to hell. He took his shaking hand out of his pocket and pressed it to the door. With an eerie moan it gave way and opened up to fully expose the room, which like the others had been ravaged by time. Its walls were faded, its infrastructure debilitated. A cool gust of wind caught him by surprise. The far wall was half gone, exposing a view of the city. But it's what he saw next that truly vexed his soul. In the middle of the rubble was a man tied to a chair; a man whom Demo knew all too well.

"*Martinez?*" Demo gasped, sprinting forward instinctively.

Martinez…Jacky's right hand man and devoted cop. Demo looked carefully at the meticulously knotted rope that bound him. This had been planned out carefully. That's when it hit him; a horrific wave of nausea and the sudden awareness that they weren't alone. Everything he knew was converging. He had a monster to slay and decades of spilled blood to redeem.

"So, is this where she died? Is this where they failed you, Dio? Is that what you call yourself now, or is it what *Angel* used to call you, you self–righteous bastard!"

Demo heard footsteps behind him but didn't turn.

"It's such a sad thing to see when the people called to protect, heal, and serve are found to be inadequate. There's no justice in failure. I should have known the doll was yours, the car's deity tied name *divine protector*, the eyes of beauty carved out of the victims, the scales of justice, the disciplined disciple—it was all there—I just couldn't see it. "

Demo could hear someone breathing behind him now; they were getting close.

"Justice? Like a father and mother who failed at raising their child; who abused hum, tortured him, betrayed him? They deserved nothing. They left a kid alone to fend for himself in a sick, sick world. But then again, he wasn't really alone, was he? He found someone with a bleeding heart he could manipulate, lie to, and deceive into taking up his cause to shed the blood of the innocent."

Demo was answered by a terrible gnashing stream of words that could only be coming from a completely unhinged, psychotic mind...

"They're *not* innocent! They're whores of perversion! Embellishers of filth! They are *nothing*! Each one deserved the end they met!"

Demo turned as Martinez began to groan. What he saw slammed an icy hammer against his heart, shattering it to pieces. He had expected almost anything, but never this. The judge stood before him, though every movement and sound he made seemed to come from someone else entirely; a monster, a demon. He was hunched over and wore a look of sheer madness on his face. In one hand he held a dingy looking pistol, in the other, a child's doll, its faded blue hat and suspenders carrying a dark message from the past. As Lyle came closer, he carefully set the innocent looking doll down. He looked completely insane.

"They're people and deserve to be judged fairly! Who gave you the right to take their lives? Who gave you the right to decide that they deserved to die?"

Lyle stepped aggressively toward Demo. He pointed the pistol at a spot right between Demo's eyes. It was then that Demo saw it. The weapon Lyle held was the same gun that had taken the life of his partner so long ago.

Where did he get that?

The judge spread his arms wide in a malicious display of pure evil.

"I was called! I was chosen! *God* gave me the right! God is in *me*! God knows justice, and I am HE!"

Demo was stunned by the metamorphosis that had taken place. There was absolutely no trace of the refined, articulate Judge Lyle Ridding in this monster before him.

"*You* are no God! You're just a sick freak! A freak who's ended too many lives for his sick and twisted game!"

Lyle let out a guttural howl that echoed through the abandoned building.

"I shall not indulge you! I'm here to open your eyes! I wish to show you the truth of all things! Don't you understand? I didn't come here to kill you; I came to set you free, to give you wings my angel!"

Demo's soul shrank into the depths of his own personal darkness. His worst fear had just revealed itself. Everything became crystal clear—terrifyingly so—Demo had been chosen as Lyle's new zealot of evil. The judge had been grooming him all along.

"I tried to tell you. I showed you myself time and time again! But your humanity blinded you. The sinners that called you friend deceived you! I was the only one who spoke the truth! I was the only one who never stopped believing in you! I gave you pieces of me in order to perfect you!"

Demo felt his insides bubbling. His darker emotions swelled, ripened, and then burst forth, leaving toxic pools of anger. His pain and loss threatened to consume him. Suddenly, Martinez spoke.

"Demo, is that you? Where am I? What's going on?"

Hearing him through a mental fog, Demo came back to reality. Despite everything, Martinez did not deserve to go out like this.

"Leave him out of this, Lyle! He doesn't concern you!"

Lyle let out an unworldly cackle that shook the walls.

"Oh, that thou should ask and receive, that the dark shall be brought to light!"

What is he talking about?

Lyle circled Martinez, keeping the gun carefully on Demo.

"Our dear Richard Martinez—cop, friend, servant to vice, and murderer!"

Martinez cringed painfully.

"What is he talking about, Martinez? Why are you here?"

With tears in his eyes he shook his head.

"I won't…I can't…don't make me do this!"

Lyle hit him hard with the back of his gun.

"Oh, ye of little faith, you poor tainted creature! You know what I can do if you disobey me!"

Martinez spat out a mouthful of blood.

"Martinez, what is he talking about? Demo screamed frantically.

"I did it! I did it, alright! I was desperate and it was years ago."

Demo stepped back. His mind was furiously trying to stitch together the new info crashing into him like a tsunami.

"Speak clearly, devil, so your sin can be made clear!" Lyle demanded. The judge was pacing faster and faster around Martinez and Demo like a bloodthirsty shark.

Martinez dropped his head onto his chest. Tears streamed down his face mixing into the thick rivers of blood gushing from his wound.

"I was a strung out druggie once, another lifetime ago. I was desperate and the door was open! I wasn't in my right mind. I was just looking to score some cash. I didn't know two cops would be inside. I didn't know that it would go down like that, I swear!"

Demo asked what he already knew.

"What are you trying to say, Martinez?"

"Yes, tell him. Purge your sins, you lying whoremonger!"

"I killed Mike, Demo. I thought you both were sleeping. I thought I could sneak in and out, no big deal. But then he woke up! He was so angry he attacked me, so I panicked. I did the only thing I could think to do. I shot him…with your gun. I pulled the trigger over and over, and watched him collapse next to you. I can't shake that image, man! I can't forget what I did! I joined the force in hopes of redeeming myself, somehow, some way, but I can't! I just can't! I didn't mean for it to happen, Demo, you've got to believe me!"

Demo's head swirled with emotion. Martinez's confession ignited a spark that was becoming a raging fire.

"*You?* You killed Mike? Why didn't you tell me? All this time I've known you, and you just looked me in the eyes and smiled! How could you do this to me? How could you do that to Mike?"

Martinez began to whimper and sobbed uncontrollably.

"I'm sorry, Demo! I just don't want my family to die; he said they'd die if I didn't believe! I'm sorry. I can't change this!"

"But *I* can. Those you held dear have abandoned you, but I never will. You are my own; you are my flesh and hands! I will set you free and give you a life you could only dream of. You will finally have what you've always wanted; a normal life! "

Lyle suddenly tossed an ornately embellished knife at Demo's feet.

"You know what you need to do to make this all goes away…all the injustice, pain, and suffering. I will call you my executor, harbinger of righteousness upon the vile evil that thinks it is safe. We will bring them all to justice; for only the chosen have the eyes of beauty, the eyes that truly see."

Demo bent over and picked up the blood-stained knife. Throughout the decades of ceremonious murder, this deviant tool had been used time and again. He stood and looked directly into Martinez's quivering eyes. Inside he could feel the darkness he now shared with Spencer clawing at his rapidly beating heart. A part of him wanted to exact vengeance. A part of him wanted to release all his years of hell in one repulsively artistic slice; one final climactic gesture to seal off all the pain. Then maybe, just maybe, he could live a normal life under the careful watch of a new devil.

"Do it! Take his life and set yours free! Become part of this righteous work! He will be the first of many that your hand shall cleanse, my angel, my perfect angel!"

"Many? What are you talking about?"

Lyle pointed into the open air of the ravaged hospital room. Demo followed his signaling gesture to see a paralyzing image of something he now could see clearly; a hospital.

"They shall be cleansed by the purity of fire, those who call themselves healers but only for profit; those who fail to bring salvation where it's needed most. They could have saved her, but wouldn't! Their insolence shall not go unpunished! I have given the sign! Now comes the calamity of God!"

He's going to blow up a hospital!

Demo pressed the knife into Martinez's throat. But there was one more thing he had to know.

"At the docks, when you pulled me out of the river, was it you that shoved me in? Was it you?"

Martinez completely broke down.

"He got to me early, told me he'd hurt my family! He told me to help you! I had a weak moment; I thought maybe if you were gone he'd leave me alone and then maybe I could get out of this! He wanted to destroy me, Demo. I'm so sorry!"

It was all making sense. Martinez had been used by Lyle. Lyle had obtained Demo's pistol through Martinez. Martinez had let him into the evidence locker where he'd seen what he wasn't supposed to see. It was the perfect set up. All the evidence would now point at Demo if Lyle didn't get what he wanted. He would be a pariah thrown to a rabid public then locked away for eternity. He knew what he had to do.

"I'm sorry, Martinez. I truly am."

Demo stalled for just a heartbeat before speaking again.

"Didn't you see it, Lyle? I left it for you, right inside your own house. What was it you said about that chess game? There's always another move? But you failed to see that there isn't another move when one side is willing to lose everything, when one side is willing to die!"

In one swift movement, Demo spun around and threw the knife directly at Lyle. In sheer panic, Lyle squeezed off a deafening blast from the pistol before Demo tackled him to the ground, sending the gun flying. Lyle screamed demonically as his surprising strength was pressing an advantage. He bit into Demo's shoulder, ripping out a chunk of flesh. The open wound sent bolts of pain into Demo's body. But he wasn't about to give up. Now more than ever he wished he possessed the strength and fighting ability of Bob Cat. Alone, he was frail and weak, even against an aged Lyle. A detail that was suddenly and painfully obvious. With a couple of well–placed head butts, Demo felt the world around him turn hazy. An intense pain erupted from his side. Lyle had found the knife.

"Pathetic creature, I was willing to give you everything!" Lyle pronounced boldly, gasping for air as he stood back up.

Demo rolled over, feeling his life essence rapidly draining out of him. His eyes fell on Martinez who sat still and silent. An errant bullet had found its mark; Martinez was dead. Despair and hopelessness crept over Demo as he remembered the hospital. All those people could still be inside. Gathering every last bit of his diminishing willpower, he pushed himself back to his feet. He pressed a hand deep into his wound to try to stop the bleeding; the pain was almost more than he could bear.

"It's over, Lyle! I'm not going to join you! You're alone, like always!"

Lyle's teeth chattered manically. He had become completely lost in his bloodlust. He held the knife firmly in his grasp and ran at Demo. Lyle slammed Demo with a powerful backhand that sent him tumbling backwards. In pure defiance, Demo fought the pain and looked at him with disgust.

"Your family, Spencer, Kevin, Martinez, and now me; nobody cares about you anymore! You will be forgotten, erased, left behind, another raving lunatic lost to the pages of history! Just another dead, wannabe god, forgotten by everyone!"

Lyle raised the knife high. A ray of sun broke through the clouds directly above his head. For a moment he looked like what he believed himself to be; a god.

"Thou shall not forsake me!"

Lyle was about to plunge the knife directly into Demo's skull when a powerful blast sounded from the shadows. An intense force ripped through Lyle's chest, leaving a mangled, gaping hole behind. With one last beat, the monster's heart stilled. The judge was dead. Demo's knees buckled. That's when he saw his savior emerge from the shadows—*Bob Cat.*

Seeing Demo's massive wound, Bob Cat rushed to his side.

"I've got you buddy. Hold on!"

Demo broke into the biggest smile he could manage. His soul felt awkwardly happy.

"You came for me?"

Bob Cat smirked.

"Of course I did, you chicken's arse! Look what happens every time I lose you for five minutes!"

Demo's smile faded.

"We've got to get out of here, Bobby. He said he was going to blow up the hospital!"

Bob Cat's eyes bulged open. With little effort, he threw the injured Demo over his shoulder to carry him from the horrific scene. Before he could take a step, there was a deafening explosion. Any windows not already broken shattered as flaming pieces of shrapnel rained from the sky. The shockwave knocked Bob Cat off his feet, dropping Demo onto the vibrating rubble covered floor. Demo glanced over as he felt his body finally beginning to succumb to his injuries, and saw the doll. Its lifeless eyes stared back at him with the forever look of a child; an abused, lonely, demented genius of a child. The doll had been Lyle's projected innocent self, for so long protected by its new deity, Lyle himself. Now it was just a doll, just a childish toy. Demo's blood loss carried him into unconsciousness.

CHAPTER TWENTY

Freak Family

Bright sunlight streamed through a large window framing a magnificent blue sky. The warming rays fell on a long hospital bed sitting dead center in the room. In it lay a waking Demo. Everything felt warm and fresh to him. It was a new beginning that had ushered in a promising life with renewed purpose. Looking around the room he saw familiar faces; Jacky, Bob Cat, Mars, and even Roslin.

'Bout time — I thought you'd never wake up," Bob Cat spoke first, smiling.

Demo was elated. He could barely contain his joy at seeing them all here together. At the same time, he felt a nagging sense of guilt for what he had done to get here.

"Where am I? How long have I been out?"

"In the hospital for a few days now…I told them not to put you on ice," answered Bob Cat smugly.

Demo looked at Jacky.

"Jacky, I'm so sorry about all of this. I'm so sorry about Martinez."

Jacky shook her head. She was still showing signs of grief, but let it fall to the wayside for now.

"It's okay, Demo…Bobby explained everything. It's just good to see that you're okay."

Demo smiled. An enormous weight had been lifted. He began to try and sit up when a sharp pain sent him back down onto the bed. He grabbed at his side and felt a thick layer of gauze.

"You got hit pretty hard, Demo. I'd give it a rest for now," said Bob Cat, pointing at the wound.

"You've done enough for now, son. Rest assured we'll have everything cleared up," Roslin added.

Roslin's face looked like he was twelve rounds deep into a boxing match. They each had their own painful reminder of their friendly companionship.

Bob Cat hits hard.

"You're a hero, Demo; a real living and breathing hero," Roslin continued. "You can be proud of that. You've saved hundreds, maybe even thousands of lives. You solved the case of the century."

"But the hospital, the people…are they—"

"They're completely safe. We did exactly what you instructed in your little note. The secret evacuation practically went unnoticed." Roslin leaned in and whispered, "But I do have to say, not that you care, that it came at an astronomical cost of time and resources. Speaking of which, you owe me some new hardware, and Jo will probably need some therapy for a while, but we'll discuss that later. I'm just glad you're alright."

Demo nodded. He had come to respect Roslin despite everything that had happened.

"I suppose I owe you an apology," Mars said, stepping in from the back of the group.

"I could have never fathomed that Judge Ridding was capable of such heinous acts. I had you pegged all wrong. I could have ended up as just another victim of his cold–blooded evil. I thank you, Demotreus Ward."

"We all owe you an apology, Demo. We should have never doubted that you could solve this," added Roslin. "You're special, Mr. Ward, very special. Now, if you all don't mind, I think Mr. Ward needs some time to rest."

Jacky clacked her heels and gave Roslin a rebellious stare, but she quickly pacified herself and reluctantly agreed.

"Yes, he's been through hell and high water. He deserves some time off."

The group began to funnel out, Jacky and Roslin predictably quarreling as they went. Only Bob Cat stayed behind. He looked happy and relaxed.

"You did good ole' boy…real good. They say that catching that guy solved one of the biggest cases in history. I guess I'm sorry about doing what I did to your face," Bob Cat said, pointing at the massive bruise on Demo's face.

Demo sniffed the air and grinned.

"Bobby, you quit! You don't smell, you're not shaking, and no gum!"

Bob Cat smiled.

"Yeah, that's right. Things are kinda looking up, I suppose."

A mischievous grin took over Demo's face.

"You and Jacky?"

"What fat lip blabbed that news? It ain't nothing…we just had a moment or two, what with all the emotions…"

"Relax Bobby, it's a good thing. Heaven knows you need it. But you do have some explaining to do. Just how did you manage to show up at just the right moment?"

Bob Cat let out a sigh and shrugged.

"That's weird…I thought *you* were the smart end of the donkey that *I'm* always asking questions to…"

Demo remained silent.

"Fine, fine, don't let me have my fifteen minutes of fame. I did what you said to do; I took a guess and ran with it."

"*Meaning?*"

"You said it, don't you remember? The guy was good—too good—and we needed to stop doing what we were doing. So when you gave me that note asking for information on that piece of crap judge's wife's hospital room, I went digging. I found it odd even for a freak like you to suddenly care so much about some dead lady. I acted the part of detective, your part, and played it as best as I could. I could then watch you from the sidelines like a cheerleader. Must of worked because that raving loony never saw it coming. I'm just glad I got there when I did. You scared the pebbles out of me. Don't ever go do that again, by the way."

"But you hit me really, really hard. Did you have to make it *that* real?"

Bob cat shrugged.

"Well, maybe I didn't fake everything. That actually felt kind of good. You have a way of not clamming up sometimes."

Demo chuckled. He was beyond relieved to have his family back together; his beautiful, freak show family.

"Freak family," he muttered under his breath.

"*What* did you say?"

"Nothing, I just need to get some rest. I'm still not all there."

Bob Cat was heading for the door when he stopped and tossed a jangling set of keys to Demo. The keys landed on the bed's crisp white sheets.

"I brought you your rust wagon. Figured you'd probably be done with walking for a while."

Demo smiled and nodded.

"Thanks, Bobby."

Once alone, Demo rested his head against his pillow. It had been ages since he'd had a bath and a clean bed to sleep in. But now he felt like he could move forward. He relaxed, shut his eyes, and for once slept like a baby.

After a few days of rehab, antibiotics, and fervent lecturing by the hospital staff about remembering to take his pills, Demo was released back into the world. But now it was a world that had nothing much left in it that he could call his own; a partially burned down apartment, a crappy car, a raggedy old suit, and a pair of worn shoes.

I need to get a real job.

When he got to his car, he pulled out the keys. Looking up, he saw a piece of paper carefully stuck in the windshield wiper. Snatching it out roughly, he let out a sigh of frustration.

"You have *got* to be kidding me. Can't I ever catch a break?"

Suddenly, the buzzing vibration of a cell phone came from inside the car.

That's not mine. My phone is busted.

Curious now, he opened the car to a surprise. Laying in the driver's seat was his old pistol, barely recognizable having been cleaned and polished. The buzzing started again. Tracing the noise to its source, he opened the glove box. Inside was a high tech looking cellphone, the likes of which he had never seen. He grabbed it and brought it up to his ear.

No one was on the other end. No cordial greeting, no breathing, nothing. He took a few deep mantra breaths to slow his reactive mind. Everything up to this point in his life had molded him into something even he had never thought possible. His work, his legacy, everything he had experienced, both good and bad, was as much a part of him as his name. An unknown future stretched before him—an ever unfolding saga of good versus evil, beckoning him to follow. This was his cause—this was his purpose—he knew that now. He was a freak; but a freak that was willing to fight; a freak willing to give everything in hopes of making tomorrow a little better. He was no hero, no saint, but he was Demotrius Ward, consultant detective, and that was finally good enough for him. Reading the contents of the crumpled piece of paper he knew what had to happen. Rubbing his dry lips together he said the only thing that mattered anymore.

"I'm ready…"

About the Author

Mikel Parry is an engineer, father, husband, and author. A storyteller since birth, he cultivated his imagination as he grew up with the hope of one day writing the stories he so loved to envision. Born in a small town in Southern Utah, he dreamed of far off places, fascinating worlds, and unconventional ideas that entertained him during his childhood. Over time his dedication and persistent efforts to realize his dream of being a writer gave him the courage to finally decide that he was ready to bring his talent out into the open.

Check out Mikel's blog, his latest projects and contact him at:

www.mikelparry.com